THE BALLAD
OF
LAUREL SPRINGS

THE BALLAD OF LAUREL SPRINGS

JANET BEARD

GALLERY BOOKS

New York   London   Toronto   Sydney   New Delhi

G

Gallery Books
An Imprint of Simon & Schuster, Inc.
1230 Avenue of the Americas
New York, NY 10020

First Gallery Books hardcover edition October 2021

GALLERY BOOKS and colophon are registered trademarks of Simon & Schuster, Inc.

For information about special discounts for bulk purchases, please contact Simon & Schuster Special Sales at 1-866-506-1949 or business@simonandschuster.com.

The Simon & Schuster Speakers Bureau can bring authors to your live event. For more information or to book an event, contact the Simon & Schuster Speakers Bureau at 1-866-248-3049 or visit our website at www.simonspeakers.com.

Interior design by Lana J. Roff

Manufactured in Italy

10   9   8   7   6   5   4   3   2   1

Library of Congress Cataloging-in-Publication Data is available.

ISBN 978-1-9821-5156-0
ISBN 978-1-9821-5158-4 (ebook)

To Penelope, with all my love.
May you learn the old songs and then write your own new one.

CONTENTS

PRETTY POLLY

GRACE
2019

Aunt Dee told me about the murder. She'd picked me up from school that day and taken me to the park. We were swinging together, when I asked if our family had any good stories. She laughed. "We got stories for sure, Gracie. What kinda story are you after?"

"It's for my language arts class. We're doing a family history project. I've already made my family tree, but we're also supposed to write a family story."

Dee nodded. I pumped my legs back and forth in the swing, and a cool breeze whipped around us. "Well, I know our family's lived here forever. We're not related to anyone famous or anything."

"Are there any family legends?"

"Hmm . . ." Dee looked thoughtful, which was unusual for her. Mom says she never thinks and just says whatever comes into her mouth. That's why she can't keep a job or a boyfriend for more than six months. But Dee's my favorite babysitter. Her hair is shorter than most boys', and she wears a leather jacket whenever it's cold out. She lets me watch PG-13 movies and stay up past my bedtime, and one time she squirted whipped cream into my mouth straight from the can. She's Mom's little sister, and Dad says Aunt Dee is still a child, even though she's twenty-four.

"Well!" she said, scuffing her feet in the mulch to stop her swing. "One of our ancestors killed somebody. That's a pretty good story, isn't it?"

"Really?"

"Yeah. It happened just up the road in the national park, but this was, like, way back before the park was built."

I relaxed my legs and let the swing slowly come to a stop.

Dee loved telling spooky stories, and she grinned as she got going on this one. "So supposedly our, like, great-great-great-great-grand-father was dating this girl. She was just a teenager, I think. And for some reason, he flipped out and stabbed her."

"Whoa."

Dee smiled. She knew I wasn't freaked out. We told ghost stories all the time. "Yeah. There's even a song about it, 'Pretty Polly.'"

She twisted in her swing to pull her phone out of the back pocket of her jeans. "Check it out," she said as she opened YouTube and pulled up a video of some old guys in cowboy hats with guitars and banjos. The one in the middle sang in a country twang:

"Polly, pretty Polly, come go along with me,
Polly, pretty Polly, come go along with me,
Before we get married some pleasure to see."

She got up behind him and away they did ride,
She got up behind him and away they did ride,
Over the hills and the valleys so wide.

The melody was upbeat, and I laughed as Dee bounced up and down in her swing to the beat.

They rode a little further and what did they spy,
They rode a little further and what did they spy,
But a new-dug grave with a spade lying by.

"Oh Willy, oh Willy, I'm scared of your ways,
Oh Willy, oh Willy, I'm scared of your ways,
Scared you might lead my poor body astray."

"Polly, pretty Polly, you've guessed just about right,
Polly, pretty Polly, you've guessed just about right:
I've dug on your grave the best part of last night."

I grinned at Dee, and we giggled at the gruesome bit.

And he stabbed her in the heart and the heart-blood did flow,
And he stabbed her in the heart and the heart-blood did flow,
Into her grave pretty Polly did go.

He threw a little dirt over her and started for home,
He threw a little dirt over her and started for home,
Leaving nothing behind but the wild birds to moan.

And it's debt to the devil, and Willy must pay,
And it's debt to the devil, and Willy must pay,
For killing pretty Polly and running away.

The musicians wrapped up, and the audience clapped. Dee reached her phone back into her pocket.

"So Willy was our ancestor?" I asked her.

"Yup. He was a Reid."

"Why did he kill her?"

"I don't know. The song doesn't really say."

"It's kind of terrible."

I must have looked worried, because Dee put her hand on my shoulder. "Hey, it's just a story. I mean, it happened a really long time ago."

"Yeah, I know."

"Forget I showed you that song. It's probably not a good idea for your paper."

"I liked the song."

"Well, I'm sorry the story ends in murder."

"Why?"

"It's not a very nice subject for a little girl." She gave me a sheepish grin. "Should we go home and get a snack?"

I nodded and we slid off our swings. But I wasn't scared by the song, and I'd already decided to write about it for my project.

Our language arts class has a special focus on history this year, because it's the 110th anniversary of the founding of our school, Tates Valley Elementary. We've learned all about what life was like in Douglas County, Tennessee, back then. Most people lived down in Douglasville, which is still the county seat, and Tates Valley wasn't a city at all yet, just a collection of farms up in the mountains. The people who lived here were really poor and didn't have electricity or anything. Children had to work on their families' farms until missionaries came and started this school so that we could get an education.

Mrs. Durham had said the next step in our project was to learn about our own individual family histories. The assignment was to make a family tree, then collect some family photos, write down a family story, and put it all in a binder. My mom helped me do the family tree and told me to ask my grandma for pictures and a story to write. Grandma gave me plenty of photos to use, but the only story she told me was something really boring about how my grandpa was born in a snowstorm. "Don't we have any ancestors who did something exciting?" I had asked her.

"We're just normal, hardworking folks, Gracie."

The next day, Dee told me the murder story. Later that afternoon when she'd dropped me off at home, I found out from Wikipedia that "Pretty Polly" probably wasn't written about our ancestor. The song is way older than that, and there are all these different versions. I called Dee to tell her about my research, but she wasn't moved. "I don't know. That's just what our grandma always said, before she passed. She said the song was about our however-many-greats-grandfather, who killed this girl way back when at Laurel Springs. But maybe she was mixed-up."

So I wrote out the lyrics and what I'd learned from the Internet, then told the story as best I could going off what Dee had told me. I decorated my binder with the pictures Grandma had given me and chose an old-timey font for my title page. I thought Mom would be impressed with my work when I showed her.

She had just come downstairs for breakfast when I handed her the binder. She's a nurse at a clinic and was wearing her green scrubs. Mom glanced at the pictures and family tree, smiling. But then she turned to my paper, and her face went dark. "What is this?"

"Dee helped me."

"Oh, Dee!" She turned away from me and muttered under her breath, "What is wrong with her?"

"What do you mean?"

"Why is she telling you to write about someone in our family being a murderer?"

"Who cares? I mean, it was, like, more than a hundred years ago."

Mom shook her head. I could see she was angry, and I didn't understand why.

"When's this due?" she asked.

"Today."

"Great, so you don't have time to change it. This is all Dee's fault!"

"What's the big deal?"

She wasn't looking me in the eye. I knew there was something she wasn't telling me. My family doesn't tell me things all the time, and it makes me crazy, especially since I'm not a little kid anymore. I'm ten. I can handle it.

Finally she looked up. "Has your dad seen this?"

"No."

"Just don't show him, okay? I don't want him to get upset."

"Why would he get upset?"

She snapped, in her serious-business voice, "Just don't show him, okay?! Now, finish your Cheerios. We're gonna be late."

Dee came over that weekend for dinner, and I could hear Mom talking to her in the kitchen while I was setting the table. "What were you thinking?" asked my mom, clearly not expecting an answer. "You weren't thinking. You never think."

"I'm sorry. It didn't occur to me it would be awkward until after I'd mentioned it." I could tell from her voice that Dee felt bad. She and my mom fight a lot, and usually she gives as good as she gets. But that day she sounded meek and regretful.

"This is a small town, you know? Everyone knows. Everyone remembers. It only happened seven years ago! Finn has worked so hard to make sure it affects Grace as little as possible. But she goes and writes a paper about someone in her family murdering someone else, and her teacher's gonna raise her eyebrows. If she gives a report on it in class, and then some kid runs home and tells his parents, they'll gossip about it."

"I get it," said Dee. "I really am sorry."

I put the silverware down as quietly as I could and crept back to the living room, so they wouldn't know I'd heard them. I didn't understand what they were talking about but realized I wasn't supposed to know about it.

Mrs. Durham handed our binders back the next week, and I was excited. I thought at least she would be pleased with my story. But Mrs. Durham gave me a B and wrote: *Grace, you always write well. But this story is disturbing and probably not even true.*

When the class went to recess, Mrs. Durham asked me to speak with her and bring my binder. She'd never done that before, and I was scared. Lily and Maria waited for me at the door to the playground, because we always hang out together at recess, but I motioned for them to go on without me.

Mrs. Durham turned to me. "Grace, I want to talk to you about your family history project."

She took the binder back from me.

"I'm sorry, Mrs. Durham. I didn't mean to be disturbing."

"It's okay, Grace. What made you want to write about something so yucky?"

"I just thought it was an interesting story."

She leaned in close to me. I think she was trying to be nice, but it made me squirm. I wanted to go play with everyone else. "I think you should talk to Miss Flores. I've made an appointment for you."

Miss Flores is the school guidance counselor. She comes to our class once a week to talk about feelings and how we shouldn't get in a stranger's car. She has long brown hair and wears tight dresses, and I think she's beautiful. But I'd never talked to her alone. The kids who go to her office have problems.

When I went to see Miss Flores that afternoon, she told me to sit across from her on a little sofa beside a ragged old teddy bear. The walls of her office were covered in posters with kittens and smiley faces. "Thanks for coming to talk to me, Grace. Are you comfortable there?"

I nodded. She had a sweet, soft voice.

"Mrs. Durham wanted me to talk to you. It's nothing to be worried about. She just wants to make sure you're doing okay. At school and at home."

I really didn't understand any of this. I hadn't written anything that bad. No curse words, just a tiny mention of blood in the song, but nothing too gross.

"How is school going, Grace?"

"Good."

"Mrs. Durham says you're a very good student."

"I like school."

"That's great. I'm really glad to hear it. She showed me your family history project, and I think you did a fantastic job on it." She stood up, opened a drawer beside her desk, and pulled out my binder. "Really, Grace. You write very well."

"Thanks. But I got a B."

She sat back down. "I guess Mrs. Durham thought you should have written about a nicer story." She leaned toward me. "But I think you should have gotten an A."

I was surprised. Teachers always went along together. "Really?"

"Yeah."

"I didn't mean to upset anyone. I really didn't think it was that bad or I wouldn't have written it."

"You may have already figured this out for yourself, Grace. But sometimes grown-ups will get upset when you do things, and it doesn't really have anything to do with what you've done. It just reminds them of things they don't want to think about. Did your parents help you with the project?"

"My mom helped me with the family tree but not the story. When I showed it to her, she got really angry. She told me not to tell my dad about it."

"Do you know why?"

I shook my head. "No one will tell me."

"How does that make you feel?"

"Annoyed."

"I understand. That would annoy me too."

"Do you know why she's so upset?"

She looked down. "You wrote about something scary and sad. Your story took place a long time ago. But it's still not the kind of thing people like to talk about."

"I reminded her of something she doesn't want to think about."

"Maybe."

"You're not going to tell me what it is either, are you?"

"To be honest, Grace, I don't really know. But what I do know is that you haven't done anything wrong."

We talked for a while after that about all kinds of things. I liked Miss Flores a lot. She was easy to talk to and seemed really interested in what I had to say. She said I could come by to talk whenever I felt like it, as long as I got permission from Mrs. Durham.

She gave me back my binder, and I was ready to forget that the whole stupid family history project had ever happened. But I made a mistake that night. Mom's always yelling at me that I leave my stuff all over the house, and I guess she's right. I must've put the binder down on the dining room table when I got home and forgot about it.

That evening Mom called me down to set the table for supper, like normal. She was busy in the kitchen, where I could hear the sound of pouring water, banging pots and pans, and the hum of the microwave. I ran down the stairs and saw Dad sitting at the table, still wearing his work clothes, quietly reading my binder.

I stopped still when I realized what I'd done. At first he didn't seem to notice me. His face was tight and serious, but I couldn't tell if he was angry. He looked up slowly. I braced myself for what he was going to say.

"This is really good, Gracie." He stood up.

"My teacher said the story was too disturbing."

He looked down at the binder and rubbed the corner with his thumb. "Well . . . just because a story isn't nice doesn't mean it's not true."

I didn't know what to say. He seemed lost in his thoughts. Finally he handed me the binder. "I'm gonna go take a shower," he mumbled, and went upstairs.

Dad never came to dinner that night, which was strange. Mom said he'd left something at work and had to go get it. She seemed sad, though, barely talking to me as we ate. When supper was over, I took the binder from my backpack where I'd stashed it and quietly went out the back door to the big trash can behind the house. I took out Grandma's pictures, then stuffed the binder under a trash bag. I never wanted to see it again.

I still don't know why everyone got so upset over that story. But I have a feeling it has something to do with my mother. Not my mom, who's married to Dad and lives with us now. My birth mother.

The thing is, that family tree I made was missing something. My mom isn't my birth mother. She's really my stepmother. I'm not even related to the "Pretty Polly" murderer by blood at all.

And I don't really care. I mean, my mom adopted me four years ago when she married my dad, and I love her and all that. I really do. I've been calling her Mom since she and Dad got engaged when I was five. They picked me up from kindergarten together one day, both laughing and smiling, and told me we were going to get ice cream. And then at Baskin-Robbins, Dad told me they were getting married. I remember she said that she would love to have the chance to be my mother. And I liked her. They had been dating for about a year, and she came over to our house most evenings. She was always nice. She cooked good food and played games with me and read stories in funny voices. I felt as excited as they did that day. I got two scoops of mint chip, and I've called her Mom ever since.

But I do remember my birth mother. At least, I think I do. I remember she had dark hair, almost black. I remember she had soft, warm skin, and I remember leaning into her and feeling safe.

I asked my grandma, Dad's mother, about her once, but she got so distressed that I never asked again. Grandma was driving me home from ballet, and I was shocked because she started to cry. "You listen to me," she said. "That woman's not your mother, Gracie. Not anymore."

She gripped the steering wheel so hard that her knuckles turned white, and I didn't say anything else until we got to the house.

I remember that my birth mother took me once to see the Statue of Liberty. Could that be right? I asked my dad if we'd ever gone to New York, and he said no. But then he stomped out of the living room, slamming the door behind him, and I had that feeling again that he wasn't telling me something.

About a week after I threw away the binder, I asked Dee about my family history project. We were back at the playground, sitting at a picnic table together, eating chips after school. She was smoking a cigarette, which I'm not supposed to tell Mom about. It was a sunny day and warm enough that she'd left her leather jacket in the car.

"Dee?"

"Yeah?"

"Why did everyone freak out about the 'Pretty Polly' story?"

She scrunched up her face, and I knew she didn't want to talk about it. "I can't tell you, Gracie. I'm sorry. I wish I could. I really do. But you're not gonna find out from me. Your mom would kill me."

"It's not fair! I'm not a little kid anymore. Why won't anyone tell me the truth?"

She smiled and tossed her cigarette onto the grass. "Don't rush into growing up. It's not all it's cracked up to be, I promise."

"It's all your fault anyway. Did you know my teacher made me go talk to the guidance counselor?"

"Oh no! Really? I'm sorry, Grace. I shouldn't have told you that story. I don't even know if it's true."

"But it's not really about that story, is it?"

"Look, Gracie. You need to ask your parents about this, okay? It's not my place to talk about it. I'm in enough trouble already."

But I can't ask my parents. I keep thinking back to the weird look on my dad's face when he was reading the binder. He looked so serious, his brow furrowed, his mouth clenched tight, like he might explode in rage or burst into tears. I think of the way my grandma gripped the steering wheel on the way home from ballet class, and of how my mom yelled at Dee in the kitchen, how Dee just took it.

———

We went on a field trip yesterday to the national park. A ranger took us to a waterfall and taught us about the plants and animals that live there. It's spring now and the woods are filled with wildflowers. Ranger Terry taught us their names: bloodroot, Solomon's seal, galax, trillium, violet, iris, geranium, phlox. A carpet of yellows, whites, and purples brightened the dark greens and browns of the forest. Ranger Terry said people come from all over the world to see these flowers blooming. We're lucky to live in such a special place.

Maria, Lily, and I walked together, jotting down notes about our observations. I like science, and I like the national park. Maybe I'll be a park ranger when I grow up. I like the feeling you could get lost in the forest, that it goes on forever, although I know not to ever leave the trail, and that it does stop eventually, of course, and give way to the motels and restaurants and miniature golf courses and houses and our school and all the other buildings and roads that make up Tates Valley.

We were walking up front near Ranger Terry, who would stop and tell us about interesting plants and bugs. She explained that the forest was still scarred by the wildfires from back when I was little. The trees in that part of the park were small and young, slowly replacing the great, tall trees that had burned down. Ranger Terry knew everything about the mountains.

"Let's take a quick break here!" she called out to the group. "Who can tell me what a spring is?"

Lily raised her hand. "It's where water comes out of the ground."

"That's right, Lily. This behind me is a spring." She was standing in front of a wet patch of ground where a trickle of water bubbled up at the base of a giant oak tree that must have survived the fires. "Fresh water comes up out of the ground here. You can put your hand in, but let me warn you, it's really cold."

That was when I noticed the small brown sign on the other side of the trail: LAUREL SPRINGS. This was the place where the murder was supposed to have happened. Some of the kids rushed up to put their hands in the water. I walked away from them all, over to the tree.

I put my hand on the rough bark, and then I noticed that someone had carved initials into it: WR + PC.

Ranger Terry came up behind me. "Some people have no respect for nature."

"How long ago do you think it was carved?"

"Don't know. It does look pretty old."

And it's debt to the devil, and Willy must pay, for killing pretty Polly and running away.

I tried to tell Dee about the initials this afternoon, but as soon as I brought up "Pretty Polly," she refused to talk about it. "Seriously, Gracie, let it go!"

But I know what I saw. Just because a story isn't nice doesn't mean it isn't true.

THE WIFE OF USHER'S WELL

PEARL
(GRACE'S GREAT-GREAT-GREAT-
GREAT-GRANDMOTHER)
1907–1908

I don't believe in witches. My granny swore a witch lived up on Jones Mountain when she was a girl, but I never took her too seriously. Seems to me folks just like to blame their troubles on someone. If your cow stops giving milk, it's probably sick, and if your horse up and dies, it's probably gotten old. It's not a witch's fault—just bad luck.

A lot of folks in these parts disagree. They say old Widow James is a witch. I'll admit, she fits the description. She's lived by herself for well on thirty years, and no one ever sees her at church. I think she likes people thinking she's a witch. It gives her a certain standing in the community, and folks are a little scared of her. I've always assumed she just wants to be left alone. She plays up her image, shooing away the children who run up into her vegetable garden on a dare, muttering under her breath when she makes her monthly visit to the general store. It suits her to be thought of as a witch, and it suits everyone else to think of her that way.

It was different with Violet Nickson. She didn't want folks to think she was a witch, and when they started saying so, it hurt her. But once an idea like that has begun to spread around, it's hard to stop.

Violet didn't exactly look like a witch. She wasn't old—just four years older than me, as a matter of fact, and I was twenty-six when the trouble started. She wasn't beautiful, true enough, but she wasn't a fright to look at either; she just had buckteeth. She *was* terribly shy—always had been—so some folks thought she was uppity, but I know that wasn't so. Perhaps because of her shyness, she had never married.

I first got to know Violet when I was only a girl. She was best friends with my older sister Polly. Violet had moved to Tates Valley as a child to live with her aunt after her mother had died and her father had gone off to work in the mines. She brought along a whole trunk of books her mother left her, and Polly told me she'd read every one at least three times. Violet would loan Polly books sometimes, or more often read them aloud to her, as Polly had never made it past fourth grade.

It was when Polly died that folks started talking about Violet being a witch. Polly's body was found in Mitchell's Creek. I was only eleven when it happened, so the more distressing details were kept from me. But I knew folks suspected she'd been killed right from the start.

Except for Mama, no one was as upset by Polly's death as Violet. She wore only black for a year after, and many an afternoon I saw her lingering by Polly's grave. I always reckoned that for such a shy girl, losing her closest friend was particularly difficult. But Mama had never taken to Violet. She thought the girl put on airs, since she was so quiet and always reading. I told Mama she was just bashful, but my mother was not one to change her opinion easily. And when Polly died, Mama was overwhelmed with grief and began screaming that it was Violet's doing. The girl had witched Polly and cursed her to die. No one took this seriously, of course. All women go near mad when they lose a child. Violet let the old woman be, and the rest of the family assured the girl we bore her no ill will. She'd always treated me kindly, and I liked her.

Not long after, rumors started going round that one of Polly's suitors, Will Reid, had murdered her. He'd been acting strange ever since her death, folks said, and then one Sunday at church he began sobbing during the sermon, yelling, "God forgive me!" for all to hear. Pa certainly believed Will was guilty and so had plans to kill him, but before he got round to it, Will up and joined the navy. We never saw him again in Tates Valley, although a few years later a little boy came to live with the Reid family, and soon enough news got around that he was Will's child. Will had been tried and hung in North Carolina for killing his wife, the boy's mother. The Reids are raising little Charlie as their own, and I try not to hold his father's sins against the boy. Though we felt for the murdered wife, the thought that justice had been served comforted our family, except for Mama, who clung to the crazy notion that somehow Violet was responsible for poor Polly's death.

It made sense for Violet to take over the one-room schoolhouse in Tates Valley when old Miss Abrams retired. Violet had no marriage prospects and had done more reading than anyone else around. And she took well to teaching. She wasn't so shy in front of children. By that time, my son Jake was old enough to go to school, and he learned to read and write and do sums from Violet. She taught all three of my children in that room at the same time, as well as most of the other children from Tates Valley. On any given winter's day, she'd have a class of thirty, aging from six to twelve.

My husband, Abel, looked in on Violet from time to time, as did my brothers and other men in the community. They saw to it she had enough firewood for winter, fixed the leaks in the roof of her aunt's old cabin, and brought her a rabbit or grouse when they had a bountiful hunting trip. That's how we lived in these parts in those days. I don't know what you might have heard, but there was no feuding here, and only a little moonshining. Most folks were good Christians who helped their neighbors.

Mama still muttered cruel things about Violet when she came up in conversation, but no one paid any mind. She ran a good schoolhouse, and no one else had cause to speak against her.

The trouble all started when Miss Elizabeth Munroe came around. The first I heard of her was from Ida Johnson, who stopped by on her way home from town one June afternoon. Abel runs a forge on the edge of Tates Valley, and we live just down the road, so I often see folks coming and going from town—if you can even call Tates Valley a town. It's really just Abel's blacksmith shop, Jonas Hickam's general store, Violet's schoolhouse, and two churches, Methodist where we attend and Baptist. Ida likes to run her mouth, so she makes a point to stop in when she's passing by.

I was on the porch shelling peas when I saw her coming down the path to the house, waving and singing an old hymn to herself. Ida was a big woman with a voice to match her frame. That afternoon she was carrying two large baskets, one on each arm.

"Hidy there, Pearl. Hit's a fine day, ain't it?"

"Sure is, Ida. You wanna set down for a spell?" She'd made it to the porch and was leaning against the railing.

"Don't mind if I do." She put down her baskets and sat in the empty rocker next to me. Without saying a word, she grabbed a hand-ful of my peas and started shelling along with me.

"You been in town?" I asked.

"Yes'm. Had to stop by Hickam's."

"You oughta send one of the boys to do your errands."

"Oh, I like to get to town now and again. Gets mighty boring day in, day out on the farm."

I nodded.

Ida leaned in. I could tell she had some news she wanted to share. "You know there's two women in a tent setting up a school down by Laurel Springs?"

"A school? In a tent?"

"Mm-hmm. They's from Atlanta. Dressed real nice. Come here to help us mountainfolk."

"What they doing in a tent?"

"They say it's just temporary. They want to build a proper school in Tates Valley."

"But we already got a school."

"They's talking about a big, consolidated school to teach children from all over the valley. They even mean to teach classes for grown men and women. Why, Pearl, you and I could take instruction in weaving—fancy that!"

I laughed. "No one bothers with a loom no more."

"I know, but these ladies say we could sell what we weave. They reckon folks in Chicago or New York would like to buy authentic mountain handicrafts."

"They told you that?"

"Yes'm. They got a real fancy way of talking, let me tell you." Ida reached into one of her baskets and fished out a magazine with a picture of a beautiful brunette lady on the cover. "They were giving magazines away. Books too."

I picked up the magazine and flipped through the pages. I'd never had much schooling myself, and trying to read gave me a headache.

"They done set up a kindergarten in the tent. The Greeleys' two boys were there doing lessons, and little Lureen McKay."

"Reckon my Timmy might like that. You think it's respectable?"

"Just about the most respectable thing to ever happen in Tates Valley. Can you believe they got a silver teapot?"

"What, in the tent?"

"Sure enough!"

That night after supper, I asked Abel about the tent women. He usually knows everything going on in town on account of his work. He'd heard about them and thought we might as well let Timmy take their lessons, since he was still too little to be much use on the farm. Abel didn't put too much stock in their grand plans to build a school, but seemed to think they were harmless enough.

It was a warm night, and we had the door open to let in air. The children were all upstairs in bed. "I don't understand, though," I said, as I sat across from my husband in the front room. "Why do they want to set up a school here?"

"It's charity, Pearl. They're missionaries."

"I thought missionaries only went to primitive places, like . . . China, or South Dakota."

Abel has a way of half-smiling at me that makes me feel a bit stupid, and he did it then. "They reckon we is primitive."

"Oh." I felt very stupid then. I looked around the cabin. It was simple. Abel had made most of our furniture except what had come from my daddy's house. I had sewn the tablecloth. I supposed we were poor, and yet because of Abel's smithy, we had more than most around here. I supposed everyone here was poor, but I'd never thought we were primitive.

Abel leaned back and drew on his pipe. "The truth is a real school would be good for the children."

"We got a real school, though. What about Violet?"

"Violet is a clever woman, but you know she ain't never been to school past eighth grade herself."

"But she's read all them books. A whole chestful! I seen it."

Abel was giving me that smile again. "I know, Pearl. She is smart, and she does a good job, I'm sure. But wouldn't you like for the kids to have more of a future?"

"You mean a future where they up and leave the valley?"

Abel took a long drag of his pipe, then nodded. "Yeah. Reckon I do."

I said nothing. I didn't know if I wanted that or not. I'd never really thought of it. The people I knew who'd left had gone to the army or the coal mines or the cotton mills, and none of that sounded worth making the trip for. But despite what Abel's half-smile implied, I wasn't stupid. I knew there was more in this world.

The next morning I got Timmy up and dressed and took him to see the tent women. Esta came along, though I thought she'd be too old for their kindergarten. She skipped ahead of us on the road down to Laurel Springs. Timmy held my hand tightly, nervous of wherever I was taking him.

"Hit's gonna be real fun!" I told him. "Don't you want to learn your letters and arithmetic?" Timmy said nothing but gave me a fearful look. He was the quietest of our children, the most frightened of strangers and new situations.

When we got near to the creek, I saw four tents set up in a clearing. Three women stood outside, talking amongst themselves, one of whom was Violet. I felt worried for her, offended on her behalf by these women coming to take over her school. The other two ladies were immaculately dressed—I could see that much even from a distance. One had a skirt that was a rich plum color, the like of which I'd never seen in a fabric. The other wore a white dress, and as we got closer, I saw that it was covered in tiny, delicate blue flowers. These two dresses were the most beautiful items of clothing I had ever seen. I looked down at my own homemade dress of faded blue cotton, thinning from years of wear and wash. I had never thought much about what I wore, but it was impossible not to compare.

When Violet saw me, she smiled and waved. I hurried up and called to Esta to stop running. Violet walked toward us, followed by the woman in the flowered dress. "Hello, Pearl! I'm so glad you've come along. Is Timmy going to stay and study in our kindergarten?"

I noted Violet's "our." "Howdy, Violet. Yep, Timmy's real excited." He squeezed my legs and tried to hide behind them. I pulled him out. "Say hello, Timmy."

Timmy looked down at the ground. The woman in the flowered dress crouched to his level. "Why, hello there, Timmy is it?"

He nodded silently.

"My name is Miss Ames. Would you like to come inside our tent? Some other children are doing lessons inside. I'm sure they'd love to see you." He stayed silent, but Miss Ames persevered. She pulled a piece of chalk out of her pocket. "I've got a slate that you can use. How does that sound?"

Cautiously, Timmy took the chalk. He gave me a look. "Go on then," I said. He followed Margaret into the tent.

Violet smiled at me. "He'll love it, Pearl. Margaret's a first-rate teacher."

"How do you know her?"

"Oh, we only met last week when she and Elizabeth"—Violet motioned toward the woman in the plum dress, who was writing something in a notebook—"arrived. But I've been mightily impressed with both these women."

Elizabeth looked up from her writing and came toward us. "Hello!"

"Hello," I replied. "Name's Pearl Whaley. My son Timmy's inside there."

"I'm Elizabeth Munroe. So nice to meet you!" She extended her hand, and I shook it. Her face was wide and pale. She had straw-colored hair and brown eyes.

"Pearl's husband is the town smith, Abel Whaley."

"Ah, I see! Yes, I've been by your husband's forge. It seems there's always a crowd of men there."

"Elizabeth and Margaret are from the Women's Federation of the Upper South. They hope to found a settlement school right here in Tates Valley."

"What made you decide on this spot?"

"We've been doing a comprehensive assessment of the surrounding counties, looking for the right location for our school. The most compelling factors leading us to Tates Valley were the community's isolation and its current lack of educational opportunities."

Violet seemed unfazed by this. In fact, she was nodding slightly.

"But Violet runs a real good schoolhouse," I said.

"I'm sure she does."

"I do what I can," cut in Violet. "But with our lack of resources, there's only so much anyone could accomplish."

She and Miss Munroe were nodding at each other now, almost as though I weren't there. "It has been such a delight to find such a naturally gifted teacher here in the mountains! We hadn't dared hope to stumble upon such a diamond in the rough."

Violet smiled and let out a sound close to a giggle. I couldn't recall ever hearing her giggle before.

Miss Munroe continued, turning back toward me. "When I found out how well-read your Violet is—why, I could scarcely believe it! I tell you, I did begin to doubt whether we had chosen the right spot for our project. Do the people of Tates Valley really need a settlement when they already have the innate gifts of Miss Violet Nickson at their disposal? But I hope we can build a school worthy of Miss Nickson's talents."

Violet was blushing now. She looked a right fool, and I felt embarrassed for her. "So you'll teach in the new school?" I asked her.

"I would like to."

"And we would love to employ her," replied Miss Munroe.

"How long should Timmy stay here?" I asked.

"You can pick him up after noon," answered Miss Munroe. "We'll serve the children a light lunch. And we can offer you some magazines to take home with you, if you like. We have some to give away."

"No, thank you. Though my daughter might. Esta!" I called. She'd run out of sight down by the creek. "I'm mighty thankful to you for learning Timmy like this. Tomorrow we'll bring you some eggs."

Miss Munroe shook her head. "That isn't necessary. We are happy to help those who need us. Besides, your generous neighbors have already begun supplying us with more eggs than two single women can possibly eat!"

Esta sprang toward us. I explained, "This here's Miss Munroe. She wants to know if you'd like a magazine."

Esta glared. "What magazine?"

"Esta! Don't be rude. Introduce yourself."

The girl sighed and stuck her hand out toward Miss Munroe, who invited her into one of the tents while I stayed outside with Violet.

"You ain't bothered that they think we're primitive?" I asked her.

"We are a bit primitive, aren't we?"

"And you ain't mad they're taking over your school?"

"They want to include me in their project, Pearl! It's terribly exciting. Why, this past week, since Margaret and Elizabeth arrived, has been one of the most thrilling of my life. We've had the most stimulating conversations."

Her eyes were shining, as though they might begin to leak. I could see her happiness was genuine, and the intensity of it made me uncomfortable. I looked away and muttered, "They seem real clever."

"More than clever," replied Violet. "*Good*. They are intelligent and good."

Esta and Miss Munroe reemerged from the tent, and I couldn't help but notice the silver buckles on the woman's shoes. They caught the light of the sun and half-blinded me.

For the next two months, Timmy spent his mornings in the tent. He seemed to like it well enough, and he was spelling words by the end of the summer. Most folks I talked to seemed taken with the tent women and their magazines and silver teapot. They were hoping to buy Old Man Kingsley's farm to build their school on. In August, they went back to Atlanta or wherever they came from. But around about October, I heard from Violet that Elizabeth Munroe was coming back. She would be staying with Violet while trying to work out the details of the land purchase. Not long after she arrived, Violet asked Abel and me to come to dinner with them.

"Where'd she get all this money from anyway?" I asked Abel in the wagon on the way to Violet's.

"Looks to me those ladies come from plenty of money."

"Sure, but silver buckles for your shoes is one thing. Buying up whole farms and building schools is another."

"Them that's got money get more easy enough."

Violet met us at the door. Miss Munroe was sitting in the front room before the fire, but she rose when she saw us, carefully placing the embroidery she was sewing upon the mantel.

"Thanks for having us, Violet," said Abel.

"Thank you for coming. Hope the children are well."

"They're with Mama," I said. Violet winced at the mention of my mother.

"Mr. and Mrs. Whaley, it's a pleasure to see you again." Miss Munroe swooped over.

"Miss Munroe." Abel nodded as he took off his hat and hung it on the rack. "How long you in town for?"

"Two weeks at the shortest, I should think. However long it takes to secure the sale of the property."

"Then when will you commence to building your school?" I asked.

"Just as soon as possible. I have made arrangements with an engineer in Knoxville who has the plans all ready."

"Progress moves so quickly," said Abel.

"It does when you make it," said Miss Munroe.

"Come along to the table," urged Violet, and we followed her into the cabin.

She had done her best to brighten up the place with pictures from magazines, mostly landscapes, on the walls. I didn't remember them from the last time I was here and wondered if they'd come from Miss Munroe's magazines. As we ate, the two women chatted back and forth like the best of friends. Violet was sounding more and more like Miss Munroe. She'd always had a schoolteacher's proper way of talking, but her accent was becoming more refined.

"Our village will never properly be able to thank you and Margaret for the kindness you've bestowed upon us."

"You know, dear Violet, that it is my pleasure." Miss Munroe carefully stabbed a green bean with her fork. "I only hope that the rest of your neighbors share your enthusiasm for the project. Mr. Whaley, I know you are a pillar of the community here."

Abel looked up from his potatoes.

"What is your sense of the people's feelings regarding our school?" she asked him.

Abel cleared his throat. "Folks are real thankful for the opportunity you're giving us. I know Pearl and me, like everyone, I suppose, want the best for our children."

Miss Munroe smiled broadly. "Of course. That is what all good mothers and fathers want. I am confident we can create a school here that will give your children a first-rate education, whether in agriculture or academics. And, you know, we hope to provide education for the entire community as well. We plan on running workshops for all ages in homemaking, hygiene, and similar subjects."

I almost choked on my beans. I was trying very hard to say nice things, but this was too much. "What in the world do you think you could teach me about homemaking?"

Miss Munroe went slightly red. "Oh, I mean no offense, Mrs. Whaley! I'm sure you are an excellent homemaker, as are all the fine women of the community. But there are modern techniques and technologies that I'm afraid no one around Tates Valley has been exposed to."

I had thought Abel would be cross at my rudeness and was surprised to hear him say, "And do you think folks here are unhygienic?"

"No, no! Oh, I should have explained more carefully. Again, it is not meant as an insult to the people or their current way of life. But we can provide medical services and instruction. There are so many simple things you can do to prevent the spread of disease, aid women in childbirth, and the like."

Violet tried to help. "Elizabeth and Margaret have shared their plans with me. I assure you both they aren't insulting in the least. Our people would benefit most greatly from the help they could provide."

Abel leaned away from the table, thoughtful. "I would caution you not to push folks too hard or too fast, Miss Munroe. People are attached to their ways. Ain't no one like to be told to change."

"Of course, of course. I understand you completely. And let me assure both of you that I have no intention of interfering with your custom. In fact, it is my greatest desire—after, of course, setting up the school for the betterment of the local people—to learn more about the culture here. What I have seen has truly impressed me. It seems to me that the people of the mountains have a real connection to our country's past and to the best of our shared heritage—and that should be treasured."

I stared at her blankly. Violet attempted to explain: "Elizabeth is a ballad collector."

"A what?" I asked.

"A ballad collector," repeated Miss Munroe. "It's a hobby, really—nothing scientific. I've been recording as many of the local songs as I can while in Tates Valley. To preserve the culture. Why, do either of you sing? Do you know any of the old ballads?"

I glanced at Abel. "I play the banjo," he said.

"Oh." Miss Munroe sounded disappointed. "An imported instrument, I'm afraid. My real interest is in the authentic mountain music."

"We had a fiddle in the attic," I mentioned. "Some say that's bad luck, but I don't put no stock in superstitions."

"You did ask for the rattle on that snake I kilt behind the barn to put inside it." Abel gave me his sly half-smile.

"Well, we ain't had no other use for that rattle, so we might as well use it to ward off evil spirits, just in case there is truth to those tales. Anyway, Jake's taken to playing it now."

"Does he play ballads?" asked Miss Munroe.

"He's been learning from my father," said Abel. "Mostly just fiddle tunes like 'Devil's Dream.'"

"I sing some to the children," I offered.

"What tunes?" she asked eagerly.

"'The Cuckoo,' 'Old Smoky,' that sort of thing."

She nodded, reached into her pocket, pulled out a notebook, and jotted something down. "Mrs. Whaley, could I stop by sometime and take down your songs?"

"I mean, I don't know anything special. Just the same old songs my mama sang to me when I was little."

"But that is exactly the sort of thing I'm after! Really, I would be most grateful."

I couldn't figure a polite way out of it. "Sure. I don't see why not."

"It's settled then—fantastic!" Miss Munroe dug into her potatoes, triumphant.

We managed to leave quickly after supper—I complained of exhaustion, which was true enough. I hadn't told Violet yet, but I was about three months along carrying a new baby. Abel was silent at first in the wagon on the way home. But then all of a sudden, as we passed the Turner place, he exclaimed, "What is wrong with that woman?"

I laughed at how irritated he sounded. Abel was a moderate man, not given to fits of temper or speaking ill of others. He looked over at me and laughed as well. I shook my head. "I can't understand half of what she says."

"I know! And what I do understand makes me madder than a wet hen. What business she got telling us we need hygiene classes?"

"And to think she wants me to sing songs for her!"

"You don't have to if you don't want to."

"I know, but how to get out of it without being rude? Besides, I almost feel sorry for her."

"Why on earth?"

"I don't know exactly. . . . She means well, don't you think? I mean, she really is trying hard to do the right thing."

"You're a kind woman, Pearl. You think the best of people."

"I try to. Hit don't always work, though."

I saw Violet the next day at church. She came up to me in front of the chapel after the service. "Pearl, I hope you had a nice time last night."

"Of course we did, Violet! Sorry to rush off—I's all tuckered out." I put my hand on my belly. "Looks like I'm expecting again."

"That's wonderful news, Pearl! I thought you had a glow."

"I don't know about that." Out of the corner of my eye I saw Jake terrorizing his little brother. "Jake! Don't hit!"

"Elizabeth really would love to hear your ballads."

"Oh yes. She's welcome to come by the house. I don't know anything special."

"She may consider it special. You know, she doesn't always know how to talk to folks around here. But she's determined to do good. I promise."

"I know, Violet." Seeing my boys roughhousing now in front of the church, I turned to them. "Boys! Stop that!"

My mother had also seen them fighting and came over to pull them apart. She yanked Timmy up by his collar and deposited him away from Jake on the grass. She was rougher with them than me.

"Well, thanks again for coming," Violet said quickly. She had already turned to go before I could reply. I knew she didn't want to speak to Mama, who was approaching us, dragging Jake behind her.

"What she want?" asked Mama.

"Just making conversation."

Mama watched Violet walk away, her face ugly with suspicion.

Three days later Miss Munroe came by to collect her ballads. It was a warm day, and I was outside hanging the washing when she stopped by. I heard her skirt rustling before I saw her on the path.

"Hullo there, Mrs. Whaley!" she cried as she came toward me.

"Hidy, Miss Munroe. How're you today?"

"Excellent! We are one step closer to finalizing the purchase of the land for the school."

"Good for you. Can I get you a cup of tea?"

"I'd love a glass of water. Hot today, isn't it?"

"Indian summer, I reckon. Come on inside."

We sat in the front room. I figured it was best to get it over with quickly. She asked me what songs I knew, and I tried to think of as many as I could. Most she wasn't interested in, but sometimes when I'd say a name, she'd stop me. I sang "Little Sparrow" for her twice, then mentioned "The Wife of Usher's Well."

"Ah, wonderful." She jotted something in her notebook. "You know that one's also known as 'The Lady Gay.' Did you ever hear it called that?"

I shook my head, and she made a note.

"Would you be so kind as to sing it?" asked Miss Munroe.

So I did. I'm not a great singer, but I can carry a tune. I sang out clear, "*There was a woman and she lived alone, and babies she had three. She sent them away to the north country to learn their grammarie.*"

Miss Munroe held up her hand, and I stopped. "I'm sorry, Pearl. Let me just get that last line. 'To learn their grammarie'?"

"That's right."

"Fascinating. Every other version I've heard begins with the mother sending her sons 'o'er the sea' instead of 'to the north country.'"

"Oh. Well, that's just how Mama taught me."

"No, it's wonderful, wonderful! It's very exciting to find a new variant. Please go on."

I cleared my throat. "*They'd not been gone but a very short time, scarcely six weeks to the day, when death, cold death spread through the land and swept them babes away*."

The whole time I sang, Miss Munroe wrote in her book. When I finished, she put down her pencil. "Thank you, Pearl—that was wonderful!"

"It's such a sad song."

"It is, isn't it? At least the children are reunited with their savior in the end."

I nodded. Then she asked if I would sing the song one more time. We did this with four or five songs. It seemed to take forever. As I finished singing "Lord Randall" for the third time, Miss Munroe looked up from her notebook and smiled. "It is such a thrill to hear these ancient songs being sung live right here in America! You know, scholars say that the Elizabethan manner of speech is best preserved in Appalachia."

I was puzzled. "What do you mean, 'Elizabethan'?"

"Just that it's how Englishmen spoke during the reign of Queen Elizabeth, hundreds of years ago."

"But how does anyone know what that sounded like?"

"Scholars have remarkable techniques for studying these things. To think you, dear Pearl, have a deeper connection to your Anglo-Saxon past than anyone else in all of the country!"

"They's just songs my mama taught me. She don't sing like she used to, not since my sister Polly passed on. Some of the old ballads turn her mind to how Polly died, especially 'Pretty Polly.'"

"I can see how a song by that name would be disturbing."

I sang it for her:

"Oh Polly, Pretty Polly, come go along with me,
Polly, Pretty Polly, come go along with me,
Before we get married some pleasures to see.

Oh, he led her over mountains and valleys so deep,
He led her over hills and valleys so deep,
Pretty Polly mistrusted and then began to weep.

"Oh Willie, Little Willie, I'm afraid of your ways,
Willie, Little Willie, I'm afraid of your ways,
The way you've been rambling you'll lead me astray."

"Oh Polly, Pretty Polly, your guess is about right,
Polly, Pretty Polly, your guess is about right,
I dug on your grave the biggest part of last night."

Miss Munroe looked unimpressed. "I've heard that one before. A murder ballad."

I nodded. "My sister Polly was murdered just like the girl in the song."

"That's horrible. Violet has told me the story. I can only imagine how awful it was for your family."

"Violet took it real hard. She and Polly were close."

"It must have been a terrible time for your family."

"It was. You know, I got married just as soon as I could. I love Abel, but I might have tried to slow him down some in the beginning if things had been differnt. But with Polly gone, Mama and Pa's house was filled with such a dark sadness, I wanted to get away as quick as I could. Losing a child is the worst thing that can happen to a soul in this life, even if you do have faith that you'll be reunited in the next."

"I can understand why your mother doesn't want to hear that song. And in any case, I'm more interested in ballads that trace back to Britain. I believe your 'Pretty Polly' is a variant of an English song called 'The Gosport Tragedy.' But it's been so transformed that the lurid American version is hardly recognizable in the original song."

"So you don't want it for your collection?"

"No. Americans have made a habit of memorializing young girls' murders in songs that are a dime a dozen. 'Omie Wise,' 'Pearl Bryan,' your 'Pretty Polly.' I'm interested in the ancient ballads that have only been preserved in a few special places, like the southern mountains. I hope to publish my collection so that these folk treasures are not lost to future generations."

The idea that anyone would want to read a book of Grandma's old songs made me want to laugh. But I held my tongue and said, "Glad I could be of help."

"Now, I do have just one more thing to ask of you, Pearl. Violet told me of your . . . condition. I hope you don't mind that I know."

"No, of course not. Everone's gonna know here purty soon." I patted my expanding belly.

"I would love to talk to you about steps you can take to ensure the health of your baby. I brought a pamphlet. . . ." She fished around in her pocket and handed me what looked like a small magazine but with no picture on the cover. "This goes over the very latest advances in prenatal hygiene. Your diet, exercise, and even clothing can affect the health of your unborn child."

"I done had three children already, Miss Munroe."

"Of course, of course. But please, just take a look, Pearl. You may find it helpful."

After she left I stuffed the pamphlet in the bottom drawer of my dresser, underneath all of Abel's shirts.

A few days later, Abel reported that the land sale had gone through, and sure enough, not long after that two engineers from Knoxville showed up at his forge, having gotten lost on their way to meet Miss Munroe and begin construction of the school. Everywhere you went in those days, folks were talking about the school. Nothing so exciting had happened around here since the railroad first came through, and that was back before I was born. For the most part, Miss Munroe was a hero, or at least a figure of great interest, larger than life. But she made some mistakes that winter.

I don't know how she first got wind of the local gatherings. My best guess is she was collecting someone's ballads, and they invited her along to hear more mountain music. The gatherings were informal parties that different folks hosted about once a month, usually in a barn or other space big enough for dancing. Everyone who played an instrument would bring it along and make music late into the night. I used to go when I was younger, and Abel and I had courted at many a gathering. Those are some of my best memories—hot and flushed, surrounded by all the other young people in the valley, dancing reels while the fiddles played. I always loved dancing. You could forget the hard work of the farm, the hot days of July or the freezing nights of January, the preacher's hellfire warnings—all of it—when you were dancing. Now, true enough, often some young men would sneak in moonshine, or show up already drunk on it beforehand, and sometimes they got to fighting. But most folks came to enjoy the music and dancing, and there wasn't anything immoral about that.

Since Jake came along, I hadn't gotten out to many gatherings, but Abel still liked to go along with his banjo now and then. He was there the night that Miss Munroe showed up, along with Violet. I don't remember Violet ever coming along to a gathering before, even when she and Polly were fast friends. She was so shy that I'm sure the thought of dancing gave her terrors. But there she was that night, escorting Miss Munroe to see the local festivities. "As though we was animals in a zoo," said Abel sourly that night as he got into bed.

I'd been asleep when he got home, but he was worked up and woke me so he could tell the story.

"You shoulda seen her, Pearl. Just standing in the corner of Hank's barn, staring at everone. Poor Violet looked embarrassed by the whole thing. But that Miss Munroe couldn't hide her disgust. She kept whispering to Violet and shaking her head. Finally she went right up to Silas Barnes and asked him if he was drinking. Can you imagine?"

I grunted sleepily. Abel was under the covers now, wrapping his arms around me. "Well, Silas just laughed and offered her some of his whiskey. She stormed out and took poor Violet with her. Violet had her head down like she was afraid to look anyone in the eye. But Miss Munroe's head was way up high in the air like usual."

The next we heard about the whole thing was from the children. They came home from Violet's schoolhouse one day with flyers, which they presented to me.

"What's this?"

"Miss Munroe came to school today and gave them to us," replied Esta. "She said to take them home to give to our parents."

"What's it say, Esta?"

"I'll read it!" shouted Jake, grabbing the flyer out of his sister's hand.

"No, I want to read it!" said Esta.

"Oh, I don't care which of you reads it—just somebody tell me what it says."

Esta grabbed the flyer back. "*December second at the new Tates Valley Settlement School building site,*" she read aloud, "*please join us for a Christian Social. Hymn singing, apple bobbing, baseball games. A celebration of Family, Community, and TEMP . . . TEMP . . .*"

"*TEMPERANCE!*" said Jake.

Esta looked up at me. "That last word is written real big."

"I can see that," I said.

"What's temp-er-ance?" asked Jake.

"It means not drinking any moonshine."

"Are we gonna go to the Christian social?" asked Esta. Both she and Jake watched eagerly for my answer.

"Reckon so."

"Hooray!" shouted Esta.

"I'm gonna play baseball!" shouted Jake.

I picked the wrong time to bring it up with Abel. It was late in the day, and he'd been at work all afternoon slaughtering and salting one of the hogs. He was worn out, and I would have been better off letting it be for the time. But I thought he'd feel the same as me: annoyed at Miss Munroe, yes, but also amused by her. I still found her harmless and knew the children would be fit to be tied if I didn't let them go.

He wasn't amused by the flyer. "The children can't go. Ain't none of us gonna go. That's just giving the woman what she wants."

"Well, we're gonna send the children to the school when it's built, ain't we?"

Abel was peeling off his blood-soaked shirt. "Only because it's the best thing for them. They don't have no need to go to this 'Christian social.'"

"Reckon that's true. They'll be mighty disappointed, though."

Abel wiped himself with the wet cloth I handed him. "Life is full of disappointment."

He marched upstairs, and I was left alone in the kitchen. That was when I realized just how set against Miss Munroe Abel had become. It gave me an anxious feeling, a rise of nerves in my belly. Not that I cared so much for Miss Munroe, but I could feel that trouble was coming. If Abel felt this way, others must too.

The next day was Saturday. Abel and Jake were working in our small field, so I left Esta in charge of Timmy and walked the two and a half miles to Violet's cabin. I knocked on her front door, and as I stood waiting, I felt the anxious feeling again and hoped Miss Munroe wasn't there.

Violet was surprised to see me. "Why, hello, Pearl! This is unexpected. Come on in." As I followed her into the cabin, she pulled off the apron she was wearing and hung it on a nail in the wall. "Can I get you a cup of coffee?"

"Thank you. That'd be nice." I gave myself a seat in the front room, worn out by the walk. As this pregnancy had progressed, I had begun to feel a dull ache in my lower back most all the time.

Violet brought in two cups and sat across from me. "Is Miss Munroe around?" I asked.

"No. She's at the building site most days now."

"I would have thought she'd have headed back to Atlanta."

"I think she's too excited by the construction to go."

"You don't tire of having her around?"

"Oh, never! It's so pleasant to have company."

Poor Violet, I thought. She must have been awfully lonely before Miss Munroe came.

"Will we be seeing you at the social next week?" she asked.

"No." She'd been about to take a sip of coffee but stopped short in surprise. I continued, "Abel don't want us to go. You know, Miss Munroe upset a lot of people at the gathering."

Violet exhaled loudly and put her cup on the arm of the chair. "Oh, that. It was silly, really. I told her she shouldn't have gone—"

"She shouldn't have, Violet! And what were you doing there with her? You don't want to get all mixed up in this business. You ain't never been to a gathering before in your life."

Her brow furrowed. "So what if I haven't? I got as much of a right as anyone!" She sounded more hurt than angry.

"You ain't got no right to judge," I said, shaking my head. "*She* ain't got no right, Violet. To come from outside and pass judgment on folks here."

"Maybe she does have the right! The effort and expense she has put forth to have the school built! Folks should be thanking her, not condemning her."

"But ain't no one asked for her help. We is thankful, of course, but still. It don't give her the right."

We hardened into silence. I stared into my coffee cup and listened to the sizzle of the logs in the fireplace.

When Violet spoke again, her voice was softer, almost dreamy. "I just wish . . . I wish that you could see how much she cares. Elizabeth has the kindest, most sensitive soul of anyone I've ever met. You know, I haven't had a friend so dear since your sweet sister Polly passed."

I gave her a sad smile. "I am glad that she has been a friend to you. But you must realize how everyone else around here sees her."

"You say she's judging the people here, but she reveres them. She says all the time that the mountaineers are the noblest race in this country."

"Why, because we talk like folks did when Elizabeth was queen?"

"She wants to help. That is her only impulse. And there is so much she could do for us. We are terribly isolated here, Pearl, you know that. We could use the help—the educational and medical help."

"Is it that we're isolated or that we're poor? If I'da goose laying golden eggs, I'd take some time to learn reading and writing. I'd take a carriage into town to have my babies at a hospital."

"So let her help you! Let her help us all. She can't make you rich, but she can see to it that your children have a better life."

"My life ain't so bad!"

"It's good you feel that way. But what if Esta and Jake don't? Shouldn't they have the opportunity for a different life if they want it?"

We were spinning in circles, and I no longer knew how to convince

Violet of anything. I wanted out of the cabin and wished I'd never come. I spoke more forcefully than I intended. "Just be careful, Violet! That's what I came here to say."

"Are you warning me? Or threatening me?"

"Don't be ridiculous. I've always liked you. I's just trying to help."

I felt sick on the walk home and had to vomit behind a rhododendron on the side of the road. I'd never had much problem with morning sickness and wondered if I'd eaten something bad. When I got home, I went right past Esta and Timmy to lie down in bed.

I felt better the next day and tried to put the whole thing out of my mind. If Violet was too deep under Miss Munroe's spell to listen to reason, there wasn't anything I could do about it. The Christian social came and went. Besides trying to ignore the children whining about having missed it, I didn't give it much thought until Ida Johnson stopped by one afternoon.

It was a bitter day, and when I let her in she went straight to the fireplace to warm her hands. "Cold day to go into town, ain't it?"

"I done run out of sugar. Milo gets awful testy if I ain't got none for his coffee."

"Well, set a spell and warm yerself."

We talked about the cold weather, and she asked how I was feeling. I knew Ida had some gossip she was getting around to.

"Didn't see you at the social on Saturday."

"No, Abel didn't want to go."

"You missed quite a show!" Her eyes were sparkling with secret mirth.

"That right?"

"Mm-hmm. Silas Barnes and the Riley boys done showed up drowning in mountain dew. Caused quite a ruckus! Silas kept following that poor Miss Munroe around singing temperance songs. She was madder'n a hornet."

Ida was laughing at the memory, but I didn't join in. The whole thing filled me with dread.

"Anyway, she done left town now."

"Really?"

"Mm-hmm. Says she went back home for Christmas, but I reckon those boys done got to her. She was probably offended they don't drink their shine out of a silver teapot!" Ida laughed at her own joke, and I gave her a weak smile.

After a moment, her face fell. "Seems Violet's taken over Miss Munroe's work at the new school."

"Well, that's only natural."

"I suppose, but she's got the old school to worry about, you know."

"I'm sure she can keep an eye on the builders while teaching as well."

"I wonder about her sometimes."

"What do you mean?" I asked.

"She ain't never been quite right, has she?"

"Violet's just smarter than the rest of us, I reckon."

"Maybe that's it. But you know, I talked to old Mrs. Barnes, Silas's mother, and her milk cow, Dottie, dropped dead last week. For no reason."

"What you getting at, Ida?"

"Violet looked awful upset when those boys was pestering her precious Miss Munroe."

"Ida, don't be ridiculous! You think Violet Nickson bewitched Mrs. Barnes's cow?!"

She shrugged. "You never know. We've had witches here before."

"You don't really believe that nonsense, do you?"

She shrugged again.

I felt the baby in my belly kick. "Abel's gonna be home soon. I best get supper ready."

Ida stood. "I know you's friends with her, Pearl. But be careful."

"I don't want to hear no more of this, Ida. Hit's foolish and mean."

She shook her head at me, as though I were the fool.

Miss Munroe didn't come back until early spring, round about when the floods had started. It was the wettest March anyone could remember. It rained every day for a week, and folks were terrified of the damage done to the crops just starting to grow. We weren't as dependent as others on our field, owing to Abel's forge, but a bad season hurts everyone here. If farmers have no crops, they have no means to have their horses shod or wagons repaired.

I started hearing other people talk about Violet besides Ida. At church, two girls yelled, "Witch!" as she walked by their pew, loud enough that Violet herself surely heard, as well as anyone else nearby. And Abel told me that some of the men hanging around the smithy had started blaming the rain on her.

"I hope you told them to take that foolish talk right out of your forge." I was churning butter as he ate his breakfast.

"They's just fooling around."

"I don't think it's funny."

Abel munched his bacon. "You get awful worked up about Violet."

"She's my friend."

Abel stood and began putting on his jacket. Esta cleared the breakfast plates from the table. "Mama, why didn't Miss Violet ever marry?"

"Not everone's lucky enough to find a man to marry."

Esta set the dishes in the washbasin and paused. "But doesn't she want a family?"

"I'm sure she probably does, but they ain't no help for it. Besides, she has all the schoolchildren to care for."

Esta looked worried, as though she had just become aware of one of life's injustices.

Later that day, I answered a knock at the door to find Miss Munroe. She was dripping wet from walking in the rain, and I had her stand by the fire to warm herself.

"How are you doing, Pearl? You've been on my mind."

"I ain't too bad. My back aches."

She nodded. "Please let me know if you need any help. I would be glad to attend to the birth, if you'd like. I'm no midwife, but I have some basic obstetric training that might be helpful."

"My mama is a granny woman."

"Oh, I see. You mean she tends to births?"

"Yes'm."

"Alright, well, still, I'd be glad to give her a hand."

"That's kindly of you. How long you back for?"

"I'm hoping to open the school in a month's time. We won't begin regular enrollment until the fall, but will run community programs and the kindergarten this summer."

"You staying with Violet?"

"For the moment. There will be a cottage on the school grounds for myself and the other teachers, like Miss Margaret Ames, whom you may remember."

"That sounds nice. How many teachers you expect to employ?"

"It will just be Margaret, Violet, and myself to start. We'll have to see how enrollment develops. We hope to attract students from all over the county."

"Well, good luck to you."

Folks seemed to have cooled down about Miss Munroe, and no one made much fuss about her return. People's anger and distrust had transferred to Violet. Maybe since she was one of us—or at least less of an outsider than Miss Munroe—people felt more comfortable slandering her. Something about Miss Munroe was a little too fancy and important to suspect of witchcraft. I never heard anyone mention it. It would have seemed silly.

Two more wet weeks, and it wasn't even April yet. It was a shock to see the sun come up one morning into a bright, blue sky. I couldn't help but stop on my way to feed the chickens, sit on the big stump behind our house, and take a minute to breathe in the cool morning air, still damp but without the oppressive threat of rain. The trees were glowing early spring green, and the birds were screeching and calling, probably just as excited by the change in the weather as I.

I let the chickens out of the coop and spread the feed on the ground, as they bobbed and squawked. I was still lost in my reverie, mindlessly humming a tune, when I felt something wet run down my leg. I knew I was by myself—Abel was at the forge, and the children at Violet's schoolhouse—and without thought, I picked up my skirts high enough to see a trail of bright-red blood sliding down my thighs. I dropped the bucket, and the chickens ran over to gorge on the mound of spilled feed. I walked back to the house as fast as I could without running.

I cleaned myself up and lay down on the bed. I felt no pain. My third pregnancy had ended in miscarriage, but that had been much earlier, before I was even showing. I was close to ready for birth now. At night when I lay in bed, I could feel legs and arms kicking, stretching inside me. I put my hand on my belly then, hoping to feel the child move. There was nothing. I went downstairs to the pantry, opened a jar of apple butter, and put a spoonful in my mouth. I waited a moment, and then felt a somersault inside me, the way I always did when I ate something sweet. I walked slowly back to the front room, relieved.

It was luck that Mama stopped by about an hour later. Her face fell when I opened the door—I must have gone quite pale, and she seemed to know something was wrong.

"Set down, set down!" she said, and I did as I was told like a child.

"I'm bleeding, Mama." I sounded scared like a child too.

"Nettle tea. That's what you need. You set right there, and I'll fetch some nettles directly."

I sat in front of the fire and waited, not sure what else to do. This was my fourth pregnancy—fifth, if you count the one that ended early. It got easier but was still hard. The first time with Jake had been pure terror. I had married Abel at fifteen and got pregnant the next year. Even though Mama was a granny woman, she'd hardly told me anything about birthing. I'd watched a cow give birth, and that was the image that played again and again in my mind as my belly grew. I even dreamed once that I gave birth to a calf. I was in labor for two days with Jake and thought I was going to die the whole time. I didn't know a person could survive pain like that. I didn't know my body would just about tear itself open to push the baby out. It was faster with Esta and Timmy, and I knew I wasn't dying when the pain started, though I still didn't know that I wouldn't die. You never do know, of course. My aunt died in childbirth, and so did Abel's sister.

When the door opened, I was surprised to see Jake instead of Mama. I'd forgotten he was coming home for lunch and then to work in the field.

"Jake! I'm not feeling well, and I need you to fetch Miss Munroe. She's probably at the new school site. You can saddle up Old Sandy."

"But I'm starved!" he complained.

"Grab yerself a biscuit then. But hurry, Jake!"

He seemed to notice the fear in my voice and did as he was told. Mama came back with her nettles. "Sorry that took so long. The rain must have drowned 'em out. The woods is usually full of 'em by this time."

I said nothing as she made her tea. And just as she handed me a mug of steaming green liquid, I heard a wagon approaching.

"Who's that?" asked Mama.

"I asked Jake to fetch Miss Munroe."

"What? Why'd you do that?"

"She has medical training, Mama."

Her face hardened. "I see. You know I been attending to women for twenty years."

"I know, Mama. But she might have learning you don't know 'bout."

She stomped back to the kitchen. The door opened, and in rushed Miss Munroe, Jake, and, to my surprise, Abel, who came straight to my side. He knelt and touched my cheek so tenderly that I almost began to cry in terror. He was never normally so gentle in front of other folks. "I's alright," I whispered. "How did you find out?"

"Saw Jake go by on Old Sandy."

Miss Munroe took my hand. "How do you feel, Pearl?"

"I feel alright."

Abel stood. "Jake, let's go on outside."

After they left, I described the bleeding to Miss Munroe. She nodded, her brow furrowed. Mama watched us from the kitchen with her arms folded across her chest.

"Can you feel the baby moving?" asked Miss Munroe.

"Yes'm."

"That's good, Pearl, very good! Now, I want you to stay in bed for as long as you can. I'm afraid it could be dangerous for your baby for you to try to get up."

"But I feel fine."

"I know, and that's a good sign. I hope this bleeding will stop soon. But we need to keep an eye on it, and you need to rest."

I nodded. She helped me up the stairs to bed and asked me where she could find cloths. She made a neat pile by the bed for me. "I'm going to stay for the afternoon, Pearl. You just try to rest. Sleep, if you can. I'll be downstairs."

I did manage to sleep after she left. When I awoke, it was dusk. Mama was standing over me with a tray. I sat up. She handed me a bowl of soup. "That woman's finally gone."

"You been here all afternoon?" I asked, taking the soup.

"I weren't going to leave you alone with her."

I heard footsteps on the stairs, and Abel appeared in the doorway. "How you feeling?" he asked.

"Alright," I said. "I'm sorry I ain't much use today."

"Don't you worry about that," he said.

"I'll stay as long as you need me," said Mama.

The next day the bleeding stopped. Miss Munroe came by in the morning, and I told her everything seemed normal again, but she wanted me to stay in bed for a few more days. By the afternoon, I could hardly stand it. Mama was making Lord knows what mess out of my pantry, and all my chores were going undone. I got out of bed and went downstairs. Mama was kneading dough in the kitchen.

"I can do that," I said.

"Thought that woman told you to rest."

"I feel fine. Why don't you go on home?"

"You sure?"

"Yes. This place ain't gonna run itself, is it? The children will be home soon."

"You know I can take care of everything just as long as you need me to."

"I know, Mama, and I thank you, but honest, I feel normal."

"At least let me make you some more nettle tea. I fetched these nettles after all."

I let her make the tea. I don't know if Mama's nettle tea is any better or worse than the medicines a town doctor would give. It didn't taste too bad, anyway.

She was gone when Abel got home, and I had just finished cooking supper. He was surprised to see me up and about. "I thought Miss Munroe said to stay in bed."

"She did, but I feel fine. It seemed like such a waste of time just lying in bed."

He looked concerned. "Miss Munroe seemed to know what she was talking 'bout yesterday. You sure you don't wanna do what she say?"

"I promise I'll take it easy. I ain't going for any long walks with this belly anyway. But I can't stay in that bed."

"Alright."

I did try to take it easy, but so many things need to be taken care of on a farm. The next afternoon, Abel was still at the forge when the cows knocked over part of a fence. I set Jake to fixing the fence and left Esta in charge of Timmy while I went after the cows. They are stupid animals, and you have to be careful not to spook them and get them to running the wrong way away from you. These two had made it almost all the way down to the creek.

Mitchell's Creek is just on the other side of the road from our place, but set down a bit, and you can hear but not see the creek when you ride or walk past. I was careful on the bank going down. The ground was still soaked through from the rains, and the last thing I wanted was to fall or find myself stuck in a laurel slick. I could hear Spotty lowing, and walked quietly toward the sound, so as not to startle her.

As I made my way through the wood, I heard another sound— human voices, women's voices speaking softly, almost drowned out by the running water. Something made me stop. I looked down toward the creek. The trees were still mostly bare, so I could see all the way to the water, even though I was high up on the bank. I stepped carefully toward the sound of the voices, away from Spotty. I was able to see around the next bend in the creek to where Violet and Miss Munroe sat on a broad, flat rock just above the water. I walked closer for a better look, keeping as quiet as I could. I can't say what made me want to spy exactly, except that I'd been worried about those two for months now. It didn't feel dishonest to come a little closer to hear what they might be saying. They were in woods belonging to no one but the railroad, after all, even if they'd chosen a hidden spot to sit.

They were sitting close and holding hands. I was surprised by the intimacy, but then I supposed they'd become almost like sisters living together those past months. The noise of the creek made it hard to hear anything they said. Stray words floated up to me: ". . . I'm afraid . . ." ". . . the school . . ." ". . . so tired . . ." I was worried to go any closer lest I be seen. Of course, I could tell them I was going after Spotty, but Miss Monroe would chide me for getting out of bed. Besides, I didn't want to spoil their private moment.

I waited, though, to turn and go after the cows. I watched them talk and smile. I noticed that Miss Munroe had taken off her boots and stretched out her naked feet in front of her. She touched Violet's hair gently, and they stopped speaking. In an instant, they were both leaning into one another in an embrace and a kiss.

It was not a sisterly kiss. It was the sort of passionate kiss that Abel had bestowed upon me when we first began courting. It lasted for a long moment. I stood as still as I ever have, though the baby started kicking my ribs.

Finally they pulled apart, and went back to talking as though nothing had happened, except that Miss Munroe was idly stroking the back of Violet's hand. Carefully, I turned and walked as quietly as possible away toward Spotty. My heart was pounding, and I felt out of breath at the strain of walking on the steep slope.

I got the cows back to the pasture, where Jake had fixed the fence, and I went in to lie down for a spell. I had always liked Violet and never believed the nonsense about her being a witch. But now I had seen with my own eyes that she was not a good woman.

I knew I should go downstairs to get supper together, but I felt awfully tired. I heard Abel coming through the front door and forced myself to sit up. Before I could get out of bed, my abdomen seized and cramped. The pain startled me. I put my hand on my belly and threw off the quilt. With each child, I was surprised by labor, never quite remembering the pain until it was upon me again. Yet this pain seemed sharper, more sudden than I recalled—or was that how it always was? It seems impossible to recall the specifics of hurt after it has passed.

I stood up and made my way toward the stairs to fetch Abel but had to stop halfway across the room. The cramping had started again—so soon! I leaned against the wall to try to catch my breath. It was then I looked back at the bed and saw the trail of blood.

"Send Jake to get Mama," I said to Abel after he'd come running to help me back into bed, saying comforting things but in a voice thick with worry.

"I will. And I'm gonna take the wagon to go fetch Miss Munroe."

"No."

"What do you mean, Pearl? She's smart, and I believe she can help you."

"I don't care. I don't want her here."

"Pearl, please—"

"No!" I screamed.

"Alright. I'll go send Jake."

He left me. I tried to breathe and not think about the blood. But then another stabbing pain. I cried out—I couldn't help it. I felt hot. I pulled off my dress and threw it on the floor. But now that I was wearing only my chemise, I began to tremble with cold. I pulled the blanket over me and tried to lie down. But the pain returned, and I had to sit up. I got out of the bed and leaned forward against the side of it. I think I was groaning.

Abel brought me a cup of water, but I didn't want it. I could see from his face that he was scared. He put his hand on my back. "You're so hot," he said.

"I'm shivering!"

"Don't you want under the blanket?"

I nodded and tried to back onto the bed. Abel stood over me, unsure of what to do. I heard the front door opening, and then Mama was bounding up the stairs.

She came to the bed and took my hand. "How do you feel, Pearl?"

"It hurts, Mama! There's more blood."

"Abel, go fetch me your ax."

"What?"

"To put under the bed. It cuts the bleeding." Mama spoke with assurance. Abel gave me a look, and I could see he didn't believe it. I didn't really believe Mama's old folkways either, but had no energy to fight her. Clearly Abel didn't feel like fighting her either, since he did as he'd been told.

Mama pulled back the covers. "Is it bad?" I asked.

"Not too much blood, honey." Her voice was reassuring, but I sensed she was lying. I was scared to look down there myself. "Esta!" she called. I looked at her in alarm. "She's old enough to help. She can boil a pot of water, can't she?"

"Am I gonna die?" My voice cracked.

"No! Of course not, Pearl. No more talk like that. This is your fourth child. You know it hurts."

"But there ain't supposed to be blood yet!"

"It happens sometimes."

"And then women die."

"No, Pearl! We are gonna get you through this."

I closed my eyes. Mama began praying, but I couldn't concentrate on the words. The pain was rushing back, worse this time. I let out a low moan, and Mama squeezed my hand. It seemed to me that we went on like that for some time, me moaning, Mama praying. Then Abel returned with the ax.

"Good!" said Mama. "Now, just put it right under the bed. That'll stop the bleeding."

Abel looked unconvinced. Esta appeared. "The water's boiling, Granny!"

"Good girl!" She let go of my hand. "Pearl, I'm gonna go prepare what we need for the birth. Come on, Esta, help your mamaw downstairs."

She left. Abel came to my side. "Pearl, I don't care what you say, I'm fetching Miss Munroe."

"No, Abel! She's a sinful woman."

"I don't care! I'm scared, Pearl. And you and I both know that putting an ax under the bed ain't nothing but an old wives' tale."

Before I could say another word, he'd left the room. I was panting, staring at the wooden wall beside the bed. I didn't have the energy to care much what Abel did. I thought Mama was lying to me. I was dying.

I don't know how much time had passed when Abel came back with Miss Munroe. I didn't want her there, but I was so weak, I couldn't fight. She just about ran up the stairs to my side, ignored Mama sitting by me, and put her cool hand on my cheek. "Pearl, dear, how are you doing?" Her voice was low and calm.

"It hurts."

"I know it does. But it will pass. The pain will pass. I think you're ready to deliver this baby. We're going to get it out as quickly as we can and then focus on stopping your bleeding. Alright?"

I nodded.

"Violet, can you bring up the water?"

I hadn't even noticed Violet in the corner.

"Alright, Pearl," said Miss Munroe. "It's time to push."

I desperately wanted it over. I summoned all my strength and pushed and pushed, hoping to push the pain away. Miss Munroe and Violet stood with me, taking turns holding my hands. At some point Mama returned too. I got on my hands and knees—it seemed easier to push that way, so I did. Every now and then, between the pushes, I would see the women looking at each other, whispering. I knew they were discussing my doom.

Finally Miss Munroe told me the head was coming. I was burning and aching and so very tired. I pushed as hard as I could. Mama was holding my hand, praying into my ear. Miss Munroe exclaimed, "You've done it, Pearl! You've done it!" and I felt that great release.

But there was no sound. No crying. I was scared to look down. Miss Munroe was speaking to Violet quietly. Mama was still praying.

Violet walked away with my baby in a blanket. Miss Munroe turned to me. "Pearl, we have to stop your bleeding now. I am going to massage your womb to try to get it to contract faster."

I didn't care what she did just then. I had never felt so exhausted in my life. I was on the edge of consciousness and knew it would be easy to close my eyes and go to sleep. Maybe forever. At that moment I didn't care if it was forever—I just wanted the rest. So I said nothing and let Miss Munroe do her work.

"Where's Violet gone?" asked Mama.

"She's tending to the child."

Mama let go of my hand and left. I barely noticed. I wasn't even worried about the baby, that's how tired I was.

"I'm sorry if this hurts," said Miss Munroe. "But we have to do what we can to stop the bleeding." I didn't answer. I was drifting off. "Pearl? Pearl? Don't go to sleep just yet. Pearl!"

I don't remember what happened after that. Some time had passed when I woke up.

Abel was beside me, holding my hand. "Pearl!" he said. I could tell from the way he looked at me that he hadn't known if I would wake up. "Pearl! Are you awake?"

I nodded weakly. I could see Miss Munroe and Violet sitting across the room, watching us.

"Where's the baby?" I asked.

Abel looked down. Miss Munroe came to me and took my hand gently. "I'm so sorry, Pearl. She didn't survive. She's gone back to her Lord."

"But I saw Violet take her away."

Miss Munroe nodded. "She wasn't alive. It was a stillbirth, Pearl."

I looked at Abel. I didn't trust Miss Munroe.

"I'm so sorry, Pearl," he said. His eyes were red. I'd only ever seen him cry once before.

"Violet and I will give you both a moment alone. We'll be downstairs. But please, if you feel worse or start to bleed again, send Abel to get me immediately."

Abel and I were silent for a long while. Finally he spoke. "What matters most is that you're alive. I thought we'd lost you, Pearl."

"I thought I was dying."

"How would I have gone on if we lost you?" He cried then, and I had to look away.

Mama came up the stairs. "Pearl!" she shouted. She ran to my side and hugged me tight.

I hugged her back and started to cry. "My baby, Mama . . . my baby's dead. . . ."

She pulled back and looked at me. "Those women—"

Abel cut her off. "Abigail! Miss Munroe just saved Pearl's life."

Mama ignored him and looked at me. "She handed Violet that baby. She handed her that baby, and it died."

"That is enough!" I had never heard Abel speak to my mother that way. "You will not talk like that in my house."

Mama gave him a cold look. "I know what I saw." She turned and left the room.

"Don't listen to her, Pearl," said Abel. "Something was wrong the whole time, you know that. It was wrong days ago even, when the bleeding started."

"I want to see my baby."

Abel nodded. "Alright."

He left the room, and in a moment Violet came up the stairs holding the tiny bundle. She laid the swaddled corpse in my arms, her face streaked with tears. "I'm so sorry for your loss, Pearl."

I stared at the round little face of my daughter. She looked like Jake had as a baby, though with more dark hair. I had wanted to know what my child looked like, but now that she lay on top of me, I didn't know what to do. I was afraid that stroking her cheek or holding her hand would break my heart.

"Please take her away, Violet. I can't . . ." I stumbled. "I can't . . ."

"Of course." Violet picked her up. "She's with the angels, Pearl."

I fell back into a deep, dreamless sleep. When I woke, it was dark. Abel was awake, beside me, holding my hand.

"How you feel?" he asked.

"Alright."

"I'm gonna carve a coffin for the child out of that white oak I took down last fall."

"Good."

"Don't listen to your mother, Pearl. She wants to fill your head with foolishness."

"Violet ain't a good woman."

Abel stared at me. "You've always been friends with Violet. I know you're tired and upset, but you can't go along with this hateful talk."

"Mama's been right all along. Maybe she is a witch."

"Pearl! You don't know what you're saying."

"I do. She killed my baby."

Abel looked disgusted with me. But I didn't care.

I lay in that bed for days after, too weak to move, milk spilling out of my swollen breasts, blood still pouring from inside me, and went over and over it all. I don't believe in witches, but I knew Violet wasn't a good woman. And my baby was dead. I let Mama tell folks whatever she wanted about my labor. She talks a lot and knows everyone, so it didn't take long for the story to get around. Folks started keeping their children home, away from Violet's schoolhouse. I told Esta and Jake I needed them home with me while I recovered. Two weeks later, a tree fell on Violet's cabin and knocked off part of the roof. Abel wanted to fix it for her, but Mama and I talked him out of it. He was upset. I think if I hadn't still been so ill, he wouldn't have given in. But he was afraid of troubling me.

Ida came by one day with the news that Miss Munroe's friend, Margaret Ames, was taking over the teaching in the one-room school-house until the big school was built. I was sitting up in bed by then, beginning to feel better, and sipping the soup she'd brought for me. "So everone's agreed to send their children back," she said.

"I'll let the kids return Monday, then."

"I never did like Violet."

"Is Miss Munroe still staying with her?" I asked.

"She can't very well with no roof on the house! Miss Munroe's gone—gone back to Atlanta, I reckon. Miss Ames is staying in the new cottage on the school grounds. Violet's all alone." Ida sounded satisfied.

"What will she do?"

"Don't know. Hit just goes to show—God is more powerful than the devil."

That summer we heard that Violet had sold her little piece of land to the logging company. And just like that, she was gone—no one knew where.

I knew Abel was angry with me, but he let it go. He'd been awfully scared when he thought I was dying. The school was completed, and Miss Ames became the headmistress. Miss Ames was gentle and kind. She didn't collect ballads or comment on community behavior. Sure enough, students came from around the county to attend the school. All three of my children attended through high school. And we all went to the community events. I even took a health and hygiene course. It wasn't so bad. I learned some useful tips for keeping the house clean.

I wasn't able to have children after that birth, which was a relief, to be honest. We went on happily enough. In other parts, blacksmiths began to fall on hard times as automobiles took over, but it was many years before folks around here began to buy cars. The logging company started buying up folks' timber rights all through the valley, and soon enough we had a railroad not half a mile from our farm.

Jake got married and joined the army, and when she was old enough, Esta went to nursing school in Knoxville. She met a young man there, and I went to the city for the first time in my life for her wedding. We stayed in a hotel on Gay Street. I could hardly believe the size of the buildings. And there were so many of them! I got a headache almost as soon as we got to the city. There was so much noise and dirt and smoke.

Esta took me to a fancy department store to buy a hat for the wedding. The building was five stories tall and we had to walk through a revolving glass door to get inside. It was just like pictures I'd seen in magazines. The huge front room was brightly lit with rows and rows of gloves, hats, and coats. A rich, rosy scent wafted through the air from the perfume counter. I felt like the hillbilly I was in my mud-caked boots and homemade dress.

I picked out a simple blue felt hat with a feather on the side and took it up front to pay. And that was when I saw her. Standing behind a cashbox, speaking to a customer. It was Violet. Her face had wrinkled, of course, and her hair was streaked white, but I knew her, sure as I know my own children. She was wearing a simple but well-made dress, and her hair was done up in a fancy style. She looked at home in the store, poised and capable, taking the young woman's cash and giving her change. I stared for a long moment. Finally, Esta nudged me. "Mama, ain't you gonna buy it?"

Before I could think to turn and find another cash register, Violet saw me. We locked eyes for a moment, and she smiled. Not a broad, friendly smile—nothing that encouraged me to approach. A small smile, a knowing turn of the lips to let me see that I didn't scare her. The sort of defiant look a witch would give the neighbors who accused her.

I put the hat down on the counter next to me and rushed to the front door. Esta trailed after. "Mama! What's wrong? I thought you liked that one!"

I couldn't speak until we were out on the sidewalk. My head was pounding. People were walking by, and the street was filled with cars. It was so loud out there.

"Mama, what's wrong?"

"Nothing," I said finally. "What if I don't wear a hat? Maybe I could do something nice with my hair?"

"Mama. If you think it's too expensive, I got some money saved."

"No, no, of course not! I just feel foolish. I don't belong in that shop."

"Don't be silly, Mama. Anyone with money belongs in there." Esta looked so sure of herself. I took her arm proudly. I was glad she'd had the chance to go to Miss Ames's school and learn that sort of confidence.

We went to a big church the next day, where Esta's boy attended, and they married in front of a crowd of nearly fifty people. I'd never seen anything like it. Esta looked so happy, and I reckon she'll have a good life in the city. But I just wanted to get back to Tates Valley. I know everyone there, and I know how things work. I don't know what you've heard, but it's a good place. Folks may not have much, but they look out for one another. That's how it's always been.

THE WAYFARING
STRANGER

MIRIAM
(PEARL'S DAUGHTER-IN-LAW)
1925

My husband returned from the dead in 1925. I was in the sitting room with my friend Evelyn Lacey, who lived two houses down and came over most evenings to dine with me. When the weather was nice, we would go out on the porch after supper, but that day it was raining, so we shared a pot of tea inside, she reading a book, I working on my embroidery. I was surprised by the sound of a knock at the door. It was awfully late in the day for company to come calling.

I recognized him at once. He looked older, of course, older even than our eight-year separation warranted, but was clearly the same man: broad-shouldered with bushy copper hair sticking out from under his black hat and almost translucent blue eyes that had the uncanny appearance of looking right through you. His face was thinner, practically gaunt, drawing attention to his curved nose in a way it hadn't when he was younger. He was dressed well in a black suit, though dripping from the inclement weather.

"Miriam," he said, stating my name with no discernible emotion.

Novelists would have you believe that a lady would faint in such a situation, but I stayed fully conscious. He had been dead but was no longer. It was plain to see.

"Jake!" I exclaimed.

He gave me a slight nod and entered the doorway, taking off his hat and shaking the excess water on the mat.

"We thought you dead these past seven years."

"I apologize for the confusion." He hung his hat on the rack and began removing his muddy boots.

"But where have you been?"

He waited to prop his boots up by the door before turning to me. "I lost my way upon my return from the war."

With that, as though having provided explanation enough for his lengthy disappearance, he strode into the sitting room with only stockings on his feet. Evelyn's reaction was more extravagant than mine. She gasped and let her book fall to the floor, covering her mouth as if in terror.

With nonsensical calm, I said, "Jacob, do you remember Miss Lacey?"

"The sheriff's daughter."

"My father passed in 1919," said Evelyn, dropping her hand back on her lap. "But, yes, he did used to be the sheriff."

Jake nodded. "Pleased to see you." He turned to me. "Is there any food I could eat? I'm mighty hungry."

So I took him to the kitchen and got him some supper.

Eight years is a long time. The first two were spent in the usual way of a war bride: worrying, writing letters, praying for my beloved's safe return. Then came the Armistice and relief that soon we would be reunited. I wrote to Jacob of my overwhelming joy and excitement, but no reply ever came.

The next years were far worse. Is any horror quite so unbearable as the unknown? Jake must be dead for he could not be found. The army could not find him. His parents and I wrote countless letters but received only vague, contradictory responses. His mother was informed that Jacob had been discharged. I was first told he was missing, then later that he had deserted. Upon further inquiry, his status was returned to missing, by which time I didn't need anyone in the army to add the inevitable "presumed dead." I had already presumed and imagined and wept. Still, what makes the unknown so awful is the hope that human nature instills in us. We are such weak creatures. I would cry for a day, then wake the next morning certain that my husband was alive and suffering amnesia in a French hospital. The other young men who'd left Douglasville for the war returned, and I tried to smile at the celebrations of those happy events. Some did not return, of course, but unlike Jake, they had funerals, which were easier to take than the homecomings because I was free to weep. I am ashamed to admit how I envied the widows wailing by the caskets of their fallen soldiers. They were lucky. They knew what had happened to their husbands.

Of course, I cannot name the moment when those dark years gave way to the more peaceful, later ones. I didn't give up hope all in one moment, but slowly it slipped away, until I found it gone entirely and my mourning finished. Jacob was dead. I was a widow. And it was an enormous relief.

My mother-in-law, Pearl, never gave up hoping, though. She came to see me once a month or so, out of some sense of duty to Jake or me, I'm not sure which. More than once, she claimed she'd seen him in the woods behind her house up in Tates Valley. "He's alive, Miriam. I can feel it. You know, I done lost a child once. I know what it is to lose a child. But my Jacob is alive."

I took her knobby hand in mine and squeezed it.

"A mother knows these things," she went on. "I feel it when my children is sick. That might sound silly to you, but it's the truth. I wish you could know the feeling, dear. I pray Jake comes back to us and makes you a mother and me a mamaw."

I tried to feel close to this woman, the only sort of mother I had left in the world, since my own had died of tuberculosis when I was just a girl. But I felt nothing for her, except pity. At first her tall tales gave me an outrageous, irrational surge of hope, but in later years I struggled not to roll my eyes in front of her. She was a true mountain woman from a different age, who believed in ghosts and witches and old wives' tales. She believed her long-dead sister haunted the spot where she'd been murdered up in the mountains, so I couldn't take seriously her notion of seeing Jake. In fact, I'm ashamed to say, I took some pleasure in recounting her hillbilly manners and expressions to my friend Evelyn for our mutual diversion.

Evelyn Lacey was a great source of comfort to me during those years of unknowing. She lived nearby in downtown Douglasville, and our fathers had been good friends. Because she was four years younger than me, we hadn't been close as children. Indeed, I remember her attending my wedding as a mere girl of thirteen. But when Evelyn returned from normal school in North Carolina to teach in Douglasville, she was a young woman, and we immediately struck up an easy, natural friendship. We saw the world, or at least our little corner of it, in much the same way. Though we always made certain to do unto our neighbors as we would have them do unto us, we also enjoyed sharing our amusement with their foibles and follies. It might have appeared that we felt superior to those around us, but it was less snobbery that bound us together than a sense of the absurd. After all, what could be more absurd than the position in which I found myself? A young woman, not yet twenty-five, perhaps a widow, perhaps not.

When my father passed away, I was left all alone in our big family house. Evelyn must have noticed my intense loneliness, for she made a habit of calling on me many afternoons. When her mother passed away a year later, it became our unspoken arrangement to dine together most evenings. It suited me and seemed to suit her as well. Though we never had any trouble making conversation, Evelyn could be painfully shy with people whose company she found less amiable. Sometimes I worried that our friendship, no matter how I valued it, was keeping her from finding a young man to marry. Evelyn was not unattractive, though one might have described her as plain. She wore her straw-colored hair in a tight bun, which drew attention to the sharp angles of her narrow face. A small amount of effort and powder would have softened her features, but Evelyn had no interest in making herself pretty. She referred to herself as a spinster, even when she was only nineteen. She said that was how she wanted it, that a husband would only oppress her. And who was I to argue for the benefits of marriage? So we came to spend our evenings together in a happy companionship, a grass widow and an old maid.

I had loved sewing since my grandmother first taught me to thread a needle, and when my father died, the needle was my salvation. At first, women from church sent me small jobs to do out of pity, but I can say in all humility that once word of my artistry and ability got around Douglasville, I was the most sought-after seamstress in the county. Most women in town were happy enough to sew basic clothing for themselves and their families. But when they needed something with extra attention to detail or embellishment, they came to me. I excelled at the special occasion—and, perhaps ironically, my favorite assignment was a wedding dress.

So life went on without Jake. Evelyn and I would complain in passing about our lack of husbands. But did we really mind? I look back on that time now, those final years of Jake's absence when I had accepted him as dead and created a new life for myself, sewing lace, spending quiet evenings with Evelyn, and it seems to me I was profoundly happy.

I made up the guest room for Jake that first night of his return, as inviting him into my bed seemed awkward and almost improper under the circumstances. After eating his supper in silence, he stood and announced he would like to retire. By that time, Evelyn had left us, whispering to me that she would come by to check on me the next afternoon.

I led him upstairs, aware of the sound of my heels hitting the wooden stairs. "I've made up this bed for you," I said, motioning to the guest room.

"Thank you kindly."

He started into the bedroom, but I cleared my throat. "Jake. Jake . . . you haven't explained your absence."

His shoulders slumped, and he looked down at the floor. "I'm awful tired," he replied. "Perhaps we can talk about it tomorrow."

With that, he closed the door behind him, and I was left staring at the blank white door.

I woke early the next morning and put on my favorite pale-blue dress with some notion of impressing him. I studied my reflection in the mirror and felt that if anything our years of separation had improved my appearance. When he'd left I'd still been a girl, but I was undoubtedly a woman now. My face was thinner, and I was more careful with my posture. I put my hand to the collar I had carefully embroidered with a pattern of roses, proud of my handiwork and still-youthful figure. Evelyn always commented on how lovely I looked in that dress.

I waited for him to come downstairs, working on a set of curtains Mrs. Hodges had sent in. When he finally entered the parlor, Jake looked better rested than the night before and less bedraggled. I had set out a stack of his old clothes for him, and he was wearing the same shirt and jacket that I remembered from the first weeks of our marriage.

"Would you like some breakfast?" I asked.

"Bread with butter will do me just fine."

I nodded and went to the kitchen. When his breakfast was ready, I sat across from him at the table, sipping on a cup of coffee.

"Are you making new curtains?" he asked.

"They're for Mrs. Hodges. Do you remember her? The Methodist preacher's wife. I take in sewing to support myself."

"I see. I suppose you've been under some financial pressure." He munched his bread.

"My father died two years ago. I own this house, of course, but do require some source of income. Luckily, I am rather skilled with a sewing machine."

"I'm glad to hear it. Please let me know if you have any debts or accounts that need attending."

"No, I'm proficient at keeping household records and have had no cause to acquire any debt." I paused for a moment, then asked, "And you?"

"What of me?"

"Are your finances sound?"

"Oh yes." He pushed his plate back and wiped the crumbs from his face with his napkin. "You are probably aware that I have recently come into an inheritance."

My eyes widened. "You know about your father, then?"

"Yes, God rest his soul."

"My condolences," I said, which didn't feel quite right since I was the one who had stood next to Pearl as they lowered my father-in-law's casket into the ground. I stood and reached across the table to take Jake's plate, just as he did the same. Our hands brushed together, and I pulled mine back in surprise.

"I can clean this up," said Jake as he turned to the kitchen.

We moved awkwardly around each other during those first days of his homecoming. Sometimes I would forget that I was no longer alone in the house, and start at the sound of his footsteps in the next room. We passed each other one evening in the narrow hallway outside the bedrooms when I was already dressed for bed, and I shuddered at the feel of his warm body skimming my thin cotton nightgown, close enough that I could smell him, a sweet, earthy scent that I recalled from our honeymoon days. I would clumsily inform him when I left the house, unsure of the correct wifely behavior, or at least the correct behavior for the wife of a ghost.

Our conversations remained painfully trivial. I danced around the obvious questions, but he never offered any explanations, and I was afraid to pursue them too aggressively. And after all those years, I had become an expert in not knowing.

When Pearl came over, it was a relief to let someone else take over communications. She plowed past me when I opened the door for her, making straight for Jake standing in the hallway, wrapping her tiny frame around him. "My boy, my boy!" she cried, finally pulling back. I couldn't be sure, but Jake's blue eyes appeared wet with emotion.

"Hello, Mama."

"I knew you were alive! I never doubted, my beautiful boy! Did I, Miriam?"

"It's true. Pearl's always kept faith."

"I'm sorry for your worries, Mama." He had not apologized to me for anything.

"That's no matter now! You're home!"

I had barely had a chance to speak to Evelyn since Jake's return. We'd had a stilted conversation on the porch that first day when she came over to check on me, and then she stopped calling at suppertime as usual, not wanting to interfere with our reunion. I missed her terribly, and when Pearl sent word that she was coming, I had begged Evelyn to join the three of us for dinner.

I roasted a chicken for our meal. Pearl was still smiling at Jake, praising God for his safe return. Jake was quiet, as always. Evelyn clearly didn't know what to say and kept arching her brow at me in silent solidarity. When Pearl's relentless commentary subsided, I tried to make conversation between them. "Evelyn teaches at the Douglasville school. She's an avid reader."

"That so?" asked Jake.

"Yes," Evelyn said. "I've been teaching for three years now."

"What sort of books do you like to read?"

"I like all sorts, but fiction is my favorite."

"I never did learn to read real well," said Pearl. "I wish I could enjoy it, but it makes my head hurt."

"That's why education is so important for our children," I replied.

"What are you reading at the moment?" Jake asked Evelyn.

"English novels, lately. *Tess of the D'Urbervilles* by Thomas Hardy just now. Do you know it? "

"I'm not much of a reader myself beyond the newspaper."

"What's a D'Urberville?" asked Pearl.

"It's a family surname."

"Oh. What's the story about?"

"A woman who is abandoned by her husband. Among other things."

I choked on my potatoes and let out an ungainly cough. I tried to catch Evelyn's eye, but she was staring at Jake.

"Sounds interesting," he replied. If he had noted any reference to our situation in her summary, he didn't let on. "Tell me, do you ever have any old books that you need to get rid of?"

Evelyn looked confused. "Certainly, upon occasion."

"I might know of someone who would be interested in them."

"I see. Well, I'll be certain to let you know. Perhaps you would be interested in reading Hardy yourself."

"If I ever get round to picking up a novel, I'll be sure to give him a shot."

Evelyn put down her fork, and I could tell she was winding herself up. She could be terribly shy but also insisted on speaking her mind when she had something she felt was important to say. Now she spoke in the delicate, biting voice I knew so well from our personal conversations. I realized I'd never heard her talk to a man in that tone. Perhaps her intimacy with me made her feel familiar with my husband. "I've been looking forward to hearing the extraordinary tale of how you came to be waylaid these eight long years." She was almost smiling.

Jake wiped his mouth and cleared his throat. "It's a dull story, I'm afraid."

"I find that hard to believe."

"Truly, there's not much to tell."

"That seems hardly possible. We're you imprisoned? Ill? Lost?"

Pearl cut in: "Jacob has seen great suffering. I'm just grateful that he's home now."

Evelyn gave me a fierce look, and I shook my head ever so slightly, in an unspoken effort to ask her to let it go. Jake seemed happy to remain silent.

Pearl smiled at him. "Tell me, do you still remember how to play the fiddle? I brought your father's in case you did."

His face lit up with a grin, and truly the man looked happier than I had seen him since his resurrection. He pushed his chair back from the table. "Where is it, Mama?"

Evelyn gave me another look, her cheeks turning red with emotion. I shrugged at her. Pearl had already gotten up to fetch the fiddle. In a moment we three women were all in the sitting room, watching as Jake played an old-time tune. Pearl began to sing as he played, *"I'm just a poor wayfaring stranger, traveling through this world below. There is no sickness, no toil, nor danger, in that bright land to which I go."*

Her high-pitched voice pierced my ears, and I felt a sick headache coming on. Evelyn stared at the ground, tapping her toe furiously, not in time to the music but clearly out of simmering rage. Jake and Pearl didn't seem to pay her any mind. He went on as Pearl sang:

I'm going there to see my father
And all my loved ones who've gone on.
I'm just going over Jordan.
I'm just going over home.

I know dark clouds will gather 'round me,
I know my way is hard and steep,
But beauteous fields arise before me
Where God's redeemed, their vigils keep.

I'm going there to see my mother,
She said she'd meet me when I come.
So, I'm just going over Jordan.
I'm just going over home.

Jake drew out the last note, then put the fiddle down. Tears streamed down Pearl's face. Evelyn's foot was still tapping.

"That was your daddy's favorite song," said Pearl.

"I know. He taught me to play it."

Evelyn stood. "It's getting late. I'd best be on my way home."

"I could make a pot of tea?" I offered.

"No, thank you, Miriam. I'm quite tired."

"Would you like me to walk you home?" asked Jake.

"Oh no. It's just down the street."

I saw her to the door and watched as she walked away into the dusk.

My union with Jake had been a love match. When we first courted, he would whisper such sweet words in my ear as I'd never heard before. Jake was the only man I'd ever loved, and it seemed a miracle he loved me in return. We first met when I was fifteen, and he was working at Frank Nelson's forge just outside of town. He'd learned blacksmithing from his father, who had a forge in Tates Valley. When old Mr. Nelson had a stroke, he hired Jake to run his shop while he recovered. Jake was only two years older than me, but strong and skilled with a hammer and anvil. He boarded at a house on our street, and I began to see him around, always unfailingly polite, tipping his hat to me on the street, opening the door for me at church. I was thrilled to meet a new boy in Douglasville, as I'd already tired of the local selection.

Father often had business at the forge and took a liking to Jake. He began inviting him to dine with us, taking pity on a young man away from home for the first time. We got along right from the start. Jake was always a quiet sort, but I seemed to draw him out. He started coming round to see me when he finished his work at the blacksmith shop. Jake would play his violin for me or I would read poetry to him. Eventually we grew bolder and held hands when we were alone, sometimes even daring to sneak in a kiss. When he asked me to marry him, I didn't hesitate.

I knew folks thought I was making a bad match. My father was one of the most prominent men in Douglasville, and though Jake's family was prosperous by Tates Valley standards, his prospects were unclear. Blacksmithing was a dying art. But my father liked him and had always been something of a romantic. He even suggested that after our wedding Jake come to live in our house with us. Father certainly didn't need it all to himself, and the arrangement suited us all, at least as long as Jake was in Mr. Nelson's employ. I was happy to remain in the only home I'd ever known, our stately white house in the center of town. We lived like that for just under a year, Jake and I deeply in love, Father happy for our companionship.

Then came the war. The moment I heard that the United States was becoming involved, I knew Jake would enlist. He did, that very week.

In the first weeks after Jake returned, I would try to force my mind back to those days before he joined the army, try to remember the boy I had loved and the life we had shared in that very house. But it seemed impossible to reconcile that young man with the older version who had returned in his place. Jake had become a stranger.

Douglasville was a small town with plenty of gossips. I could feel their eyes on me in the general store, on Sundays at church, or when I went on a morning stroll through town, as was my habit in nice weather. Sometimes I even caught snatches of conversations. A rumor went around that Jake had killed a man in Kentucky and was on the run from the law. Some folks said he'd been living with another wife in France this whole time. Once I heard someone say he'd taken up with a colored woman right here in Douglas County. But I didn't pay any of it any mind. I didn't care what folks thought. The good people of Douglasville had been whispering about me for years. They whispered when I, the daughter of a judge, chose to marry a smithy. They whispered when the smithy disappeared. They whispered when I chose to spend all my evenings with the school-mistress. I had given up heeding what people said a long time ago and felt it safe to assume that none of them had any more information about Jake's disappearance than I did.

I tried to go about my business. Most mornings I went for a long walk, enjoying the exercise and fresh air. Though I have not had the opportunity to travel far in my life, it is hard to imagine that any town in the world is situated in a more beautiful spot than Douglasville. We live in the foothills here; the mountains loom above and beyond, forbidding yet breathtaking. The tallest, Jones Mountain, rises in the distance, always looking over us in ever-changing shades of blue, reflecting the weather and season. Snowcapped in winter, mist-shrouded when the air is heavy with damp, brilliant in the sun, always majestic, a reminder of the eternal. I will never tire of the view.

Since Jake's reappearance, I felt myself lingering outside on my walks, dreading the return to our house. One morning I could see him on the porch in the distance, and I slowed my steps, delaying the inevitable as long as I could. He nodded as I walked through the gate. "Nice morning for a walk."

"Yes, it is."

He stood up from the rocking chair as I approached and opened the door for me, an echo of his youthful chivalry. "This scrollwork above the door is so lovely," he said, following me inside.

"I've always admired it."

"Do you know who the carpenter was?"

"Oh no. I was just a baby when the house was built. Would you like a cup of tea?"

"No, thank you."

I darted into the kitchen to put the kettle on; to my surprise, he followed me.

"What happened to the maid? Miss Dora, if I rightly recall?"

"Oh, I had to let her go when Father passed." I turned to light the stove.

"I see. I'm sorry to hear that."

"No, don't be. I had no real need for a housekeeper living by myself."

"I know I left you in a position of hardship."

I turned back to him. Perhaps he was trying to apologize. "I've gotten by."

"Yes. You have. And I want to talk to you about my plans moving forward."

"What plans?"

"For my father's forge. It belongs to me and Tim now."

Tim, his younger brother, was a kind man who had always looked out for me in Jake's absence.

"Are you going to sell?" I asked him.

He shook his head. "We want to turn it into a gasoline filling station."

"A what?"

"A filling station. For automobiles."

I laughed. "No one in Tates Valley has a car!"

"Not now. But things are changing. There's talk of building a national park."

I nodded. "Yes, I've heard the talk. But that's all it is so far."

"Powerful men mean to see to it that there's a park, and a good portion of it is in Tennessee." He reached into the pocket inside his jacket and produced a brochure, which he handed to me. *PRESERV-ING OUR EASTERN MOUNTAINS*, it said in large block letters on the front. I opened it and saw a map of the proposed park. It straddled the Tennessee/North Carolina border and went right up to Tates Valley.

"But people live all over those mountains," I said.

"The government will buy their land. And they'll have to sell."

"That doesn't seem right."

"Have you seen the hillsides in the mountains after they've been skinned alive by the timber companies?" He spoke with a surprising passion. "Stumps as far as the eye can see. That's not right." I hadn't seen him express such emotion about anything since returning to Douglasville. "The logging companies have raped this land, God's country. I support the effort to protect it."

"But you can't mean to go all the way to Tates Valley every day to run this filling station."

"No, we will be moving to Tates Valley."

The kettle began to whistle. I extinguished the flame and tried to catch my breath. I had lived in this house, in Douglasville, for as long as I could remember. I turned back to him. "But what of this house?"

He looked at me with sympathy and replied in a soft voice, "We will have to sell."

"No, I couldn't. We can't."

He said nothing, but kept looking at me in a pitying way. I poured hot water into the teapot. He took a step toward me. "I know I have failed you as a husband these many years. But I mean to make it up to you. You no longer need to concern yourself with financial matters. I have it in hand. And I assure you this is a wise venture. Charlie Reid is building a hotel, just down the road from Daddy's forge. Tates Valley is changing."

He put his hand on my arm. I think it was meant to be comforting. It was the first time he had intentionally touched me since his return. I stared down at his rough, red hand. "You could sell the forge. Open a filling station in Douglasville."

"Tim and I have made up our minds to go into this venture together."

I didn't even know when he had spoken to Tim. Perhaps when he left the house during the day. I never asked where he went, and he always returned for supper.

I poured myself a cup of tea. "Excuse me," I said. "I'm going to work on Jane Wilcox's wedding dress."

I went to the sitting room and took up my sewing.

I had a note from Evelyn that afternoon, inviting me to lunch on Saturday at her house, which filled me with relief. I hadn't heard from her since the awful dinner party, and was acutely in need of a friend in whom I could confide my troubles.

I tried to go on about my usual business for the rest of the week, but was nagged by a growing sense of doom. Jake began making casual references to his business venture and our impending move. I could scarcely bear to look around that sweet, sturdy house, which had provided me with hearth and home since childhood. When I thought too long of life in Tates Valley, I was overpowered by despair. I envisioned living in a primitive structure in the forest, the canopy blocking out light, making us as blind as moles. I knew it was a fantastical notion, but my dread was real.

Saturday was a fine day, and my anxiety faded as I walked down the street to Evelyn's house. Despite the threat of moving to Tates Valley and the strain of living with my reinstated husband, there was momentary happiness at the prospect of spending the afternoon with my friend.

Evelyn greeted me at the door. I gasped to see she had bobbed her hair. "Do you not like it?" she asked, ushering me inside.

"I'm just surprised. It's quite becoming! And very modern."

She smiled and led me to the dining room. I was surprised to see a woman sitting at the table, an older woman I knew from church, Violet Nickson. She had recently moved here from Knoxville to teach in the school. Evelyn had mentioned her now and again, but I didn't know they were particular friends. Violet sat up straight and tall, her gray hair tied in a tight bun on top of her head, her face made slightly ridiculous by buckteeth.

"You know Miss Nickson, don't you, Miriam?"

"Pleased to see you," I said.

Violet smiled at me. "And you. Evelyn's been telling me all about your long-lost husband."

I glanced at Evelyn. "I hope you don't mind," she said. "Violet is discreet and most understanding."

"Of course. The situation is complicated."

"You still have no idea where he's been all this time?" asked Evelyn.

I said nothing for a moment, annoyed at her lack of discretion.

"You don't have to talk about it in front of me," Violet said. "It's none of my concern."

"The situation has not changed," I said, sitting at the table.

"I am sorry to hear it," said Evelyn.

"No matter," I said. "Tell me, how are things at the school?"

"Very well," said Violet. "It's a great pleasure for me to be back in the classroom. I taught school as a young woman, but for many years circumstances kept me from it. I feel I've returned to my true vocation."

Violet was a pleasant enough conversationalist, but I couldn't help but feel disappointed at not having Evelyn to myself. I had looked forward to her confidence all week but had no desire to share the details of my situation with this other woman. Finally, perhaps unescapably, when we retired to the front room for coffee, the conversation turned back to the state of my marriage. We sat around the coffee table, sunlight streaming through the large bay window.

"Does your husband have any plans for employment?" asked Evelyn.

"Yes. He intends to turn his father's old forge into a gasoline filling station for automobiles."

"In Tates Valley?" asked Violet.

"Yes."

"That's a clever idea," she replied. "Automobile traffic is bound to pick up when they begin construction on the national park."

"That is Jacob's thinking."

I looked over at Evelyn, and our eyes met. "Will you move to Tates Valley?" she asked.

"That is what he intends."

I could see that the news affected her deeply, and indeed I felt a sudden urge to cry at the harsh reality of moving away from my dearest friend. "I am very sorry to hear it," she said in a small voice.

"I grew up in Tates Valley," said Violet. "In fact, I used to be well acquainted with your husband's parents. I remember him as a wild young boy."

"I didn't know that. You were friends with Pearl, then?"

"More principally her sister Polly. But that was many, many years ago."

"Was Polly the young girl who was murdered?" I asked. Pearl loved to tell sensational stories of her sister's death.

"Yes," replied Violet.

"I'm sorry," I said.

"Losing a friend can be heartbreaking," she replied.

I looked over at Evelyn and saw a tear slide down her cheek.

I often heard my husband call out in the night. I am a light sleeper, and most nights since Jake's return I would wake to the sound of screams coming from the guest bedroom. Usually the sounds died down after a minute or so, and I assumed he had wakened from his nightmare. I knew this affliction occurred in some men who had been in the war, having read about the long-term effects of shell shock in the newspaper.

One night I heard the sounds as usual, but with a greater volume and intensity. After a minute, Jake seemed not to have found any solace from the terror, and I felt I must go to his aid. I lit the lamp on my bedside table and carried it down the hall. Carefully opening the door to his room, I saw him writhing in his nightshirt on the bed, screaming and grunting as though in excruciating pain. I put the lamp down and ran to him, gripping his shoulders tight to try to hold him still. "Jake! It's alright. You're just dreaming."

His eyes blinked open and his body relaxed. He looked up at me, wide-eyed. "I had a bad dream."

"I know. I'm sorry. I felt I should wake you."

"Yes. Thank you."

I removed my hands from his shoulders and stood to go.

"Wait! Miriam . . ."

"Yes?"

"Could you stay with me a moment?" His voice was small and desperate, almost childlike.

"Of course." I sat back on the bed beside him.

"Thank you." He closed his eyes. His breath slowed and deepened into a sleeping rhythm. His body slackened. I watched him until I felt certain he was asleep, then tiptoed back to my room.

I was sewing on the porch one afternoon when I saw Evelyn coming down the street. I put down my work and waved to her with a broad smile. "Hello!" I called. "Won't you come in for a cup of tea?"

She nodded and came up the steps. When she was near enough to me on the porch to lower her voice, she asked, "Is Jake about?"

"No, he's in Tates Valley today and tomorrow."

She let her shoulders relax and finally returned my smile.

For a brief moment it felt just like old times as we sipped our tea in the sitting room, chatting about the goings-on in Douglasville. I felt a sense of contentment I hadn't in some time. "Would you like to stay to dinner?" I asked.

"I'd love that."

Evelyn followed me to the kitchen, and we chopped vegetables sitting together at the table, as we had on countless evenings in the past, me in my pink apron, she in the one covered in daisies that she'd always preferred. As I chopped onions, I saw her looking over at the stand in the hallway where Jake's hat and jacket were hanging.

"He must've forgotten his hat," I remarked.

"You know, I've been thinking." Evelyn put down the knife she was using to cut carrots. "It seems like quite a coincidence."

"What does?"

"Jake returning right after his father dies. It's awfully convenient that he got back just in time to receive his inheritance."

My stomach twisted into a nervous knot. I knew she hated him and had hoped to avoid the subject. "What does it matter?"

"Well, maybe he's been around all along, just biding his time. Pearl always said she'd seen him in the woods. Maybe she's not such a crazy old bat after all."

"She's been though a great deal."

Evelyn raised her brow. I looked down at the onions, which were making my eyes water.

"How can you not want to know the truth?" she asked.

"Of course I want to know. But he doesn't seem to want to tell me.

And what good is knowing going to do me? What good would any possible answer do me?"

Evelyn spoke low and calm. "Grounds for divorce."

I let out a gasp that was almost a laugh. "No one in Douglasville has ever gotten a divorce!"

"Your father knew every lawyer in the county, and any one of them would be glad to represent you."

"Then what?"

Evelyn made a fist and hit the table. "You could keep this house! You could stay in Douglasville! We could go back to the way things were."

Her eyes watered, as did mine, not just from the onions anymore. "A spinster and a grass widow?"

"Yes!"

"Think of the scandal."

"Everyone knows what he put you through. And he's yet to provide an explanation! Yes, there would be a few old crones who gossiped, but what do you care about that sort anyway? Why stay in a marriage that is only causing you sorrow? A marriage where there is no love?"

"But I did love him. And he's still my husband."

"The way he's treated you! And I've never been anything but good to you!" Evelyn was trembling.

"Why must I choose? Why do you put me in this position?"

She hung her head for a moment, then stood up. "I've only ever tried to help you." She removed the apron and hung it on the wall.

"Evelyn, please sit down."

"I'm going, Miriam."

I stood, frantic, with hot tears now streaming down my cheeks. "Evelyn, please don't go!"

But she was already at the door, letting herself out. She didn't look back; she didn't say good-bye. I sat down on the floor in the hallway and cried.

I was in a haze for the next two days, going back over our conversation, trying to figure out what I could have said to keep her there. I had felt so happy when it was just the two of us, talking about anything, everything besides my marriage. I tried to pinpoint the exact moment when everything went wrong. But then I would feel angry. Evelyn wanted too much from me, more than was reasonable. Yet she made me feel as though I were doing something wrong. I went round and round it all, ricocheting between despair and rage. By the time Jake got back from Tates Valley, I was in a state.

It was late, and I had already retired to bed. But when I heard him come in the front door, I got up, put on a dressing gown, and went downstairs to the sitting room.

"Hello there," he called from the hallway, where he was taking off his boots. "I hope I didn't wake you."

"Where were you?" I asked.

He slowly walked into the sitting room and gave me a quizzical look. "Tates Valley. You knew that, I'm sure."

"No. Not yesterday. For the past seven years! Where were you?!"

His face drooped, and he sat down on a chair, though I was still standing in the corner. The room was dark, illuminated only by the light of a full moon coming through the window.

"It doesn't matter. I'm here now."

"It matters to me!" My voice was louder than I knew I could make it. "I loved you so dearly. I cried and cried! More tears than you can ever imagine, I cried for you."

"I'm sorry, Miriam."

"I wore widow's weeds. I cursed the army. I tried to make a new life for myself because you were dead. Where were you?"

"I'm sorry, Miriam. I can't explain it. I couldn't come home."

"Where were you? Where were you?" I was sobbing now and covered my face with my hands. He came to me and tried to put an arm around me, but I pushed him away with my elbow. "Where were you?!" I shouted again, then turned and ran up the stairs to my bedroom and slammed the door.

We didn't speak after that. Before we had barely spoken, but now our silence was total. I served him meals in silence; we ate them together in silence. Silence grew and expanded around us, like a living thing. I became acutely aware of the sounds of the house, creaking boards, forks on plates, rain on the roof, as well as the sounds of our bodies, stepping, chewing, breathing. The longer our silence went on, the more powerful it became.

Finally, after a week, Jake spoke to ask if I would accompany him to Tates Valley in order to inspect the forge and family home site. I simply nodded in reply. Tim drove down to Douglasville in his wagon to pick us up. Tim had been only a boy when Jake went off to war, yet during the years of his brother's absence, he'd made a point of looking in on me once a month or so. I'd always enjoyed his visits. Except for the pale-blue eyes they shared, Jake and Tim had little in common. Tim was plump and gregarious, a great talker and teller of jokes, and he knew how to coax a smile out of me even in the darkest days of my supposed widowhood.

That day I would prove an even greater challenge.

As he drove us out of Douglasville, Tim made cheerful conversation. "I've been cleaning out the forge these past weeks," he told his brother, "tryna get a sense for how we can arrange the filling station."

"Thank you, Tim," replied Jake. He was sitting beside Tim at the front of the wagon. I was just behind them, facing the opposite direction.

"Mama's about beside herself at the thought of you moving back to the old house."

I turned to look at Jake. He hadn't mentioned that he planned to move into his mother's house. He was gazing straight ahead at the dusty road.

As we got farther from town, the farms grew more spread-out, and eventually gave way to thick forest as we climbed into the mountains. Tates Valley was only fifteen miles from Douglasville, but it felt like we were traveling back in time. I half-expected Davy Crockett or Daniel Boone to wander past, or perhaps a Cherokee chieftain. The village had built up some since the last time I'd been there, due mostly to the traffic of the timber companies. Tim pointed out a large building under construction on the river. "That's where Charlie Reid's building his hotel."

All it looked like to me was mud and some sticks in the ground.

We came to the forge. I'd seen it before, of course, but never given it much thought. The log building appeared ancient, weathered by time, antique in its purpose. Jake helped me out of the wagon, briefly placing his hand on my waist. I could feel the vibrations of the wagon in my body even as I stood still on solid ground. I followed the men inside. It was dank, and everything seemed scarred by fire or the searing tools that Tim had collected in a stack beside the anvil.

"With luck, we can sell some of the equipment," said Jake.

"We can try, but ain't nobody go into the blacksmith trade these days." Tim leaned against the far wall. "The building needs a new roof. And this wall has water damage. It might be easiest to tear the whole place down."

Jake nodded. "Fresh start."

They wandered around, planning in this way, and I feigned interest. I found the place dark, almost sinister. I used to stop by Mr. Nelson's forge to watch Jake at work, when we were newly wed, admiring his skill and marveling at his ability to take one solid thing and change it into another. But this did not seem like a site of creation. Perhaps it was my imagination or the remnants of flame and ash, but the air smelled acrid and deathly to me. When the brothers stepped back out into the sunshine, I was glad to leave the oppressive forge behind.

Tim went over to the wagon and produced a small brown box, which he gingerly carried back to us. As he opened it, a lens appeared. A camera.

"Where'd you come by that?" asked Jake.

"Got it in Knoxville. I want to get a photograph of the two of you in front of the forge. Before the place is gone."

"Oh, I'm not dressed for a photograph," I protested.

"Nonsense, you're lovely as always, Miriam," said Tim, motioning for us to stand back. Jake came up beside me, and we looked at Tim for direction. He was staring into the box.

"Alright," he said. "Smile!"

Neither Jake nor I changed expression. Tim put the camera down gently on a stump and pointed to the cherry tree beside us. "The pumps could go there."

"That's a fine tree." Jake turned to me. "How would you like a cherry dining table?"

In fact, my father's dining table was in ill repair with water stains and scratches all along its surface. I nodded.

"Daddy used to say he wanted that tree for his coffin," said Tim.

"I never heard him say such a thing."

"I'm sure you did, you just don't recollect. He loved to tell folks that. Said he'd planted the tree to use for his coffin."

"Should we exhume him and build a coffin of it for him now?"

Tim shook his head. "Hit was nothing but a joke. Daddy would never have abided wasting this fine cherry on a box meant to be buried in the dirt."

We bumped along in the wagon. The road to Pearl's house ran parallel to the railroad track, an incongruous example of technological progress in that timeless landscape, built to strip the hills of their timber. I watched as a small engine passed us carrying a cargo of giant hardwoods lying prone on flatbed cars. As the train chugged off into the distance, I realized that Jake was singing softly, under his breath, a tune I'd never heard before. "*Love, oh love, oh careless love, in your clutches of desire, you've made me break a many true vow, then you set my very soul on fire.*"

He didn't seem aware that I was listening or perhaps even that he himself was singing. He seemed more alive here in the mountains than in Douglasville. More fully resurrected.

As Tim turned in to Pearl's farm, I took it in, trying to imagine a life there. She had chickens and a couple of milk cows in the barn. I was a town girl through and through, and a little frightened of cows, to be honest. I certainly didn't know how to care for them. The house was simple but well-kept, two stories with a broad porch at the front, where Pearl was waiting to greet us. When we got off the wagon, she embraced Jake as if it was her first time seeing him since he'd returned. Tim and I stood by, waiting to enter the house.

"I'm back, Mama," said Jake. "You don't have to worry. I'm back now."

I tried to be sociable during supper, but I am certain the strain between Jake and me was showing. After the meal was done, as I helped Pearl clear the table, she suddenly put her hand on my arm. "I know how hard this has been for you. But we must be thankful that the good Lord has returned Jacob to us. What you need now is to start a family. Have a child, Miriam."

I nodded and put down the dirty dishes in the sink.

Though I had never heeded my mother-in-law's words before, her advice stayed with me all through the long ride back to Douglasville. It was a dark and clear night. I could see the stars through a gap in the wagon's curtain. My situation was fixed, and the future seemed to have been determined for me by Jake or fate or God. I ought to make the best of it.

We were both tired when we returned home that night and immediately retired upstairs. But before Jake had gone into his room, I inhaled a deep breath and spoke to him directly for the first time in ten days. "Would you like to join me in this room tonight?"

He looked over in surprise. Our eyes met and connected for a long moment. "Yes, thank you."

On our wedding night, I had felt the usual nervousness when I first approached the marriage bed. When we first married, Jake had been desperate for my body, and I welcomed his embrace. There was great joy and pleasure when he took me to bed in that flush of young love. All these years later, it was different. We were reserved and dutiful. I could see he still wanted me, but the desire came with a certain sadness. I resigned myself to the situation. If I was to live with Jake as his wife, then I must truly inhabit the role. And Pearl had given me a goal to work toward, something that could be mine, a source of hope in all this misery, a baby.

We moved a few weeks later. I boxed up all my worldly possessions and watched as they were hauled off, up into the mountains. Tim came to pick me up last in his wagon. As we drove away from my father's house, I saw Evelyn on her own porch, gently rocking, a book open on her lap. The sun shone on her face, and her hair glistened in the afternoon light. Violet was beside her, and the older woman nodded at us as we drove by. I waved farewell, but Evelyn did not look up.

CARELESS LOVE BLUES

FRIEDA
(MIRIAM'S "STEPDAUGHTER")
1937

My mother never told me who my father was, and I never asked. When I was little, I hardly noticed that I didn't have a father. My childhood was happy. I had two older siblings, Ramona and Mickey, and we lived on a little patch of land at the end of Venton's Cove, on the other side of Jones Mountain from Tates Valley. Mama had inherited the small farm from her parents, who both died prematurely when she was only a girl. We had a couple dairy cows and a large collection of chickens but otherwise were alone, just the four of us, with our nearest neighbor half a mile down the hollow. My brother and sister and I ran wild through the woods, and even though I've never been past the county line, I can't imagine there's anywhere more beautiful in all the world. Mountain peaks rose above us in every direction, snowy in winter, green and greener in the warm months, and explosive in autumn with yellow, red, and blazing orange.

As I got older, though, I became aware that it wasn't conventional to not have a father. I asked Ramona about it when I was around five. Her reply was fast and fierce. "We ain't got no daddy. That all they is to it. Don't you bother asking Mama. She got nothing to say on the matter."

Three Negro families lived in Venton's Cove when I was a child. Mama said her grandfather had come here at the end of the Civil War along with another freed slave from a farm just outside Knoxville. After Emancipation, they headed into the mountains to find a place where they could keep to themselves, and Venton's Cove was far away enough from everywhere else that no one bothered them. My best friend was Eugene Raymond, great-grandson of my great-grandfather's fellow settler. Eugene lived at the next farm down from ours and was just between Mickey and me in age, so we often all played together. But Eugene's older sister wasn't so agreeable. One day she threw a rock at me and called me a "little bastard." She thought I'd stolen her comb, though Eugene told me she realized she'd simply lost it when it turned up later that week in her bedroom. I was too mortified to tell Mama about what she'd called me. Instead, I went to Mickey, who told me it was a very bad word and to never say it again. It was another year or so before I figured out what it meant, and by then I was pretty sure that I was one.

Maybe it's odd that I never asked Mama once and for all who my father was. But the older I got, the bigger the question grew, and the fact that she had never volunteered the information made me realize she had no desire to do so. She talked plenty about her own family, though. Her father had been the most skilled carpenter in Douglasville. You could walk around the town and see house after house that he had worked on, though I wouldn't know because I've never been the twenty miles to Douglasville. You could tell that Silas King had worked on a house because of the decorative details: curli-cued pediments, ornamental columns, geometrical trim. Everyone with money had wanted my grandfather to work on their houses, including the richest family in Tates Valley, the Eliots, who lived out by Mitchell's Creek. Our own simple two-bedroom had delicately carved doorways and window frames throughout, as well as the fanciest transom you ever saw on the front door of a mountain cabin. The door itself had been carved in the Victorian gingerbread style, with two faux columns on either side of a window and an intricate seashell pattern below.

My grandmother had died giving birth to my mother, and my

grandfather used the income from his business to educate his daughter as best he could in Venton's Cove. He bought her books and magazines, and from a young age she took to teaching herself from them. We had a shelf of books at home, which were Mama's dearest treasures: the Bible, of course, the collected poems of Henry Wadsworth Longfellow, five plays by Shakespeare, *The Adventures of Tom Sawyer*, *Great Expectations*, *Jane Eyre*, *Robinson Crusoe*, *The Hound of the Baskervilles*, *Up from Slavery*, *The Souls of Black Folk*, *The Call of the Wild*, and my favorite, *Little Women*. I wasn't allowed to touch them until I turned eight, and then I had to use the utmost care. The pages were soft with age and worn, some of the covers ragged. They had been passed down and carefully collected through the years. Mama read most every night before bed, and I believe she longed for nothing so much as new books. She taught all of us to read at an early age, insisting that Mickey keep up with his schooling even when he was old enough to work the farm.

We never had much money, but we got by. Mama cooked hot meals at the logging camps, and once a week one of us would go into town to sell our milk and eggs and buy whatever we might need and could afford from Hickam's general store. Mama taught us not to talk to anyone unless spoken to and never to look a white person in the eye. And once a month, on Saturday, Miss Ames, the teacher at the Tates Valley Settlement School, held an open day for colored children. She took a special liking to me because I was good at doing sums and multiplication in my head and would loan me books to take home each month. I knew Miss Ames meant well, but I hated the way she looked at me with a mixture of amazement and pity. She often told me I was the brightest colored child she'd ever met.

When I was twelve, everything changed in Venton's Cove. Surveyors started showing up, white men in suits and hats tramping on our property with maps and rods. Rumors began to circulate. They were government men, from the Department of the Interior, come to draw boundary lines for the national park they were fixing to build. Venton's Cove would be entirely within those lines.

The only grace in Mama's premature passing is that she didn't live long enough to see us have to sell her little farm. She caught pneumonia when I was fourteen and died within two weeks, just like that. We buried her in the little family graveyard on the hill behind our house next to my sister Patricia, who died before I was born, when she was less than a year old. Ramona, Mickey, and I held hands as Reverend Hale read from the Bible. He came all the way from Douglasville to preside, because he'd been friends with my grandfather. We'd never attended church regularly, since the nearest Negro church was Reverend Hale's in Douglasville, but I knew the Bible inside and out. Still, I couldn't tell you what passage he read that day. I was staring at that box in the ground containing my mother, who just a few weeks prior had been still youthful in her face, bright and beautiful. She'd loved to sing as she worked in the house or garden. She'd still kissed me at night before bed, and even though I was mostly grown, I had treasured the comfort of her embrace.

Now I would never get to ask Mama who my father was.

Ramona got married not long after to a boy down the hollow and moved to Cleveland, where he found work in a steel mill. She begged Mickey and me to come too, but neither of us wanted to leave the mountain. We were getting by—Mickey tending the farm as best he could, me using what I'd learned from Mama to get a job cooking hot meals for the Civilian Conservation Corps that was building the national park. But we'd already signed over the deed to our land and knew we only had a few months to find someplace to live.

I was always able to set aside enough of my cooking for the workers to make sure Mickey had a good supper at the end of the day. We were eating together one evening in comfortable silence when a knock interrupted us. Mickey put down his corn bread and went to the door. A tall, gaunt white man was standing there, in a jacket, tie, and hat. He looked middle-aged or possibly older, with a worn expression and piercing blue eyes. Mickey didn't register surprise at seeing him, which surprised me.

"Hello, Michael," said the man, but Mickey just half-nodded, head held high, eyes full of contempt. Mickey's expression was insolent, rude even, and I was shocked. But the man didn't seem bothered. "Can I come in?"

Again Mickey said nothing, but held the door open. The white man came into our front room and looked over to where I was still sitting at the table. "You must be Frieda."

I had no idea how he knew my name.

"It's good to see you," he said, removing his hat. Mickey motioned him toward a chair by the fireplace. "No, thank you. I don't intend to intrude on you for long. But you do know you have to leave this land by spring."

"We know," said Mickey.

"I thought you might be in need of a job. You can work for me at the filling station if you like."

Mickey was expressionless.

"I think I can find a house for the two of you as well, just outside Tates Valley."

"No, thank you."

"Do you have other plans?"

"Yes, sir," said Mickey, but I knew that was a lie.

"I see. Well, the offer stands, iffen you change your mind. Come by the filling station anytime. I'll sort you out." He put his hat back on and went to the door, then turned back to me. "Evening, miss."

"Who was that?" I asked, after Mickey shut the door behind him.

Mickey gave a rueful sort of snort. "Our father." He came back to the table and dug into his pork and beans.

"What?"

"Our father. He owns the filling station in town."

"What's a filling station?"

"Where folks get gas for they automobiles."

"I don't understand."

"You gotta have gas to run a car."

"No. How is he our father?"

Mickey gave me a look as though I was the stupidest creature he'd ever seen. "Round 'bout sixteen years ago, he and Mama had relations. Then you's born."

"But, Mickey, he's white!"

"Look in the mirror, Frieda! If you was but a shade lighter, you could pass."

It seems foolish now, but I had never considered that our father could be white, despite my light skin and wavy hair, despite even Mickey's blue eyes. I had never had a real conversation with a white person other than Miss Ames, and as far as I knew, neither had Mama. "How long you known?"

"Few years now. Mama took me to the filling station when I's about ten to meet him."

"Why you never tell me?"

"Weren't much to tell. Look, she never told me he was my father in so many words, but I put it together—why else she want me to meet this ornery old white man in town?"

"But why didn't she take me? Did Ramona know?"

"Ramona probably knew more'n either of us. I think she can remember when he would come around, before you were born."

"Who is he?"

"Jacob Whaley. He has a wife and two daughters who live in Tates Valley. I don't know much more'n that. And he can go to hell for all I care." Mickey had been stuffing food in his mouth angrily during this whole talk, and now his plate was clear. I hadn't taken a bite since Jacob Whaley appeared at the door.

Mickey looked over at me. My shock, hurt, and confusion must have been all over my face. He slumped in his chair, and his tone softened. "I think Mama thought I needed to meet him 'cause I'm a boy. I ain't never told you, because I didn't want to hurt you. Didn't you ever wonder how Mama could afford our new shoes every year, or candy at Christmas? Or where all her books come from?"

"He gave them to her?"

Mickey nodded.

"But you hate him."

He shrugged. "I don't know him. But I know he got a woman pregnant four times without marrying her."

"Well, I hate him." The words surprised me as I said them.

"Don't bother. It ain't worth the trouble."

"They more important things in the world than new shoes."

"Only someone who got new shoes every year would say that."

We shared a smile. "But why did Mama do it?"

"I don't know." And with that he got up, taking his plate and fork with him to the sink.

I spent the next couple days in a daze, burning a batch of biscuits, cutting myself peeling potatoes. I couldn't stop thinking about Jacob Whaley. I knew what I really needed to be thinking about was where we were going to live in the spring, and I tried to focus my mind in that direction, but it kept returning to that strange blue-eyed man in the front room and the mystery of what his relationship with my mother could have been. My tall, proud mother had been so warm, so easy to smile and quick to make you laugh with a joke and a wink, that I couldn't picture her beside that man with his serious face and icy demeanor. What could have bound her to him? If Ramona hadn't moved all the way to Cleveland, I could've asked her. If Mama were alive, I would've asked her. But they were gone, and that left only one other person to talk to. I made up my mind to go to the filling station.

The next day, I packed up my lunches onto our mule, Dusty, and took them to the work camp earlier than usual. When I'd distributed the food and collected my pay, I rode Dusty down the mountain toward Tates Valley. The road led past Eugene Raymond's farm, and I could see him, tending to his hogs, as I went by. He noticed me and waved, motioning me to come over.

"Can you come inside for a cup of coffee?" he asked. "I could use a rest."

"Yes, thank you."

Eugene wiped his hands on his overalls and helped me dismount. He had a kind face and a strong grip, and as he took my arm, I felt at peace for the first time since Mr. Whaley had stopped by our house. Eugene had shared his house with four siblings and his father, but they had all moved to Knoxville, leaving him to handle the sale of the property. They'd taken most of the furniture with them, giving the cabin a sad air of abandonment. I sat at the small kitchen table that they'd left behind.

"I been wanting to talk to you," said Eugene as he put a kettle on. "Have you and Mickey made plans yet?"

I shook my head.

"They ain't much time left, Frieda."

"I know. I can't get Mickey to talk about it. Reckon if worse comes to worst, I can join Ramona."

He sat across from me. "You don't want to move to Cleveland, do you?"

"No." Truth was, I could hardly imagine Cleveland. I knew there would be buildings in all directions and hardly any trees. People living squeezed into apartments, right up next to each other, their laundry hanging from neighbors' windows. And most likely, I would never see Eugene again.

"Let me talk to Mickey. We'll make a plan together. My brother's found work in Knoxville. And you know the River Vista Motel could use someone in the kitchen. That'd be perfect for you, Free."

"But where I gonna live?"

"I might be able to help with that too." The kettle began whistling, and he got up to tend to it.

"You know anything about the man who owns the filling station in town?" I asked.

He turned to look at me from the kitchen, and I could tell by his expression that he did.

"He came by our house a few days ago to offer Mickey a job."

"Did Mickey tell you who he was?"

"Yes. So you knew?"

"I heard rumors."

"I must've been the only person in Venton's Cove who didn't know."

He brought over two cups of coffee and put them down on the table. "I ain't know for sure. I just heard rumors. What did Mickey say?"

"He don't want nothing to do with him."

"I suppose it's nice that he offered."

"I suppose." I paused. I wanted to confess my plans but was nervous all the same. I looked over at Eugene, and the soft look of concern in his eyes put me at ease. "I want to talk to him. I was headed that way when I ran into you."

"To the filling station?"

"Yes."

"Well, let me get cleaned up, and I'll take you."

"Oh, you don't have to do that, Eugene."

"It's no trouble. You can go to speak to him by yourself, but I'll wait in town, just in case."

"In case what?"

"In case you need me."

I wanted to say that I didn't need him, but I did feel a comfort in knowing he would be nearby. "Don't you have work on the farm?"

"We gotta sell the farm in a few weeks anyway. Don't know why I keep bothering."

When we'd finished our coffee, Eugene saddled his mare to ride with me down to Tates Valley. Just as I was about to mount Dusty, he pulled something out of his pocket and held it out for me. It was a switchblade. I looked up in surprise.

"You never know what might happen," he said.

"I don't understand."

"Just take it. For your protection."

I took it and slipped it into my jacket pocket, though I barely knew how to use it and couldn't imagine why I would need to. We rode to town in silence, the clobber of the animals' hooves too loud to comfortably speak over, which was fine with me, as I was lost in my own thoughts. Eugene led me right up to the filling station, a boxy building with some sort of contraption out front where people could fill their cars with gasoline. He helped me off Dusty and asked if I needed anything before I went inside. I shook my head.

"I'll be waiting for you," he said.

A sign hung on the front door that read: WHALEY BROS. GASOLINE & SUPPLIES. It let out a rusty squeak as I opened the door. Inside was a small shop selling odds and ends, Coca-Cola, newspapers, candy. Behind a counter a different middle-aged white man sat on a stool, this one rounder, friendlier-looking than Jacob Whaley. "Can I help you?" he asked.

I couldn't think of anything to say. I'd imagined Whaley would be right there when I opened the door. I must have looked confused.

The man spoke in an understanding voice, "Are you looking for my brother? Jake?"

I nodded.

"He's in the back. Come." He motioned for me to follow him to a door in the back of the room, and opened it to reveal an office that appeared to double as a stock room, piled high on all sides with boxes and crates. Jacob Whaley was sitting at a desk in front of a large ledger. He looked up as we entered and removed his small reading glasses.

"Jake, this young gal came to see you."

"Of course. Thanks, Tim. Come in, Miss King."

Cautiously I walked toward him. He looked different now, without his jacket or hat. He cleared a pile of papers from a chair beside him and motioned for me to sit. His brother went back into the shop and closed the door behind him. Jacob Whaley and I were alone.

"Can I get you anything, Miss King? Believe it or not, I have an electric pot somewhere in this mess. Marvelous invention. You can make a cup of soup in minutes."

"No, thank you." A white man had never addressed me as "miss" before. When I sold my food in the work camps, everyone called me by my first name or just "girl."

"Alright then, how can I help you? Has your brother changed his mind?"

"No, sir."

"That's a shame. What are y'all planning to do?"

"Don't rightly know, sir."

"Well, I'd offer the job to you, but it ain't work for a woman."

He looked at me with his sharp blue eyes, and I had no idea what to say. The office was dark, with no windows and only one electric bulb hanging from the ceiling. The air smelled sharp and acrid. Finally Jacob Whaley asked, "Do you like music?"

I nodded, though it seemed an odd question. Music wasn't something that you had any choice in liking, as far as I knew; it was just part of life, mostly provided by your own lungs and those lucky enough to have talent with instruments. He got up and moved some crates to reveal a phonograph. I'd never seen one before, and watched in amazement as he carefully picked up a record from a pile on a shelf beside it and placed it on the player. "I keep this here at work. It's a bit selfish, but I find listening to music makes managing accounts much more pleasant."

He put the needle down and the sound of horns squawked out, followed by a woman's voice, loud and powerful: "*Love, oh love, oh careless love, you've fly through my head like wine, you've wrecked the life of a many poor girl, and you nearly spoiled this life of mine.*"

The record scratched and sputtered, and it was hard to make out the woman's words at first, but as she sang, I realized I knew them, because my mother used to sing this song when I was a girl. "*Love, oh love, oh careless love, in your clutches of desire, you've made me break a many true vow, then you set my very soul on fire.*"

My mother's soft, wavering voice had been nothing like this woman's, which was strong, rich, full of power. Still, the song brought back memories that caught me up short. "*Love, oh love, oh careless love, all my happiness bereft, you've filled my heart with weary old blues. now I'm walkin', talkin' to myself.*"

"I know this song," I said. "My mother used to sing it."

The knowing look on his face told me that he was already aware of that.

"*Love, oh love, oh careless love, trusted you now, it's too late. You've made me throw my old friend down, that's why I sing this song of hate.*"

"Bessie Smith," he said.

"Excuse me?"

"The singer. Her name's Bessie Smith."

"*Love, oh love, oh careless love, night and day, I weep and moan. You brought the wrong man into this life of mine, for my sins, till judgment I'll atone.*"

He took the needle off as the song finished. "From Chattanooga. Greatest blues singer that ever lived, man or woman."

He came back over and sat across from me. "The blues is my favorite type of music. I play the fiddle myself, which is more suited to old-time tunes. But the blues has more truth in it than most of the old mountain music."

"I guess I don't know much about music. Mama always sang around the house, but I never had much of a voice."

"Me either. That's why I took up the fiddle. I first heard the blues when I joined the army—just a man with a guitar on a street corner, playing for pennies, but I couldn't look away. After the war, I spent some time in New York and went to the colored nightclubs where you could hear the finest music in the world. Beautiful music requires pain and sorrow, which is why colored music is the best. But jazz is too easily corrupted by popular whims and fancies. Blues is the truth."

I didn't know what to say to that, and honestly didn't know the difference between white music and colored music either. I just knew the songs my mother had sung around the house. Jacob Whaley seemed unperturbed by my silence. He went to another corner of his office and produced a fiddle from a high shelf.

"What sort of songs do you like best?" he asked. "Hymns, reels, ballads?"

"Ballads," I said, just to say something.

"Alright, then. Now, don't forget I warned you I can't sing." He brought the violin to his shoulder and began to play a haunting tune with practiced assurance. He embellished the melody as he went and gave it a propulsive rhythm that compelled me to tap my foot. He played it through once, then sang as the tune began again. "*Polly, pretty Polly, come go along with me, Polly, pretty Polly, come go along with me, before we get married some pleasure to see.*'"

His voice was thin and reedy, yet he imbued the words with a sense of menace. "*She got up behind him and away they did ride, she got up behind him and away they did ride, over the hills and the valleys so wide.*"

His eyes stayed focused on his fingers, lightly dancing their way up and down the fiddle. "*They rode a little further and what did they spy, they rode a little further and what did they spy, but a new-dug grave with a spade lying by. 'Oh Willy, oh Willy, I'm scared of your ways, oh Willy, oh Willy, I'm scared of your ways, scared you might lead my poor body astray.'*"

The performance was so strange and intimate in the cramped space that I couldn't look away:

> "*Polly, pretty Polly, you've guessed just about right,*
> *Polly, pretty Polly, you've guessed just about right:*
> *I've dug on your grave the best part of last night.*"

> *And he stabbed her in the heart and the heart-blood did flow,*
> *And he stabbed her in the heart and the heart-blood did flow,*
> *Into her grave pretty Polly did go.*

He threw a little dirt over her and started for home,
He threw a little dirt over her and started for home,
Leaving nothing behind but the wild birds to moan.

And it's debt to the devil, and Willy must pay,
And it's debt to the devil, and Willy must pay,
For killing pretty Polly and running away.

His voiced trailed off, but he played the melody one last time, ending on a drawn-out note. He put the fiddle down and looked up at me. I didn't know what else to do, so I clapped.

"They say that song was written about my aunt Polly. She was killed up by Laurel Springs. Do you know the place?"

I nodded. "Was she murdered like the song says?"

He put his fiddle and bow back on the shelf. "Yes, I believe she was. My mother didn't like to talk about it." He sat again in his chair. "My brother, Tim, says it's 'The Knoxville Girl' which is about Aunt Polly, but I don't reckon that could be right, since she never set foot in Knoxville as far as I know."

"Is that another ballad?"

"Yes. Another murder ballad. But I won't subject you to any more of my singing. Besides, the melody ain't near as attractive."

"Do you know many songs about murder?" I asked.

"Reckon I do. It seems to be a favorite subject in these parts. But you mustn't think my family's history is all so dark. We have more than murder victims in our background. There's plenty of war heroes and frontiersmen too. We've been here since before the Revolution and helped to found Douglas County."

"Are you a war hero?"

"I fought in the Great War, but I've never been accused of heroism. My great-uncle died in glory at Antietam. Daddy always told me that was the noblest death a man could aspire to."

"Is that why you joined the army?"

"Reckon so, but I was going to be conscripted anyway. Like I say, I was never the heroic type. But my daddy was a powerful influence on me."

He seemed lost in thought for a moment. I tried to summon the words to ask the questions I had. But what could I say? *Did you love my mother? Did she love you? How did you meet her? How long were you with her? What do I mean to you?*

I couldn't ask anything of the sort.

"You sure you don't want a cup of coffee?" he asked at last. "I'm making one for myself."

"No, thank you."

He produced the electric pot from a shelf and flipped a switch that made it begin to purr.

"You're a good listener," he said, turning back to me. "I find it real easy to talk to you."

"Thank you," I said.

"My wife says I never talk. I reckon that's true enough. I have very little I want to say to her." He dumped some instant coffee into a cup. "Miserable woman, my wife," he mumbled into the mug.

I shifted uncomfortably in the chair. I no longer had any idea why I'd come here or what I could possibly have hoped to achieve.

After he poured boiling water into the mug, he looked up at me. "Do you have a fella?"

I hesitated, thinking of Eugene waiting outside somewhere for me. We had never so much as held hands or said anything romantic to each other, but I knew he cared for me. "Not really," I finally answered.

"Hmm. Sounds like there's at least a contender." He sat back down, holding the steaming mug. "I don't think you can know a person before you marry them, live with them, not really. Not at your age, anyway, before life has had any time to weather you. Some married folks I know get on just fine, but others are stuck with a person they fancied once but didn't understand. I think most husbands and wives still barely know each other even after years together. Everyone keeps secrets. My mother didn't know my father at all, that's for certain. She thought he was a kind, respectable sort of man, which he was at home in front of her. But he was completely different around other men, which he revealed to me when I got to a certain age."

"Was he not kind and respectable?"

"Daddy was the village blacksmith, and this place was his forge.

Men were always coming and going, and tended to linger longer than necessary. There weren't much to Tates Valley back then and this was a gathering place. Naturally, as a boy I loved to come here and be surrounded by grown men, smoking, laughing, telling ribald tales. Daddy began teaching me to smith, and I was something of an apprentice."

He held out his hands, which were rough and scarred. "I got the scars to prove it. In a smithy you best be careful not to pick up a nail that ain't cooled yet."

He lowered his hands. "Turns out I was apprenticing for a skill that was about to go extinct. We didn't realize that yet up here in Tates Valley. But I learned plenty from those years in my daddy's forge about the ways of men when women ain't around."

He sipped his coffee. "I'm sure you've heard tell of your mother's father, Silas King. There weren't a finer carpenter in all of Tennessee. Everone knew it. All the fine families in Douglasville hired Silas to decorate their homes, including my wife's parents. Silas King was respected in Douglasville, but things were differnt up here in Tates Valley. Folks couldn't afford fancy carpentry, and they resented a colored man making good money from his skill. Silas knew it and kept his business in Douglasville."

I didn't understand what my mother's father had to do with his father or where this rambling was headed, but he continued without pausing. "I was twelve years old when Silas King came into my daddy's forge one afternoon. There were around ten men here, idling in the usual way, but you coulda heard a pin drop when Silas came in the door."

He stared into the distance, lost in his memory. "He was as polite as a man could be, took off his hat, nodded to the crowd, and asked if my father could repair the ring on his wagon yoke. All eyes were on Daddy to see how he would react. He said nothing but nodded, took the yoke from Silas, and placed the ring in the hearth. It was a simple job, and when he'd got the iron hot enough he hammered it back into shape, then cooled it. Silas nodded and thanked him, then asked how much he owed. Daddy looked at him calmly and replied that it would be twenty dollars.

"I reckon I don't have to tell you that was an even greater fortune in those days than now, and Silas, rightly, laughed. But no one else did. That's when Silas began to look scared, and all those other men, my father's friends, began to look mean in a way I'd never seen before. Their faces seemed to darken and twist at once, and suddenly I saw clearly the capacity for violence in their strong arms and hard fists."

Jacob Whaley told his story without pausing, hardly registering my presence at all. The room no longer felt cold to me, but stiflingly hot. I couldn't breathe.

"Silas looked to my father and asked in a desperate voice, couldn't he be reasonable? He didn't mean to cause any harm. Just wanted a fair price. But my father had the meanest look of all those men. 'Twenty dollars,' he said. 'That's what you owe.'

"Silas looked down. 'You know I ain't got that.' My father stepped forward still holding the yoke. 'Then you got to pay some other way.' He kicked Silas hard, so that he fell to the ground. I's only a few feet away and heard the sound of his head hitting the hard-packed clay. At that, my father's friend all began to cheer and hoot, letting out all the pent-up anxious energy of the past ten minutes. My father kept kicking, and Silas moaned as blood sprayed from his mouth."

Jacob Whaley looked possessed by this memory, his blue eyes wide with emotion. I wanted to run out of the room, but I couldn't move. My hands were in my lap, and I could feel a hard object in my jacket pocket. The switchblade.

"When Daddy had finished with him, Silas could barely crawl out of the forge with his yoke. I don't know how he made it up to Venton's Cove. Some men enjoy torture for sport. I saw that in the war as well. The majority are afraid to admit that it repulses or terrifies them, so they go along with the torturers, like my father's friends did as he beat poor Silas King. But my father was the kind of man who enjoyed inflicting pain. So to answer your question, no, he was not kind nor respectable. My mother didn't know my father at all."

I thrust my hand into my pocket and held the blade tight.

"But I learned the truth about my father that day. Still, I didn't have the gumption to turn away from him until the war gave me the opportunity. Then when it was over, I couldn't face returning. I never wanted to see the bastard again. And as for my mother and my wife, I suspected they wouldn't want to see me, not as I had become."

He finished his coffee and put the mug down.

"Do you understand what I am trying to say to you?" He stared at me intently, his blue eyes pale but fierce. I nodded, though in truth I didn't understand any of it. Was this an explanation? An apology?

I didn't understand him, but I especially didn't understand my mother. I recognized the truth in at least that part of what he was saying: you could live with someone for years and yet not know them.

He could have forced her once or even more than once. But my brother, sister, and lost sister were separated by five years in age. If she had not wanted him, surely Mama could have escaped at some point. Yet my siblings and I shared the unmistakable features of this man—my sloping nose, the auburn shine of Ramona's hair, and, of course, Mickey's improbable blue eyes. Why had she been with Jacob Whaley for five years at the least?

"You're like me," he said. "You don't talk much. I know I've been going on today, but usually I'm the quiet type. My wife isn't wrong. I ain't said more than eight words to her in the past week. I can tell you don't want to talk, so I'm talking for you. That's what you came here for, right? So we could talk? Is that what you came here for?"

I gripped the switchblade. "I don't know why I came here."

He said nothing in reply, but studied me intently. We both looked up at the sound of the door opening. A little white girl walked in, humming a tune to herself, carrying a large basket filled with parcels.

"Mama and me picked up some things at Hickam's. Can we leave them with you to take home?"

She deposited the basket on the floor, and noticed me only as she straightened up. With a look of surprise, she turned to Jacob Whaley.

"Of course, Polly. Just leave it there." She stood in the doorway, staring at me and her father. "This is Miss King. She's come to me about finding a job for her brother. Heard we might need help."

"Oh," said Polly.

"Pleased to meet you," I offered.

She nodded in a distracted way. The door opened behind her, and a white woman stuck her head in. She had dark eyes and a tired expression. "Come on now, Polly. Let's get home."

"Yes, Mama."

The woman turned away before noticing me, and Polly followed. Whaley looked back at me. "My wife and youngest daughter, Polly, as I reckon you already surmised."

My hand relaxed, and I let go of the knife.

"Does your mother have a headstone?" he asked.

I shook my head. "We didn't have the money."

"I'd like to buy one for her. Let me know if there's anything in particular you'd like on it. And please, Frieda, let me know as well if you need any money or assistance."

"I'm fine, sir." I found I had regained the ability to move, and stood up. "I should be going."

He stood as well. "Thank you for your visit, Miss King. I hope I didn't wear your ear off."

I half-smiled and made my way to the door. I knew only that I wanted out of the room and never to see Jacob Whaley again.

I rushed out into the cool air and headed across the road from the filling station, desperate to get away. Once on the other side, I closed my eyes and took a deep breath. When I opened them, I saw Eugene standing in front of me.

"You alright?"

I nodded.

"Ready to head home?"

"Yes."

We rode in silence back up the mountain. When we got to Eugene's place, I stayed mounted on Dusty, not wanting to impose any further on him. He lingered on his horse beside me. "I been thinking, Free."

"What about?"

"You. And me. I know you don't want to move to Cleveland. Why don't you marry me instead? I ain't sure where we'll live, but I can figure something out." He looked at me intently, and I could see the depth of the feeling behind it.

"I'd like that, Eugene. I'd like that very much."

He gave a little hoot of happiness, and we both laughed. "I'd give you a kiss, but I'm stuck on this horse!"

We both got down, and he gave me the kiss he'd promised, and then another.

By the time we said farewell for the evening, the sun was setting. I rode the short distance home on Dusty as though I were floating on the air. Without thinking about it, I began singing softly to myself, *"Love, oh love, oh careless love, you've fly through my head like wine, you've wrecked the life of a many poor girl, and you nearly spoiled this life of mine."*

The words were inappropriate for what I was feeling, and my voice was a fright, but the song was caught in my head and brought back a strong, clear memory of Mama, hunched over the washing board, singing in her own soft voice, *"Love, oh love, oh careless love, in your clutches of desire, you've made me break a many true vow, then you set my very soul on fire."*

I was down on earth again, bumped and jostled by Dusty, my happiness mellowed by the great aching loss of my mother. And as I approached our house in the dusk, I felt the ache deepen at the thought that it too would be gone in a year or two, my grandfather's careful artistry torn down to create the illusion of untouched nature.

Mickey was inside, sitting in front of the fire. I was ready to shout out my news, but before I could, he asked, "Did you get the story you wanted?"

I must have looked confused.

"About our father. Did he tell you what you wanted to know?"

In my excitement, I'd all but forgotten Jacob Whaley. I shook my head. "How you know?"

"I had to go to town this afternoon and ran into Eugene."

"Oh." I slumped into the chair across from him.

"Well, did you? Get the story you wanted?"

"No."

"What story *did* you wanna hear? One about the blue-eyed soldier who came back from the war unable to face his wife or family? He stumbled upon a little farm and a beautiful woman at the end of a holler? The soldier figured it a good place to hide away from the world and fell in love with the woman. In time, he even come to think she his true wife, the only woman he ever loved. He wanted to stay with her forever, but eventually had to face up to his responsibilities and return to his own people. She protected his secret, because she loved him, not even telling her children the truth about who they father was."

I thought perhaps he had known more than he let on. Maybe Mama had explained to him how Jacob Whaley came into her life. But then he continued, "Or did you want the other story? The one about the man who couldn't leave the rage of the battlefield behind and took it out on an innocent girl? He found her living alone up in the mountains, her parents dead and no one to protect her. The man abandoned the woman he'd married, then ruint this other woman, seducing her with pretty words, forcing her to his will, and then trapping her in a prison of shame she couldn't escape. She too humiliated to ask for help from any of her own people or even admit to her children how they was conceived. When it was convenient and he tired of her, the brute went off to claim his inheritance and leave his responsibilities behind."

He fell silent, his blue eyes shadowed, his jaw clenched.

"Which is it?" I asked.

His let his face relax. "I don't know. I don't know any better than you do."

We sat in silence by the crackling fire. I would wait to tell him about Eugene until the next day.

I would go to Eugene to say that I knew a way we could stay in Tates Valley. And then I would go back to Jacob Whaley, even though I dreaded the thought of returning, and ask if he had a job for my fiancé. Eugene would go to work at the filling station.

I didn't want my father's help. But I wanted to help my future husband. He was a good man, better than anyone I'd ever known. Jacob Whaley might be right about some couples, but not us. I knew Eugene as well as I knew myself.

I would get a job at the River Vista. I would ask my father for help finding us a place to live. I would see to it that our home was tidy and well-kept, wherever it might be. I would be a good wife and someday a good mother.

Eugene would work hard and Jacob Whaley would treat him fairly. Business would be steady. Whaley would dote on our children as best he knew how, filling their Christmas stockings, replacing their winter coats, leaving books at the station for Eugene to take home. Folks would whisper, but it wouldn't bother us. We would have a happy life.

This house and my grandfather's handiwork would be torn down. The Civilian Conservation Corps would restore the wilderness that my forebears had fought to keep at bay. The forest would reclaim our farm, and it would become part of the Great Smoky Mountains National Park. All the hillsides that the timber companies had laid bare would become green again, thick with trees, laurel, birds, and bears.

I would spend years trying to form the questions I had for my father, but the words would never come. I would avoid him, avoid the question, avoid the past. I would find it easier to live without knowing, rather than risk discovering a truth I didn't want to hear. I would never know the true story of my parents' love, if that's what it had been. The truth would be reclaimed by the past, obscured just as surely as our vegetable garden would be by brush and pine. Best to leave it behind, walk away from what I cannot possess, eyes focused on the path ahead into the future.

DEVIL'S DREAM

POLLY
(FRIEDA'S HALF SISTER)
1942–1962

The first time Jeremiah Carter spoke to me was in the woods on Jones Mountain, out by Laurel Springs. He'd been following me, thrashing around in the branches, so that a deaf man could have heard him coming, but I hadn't let on that I noticed. It was Sunday afternoon, and Mama had said I could walk home by myself after church if I promised not to get into trouble. I certainly didn't intend to, though I reckon talking to Jeremiah was trouble of a sort, and I'm sure Mama would have agreed.

It was a warm September day—hot in the sun but cool in the woods. I had walked out of my way, into the land reserved for the new national park. Building crews had been in town for years, working on roads and trails across the mountains. A lot of folks had to sell their land to the government, whether they liked it or not, and their houses had been torn down, one by one, so that the land would look natural again.

The tips of the leaves had just begun to yellow, and winter still seemed like a promise rather than a threat. I was singing one of the old ballads Grandma had taught me when I was little—softly, since I knew Jeremiah was listening, but in a high, clear voice: *"I remember when I first courted, and his head lay on my breast, he could make me believe with the fall of his arm, that the sun rose up in the west."*

When I got to the springs, I stopped and sat down on a rock that I knew well from previous afternoons spent crawling around the woods. The rock was broad and dry, covered with rough gray moss, which I could feel prickling through my light cotton skirt. Icy water bubbled up beside me at the base of a huge oak tree. I put my hand in for just a moment, until the joints in my fingers began to ache, then pulled it out and drank a handful of springwater. Jeremiah came out from behind the bush where he was none too successfully hiding and looked at me. "What you want, Jeremiah?" I called out, still staring down at the tumbling water.

He was two years older than me and trying to grow a beard, which didn't yet consist of much more than a few patches of fuzz. He'd stopped going to school a while back, but I remembered his odd, quiet way and how the other boys would tease him, though he never seemed to notice.

"Don't you know this place is haunted?" he asked. "Ain't you scared?"

"I don't believe in ghosts."

He stared at me as though I'd said something confusing. I looked him back in the eye. "Why'd you follow me here?"

He didn't reply, but his head bobbed up and down slightly. The kids at school used to call him Turtle because of the way it jutted in and out from his hunched shoulders.

I stood up. "Well, I'd better get home. You can go on and follow me if you like."

I began to walk away from him, but he scrambled behind me. "Wait—it is haunted! You see those initials on the tree?"

I glanced where he pointed at the oak. WR + PC was carved into a flat spot in the bark. The letters were dark and smooth, obviously carved a long time ago.

"Do you know the story?" asked Jeremiah.

"I know lotsa stories, but they ain't true. Folks just tell them to scare little children."

"Not this one. It is true. My granddaddy told me about it, and he was there."

"Fine, then. Tell it."

We were walking side by side. He straightened up and held his head still. "It happened a long time back. There was this real pretty young girl living with her family where the Eliots' farm is now. Her name was Polly."

"No it weren't!" I knew he must be making it up, because I had never met another Polly or even heard of there being one anywhere around Tates Valley.

"It was so—Granddaddy told me. Anyhow, she had a boyfriend who weren't from around here, name of Will. He'd come over from North Carolina and was working for Polly's daddy on his farm. Will and Polly was real sweet on each other and would sneak up here to the springs to be alone, 'cause her pa didn't approve. Will was a good worker but he didn't have a penny to his name, and Polly's pa wanted better for her."

I glanced over at Jeremiah as he spoke, but he hardly seemed to notice me, consumed as he was with his tale. His voice became deeper and more confident with the telling; he sounded grown, less awkward and fidgety.

"Well, one evening Polly's pa saw them running off together into the woods and decided to follow 'em. He took his shotgun, thinking maybe he could give Will a scare to convince him to stay away from his daughter. He followed them up to the springs and hid behind some bushes to see what they'd get up to."

"Hope he was better at hiding than you," I interjected.

Jeremiah ignored me and continued, "Well, what he saw upset him mighty bad. 'Tweren't no time 'fore Polly and Will was in a romantic embrace, such as no respectable woman ought to be caught in with a man who ain't her husband."

I looked directly over at Jeremiah now. He didn't let on that he noticed, but his lips turned up ever so slightly into a smile. He knew he'd gotten my attention. "Consumed by rage, Polly's pa took out the shotgun and resolved to shoot Will for taking his daughter's virtue. He was an excellent shot, her pa, known throughout the county. But his emotions was running high, and this time he missed his target. Polly was shot in the head and died instantly in her lover's arms. Her daddy was horrified by what he'd done and tried to run away, dropping his gun behind him. But Will jumped on him, and in a fit of anger, he beat the old farmer to death."

Jeremiah took a breath, pausing to let the weight of this violence sink in. I was impressed by the dramatic story, though not convinced that it was true.

"Folks say that Will never came back down the mountain but lived up there by the springs, deranged by his grief and anger. Eventually he died, and now his ghost haunts the springs, calling out for his Polly, or howling into the night in despair. My granddaddy done heard the howls and seen the ghost once too. And so did Rocky Gates one time last summer, scared him almost half to death. Said the bushes around the springs kept moving, but there weren't no one there. Then he heard a horrible noise almost like a wildcat screaming, but deeper, more human."

"Wait. How do folks know what happened when Polly died if no one but Will saw it, and he never came down from the woods?"

Jeremiah's brow furrowed. "Well, I reckon they found the bodies and pieced it together."

"What if Will killed Polly and her daddy both and was hiding out from the law?"

"Well, I don't rightly know, but I'm sure there was some kind of evidence as to what happened. The ghost is real, anyway. You scared now?"

"No." I skipped ahead of him toward the clearing that led to the road. He stopped walking, but I could feel him watching me. I didn't look back until I got to the road. Jeremiah was still standing at the edge of the woods, staring after me with his empty expression.

That night after dinner I asked my uncle Tim about Laurel Springs. Tim and my father ran the filling station in town together. My uncle had never married and came to our house most nights for supper. He was the sort who thoroughly wore out already-tired jokes on us children, always grinning, generous, patient, and kind. My father was none of those things, so I often went to Uncle Tim instead of him for paternal guidance.

My sister, Katie, was in the kitchen helping Mama clean up, and Daddy was playing his fiddle out on the porch, as he often did in good weather, so it was just me and Tim in the living room. Tim was sitting in the big rocking chair, a framed photograph of my parents in their youth glowering down on him from the wall above. He was reading a Knoxville newspaper, full of bad news of the war in Europe, and his normally twinkly eyes were downcast and serious. I sat on the floor beside him and waited for him to notice me. When he looked up from the paper, he smiled.

"Have you ever heard that Laurel Springs is haunted?"

"Who told you that?" he asked.

"Jeremiah Carter."

Uncle Tim scrunched up his face, so that his long nose dipped into his thick gray beard. "He's a strange case, that Jeremiah, ain't he? I seen him in town, always real quiet, never smiling at nothing or nobody. I wouldn't let him scare you."

"I ain't scared. I was just wondering if you'd heard stories."

"Reckon I have." Tim set down the paper and picked up his pipe. "Your granny Pearl's sister was killed up there."

"Was her name Polly?"

"Yes, it was, as a matter of fact."

"No one ever told me that!"

"Maybe your mama didn't want you to know you were named after someone who was killed."

"Did her father shoot her on accident?"

"Papaw Collins?! No! Where'd you get such an idea? She weren't shot. Her boyfriend drowned her."

"Why?"

Tim shook his head. "No one rightly knows. They say folks hear things up there and see things too—things that can't be explained."

"You ever seen anything?"

He sucked on his pipe and took a moment to reply. I didn't think he'd ever seen a ghost but figured he was making something up to impress me with. He took the pipe out of his mouth slowly.

"One time I was up there hunting with your daddy. We heard all kindsa noises coming from the spring and thought we'd found us a bear. Then it screamed and didn't sound like no bear at all but more like a panther. I's a little shaken up but didn't want to let Jake know that, so

I followed the noises with him right up to the springs. Well, what do you know, but there weren't nothing there! We searched all afternoon for that wildcat but couldn't find it. Like it had just disappeared."

He bent down toward the floor, his face closer to mine, and finished in a loud whisper: "We did find tracks. But these weren't the tracks of no panther nor bear neither. They were cloven, about the size of a goat's hoof, and we realized we were looking at the footprints of the devil hisself!"

Uncle Tim leaned back triumphantly with a smile. I didn't believe a word of it, except for the part that he and my father had hunted together, but I made sure to look properly impressed.

Tim stood and cracked open the door. "Come in here, Jake! Play us a tune."

Slowly my father made his way inside. His thin frame stood rigid by the fireplace as he brought the fiddle to his broad shoulder and began to bow. Rich music filled the room. I knew the tune well: "Devil's Dream," one of Daddy's favorites. A reel that he would start slowly, then speed up until his fingers were flying across the strings. His pale-blue eyes stared at the space in front of him with an expression of something like joy, if my father could even feel such an emotion. Uncle Tim once told me that Daddy was a different man before the First World War. Apparently he was funny and kind, full of joy. But the only time I ever saw him joyful was when he played the fiddle.

When he finished the tune, Daddy put down the violin. "It's late. Reckon I'll head on up to bed." With no further good nights, he went up the stairs to the room he shared with Mama, though they slept in separate beds.

I would hear folks at church talk about my father, allowing as how he was a good man for helping his neighbors who were in need. He'd even hired a colored boy to work in the filling station, a boy who'd lost his farm in Venton's Cove when the government took it for the national park. But he never showed any kindness at home.

"I best be heading out." Uncle Tim winked at me. "Don't let me catch you wandering round Laurel Springs now, ya hear?"

"I ain't scared of ghosts."

He ruffled my hair. "That's my girl. You remind me of Ma, your grandmother Pearl. She weren't scared of nothing." Uncle Tim often told me I reminded him of Grandma Pearl, which always irritated Mama, who didn't think much of her in-laws.

I wasn't scared of Laurel Springs. It was still my favorite spot to walk to in the woods, when I had a spare moment between school and my chores. I would go up there every other day or so, and mostly had the place to myself. I liked to listen to the sounds of the forest—birds chirping, the spring gurgling, wind rustling through trees—and lie on the damp soil, thinking. Every once in a while, though, I would hear footsteps in the woods and catch sight of Jeremiah, hiding up behind the springs, watching me.

"What you doing back there, Jeremiah?"

He stayed hidden at first. I leaned back into the soft earth and yawned. "I know you're back there," I called out. "You're about as sneaky as a freight train."

He stepped out into the clearing and gave me that queer look. I couldn't stand it and had to turn away.

"Why you always come up here?" he asked.

"Why are you always following me?"

He shrugged. "Just wanted to see what you're doing."

"Well, you done seen."

"You should be careful." He spoke solemnly, his head momentarily still.

"Why, 'cause of the ghost?" I rolled my eyes.

He looked at me for a moment, still serious, then turned to walk away.

"Well, good afternoon to you too!" I shouted after him. He didn't turn back. I ripped at the grass beside me, angry with Jeremiah for disturbing my peace. He had no manners.

The next day Katie and I were walking home together from our school on Mitchell's Creek. Katie was three years older than me, and folks were already talking about her, allowing as how she had become quite a beauty. Sometimes I would catch her sitting in front of the mirror, just staring at herself and brushing her hair for hours. I was so thin that I looked like a boy, but Katie had an hourglass figure and fine features, like a porcelain doll. She had two boyfriends, though Mama and Daddy didn't know about either one, and the boyfriends most certainly didn't know about each other. She had threatened to cut off all my hair in my sleep if I told anyone, and I'd said, why would I want to tell anyone, anyway—if she wanted to be the town tramp, that was her business. Then she'd started throwing rotten eggs at me, and I'd had to run out of the chicken coop to get away from her.

That day she was being nice, though, and we were walking together, singing a song from the radio, "*Jeepers creepers, where'd ya get those peepers?*" when we came upon Jeremiah leading a pig down the road. Katie saw him and nudged me. We both stopped singing and began to laugh. "That's a real nice pig you got there, Jeremiah!" Katie called out. She loved to tease boys, and they loved it when she teased them. Most of the young men in town would turn all red when she talked to them or else smile a lot and try to impress her. But Jeremiah didn't seem concerned with Katie at all.

"This here's my pa's pig," he said.

Katie smiled at him. "Well, I'm glad to hear you didn't steal it."

Jeremiah looked at her blankly, like he didn't realize she was joking. Then he turned to me. "How you doing, Polly?"

"I'm fine."

He nodded, or rather his head jutted in and out in something resembling a nod, and he went on his way.

Katie looked at me in confusion. "Why, I do believe Jeremiah Carter is sweet on you!" Her voice was filled with disbelief, which was annoying, but I was too flustered by her words to be upset by her tone.

"What are you talking about?"

"He didn't give me a second look, but did you see the way he was staring at you?"

"But he's just strange like that. He stares at all sorts of things."

She gave me a knowing smile. "Mm-hmm. I think you just might have yourself a boyfriend!"

"I do not! Shut your mouth!" But she wouldn't stop teasing me about him for the whole rest of the trip home.

When we got to the house, Mama was sitting in the front room with her embroidery hoop on her lap, glasses on her nose, gray hair pulled back into a tight bun, fingers moving with deft precision. She was an excellent seamstress. Our dining table was draped with her delicate linens, the windows were covered in her intricate crochet lace, and Katie and I were the best-dressed girls at school because of her skill. No doubt she could have made a good living sewing dresses for fine ladies if we'd lived in a city. As it was, she took in enough sewing to provide extra income for the family. Times had been hard for us during the Depression.

"The eggs need collecting," she said, before we'd had time to set down our books.

Katie turned to me. "You do it, Polly."

"I ain't gonna let you laze around while I tend to the chickens!"

"Don't say 'ain't,' Polly." Mama's voice was soft but firm. She insisted we always speak properly and tried to keep us from developing "mountain habits," as she called them. Mama had grown up down the road in Douglasville and never quite fit in with the folks in Tates Valley. She looked down on most of our neighbors, though she reserved her fiercest disdain for the man who'd brought her to Tates Valley: our father.

"I'm not going to laze around. I'm getting supper started." Katie had already headed to the kitchen. I looked to Mama, but she was focused on her embroidery. I shuffled back out the door, seeing there was no escape from the chickens.

About a week later I went up to the springs on a Sunday afternoon. It was October now, but still hot—fall came late that year. I drank as much of the frigid springwater as I could stand and lay down on my back on a flat patch of ground. I could feel the wet earth pressing into my back and could smell it too, a rich scent of decay. I turned my head on its side and watched a woolly worm crawl away from my arm. The air was still but brisk in the shade of the forest. I closed my eyes, and my mind wandered away toward sleep.

I had a bad dream. The ghost was chasing me through the woods— at least, I thought it was the ghost. I couldn't see it; I could just hear it behind me—leaves thrashing, twigs breaking, and a horrible animal scream echoing through the forest. I was running deeper and deeper into the woods, over hills and valleys I'd never seen before, with branches tearing at me, and the undergrowth finally pulling me down to my knees. I woke with a start, confused to find myself lying on the ground. I opened my eyes and saw Jeremiah Carter sitting not a foot away from me. He was perched on the rock above my head, staring down at me in his funny way. I flinched under his gaze.

"Jeremiah, what are you doing?"

He didn't say anything but leaned down toward me. Before I could realize what was happening, he'd begun kissing me right on the lips. His mouth jammed up against mine, rough and hard, but then his tongue in my mouth was soft and plump. The sensation was so surprising that I didn't know quite what to do, so I lay still and let him go on kissing me. His hand began sliding up and down the side of my dress, as he moved to lie beside me on the ground. His fingers reached up the side of my stomach, and I laughed.

"Stop it, that tickles!"

He dropped his hand and stared down at me. His face was so close to mine that it looked huge and distorted. He had a hungry expression, serious and perhaps desperate—it frightened me.

"What are you doing?" I asked again, in a weaker, wavering voice. Still he didn't reply. He began to kiss me again, and I felt his hand on my breast. I pulled my mouth from his.

"Jeremiah!"

He stopped. I don't know why I didn't run away that instant—it would have been easy enough—I've always been fast on my feet. But I felt heavy, as if weighed down by something I couldn't see or name, and unable to move. As soon as I went still, he started kissing and touching me again, and that went on for some time—me pulling and pushing away in starts and fits but never making a concerted effort to escape, his hands searching down and around the worn cotton of my dress. He began pulling down his pants, but I didn't really know what was happening—I'd caught Katie with one of her boyfriends in a similar position once but had been too scared to ask her about it. When Jeremiah tried to push my legs apart, I shoved away from him, harder this time. But he yanked me back down, just as forcefully, and held me there.

I didn't try to pull away after that. I don't know why. I went over and over it afterward and couldn't figure out why I lay there like that and did nothing to stop him. It hurt, but I didn't cry or yell out, I just closed my eyes and bit my lip. I tried to concentrate, to see if I could make out the ghost's sounds coming from the forest, but I couldn't hear anything except Jeremiah on top of me and a bird chirping.

After, Jeremiah stood up and walked away from me. He was still, facing away from me and the springs. It was then I began to cry—hard, heavy sobs. He turned around. "I'm sorry," he said. "I didn't mean to hurt you." Then he walked away into the forest.

I rolled over to the springs and dunked my head in the cold water. I took handfuls of it and poured it all over myself, until my dress was soaking wet and I was shivering all over. When I got home, I told Mama that I'd fallen into the creek.

I tried to act normal, as though nothing had happened. I couldn't imagine what would happen if anyone ever found out what I'd done, especially that I'd done it with someone as strange as Jeremiah. No one seemed to notice any difference in me, though. I stopped saying my prayers at night, because I was too ashamed to admit my sins, even to God.

I also worried about seeing Jeremiah again. I knew I was bound to run into him sooner or later, and the thought of it made me shiver with fear. How was I to act? How could I look at him after that day at the springs?

Luckily, the next week at church I overheard some folks talking about him after the service. Just the day before, he'd gone off to Knoxville to join the army. He planned to lie about his age, since he was still too young to enlist. Best thing for the boy, folks reckoned—maybe the army would knock some sense into him.

I felt a tremendous sense of relief. I might never have to see him again—at least, not for a long time.

After that, acting normal wasn't so hard. I stopped going up to Laurel Springs. Mama said it was time for me to grow up anyway, stop running around the mountains by myself like some sort of wild child. And so I did. I stopped thinking about what had happened.

Except sometimes at night lying in bed when I couldn't sleep, I would remember. I would remember and feel ashamed, but at the same time excited to have this secret all my own, pulsing and beating inside of me.

Twenty years passed before I saw Jeremiah Carter again. It was spring when he returned; his father had just passed away. Since no one had seen him in so long, folks speculated that he'd had a falling-out with his father or might even be dead. But sure enough, I saw him in Tates Valley one afternoon as I headed home from my job at the Pancake Chalet, where I waited tables part-time. He was standing on the other side of Main Street, leaning back against a lime-green Chrysler and wearing sunglasses as though he were a movie star. He was a man now; his body had filled out and grown taller, making him less awkward, even powerful. His brown hair was cropped close to his head, and he wore a navy suit with the jacket off, slung back over his shoulder.

I knew exactly who he was as soon as I saw him. I remembered that face pressed next to mine, and felt dizzy as I quickly turned back toward the store. I wondered if he recognized me in my uniform, a black flannel dress and white apron, with my hair wrapped up on top of my head. Even after bearing four children, I was still almost as thin as I had been as a girl; there was too much work to be done on the farm to get fat. My body was taut but wrinkled, and I knew I looked older than my actual thirty-three years.

I called Katie when I got home, pretending to ask for a broccoli casserole recipe but really hoping she'd heard the latest gossip in town. Katie, who everyone but me now called Kate, had married the town doctor and always knew everything that was going on with everyone in Tates Valley.

"It's true," she said, when I mentioned seeing Jeremiah. "Came back to bury his daddy. Seems he's made a real good life for himself down in Atlanta, become some kind of businessman. It's strange—he was such a peculiar boy."

"People can surprise you."

"I suppose that's true. Now, tell me, Pol, how are you and Zach doing? Do you need anything? Any new clothes for the kids?"

"We're doing fine," I said, which was mostly true. We had enough to eat and had never had to resort to using government food stamps. Zach was too proud to consider taking charity from anyone, even my sister, but she always offered anyway—more to remind me that she had more money than us, than in a truly Christian spirit of giving.

Zach Garland and I had been married for sixteen years. He's seven years older than me, and though he'd grown up not more than four miles away, I didn't get to know him until he came back from the war. He was short but strong and had dark hair—almost black—and dark eyes. And he was the first man to ever pay me much attention—besides Jeremiah. Because my father had owned the filling station, we were one of the more prosperous families in Tates Valley, and I knew folks gossiped that it was a shame I'd made such a bad match. But that's not how I saw it. In the ways that matter most, Zach was the opposite of my father: poor and kind. Zach was nothing more than a farmer who did the best he could with the parcel of land on Mitchell's Creek that his family had been working for generations. Every year, more and more folks gave up on farming in Tates Valley, either selling their land to developers or trying their hand at building motels and restaurants themselves. But Zach loved the land and had no interest in tourism. He was a good husband—never drank, only swore on occasions when it was truly merited, and worked from dawn to dusk to provide for the children and me.

"Have you heard from Daddy?" Katie asked.

"No. You?"

"I got a postcard last week from Egypt. No message, just signed his name."

"Egypt?"

"Sure enough. The Sphinx."

A stroke had killed Mama three years earlier, and Uncle Tim died of a heart attack a year after that. Within six months, our father had sold the gas station. He didn't ask me and Zach if we had any interest in taking over. Even after a lifetime of his lack of affection and consideration, I was still shocked, and, as my grandma would say, madder than a wet hen. If Zach had wanted to stay on at the farm, I would have run the filling station. It was practically minting money these days, as more and more folks drove their cars into town from Georgia, Virginia, and Ohio. When Daddy announced at Thanksgiving that he was going on a trip around the world, I told him not to bother saying good-bye.

That afternoon I couldn't stop thinking about Jeremiah. I shook flour into a bowl for biscuits and wondered what he'd done to become successful. Atlanta seemed worlds away from Tates Valley—I'd only been out of the state once, and the biggest city I'd ever seen was Knoxville. What kind of man had he become? Did he have a wife or children? Did he remember me and that day up at Laurel Springs?

When the girls got home from school, I had just put the biscuits in the oven and was softly singing to myself: "*If I'da known when I first courted, that love was such a killing thing, I'da locked my heart in a box of golden, and tied it tight with a silver string.*" Abby and Sarah giggled from the living room. I stopped singing and looked up from my task.

Abby shook her head. "Listen to Mama, singing those hillbilly songs again."

"You'd do well to listen to these old songs," I told her. "They were good enough for my grandma, who didn't have a radio like us."

"Yeah, but why can't we have a TV like Aunt Kate?" asked Sarah.

"Because we ain't rich like Aunt Kate," answered Abby for me. She was twelve to Sarah's ten, and felt infinitely wiser.

"Don't say 'ain't.' We *aren't* rich, but neither is Aunt Kate."

"She's richer than us," insisted Abby, and that I couldn't deny.

I was reading *Life* magazine in bed that night, when Zach curled up beside me. He put his right arm around my stomach so that I had to put down the magazine and face him. He reached his hand up toward my breast, but I grabbed it before he could get there. I gave him a quick kiss, said, "I'm tired," and turned away.

But I couldn't sleep. I listened to Zach's slow breathing in the dark and remembered the feeling of Jeremiah Carter's rough kisses and his weight on top of me in the forest all those years before.

I wondered if he would go to church that Sunday. The possibility was on my mind all morning as I got all the kids into respectable clothes and combed their hair. I saw him as soon as we walked into the chapel, sitting by himself near the back. He saw me too, and nodded politely.

I looked away immediately, followed Zach to our seats, and busied myself with situating the children. But when we stood up to sing the first hymn, I cast a quick glance back in his direction. He was standing and looking down at a hymnal, tall and striking—almost handsome.

After the service, I took the kids out to the yard to play while we waited for Zach to finish talking with some of the other farmers. I was watching Elijah chase Davy, and Abby and Sarah talk with some other girls, when Jeremiah came up to me from behind. "Polly?" he asked quietly.

I turned, panicked to see him up so close. I felt thirteen again, and my palms began to sweat. "Hello, Jeremiah. I'm sorry to hear about your father."

"Thank you. We're having a funeral here tomorrow at two o'clock if you'd like to stop by." He said it casually, as though he were inviting me over for dinner.

"Alright," I said, unsure of the appropriate response. "I heard you're living down in Atlanta."

He nodded. "I sell furniture."

"That's nice."

"It's alright, I reckon. Tates Valley sure has changed."

"There's motels popping up all over the place. Jimmy Reid owns six of them, and he just got elected mayor. You should see what it's like in July—traffic's bumper-to-bumper all through town. Buddy Cox has built a miniature golf course and amusement park. We got a wedding chapel for honeymooners, a ski lift, a petting zoo, and more restaurants and gift shops than you can shake a stick at."

Jeremiah looked around the churchyard. "Those are fine-looking children you've got."

"Thank you. Do you have any of your own?"

"Children? Oh, no. I never married."

Zach came up beside me. "Jeremiah, this is my husband, Zach Garland. I don't know if you two know each other."

They shook hands. "I'm sorry to hear about your father," said Zach.

"Thank you," said Jeremiah. Then he turned abruptly and walked off. I'd half-expected him to repeat his odd funeral invitation to Zach and was relieved that he hadn't.

It was warm enough to roll the windows down on the car ride home. Zach drove with his elbow balanced on the frame. "That Jeremiah Carter was always a strange one, wasn't he?" he said.

I shrugged. "He was real quiet. All the kids made fun of him at school."

"Something about him gives me the willies."

"Guess he's a right successful businessman. He asked me to come to his daddy's funeral tomorrow."

Zach turned toward me. "Want me to go with you?"

I shook my head. "No, I'll be fine on my own. Don't want to take you away from the farm."

I hadn't been sure that I was going to the funeral until I said it out loud. I was hardly a friend of the Carter family. Then again, what harm could it do? It was a nice, neighborly show of respect.

I wore my good black dress the next day and drove myself to the church. As I parked the car, it occurred to me that maybe I had come at the wrong time, because there was only one other car in front of the chapel. Jeremiah drove up beside me as I was getting out of the car, and I waited for him.

"Thank you for coming," he said.

"You're welcome."

We walked into the chapel together and saw Pastor Davis waiting by the pulpit, looking down at the coffin. Jeremiah went up to him, and I sat down in one of the front pews. After a moment, Jeremiah sat down beside me. And when the preacher went up to the pulpit, I suddenly realized that no one else was coming.

Pastor Davis looked as awkward as I felt and kept the service short. He prayed for the soul of Lucas Carter, read the twenty-third psalm, and said some kind words. I'd never actually met the man—he'd kept to himself and had only come to church when Jeremiah's mother was still alive. Jeremiah was quiet throughout the service. He didn't cry or show emotion. His head didn't jut back and forth anymore, and he sat still and tall beside me, staring intently at the preacher.

Jeremiah turned to me when the service was over. "Thanks again for coming. This way Pa got a proper funeral." The way he said it was so sad, I could barely stand it.

"You're going to bury him now?" I asked.

Jeremiah nodded. His family's cemetery was up on Jones Mountain, just outside the national park.

"Would you like me to come along?'"

"I hate to keep you."

"It's no trouble."

I asked myself why I was helping this man I hated. I'd put it out of my mind for years, but all the same, I hated him for what he'd done to me. I tried to convince myself that I was just being decent and Christian, but I knew that I wasn't driving up that mountain because I loved my enemy or wanted to turn the other cheek. I wanted to be near him. I'd lived with the memory of his touch for so long, and now that he was back within my sight, I couldn't turn away from him.

I followed the big black hearse and Jeremiah's lime-green Chrysler up to the grave site. The road wound back and forth through trees just beginning to fill with summer greenery.

We said a quick prayer over the grave, and the men set to lowering the coffin into the ground. Jeremiah's face was dark, his lips clenched, as he watched his father's descent. He turned to me. "We don't have to stay here."

"Would you like to go for a walk?" I asked, feeling bold, reckless, and he nodded.

We walked through the park entrance. I doubted that I would recognize the old trails that I had walked so often as a child, but everything was clearly signposted now and maintained for hikers. It was a fine day, and the woods were alive with new buds, leaves, and flowers. I teetered a bit on some twigs in my nice black shoes, and Jeremiah caught my elbow. His touch shot through my arm, and my whole body tingled. We walked in silence. We both knew right where we were headed without having to say it.

The springs looked just as I had remembered. I went straight over to my rock, sat down, and cupped the icy water into my mouth. Jeremiah was standing a few feet away, staring at me, just as he used to stare when we were children. When I looked into his eyes, I knew exactly why I had gone to the funeral. I knew why I had followed him up Jones Mountain to bury his daddy and lead him into these woods. I motioned with my hand for him to come toward me.

He walked over in slow, halting steps, the awkward fifteen-year-old reemerging. He stopped about a foot from me, and I stood up to face him. I don't remember thinking at all; I only remember my actions, which were direct and determined. I put my arms around his shoulders, pulled my face up to his, and kissed him, in a fierce way I had never kissed Zach. My hands trailed up and down his back, his head, his chest, and then lower, into the front of his pants, and at that point he took me in his arms and laid me down against the bank, the same bank where he had taken me when I was thirteen, only this was not the same at all, because I was taking him, and I wanted him. I felt like I was drunk or crazy, able to do things I would never dream of with my husband, able to feel more than I ever had before, and my cries echoed through the forest.

Neither of us said anything when we were done. I lay against the wet earth and caught my breath, inhaling fresh blossoms and rotted wood. Jeremiah lay beside me—his body long and naked, his skin damp against mine, his heart thumping.

When I retrieved my dress, I saw that it was badly torn—my one good black dress. I had no choice but to put it on. Jeremiah and I parted ways back at the cemetery. He said he was headed back down to Atlanta on Wednesday, and I told him to have a safe trip. I left him at his father's grave and went back to the car. I drove down the mountain fast, skidding around the curves, wondering what I had done.

When I stopped for gas at the filling station, Eugene Raymond, the colored fellow Daddy had hired back when I was just a girl, was working the cash register. I must have looked a fright in my torn funeral dress, because he asked, "You alright there, Mrs. Garland?"

"Just coming home from a funeral."

"I'm sorry to hear that."

As I handed him my money, I noticed that the wall behind the register had been covered with a series of postcards. Some were of places I knew, others I didn't. Big Ben, the Eiffel Tower, camels walking along giant sand dunes, skiers speeding down snowcapped mountains, the Pyramids. Eugene saw me looking. "Your father must have been sending these to you too."

"My father sent you these?"

"Yes, ma'am. What an adventure he is on!"

Daddy hadn't sent us a single postcard. But I didn't have time to give it much thought. It was almost six when I got home, and I hadn't made any supper. I raced upstairs, hoping to avoid the kids and Zach, and got out of the damaged dress. Abby and Davy were in the kitchen when I got downstairs.

"Where you been, Mama?" asked Abby.

"I had to go to a funeral," I replied, looking around desperately for some kind of food to prepare. I grabbed a loaf of white bread from the counter and some bologna from the refrigerator.

"What's for dinner?" called out little Davy.

"Bologna sandwiches."

"Eeew! That's not supper food."

"It is tonight."

Zach and the children talked like they normally did all through dinner, but I hardly heard a word. My mind was back in the woods with Jeremiah. I replayed it over and over all evening, until I was lying in bed, sleepless.

I was a good woman. Except for the one other time with Jeremiah, I had never sinned before, except in the small, usual ways. I wished he were back in Atlanta already. I wished he'd never returned to Tates Valley. But I couldn't stop thinking about him and all the unspeakable things we had done.

The next afternoon I was out on the porch, mending Zach's nice pants, when he came up from the back field, sweaty, in his coveralls. "You done with those?" he asked. "I need to go into town."

"Not quite. Are you headed to the bank?"

He wiped his brow with the back of his hand. "I'd better. Don't worry about it, though, I can wear my old gray pants."

He walked past me into the house, but came back downstairs a few minutes later, holding my black dress with a dark expression on his face. I dropped my needle, realizing that I'd left the dress in the wardrobe, right next to his pants.

"What happened to your dress?"

"Oh," I said, bending down in my rocking chair to hunt for the needle. "Didn't I mention it? I took a nasty spill yesterday at the Jones Mountain graveyard."

"You didn't tell me." He was holding up the dress, examining the large tears on both the front and the back, made by mountain brambles or Jeremiah's hands. "This was a store-bought dress," said Zach, and I could hear the reprimand in his voice.

"I'll see what I can do to mend it."

"How'd you fall? You must've been hurt."

"The ground up there's uneven. I was wearing my fancy shoes." I have never been a good liar, and my hands were shaking as I picked up the needle. I dropped it again. "Damn it!" I cried, and then looked up at Zach, startled with myself. He was eyeing me suspiciously, as though I were a rattlesnake ready to bite. I couldn't recall ever having cursed in front of him before.

"You're lying to me," he said in a low voice.

My whole body was beginning to quiver. I hadn't slept at all the night before and had been thinking about Jeremiah so much that it was about to burst out of me anyway. I began to cry, and I never cry, hadn't cried in three years since Mama passed.

Zach dropped the dress and knelt beside me. "Pol, what's wrong? What happened?"

I couldn't speak but sat still, crying. He put his arm around me and spoke in a soft, tender voice. "I'm not angry, Pol. Just tell me what's wrong."

"Something terrible happened up at Laurel Springs." I looked up at Zach and wiped my eyes.

"What happened?"

My head was throbbing with the pressure of the tears. I took a deep breath and managed to stop crying. "Jeremiah asked me to walk with him after they buried his daddy. He took me up there, and . . . and . . ."

Zach's eyebrows knotted, and his jaw clinched. "What did he do?"

"I can't say, Zach. I can't say it!"

"You have to tell me, Pol."

"He forced me . . . he forced me to . . ." I couldn't look at Zach, struggling to get the words out of my mouth. "He forced himself on me."

I began to cry again and squeezed my eyes shut so that I couldn't see Zach, as the tears poured out of me. Zach's footsteps thumped away behind me, and suddenly I heard something smash. My eyes opened, and I saw him standing beside an eruption of wire mesh and splinters, blood dripping from his right hand, which he had used to punch in our screen door.

"Your hand," I said, and got up and walked past him into the house to fetch a washcloth and bandages.

He was still standing in the same place when I came back. I took his injured hand in mine and cleaned it. I had stopped crying.

Zach slowly turned his head toward me. "Are you . . . hurt?" he asked so softly I could barely hear.

"No." I dried his hand and wrapped a bandage around it.

"Does anyone know what happened?"

"No." I knotted the bandage tight across his knuckles and around his palm.

Zach pulled his hand away from me and turned toward the front steps. "I've got to go into town," he said. "Don't expect me back for supper."

There wasn't much time to think about the lie I'd told or what Zach was planning to do about it. I had to finish mending his pants and peel potatoes to make soup, and then the kids got home and were running around the house, shouting and fighting with one another. After supper, I cleaned the kitchen—scrubbed the stove, mopped the floors, scraped out the oven. After the kids were in bed I set to work on the living room, and when there was no cleaning left to be done, I collapsed into a chair at the kitchen table. My head ached, my eyes were swollen from crying, and my limbs felt weak and useless. Every joint in my body was sore. I sat up straight and with my fingers traced the grain of the wood on our old cherry table. My father had made that table before I was born as a present for my mother.

I sat like that for some time, until I heard the sound of voices out on the porch. Zach came in the front door with his friend Mac Folsom behind him. Zach's eye was half-shut, puffed up, and purple, and fresh blood had soaked through the torn bandage on his hand. Mac's cheek was scarlet and bruised. They were both dirty and sweating, and Zach's shirt was streaked with dark burgundy stains.

"Are you alright?"

"Could we get some water?" asked Zach.

I nodded and went to the kitchen. When I came back, they had both taken off their shirts. Mac wiped his face with the plaid flannel. I handed them tall glasses.

"Mac's just gonna wash himself up here 'fore he goes home. Could you get him one of my shirts to change into?"

"Alright." I went upstairs, not asking any questions because I was too scared of the answers.

After Mac was gone, Zach stayed still on the sofa. "Let me get you some ice for that," I said after a few moments of silence. Returning, I knelt in front of him with an ice-filled towel and placed it gently on his eye. "Here. How does that feel?"

"Stings." He put his hand over mine. I let him take the ice and stayed in front of him, on my knees. His gray pants were caked with mud—I could smell it, raw and earthy. He pulled the ice away from his face and took my hand. His off-kilter eyes met mine. "You don't never have to worry about Jeremiah Carter bothering you again."

I didn't move or say anything. Crickets chirped outside in a perpetual rhythm. After a moment, Zach dropped my hand, stood up, and walked away. We never spoke again about what had happened.

The other night, while I was tucking Sarah into bed, Abby kept jumping up and down around me, chattering away. "Winnie's having a sleepover this Friday, can I go, Mama?"

"Be quiet, Abby, I'm trying to get your sister to sleep."

"I'm not tired!" said Sarah from under the covers.

"Yes, you are," I told her.

"But can I?" asked Abby in a loud whisper.

"I'll have to discuss it with Daddy. You need to get ready for bed too, young lady."

"I am ready!" Abby called out, dancing in front of me in her yellow nightgown.

"Fine. Then get in bed."

"Will you tell me a story?" asked Sarah in a babyish voice.

Abby chimed in, "Tell a ghost story!" She climbed into bed in preparation.

"I don't want to scare your little sister."

"I like ghost stories." Sarah's voice deepened in an attempt to sound grown-up.

"Oh, I don't know any." I stood up, exhausted. "Just go to sleep, girls."

I turned to the doorway but heard Abby's voice behind me: "Do you know the one about Laurel Springs?"

I stopped. My heart leapt, and my fingers felt numb. I turned back to the girls and spoke in my darkest, most commanding voice. "Listen to me, Abigail. I don't want to ever hear you talking about Laurel Springs again. And I don't want either one of you to ever, ever go to that place, under any circumstances, do you hear me?"

"Yes, Mama," said the girls in tiny voices. I hardly ever spoke so harshly to them.

"Good, then." My cheeks and neck were flushed and throbbing.

"Is it really haunted?" whispered Abby.

I met my daughter's wide, frightened eyes. She looked very small, buried beneath quilts and blankets. I kept my voice steady. "It's an evil place, and that's why I never want to hear another word about it. Hush now, and go to sleep." I turned off the lights, but paused in the doorway and added, "The devil himself lives there."

LITTLE SPARROW

SARAH
(POLLY'S DAUGHTER)
1974–1975

I moved home a year and a half ago, after graduating from college, because my father was dying. Everyone else was gone. My brother Elijah was in the army, Davy was driving a big rig across the country, and Abby already had kids of her own in North Carolina. I helped Mama during those final months, as the cancer slowly did its work on my father's withered body, and waited for him to die so the rest of my life could begin.

Little Sparrow, Mama's always called me, after her favorite song. Partly because I'm the youngest; partly because I've always had my mind set on flying away. Night after night, she would sit on the edge of the bed I shared with Abby and sing in a wavering alto, *"I wish I were a little sparrow, and I had wings that I might fly. I'd fly away to my false true lover, and when he speaks, I would be nigh."*

So it's funny that I was the only one still around when Daddy died. He was just fifty-three. Our neighbors baked casseroles and called daily for the first week. Abby and Davy came home, and my boyfriend, Bob, drove up from Knoxville. We sat in silence at Mama's old cherry dining table, surrounded by more food than we could ever eat, while my aunt Kate fussed over Mama. Pastor Davis, who'd baptized me as a baby and couldn't be a day under eighty, performed the service for Daddy's funeral in a faltering voice, looking unsure on his feet and half-blind. I couldn't help but think it wouldn't be long before his own funeral, and who would preside over that? Maybe because I was so distracted by worrying that the old man would fall from the altar, I felt unmoved by the ceremony. Or maybe it was because I had sat by Daddy, watching him die, for so many months that his actual death almost seemed like an anticlimax.

My brother and sister left after the service, and it was just me, Mama, and Aunt Kate. The next day Kate went back to her own house, and the two of us were left alone. Mama would sit in front of our little black-and-white TV, staring at game shows and soap operas without really seeing them—my mama who was usually in constant motion, weeding the kitchen garden, kneading dough, sewing all the family's clothes on her little Singer in the corner. But after Daddy died, she even stopped singing.

It was six days after the funeral that she got her first offer on the farm. Of course, everyone in Tates Valley was speculating. I didn't know the details, but my parents were obviously broke. Mama had been waiting tables at the Pancake Chalet, but quit to take care of Daddy when he got sick. Aunt Kate had begun surreptitiously leaving envelopes on Mama's dresser, and I knew things must be bad, because she took them without any protestation. I was sure Mama could get her job back or find work somewhere else in town, but I hadn't had the heart to discuss it with her yet. I was selling some of my paintings at Hickam's store in town, but that hardly brought in enough money to help. I'd applied to graduate school for the fall and was expecting to move, I hoped to Chicago, in a few months, so I didn't see much point in looking for long-term work.

The farm was in bad shape. Daddy had let things go since he got his diagnosis, and Mama had spent every waking moment by his side. Now she seemed unable to consider what needed tending to, and I didn't much want to think about it either. I'd always had chores to do and knew the basics of milking a cow and driving a tractor; but as the youngest and least interested in farm life, I'd avoided doing as much work as my siblings. By the time they were leaving home, I was doing well enough in school that my parents wanted me to prioritize my studies.

Jimmy Reid was the first neighbor to make a move. Mama heard him out. He said he wanted to get the farm back up and running, just like Daddy would have wanted. Mama nodded politely. But as soon as the door had shut behind him, she spat on the floor. I was shocked. She was normally well-mannered and fastidious. "Jimmy Reid will turn this place into a parking lot faster than grass through a goose. You know he just started construction on a new motel, not one mile from here! He ain't no more a farmer than I'm a ballerina."

Over the next couple weeks, at least three more of the wealthier men in town stopped by to inquire pointedly after Mama's well-being and her plans for the future. She politely offered them coffee and listened to their pitches without revealing anything of her plans. Mama's no fool.

Next came Mac Folsom. He'd been friends with Daddy, and Mama was at ease with him in a way she hadn't been with Jimmy Reid. They sat together on the sofa, and she even turned off the incessant chatter of the TV to listen to him. Mac still had dark-brown hair and heavy-lidded eyes. He regarded Mama with sympathy, in her home-made dress and polyester apron.

I sat on the bottom step of the staircase, so I could hear them.

"Polly, I'm gonna speak frankly, if that's alright."

"Please do."

"You can't afford to stay here the way things are. We both know that. It's the sad truth. Life ain't easy for a farmer's widder."

A moment of silence passed between them; then he spoke again. "It might not seem that there's a silver lining to your situation right now, but things could be a lot worse. The good news is that these acres are worth a lot of money. Don't let anyone come in here and sell you short, Polly."

"I won't."

"I know it. I don't have to tell you Tates Valley is changing. You're not on the highway, but you're awful close. The right entrepreneur could make a lot of money here."

"You ain't that entrepreneur, are you, Mac?"

He chuckled. "I'm a farmer. Same as Zach was, rest his soul. I would be more than happy to lease this land from you to work. I can't afford to buy it from you for what it's worth, but since it backs right into my farm, I could use the land. But listen, Polly, if you want to sell up, you should do it."

"Thank you, Mac. I'll think about your offer."

When I heard the front door shut, I came back into the living room. Mama was tidying up the coffee cups.

"Are you gonna sell the farm?"

She straightened up and looked out the front window absently. "Reckon I'll have to afore long."

She took the cups to the sink and began washing them. Even before Daddy died, Mama had never been the type for long conversations.

Not long after Mac's visit, the weather changed. It was only the first week in March, but a warm front made it feel as though spring was here to stay. I was desperate to get out of the stuffy house, which smelled of too many chicken potpies, so I went for a walk by Mitchell's Creek, off the road through the neighbor's woods. I was enjoying the warm air, listening to birds and wind and rustling rhododendron, when I heard the sound of girls laughing and voices, young though not quite childish, echoing up the creek bank. Curious, I made my way downslope toward the water. Three young women around my age were sitting on a broad rock beside the stream. Two of them had long hair, down to their waists; the third had tight, natural curls that formed an orb around her head. She was wearing a muumuu. The long-haired girls were in jeans, one with a tight T-shirt, the other a peasant blouse.

The one in the T-shirt noticed me first. She smiled and motioned for me to come over. "Hi there!"

"Hi," I said, cautiously approaching.

"Are you our new neighbor?"

"Um, I don't know. Do you live here?"

They nodded. The curly-haired one spoke up: "We just bought Blackberry Acres."

"You bought what?"

"The farm up the hill."

"Oh." I hadn't realized the Eliots had moved. And I had never heard of anyone around here naming their farm before.

"My name's Marie," she said, extending her hand, which I was now close enough to shake.

"I'm Sarah. Pleased to meet you."

"This is Joy and Sunshine."

"How uplifting." I couldn't hide my sarcasm.

"My given name is Bertha. I changed it to Sunshine," said the one in the T-shirt.

"Fair enough. Is it just you on the farm?"

"Oh no," said Joy. "We're part of a collective. There's nine of us at the moment, but we expect more friends to join soon."

"Oh, I see." I smiled to myself at the thought of a hippie commune in Tates Valley.

"Do you live on the farm to the west?" asked Marie.

"Yeah. Well, my mother does. I'm just staying with her for a few months."

"You should come eat dinner with us," said Joy. "Tonight or anytime. Our door is always open."

"Thank you."

Marie stood up, and I realized for the first time that her muumuu concealed a heavily pregnant belly. Surprise must have registered on my face, because she patted her stomach and smiled. "I'm due in May. Sunshine is my midwife."

I looked back at Sunshine, who, true to her name, was beaming. She looked like she could barely be out of high school. "Have you delivered other babies?" I asked.

"I've assisted at a number of birthing experiences."

"I'm going to have a water birth in a bathtub. I wish we could do it right here in this river!"

"That doesn't seem safe," I suggested.

Sunshine nodded. "The trouble is the pollution these days."

Pollution seemed the least troublesome thing about the idea to me. "Well, I'd better be getting home."

"It was so nice to meet you!" said Joy.

"You must really join us for supper," added Sunshine. "Anytime. I'm sure Freddy would love to meet you."

"Freddy?"

"Our community leader," explained Marie. "He founded Black-berry Acres."

"I see. Yeah, that sounds great. I'm sure I'll see you around."

Despite the circumstances, I took a devilish delight in telling Mama about our new neighbors at dinner. "And they all just live together?" she asked, bewildered. "Unmarried girls and young men?"

I nodded. "It's called a commune."

"Like Communists?!"

"Kind of. They all work together and share their money and possessions." I dug into my mashed potatoes, enjoying Mama's outrage.

"What is this world coming to? Have you seen what Jimmy Reid is up to at the end of Mitchell's Hollow? He's got that earthmover out there, digging up an entire hill. Last week there was a hill there, this week there ain't."

"You know what he's building?"

"No idea. Some sort of amusement for Yankee tourists, come to gawk at us ignorant hillbillies, no doubt."

I hated to see the development as much as my mother. Even though I'd been talking about leaving Tates Valley just about since I spoke my first words, it still pained me to see the old farms bulldozed, forests replaced with concrete. "I'm sorry to hear it."

"In my daddy's time, it was the loggers coming in, taking our timber, and leaving the land barren and destroyed."

"At least the national park is protected."

"But we can't live in the park." She sat back in her chair, crossing her arms before her.

"Mama, you gotta eat something."

"I'm not hungry."

I didn't know what to do about Mama. I tried to find activities to get her out of the house, but she resisted, content to watch *The Newlywed Game* in silence. I even missed her singing, which had always driven me crazy. She sang constantly, all through my childhood. I don't think she realized she was doing it—singing was like breathing to Mama. Occasionally she would hum popular songs from the radio, but mostly it was the old-time mountain music she'd grown up on. *"Come all you fair and tender ladies, be careful how you court your men. They're like the stars on a summer's morning, first they appear, then they're gone again."*

She sang to us every night before bed, and that was her favorite song. Only when I got older did it occur to me how inappropriate it was to sing to little girls, with the message that all men are dogs and will break your heart. *"They'll tell you that they love you only; they'll tell you that their love is true. But then they'll go and court another. That's all the love they've got for you."* The singer is like a crazy, drunk lady at a bar whom you know to stay away from, or she'll talk your head off about how she's been done wrong. When I pointed that out to Mama, she rolled her eyes. "It's just a song. Folks been singing this song longer than you or I know."

The weather stayed nice that week, so I decided to go out to the barn and do some painting. Not great art, but small mountain scenes that I could sell in our friend's shop in town. I knew my limitations as an artist. I had the skill to reproduce a pleasing vista that a tourist would pay a small amount of money for. But I didn't have any true originality. When I first got to the University of Tennessee, I'd thought maybe I'd become an artist, mostly because everyone had been telling me how good I was at drawing since I was a kid. But when I took art history that first semester, I knew immediately that I didn't want to make art; I wanted to study it. Sitting in the dark, looking at slides projected on a screen of the most wondrous examples of classical art, I felt a sublime sort of contentment. I was transported to long-lost worlds, into the ancient myths. By the time Daddy died, I had applied to four graduate programs in art history, and I was hoping for the Art Institute in Chicago.

I was lost in thought, painting a riverside scene, when I heard footsteps approaching. My first thought was that Mama had come outside, but no. A young man was standing in the open doorway of the barn. An untucked shirt hung off his skinny frame, and long red hair brushed his shoulders, matched with a bushy beard. He was holding a small basket.

"Hi there!" he said. "Excuse me for interrupting. I just wanted to come by and introduce myself. I brought some muffins." He held the basket out toward me.

I put down my paintbrush and wiped my hands on my jeans. "Hi. I'm Sarah."

"I know. The girls told me all about meeting you." He spoke with an assurance that made me uneasy, as if he knew something that I didn't.

"You must be Freddy." I extended my paint-splattered hand.

He shook it, seemingly unmindful of the paint. "Freddy Abbott, pleased to meet you." I took the muffins and set them on the ground. He leaned back against a bale of hay and examined my painting. "You're an artist?"

"Well. Just an amateur."

"I saw one of these for sale on the strip," he said, pointing to my canvas.

"I sell out of Joe Hickam's shop."

"Sounds professional to me."

"I make pocket change."

"We want to make handicrafts on the farm to sell in town."

I couldn't help but smile at the thought of his girls knitting or whittling wood. "What? Like handwoven baskets?"

"Sure. Anything traditional."

I had begun our interaction with every intention of being polite, but something about Freddy's placid self-confidence bothered me. "What do you know about the traditions here? I guess you've read *Foxfire*."

"I have. I'd love to talk to you and your family as well to learn more."

Even the way he asked for help struck me as arrogant. "It's just me and Mama these days."

"Do you think you could introduce me to your mother?"

"Sure. I should warn you that she doesn't have much use for hippie types."

"Am I a hippie type?"

"You lead a commune, don't you?"

"No. I'm not a leader. We don't believe in hierarchy."

"Well, your acolytes told me you were their leader." Somehow, I just couldn't help myself.

"I coordinate." He paused, but kept looking me in the eye. His eyes were a luminescent green. I felt uncomfortable but held his gaze. "You don't like me much, do you?"

"Look, I just met you."

"I get the feeling I'm not making a good first impression."

"Well, you know us mountainfolk don't like outsiders."

"I mean no disrespect. We've come to Tates Valley because of our deep love for the country and people."

"You can't love something without understanding it."

"My deepest love is for things I don't understand." His eyes were drilled on me, as though we were in a staring contest. I was flustered, unsure how our conversation had progressed to this point. I don't make a habit of antagonizing strangers, but there was something about Freddy Abbott that got my back up.

We both turned at the sound of singing. My mother's voice, which I hadn't heard carry a tune since Daddy's passing, warbled softly, "*I remember when I first courted, and his head lay on my breast, he could make me believe with the fall of his arm, that the sun rose up in the west.*"

She appeared in the doorway to the barn, overbundled in her house cardigan with one of Daddy's jackets on top, as though she'd forgotten how to dress for spring.

"Mama, this is Freddy Abbott. He's moved into the Eliots' place. He brought us muffins."

Mama looked him up and down. She was only in her mid-forties, but a life of constant work had aged her. Her short hair was completely white, and her small frame appeared further shrunken by the layers of clothes.

Freddy shook Mama's hand. "Pleased to meet you, ma'am."

She gave him a nod.

"What was that tune you were singing?"

"Oh, I don't rightly know. Was I singing?"

"Yes," I said. "Your favorite song, 'Little Sparrow.'"

"I don't always realize I'm singing aloud."

"It was lovely," said Freddy. "I'd like to hear more."

"Oh, I'm not a real singer. I just hum to myself."

"You have a beautiful farm. We're so happy to have found this little corner of paradise."

"I didn't realize the Eliots had moved. Did you keep their cattle?"

"No. We are working the land and hope to be self-sufficient, with some additional cash crops. But we aren't planning to raise livestock commercially. And we don't believe in eating meat."

"What do you eat, then?"

"Vegetables, of course, with legumes and soy for protein."

Mama looked troubled.

"Thank you for the muffins, Freddy," I said.

"You're welcome. We would love to have you both over to dinner soon."

"Thank you. That's most kind," said Mama.

When Freddy had gone, she turned to me. "How many girls does he live with?"

"I'm not sure. There are other men there as well, I think."

"Communists who don't eat meat?"

"Something like that."

Part of me thought I should try to make friends with Freddy and the hippies. I'd been lonely through the months of Daddy's illness. Though I spent most all my time with him or Mama, I longed for the company of other young people and had called on my old high school friends. They were all married, though, with one or more children running around. Only one other girl from my circle had gone to college, and she'd moved to Nashville. I didn't know how to talk to the girls with the husbands and kids who now seemed a generation older than me. And they didn't much want to talk to me. But before I was driven to socializing with the bohemians, my boyfriend drove up from Knoxville for a visit.

I was especially hoping Bob would cheer up Mama. She liked him and was anxious for me to settle down and start a family. Most people liked Bob. I had adored him when we first met, though my affection had since mellowed into something more sustainable. We'd been going out since my sophomore year at UT. Bob was a catch—good-looking, with a strong jaw and a thick head of blondish-brown hair and matching mustache, ambitious, and popular, a smart aleck who kept his friends entertained. By the time of Daddy's illness, I'd begun to take Bob and our assumed future together for granted. He was working at the *Knoxville Journal*, but eager for bigger and better things. Our loosely agreed-to plan was to move to Chicago that summer, and somehow he'd been managing to set aside money from his meager paychecks to pay for our move. If I got into the master's program at the Art Institute, he'd look for a job at one of the Chicago papers.

Bob had grown up in Knoxville, and to him Tates Valley was a foreign country, even if it was only forty miles away. He referred to my parents as "the Clampetts" and loved to make fun of the hillbilly words I'd failed to scrub from my vocabulary: *holler, young'uns, britches*. Though Bob was unfailingly polite to my parents in person, I couldn't shake the feeling that he viewed them as anthropological specimens of a forgotten race.

We decided to take advantage of the nice weather and go for a hike, then join Mama for supper. Bob had only been to visit my family a handful of times, so I played tour guide as we drove through Tates Valley in his Beetle. I pointed out the shop that sold my paintings, the most garish of the new tourist traps, my old high school. "I would have liked to see you in your majorette uniform," Bob teased.

"I've still got it at home in the closet."

"You may have to give me a fashion show later." Bob loved to hear tales of my glory days at Tates Valley High, though I found it embarrassing. I had been a big fish in a small pond, a fact that became brilliantly clear to me the first week I arrived in the big lake that was the University of Tennessee. I was smart enough and attractive enough to be homecoming queen in Tates Valley. In Knoxville, I was nobody much, a scholarship kid from the boonies with a hick accent, until I started going out with Bob.

He pulled up to a stoplight and put on his blinker. "No," I corrected. "It's straight on to the park."

"I need gas."

I looked over at the Shell station he was preparing to turn in to. "You can't go there."

"Why not?"

"My grandfather sold it out from under my parents."

"Excuse me?"

"My grandfather used to own that filling station but sold it when I was little, instead of giving it to my parents. Mama is extremely bitter. You can go to the Phillips Sixty-Six up here."

"Wow. I didn't know your grandpa was a businessman. Owning a gas station—that's pretty high-class for Tates Valley!"

"Ha-ha-ha. He was pretty successful. My dad, rest his soul, not so much."

Bob turned off his blinker and looked over at the Shell station. Eugene Raymond was cleaning the front window of a tourist's Chevy. "Look at that—a Black attendant. Tates Valley is full of surprises."

"Eugene's worked there forever, even back when my grandfather owned the place."

The light changed, and Bob did as I'd told him, driving straight. "I didn't know there were any Black folks in Tates Valley."

"There's not really, just Eugene's family."

He turned in to the Phillips 66 and pulled up at a tank. "So why didn't your grandpa pass the gas station on to your folks anyway?"

"Greed, I think. He was a real SOB. He died when I was twelve, but when he was alive, I was completely frightened of him. Mama has a photo of him and my grandma from the twenties on the wall at home that I'll show you later—they both look terrifying."

"Then what happened to the money from the sale?"

"I don't know. My mom got a little when he died, but not as much as she'd hoped."

"Have you ever asked her about it?"

"Are you kidding? I can barely get her to tell me where's she's planning to live now that Daddy's gone."

"Well, maybe it's for the best. Hell of a time to be in the oil business." He turned off the engine.

We drove into the national park and decided to hike up the Laurel

Springs trail. It was colder at the high elevation and the trees were still bare and wintry. We walked at a leisurely pace, talking as we went. I was eager to tell Bob about the hippie commune, knowing it would amuse him.

"It's not a Charles Manson–type situation, is it?"

"That wasn't the impression I got. I think Freddy's just a run-of-the-mill hippie."

"What does Mrs. Clampett make of it?"

"Mama is properly horrified. And maybe a little intrigued."

"How is she doing?"

"Not good. She's taken up watching TV. All the time."

"Everyone grieves in their own way."

"I know. But there are financial realities to deal with. The farm is going to hell, and she's broke. She needs to sell it and find a job."

"Maybe I could try to talk to her about it."

I ignored what he'd just said, pointing to the giant oak tree up ahead. "The spring's just there at the base of that tree."

"What's so special about this spring anyway?"

"Well, it's haunted, of course."

He grinned. "Of course."

"Actually, Mama didn't allow us to come here when we were kids."

"I didn't realize she was that superstitious."

"Not about most things. But she hates Laurel Springs." I sat on one of the large, broad roots of the tree, and Bob stood above me.

"So what's the story?"

"I don't know. She would snap my head off if I even mentioned this place as a kid."

"No, I mean the ghost story."

"Oh. Well, a girl was murdered here, I guess. By her boyfriend." I picked up a stick and dug into the ground absently.

"Why would he do a thing like that?"

"Don't know. Maybe she cheated on him? Maybe he was just a psycho. We're related to the girl, though. She was my great-grandmother's sister."

"Maybe this isn't the right place after all, then."

"The right place for what?" I looked up and saw that he had pulled a small box out of his pocket. He knelt on one knee. "Bob, you don't have to do that. You'll get your slacks all muddy."

This was his third proposal. The first time he'd asked me, we'd only been going out for four months. I didn't know if he really meant it, but I didn't take it seriously. I thought it meant that he loved me, and I knew it meant that he wanted to take me to bed, but I wasn't sure if it meant that he wanted to get married. I'd told him I wasn't going to think about marrying anyone until I'd finished my degree. He'd said that he loved that I was a liberated woman. He waited to ask again until a month before my graduation. But he didn't know that Mama had just called that morning to tell me about Daddy's diagnosis. I'd burst into tears when he asked me and told him I had to go home to be with my parents.

Now he was on his knees at the base of a huge oak tree. He let his slacks get muddy. "Sarah, will you do me the honor of marrying me?"

"Yes," I said. We stood and kissed. I felt happy, if not elated. I had known the proposal was coming sooner or later and felt the comforting sensation of my life proceeding just as I thought it should.

"I was thinking we could do it this summer, before we go to Chicago. Something to cheer up your mother."

"That's a nice idea. But I still don't know if I'll get into the Art Institute."

"You will." He kissed me again. We walked back to the Beetle, where we had hurried, uncomfortable celebration sex before heading home.

We told Mama as soon as we got back to the house. She smiled, a big, broad smile the likes of which I hadn't seen in months. Then she set to cooking, declaring we needed a meal worthy of the celebration. "Chicken and dumplings," Mama declared. "That was always Sarah's favorite when she was a little girl."

The three of us peeled, chopped, and stirred together in the kitchen, talking, laughing, discussing where we should have the wedding and who to invite. Mama insisted that I just needed to pick out a pattern and she would sew me a dress. I felt a great wave of contentment wash over me. Each laugh seemed to crack away at the ice that had settled over Mama and that house, until it began to melt away. We sat at the table and held hands as Mama said grace: "Dear Lord, we thank you for your many blessings and ask you to keep Sarah and Bob close to you for all their days." I gave her hand a firm squeeze.

"So how did you pop the question, Bob?" she asked as she spooned beans onto her plate.

"We went for a hike up to Laurel Springs. I asked her there."

Mama's face fell. I glared at Bob. She turned to me. "Why did you take him there?"

"We just wanted to go for a walk someplace close." I saw the look she gave me, and tried to reassure her. "I don't believe in ghosts, Mama."

"It ain't about ghosts. It's just not a good place." Mama's face was knotted with disapproval.

"Don't be ridiculous, Mama."

Bob looked sheepish. "Do you think your pastor would perform the ceremony?" he asked her, in an obvious attempt to steer the conversation in a different direction.

Mama said nothing, so I answered. "I'm sure Pastor Davis would be happy to. If that's alright with your family."

"As long as there's no speaking in tongues or snake handling."

"Not at the Baptist Church." I gave a weak chuckle.

Mama was stone-faced; the jovial atmosphere dissipated, and she sank back into the dark, untouchable place where she'd been residing since Daddy died. When Bob left to drive home to Knoxville, she fell back into her armchair in front of the TV.

The next morning we were eating breakfast together when we heard a knock at the door. I got up to find Sunshine on the doorstep, wearing the same outfit I'd seen her in the other day and looking as though she hadn't taken it off in the interval.

"Hi, Sarah. We were hoping you and your mother could come to supper this evening at Blackberry Acres."

I looked back to see that Mama had gotten up and was standing behind me. "Hello there," she said to Sunshine. "I'm Polly. We'd be glad to join you. Should I make some corn bread?"

"Only if it's no trouble. We have more than enough for everyone."

When I closed the door behind Sunshine, Mama muttered under her breath, "She looked rode hard and put away wet."

"I didn't think you'd be interested in dinner in a hippie commune."

"We ought to be neighborly."

"Just remember not to use any lard in the corn bread."

"Why not?"

"They're vegetarians."

"You mean they don't even eat bacon grease?"

I was looking forward to Mama meeting the commune. I knew I was childish to take such delight in the inevitable culture clash and discomfort it would cause my mother, but given how dreary the past few months had been, it seemed like a relatively harmless pleasure.

The Eliots' former house was a large, three-story Victorian. At one time, they'd been the most prosperous farmers in Douglas County. A hand-painted sign now hung on the front porch: BLACKBERRY ACRES. Inside was a mishmash of furniture, old and new, with a bizarre assortment of artwork on the walls: abstract paintings on canvas, psychedelic posters, swaths of Middle Eastern fabrics hung for decoration. The commune members were strewn about the living room and smiled at us as we walked in. Freddy came out from the kitchen to greet us. "Welcome! We're so pleased you could join us."

Mama handed him her pan of corn bread, and he led us to the large dining table, long enough to seat twelve and covered with more exotic cloth and candles. We sat at the end of the table next to Freddy and Marie. Slowly the other hippies came in to join us, some carrying bowls of food to put on the table.

"Welcome to our neighbors, Polly and Sarah," Freddy intoned when everyone was seated.

"Welcome," muttered the assembled flower children.

An assortment of serving dishes went around the table, mostly filled with roasted vegetables, although there was a tofu curry that Mama sniffed at suspiciously before passing it along. But other than that, she seemed to warm to the hippies immediately and took a special interest in Marie's pregnancy. "Is Freddy your husband?" she asked innocently.

Freddy smiled. "We don't believe in marriage."

"Oh. So how do you manage things?"

"We'll all help raise Marie's child together here. Every member of Blackberry Acres will be his parent."

"Or her parent," corrected Marie.

I knew Mama must have a lot of thoughts about this, but she managed to keep them to herself. Instead, she said, "Good for you, dear. Heaven knows when Sarah will ever bless me with a grandchild."

"Mama, I'm going to graduate school. You know that. Besides, Abby has three kids already."

"But they aren't here."

"Well, I won't be here for long either."

"Where are you headed?" asked Marie.

"Not sure yet. Chicago, I hope."

Mama looked down the table at the assembled crowd. "How many of you'ns live here anyway?"

Freddy put down his fork. "The community currently has nine members, but we hope to continue expanding."

Mama looked impressed. "You're gonna run out of room. Why did you decide to live in Tates Valley?"

Freddy replied, "It's the most beautiful place I've ever seen."

"Goodness," said Mama.

As I lifted my water glass, Marie pointed to my hand. "Is that ring new?"

The ring had belonged to Bob's grandmother. It was simple, but the small diamond glittered in the candlelight.

"Sarah got engaged yesterday," Mama announced.

"Congratulations!" said Freddy.

"Thank you. Even if you don't believe in marriage."

Mama turned back to Marie. "When are you due, sweetheart?"

"May."

"My brother-in-law is a doctor in town. He's birthed many a child in Tates Valley. Dr. Mason."

"I'm planning a home birth."

"Sunshine is her midwife," I explained.

"Oh, I see. Don't you want medical care?"

"I prefer to experience childbirth without medical intervention."

"Well. That is how I experienced my first birth, though it wasn't because I preferred it."

I looked over at her. I hadn't known that.

"Sarah's brother Elijah came early, and Zach, my husband, was in Douglasville on business. I tried calling my sister, but couldn't raise her on the phone. Luckily, my mother stopped by that afternoon, or I don't know what would have become of me."

"You never told me that!" I said, shocked. "What did Grandma do?"

"All she could do at that point was hold my hand and catch Elijah when the time came. She didn't know how to drive, and I was too far along for much anything else anyway."

"Grandma Whaley delivered Elijah?!" Mama nodded. I tried to explain to Marie and Freddy how surprising this was. "My grandmother wasn't the warmest person. Or very comfortable with the human body."

"It's true. She weren't much help. But at least I knew someone was there in case I didn't make it."

"Well, thank goodness you did, Mrs. Garland," Freddy said.

"Please, call me Polly."

I was still digesting her story. "Grandma wouldn't even set foot in the chicken coop. She hated animals."

"That must have been difficult, living on a farm," said Marie.

"Mother grew up in town in Douglasville. She moved here with my daddy, but he didn't farm really. He ran a gas station."

"In Tates Valley?" asked Freddy.

"The Shell station on the strip. Sold it before he died, though. It's run by some foreigner now."

"By 'foreign,' she means he's from Georgia," I clarified.

"I'm from Atlanta," said Freddy.

"Oh," said Mama. "Well, I reckon there ain't nothing wrong with that."

Freddy grinned. I could tell he liked her. She was adorable in her way, a tiny, feisty hill-woman who drove me nuts. And for whatever reason, she seemed to be enjoying the company of these people. Maybe it was because they were so different from anyone else she knew. They couldn't remind her of the things that made her sad.

When we had finished eating, everyone moved into the living room for tea. There weren't enough chairs, so I sat awkwardly on an over-stuffed pillow on the floor, while Mama perched on the edge of the sofa. Sunshine passed around a teapot, steaming with a bitter com-bination of herbs. As I cautiously dipped my tongue into the murky liquid, I heard a plinky-plonky sound coming from upstairs. I looked up to see Freddy slowly making his way down the staircase, playing a mandolin. The instrument looked like a miniature guitar, and the contrast with his height created a ridiculous effect, like someone wear-ing an outgrown shirt or clown shoes. He stopped in front of the sofa.

"Sometimes we play music together after supper. I would be thrilled if you would sing us one your folk songs, Polly."

"Oh, I don't sing for people really. Just to myself."

A young man wandered over with a banjo, and he and Freddy began to play together, a melody I didn't know. The banjo player was excellent, and Freddy was obviously struggling to keep up. When they finished, everyone clapped and hooted.

"Any requests?" asked the banjo player.

When no one replied, he played the opening line of "Dueling Banjos" from *Deliverance*. Freddy smiled and played the reply on his mandolin. They went back and forth, speeding up, and I couldn't help but tap my foot, even though I hate that song. Freddy wasn't a great player, but he was a natural performer, mugging at those of us crowded around the sofa as he played, cocking his eyebrow, pulling faces, winking at Mama.

I knew I should leave well enough alone. But something about Freddy's smug expression and ridiculous mandolin wouldn't let me. "You know, we don't care much for that film around here," I said when he'd finished playing.

"Don't be so uptight," said Freddy. "It's a brilliant dissection of modern masculinity."

"Yeah, it's also a hateful stereotype of southern Appalachians."

"What film?" asked Mama.

"*Deliverance*," I answered. "It's about men from the city who go white-water rafting in the mountains and get raped by inbred hill-billies."

"Sarah! What a thing to say!"

"Well, that's what it's about."

Freddy put down the mandolin and sat by Mama. "Come on, Polly. Sarah doesn't dig my songs. Why don't you sing us one?"

"She doesn't 'dig' my songs either."

"That's not true, Mama."

"What was that you were singing the other day?" asked Freddy. "'Come All You Fair and Tender Ladies'?"

Mama nodded. "But we called it 'Little Sparrow' back in my day."

"I'd love to hear it."

I could tell Mama wanted to sing. She was enjoying Freddy's attention but felt she had to put up this show of humility. She cleared her throat and began, *"Come all you fair and tender ladies, be careful how you court your men. They're like the stars on a summer's morning, first they appear, then they're gone again."*

Her voice, though untrained, was strong, and the room was riveted. On the second verse, the banjo player began gently accompanying her, and I have to admit, it was lovely. Despite her protestations, Mama had some stage presence of her own. She held the notes of the final verse for effect: *"If I'da known when I first courted, that love was such a killing thing, I'da locked my heart in a box of golden, and tied it tight with a silver string."*

The banjo player followed her lead and trailed off to silence. For a moment, no one said anything. But then someone whistled, and everyone burst out in shouts and applause, including me. Mama glowed.

The night was cloudy, and if the two of us hadn't both spent decades memorizing the lay of that land, we would have struggled to find our way home in the darkness. "You sounded really nice with that banjo, Mama."

"I always did love music. My father played the fiddle when I was child. You know, he was a hard man, and that was just about the only time I felt close to him."

"The hippies loved you."

"They seem like good people, even if their lifestyle is unusual."

"I had no idea you were so liberal in your attitudes."

"I don't have to agree with them about everything to like them."

"You're right. They do seem nice. But still, be careful around them," I warned.

"What on earth do you mean?"

"I don't know. I just don't trust that Freddy."

"Oh, don't be silly, Sarah," she scoffed. "He's harmless as a kitten."

"I don't know, Mama. He's talked an awful lot of young girls into coming to live in a house with him."

"Well now, that is unusual, I'll admit. I hope that girl Marie will be alright. You know, there was a woman in town when I was growing up who'd come from away somewheres in Kentucky. Her boy didn't have a father, and she claimed to be a widow. But most folks reckoned he was a bastard."

"Glad you didn't share this story at supper."

Mama sniffed loudly. "Of course not, Sarah. I'm not cruel. Or even stupid, like you probably think. But that girl did remind me of her. The thing is, with the Kentucky woman, no one seemed to much mind that she was raising her boy alone. She was a good person and went to church every Sunday. So folks liked her and gave her a helping hand."

"Is she still around?"

"She passed years ago. The boy was a couple years older than me, and he died in the war."

"That's sad."

"There was a lot of sadness back then." She was matter-of-fact. "I always figured if some man had got her pregnant and abandoned her, that was just about as bad as being widowed. Some would say a good girl should know better than to get herself in trouble. But I know how men can be."

I could barely see her face, though we were walking arm in arm, but I heard a tremble in her voice that hinted at something I didn't want to question. Somewhere in the distance, a fox screamed, and I startled, squeezing Mama's arm despite myself.

"We're almost home," she said, as though I were still a little child. "Don't be scared."

———

The headlines in the wispy *Douglas County Register* usually consisted of school board decisions, new business openings, house fires, and automobile accidents. But that spring, real news happened in Tates Valley. Two teenage girls were killed at a campsite on the river, just at the edge of town.

At first the sheriff's office released scant details, which of course set everyone in town conjecturing about what had happened, their own gruesome stories filling in the blanks. Cause of death was strangulation in the case of one girl, and blunt-force head trauma in the other. They were out-of-towners, traveling together from Ohio. The most tantalizing aspect of the crime was that no one knew who did it.

Mama hadn't picked up a paper since Daddy died, as far as I knew. But she pored over the articles about the murders with a worried look on her face. "What is this world coming to?" she would say, obviously not expecting an answer from the likes of me.

A couple days after the news broke, I took Daddy's truck into town to buy groceries. No fewer than three of our acquaintances stopped to say hello while I was shopping, cordially asked after Mama, then quickly segued into murder gossip—the most surprising of them being old Pastor Davis, who had a theory involving a man he'd seen at last week's late service.

"He must have been from away. I ain't never seen him before."

"Just because he's a stranger doesn't mean he's a murderer," I pointed out.

"The wicked often hide behind Christ."

I politely wheeled my cart on by the reverend.

Back home, as I unloaded groceries from the back of the truck, I was surprised to hear laughter coming from the house. I hoisted a paper bag on my hip and opened the front door to see Freddy sitting across from Mama in the living room. I noticed his mandolin leaning against the fireplace.

"Hi there, Sarah. Freddy's been entertaining me."

He stood. "Can I give you a hand with those groceries?"

"Oh no, thanks. I got it."

Even before I finished unloading the bags and joined them, I heard Mama singing: "*She fell down on her bended knees, for mercy she did cry. 'Oh Willy dear, don't kill me here, I'm unprepared to die.' She never spoke another word, I only beat her more, until the ground around me within her blood did flow.*"

"Geez," I said.

Freddy turned to me. "You know this song?"

I shook my head.

"It's a murder ballad," he explained.

"Yeah, I got that much."

"It's called 'The Knoxville Girl.' Some folks say it's about my great-aunt," said Mama, "but I'm not sure. She never even set foot in Knoxville, as far as I know."

"Was she murdered?" asked Freddy.

"Yes. Long before I was born. She was just a girl herself."

"That's heavy."

"Speaking of which, everyone at the store was talking about the murders," I said.

"What murders?" asked Freddy.

"Have you not read the papers?!" asked Mama. "Why, it's been on the Knoxville evening news the past three nights."

"We don't have a television or subscribe to any mainstream news sources." Mama looked puzzled. "It's all government propaganda," Freddy explained, which didn't seem to help.

"Two girls staying at the RV park were killed," I told him. "They don't know who did it."

"Here in Tates Valley?" he asked. I nodded.

"What is this world coming to?" asked Mama.

We were all silent for a moment. "Do you remember the rest of the song?" Freddy finally asked.

"Of course," said Mama, and she began to sing again.

As I started boiling water for supper, still listening to them from the kitchen, I tried to get used to this new version of my mother. She and Freddy shared a genuine mutual admiration. She wasn't bothered by his long hair or nontraditional values, just as he didn't laugh at her homemade clothes or hillbilly ways. Mama seemed happier in

Freddy's presence than she had been in months, and he hung on her every word and note, slowly wrenching her out of her melancholy with questions about her songs and her life.

I'm just a poor wayfaring stranger,
Wandering through this life of woe.
There'll be no sickness, toil, nor danger,
In that fair land to which I go.

I'm going home to see my father.
I'm going there no more to roam.
I am just going over Jordan.
I am just going over home.

Mama's voice was clear, but her eyes were glistening, and I knew she was thinking of Daddy.

"I love that one," said Freddy.

"It was my father's favorite song," said Mama. "He would play it on the fiddle, real slow and mournful-like. That's Daddy there." She pointed to the framed photo on the mantel that showed my grandparents sometime in the 1920s, standing beside a cherry tree in front of a log cabin, looking miserable.

I cleared my throat. "I've made some spaghetti, if anyone's hungry. Would you like to stay for dinner, Freddy?"

"Thank you, Sarah. That would be great."

"I didn't even realize you were cooking back there!" Mama said. "Sarah takes good care of me," she added as we all sat together at the table.

"I'm glad to do it, Mama."

"Are you planning to stay on the farm when Sarah leaves?" asked Freddy.

Mama took her time answering, slowly swallowing a big mouthful. "I reckon I'll have to sell."

"Have you thought about any of the offers you've gotten?" I asked, hoping this might be the opening I'd been looking for.

"Not particularly. But I know I need to sooner or later. It doesn't make sense for me to stay here, letting the land go to rot, when we can get so much money for it."

"It's a shame," said Freddy. "I can't imagine this place without you."

"I've been here a long time, it's true. But I need the money."

"You could always join Blackberry Acres," said Freddy. I almost spit out my salad. "All like-minded souls are welcome," he continued.

"My sister has offered to let me stay with her."

"That's good," I said. "We should advertise the farm properly when you do put it on the market. Make sure you get competitive offers."

"I just hope no one builds one of those mini golf courses here," she fretted.

"Me too," I said.

"I wish we had enough money to make you an offer," said Freddy. "I'd love to be able to extend the community and protect this land."

"I'd like that too," said Mama, and she gazed at Freddy with a look of admiration and affection so powerful that I felt awkward to be witnessing it. I had the unsettling thought that it was almost how she used to look at Daddy.

When we'd finished eating, Mama said her good nights. Freddy insisted on staying behind to help me clean up. I scrubbed the dishes and handed them to him to dry. We worked in silence for a while. I didn't trust him, or even like him, but I appreciated that he seemed to be able to comfort my mother in a way that I couldn't, for whatever reason.

"Thanks," I said as we were finishing up.

"Don't mention it. It's the least I can do after you made supper."

"No, I mean for spending all this time with my mother. It's been really hard for her since my dad died. But you seem to cheer her up."

"It's my pleasure. Your mom is wonderful."

"Yeah. She is. I guess you don't always appreciate the people closest to you."

"Well, she sure appreciates you. She went on and on while you were out this afternoon about how smart you are, how well you did in school. And it means so much to her that you took time away from all that to be with your dad when he was ill."

I didn't want to cry in front of Freddy, but I felt my eyes stinging, my nose getting hot. "What else could I do?" I asked, passing him the last dish to dry.

"I didn't mean to upset you."

I shook my head. "No. It was nice of you to tell me." I looked over at him. We were standing very close to each other. He couldn't have looked more different from Bob, with his neat haircut and tidy clothes. Freddy's jeans were grass-stained and ragged; his beard badly needed a trim. But there was something compelling about him—probably the same something that kept all those girls living at Blackberry Acres.

"Would you like to come over? If you're not ready for bed yet?"

"Sure."

I hadn't thought to put on a jacket and crossed my arms to ward off the cold as we walked through the gloaming. Without saying a word, Freddy put down his mandolin, then took off his peacoat and put it over my shoulders. "Thank you," I said.

"No sweat." The night air thrummed with a chorus of calling frogs.

People were lounging around the living room at Blackberry Acres, just as they had been when we'd gone to dinner. The banjo player was sitting on a chair, gently strumming. I gave Freddy back his coat and followed him to the sofa. A girl I remembered from the other night promptly handed me a joint. I took it but hesitated, honestly not entirely sure what to do. The girl looked amused. "Have you never smoked pot?"

"No," I admitted.

"Just suck it into your mouth, then breathe it in. Be sure not to blow the smoke out your nose." I did as I was told, and of course started coughing immediately.

"It gets easier," Freddy said, sidling up to me to take the joint. He took a drag, looking me in the eye the entire time, then handed the joint back to me. I tried again and managed not to cough until after I'd properly inhaled.

I waited. "I don't feel anything."

"Sometimes you don't get high the first time," said the girl who'd given me the joint. "Wanna try again?"

I did.

That guy with the banjo could really play. The music was heart-achingly beautiful. "What is that song?" I asked him when he paused.

"It's an old fiddle tune called 'Devil's Dream.'"

He played it again, and I watched his fingers dance up and down the strings.

I don't know how long I listened, but at some point I nudged Freddy and whispered, "I think something's wrong with my heart. It's beating too hard."

He held my gaze in that way of his and gently pressed his hand on my chest, just above my left breast. After a moment, he leaned into me. "Your heart is fine. You're just stoned."

"Oh." I wasn't convinced.

"Do you want to get some fresh air?"

I nodded. He led me outside. It didn't seem cold to me anymore, even though I still had no jacket. We sat on the front porch step. "I think something's really wrong," I said. "Can pot give you a heart attack?"

"No, but it can make you paranoid. I'm sorry. Try to focus on something else. Do you sing like your mother?"

I laughed. "Hell, no!"

"You must know some of her songs. Try singing."

I laughed harder. I've always been a terrible singer. I usually just mouthed along to the hymns in church. "No way. I can't sing."

"Alright, then I'll sing: *Come all you fair and tender ladies, take warning how you court your man. He's like a star on a summer's morning, first he appears, and then he's gone.*"

He had a rich tenor voice, and as he sang, I stopped thinking about my heart. I listened to his voice and looked up at the great, dark sky full of stars. I thought about all the times Mama had sung those words to me, how they echoed through my childhood. When he finished, I told him, "Mama called me her Little Sparrow when I was a girl."

"That's sweet."

"The day Daddy died, he took my hand and squeezed it and said, 'Fly away, Little Sparrow.'"

"He was giving you permission to leave."

"I haven't told anyone that. I don't know why I just told you."

"I'm glad you told me."

"I miss Daddy."

"What was he like?"

"Hardworking. Always working, until he got sick. And kind. He was good with kids. He wanted the best for us."

"I'm sorry I didn't get to meet him."

I watched an airplane blink across the night sky. "I think I want to go home."

"I'll walk you." He sang the song again, softly, as we walked. At some point, I became aware that we were holding hands, though I couldn't remember him taking mine or me taking his. His was warm, his fingers slightly rough. He gently rubbed the inside of my palm.

As we neared the house, he stopped singing. "Do you feel better?"

"Yes. Thanks for walking me."

"No sweat."

I lingered. We were still holding hands, like teenagers at a school dance. Again, he wouldn't break my gaze. Finally he said, "Good night, Little Sparrow," let go of me, and disappeared into the darkness.

I didn't feel great the next morning. I struggled to get out of bed, and when I finally did, a lethargy settled over me that I couldn't shake. I stayed at the kitchen table long after finishing my breakfast, still in my bathrobe, drinking my third cup of coffee, staring out the window at the soft rain.

I didn't exactly feel guilty. I knew Bob would not have liked last night's scenario, but holding hands with Freddy was too ridiculous to feel guilty about. I didn't have feelings for him, and he had feelings for all the girls at Blackberry Acres as best I could tell, so a bit of flirting didn't mean anything. I felt certain that had I shown any interest, he would have taken me to bed last night. But at the same time, he didn't seem really interested in me. The person in our house he actually cared for was my mother. I was merely a physical substitute for her spiritual being.

Still, the whole episode had unsettled me. I didn't make a habit of getting stoned at hippie communes.

Mama noticed that it was nearly noon, and I wasn't dressed. "Are you feeling alright?"

"I'm just tired today. Mama, can I ask you a question?"

"Surely." She sat across from me at the table.

"Did you always know you were gonna marry Daddy? Did you ever have any doubts?"

"Oh, Sarah! You seemed so settled with Bob."

"I am. I'm just curious."

"Well, Zach was the only man who ever asked me. And I didn't expect to be getting more proposals down the line. Besides, I knew he was a good man."

"Did you love him?"

"Of course," she said, as though it were an obvious fact.

"Sometimes I'm not sure I want to get married at all. Things are different now, you know. A woman doesn't have to get married. I could just go to grad school on my own."

"Don't be ridiculous."

I swilled the last dregs of coffee in my mug. "Did you have secrets from Daddy?"

She straightened up in her chair and crossed her arms. "What a thing to ask!"

"Really? Everyone has secrets, don't they?"

She slumped back down a little. "I suppose so. There are things you keep to yourself in a marriage. Then there are secrets you keep together."

"Like what?"

"Nothing. Just the things that only you and your husband know." She got up.

"What secrets, Mama?"

"I don't have time for any more of this nonsense. You're going to be very happy with Bob."

She went out the front door into the rain. I had no idea where she was going. I had clearly upset her and felt like I should follow, make her come back inside. But I wasn't even dressed. I closed my eyes and put my head in my hands.

Freddy started stopping by with his mandolin every few days after that to sit with Mama and sing and talk. Her whole body seemed to lighten when he showed up. I avoided him as much as possible without seeming rude, usually coming up with some excuse to leave the house not long after he arrived. I was still suspicious of him, and even though I was glad he made Mama happy, being around him made me feel embarrassed.

I made my excuses and headed to Hickam's store to drop off some new paintings one afternoon shortly after he'd come over. Nancy Hickam was perched on a stool behind the counter as usual and smiled broadly to see me. She was around Mama's age and had been running the general store with her husband for as long as I could remember.

"Hi there, Sarah! You got some more of them paintings?"

"Yeah. How's the last batch doing?"

"Sold out. The out-of-towners can't get enough of them. I been putting 'em in the front window there and they attract foot traffic. Folks come in for the paintings and then decide they need some peanut butter and milk."

"Just what every fine artist aspires to!" I could see that my comment puzzled her. "Thanks again for letting me sell them here."

"Of course, Sarah. How's your mother doing?"

"Alright. She's struck up a friendship with our new neighbor."

"One of them hippies?"

I nodded. "Freddy Abbott. He's interested in folk music."

"What's that got to do with Polly?"

"She loves to sing old mountain songs."

She crossed her arms tightly across her chest. "I don't know about that, Sarah. You tell her to be careful."

"Why?"

"Folks been talking about them hippies. Something don't seem right."

"What something?"

"Well, they moved in, and not a month later them girls was murdered."

"That's a coincidence."

She shook her head. "Martin Blalock saw that Freddy hanging around the RV park before the murders." Blalock owned the RV park.

"Really? He said that?"

She gave a solemn nod.

"Freddy's not a bad guy. He doesn't even believe in killing animals."

"How many young women has he got living there with him?"

"There's nine of them altogether. Men and women both."

She shook her head as though no more need be said on the subject.

I took my time in town, hoping Freddy would be gone when I got back, treating myself to a chocolate malt at Houghton's ice cream parlor next door to Hickam's. Old Mr. Houghton handed me my malt with a sigh.

"What's wrong?" I asked.

"You see that building for sale across the street?"

I looked out the storefront window and saw a realtor's sign.

"Some Yankee just bought it. Plans to open a Baskin-Robbins franchise."

"Oh. I'm sorry to hear that. Everything's changing around here."

"Ain't that the truth."

I sat on a stool facing the window so I could watch the tourists go by with their sunglasses on their heads and cameras around their necks. Then I noticed Sunshine. She looked even more bedraggled than usual—hair greasy and unbrushed, shirt wrinkled, jeans dirty and fraying. I tapped on the window as she passed and waved. She broke into a smile when she saw me and came inside.

"It's been a hard week," she told me. "Did you hear about Marie?"

I shook my head.

"She had an emergency cesarean yesterday in Douglasville."

"Is she okay?"

"Yeah. She had a healthy girl."

"Thank goodness."

"She labored at home for twenty-five hours before I convinced her she needed help."

"Freddy didn't mention it when he came over to see Mama."

"Freddy hardly noticed. I guess birthing babies is women's business." The bitterness in her voice surprised me.

"Is it his baby?"

"Oh no. Marie was already pregnant when she came to us. Between you and me, the father is older. Marie's father's business partner."

"Oh."

"Poor thing. I don't think she's even ever had a boyfriend her own age. This old lech had been going at it with her since she was a freshman in high school. And of course he's married with three kids of his own, all older than Marie."

"That's awful."

Sunshine nodded, but then her face lightened. "But she's safe with us now."

"Yeah. Do you want any ice cream?"

"It looks great." She didn't make a move to order or anything.

"Do you need me to spot you some change?"

"Oh, I couldn't ask."

"No, it's fine. Here." I handed her some quarters from the bottom of my purse.

Sunshine seemed like such a mess, dirty, clearly hungry, devouring her ice cream like a greedy child. I gave her a lift home to Blackberry Acres when we were done, then returned to the house.

Mama and Freddy were in their usual spots by the fireplace, grinning at me as I came in the front door. Mama stood up as I entered. "It's time for celebrations, Sarah!" she exclaimed.

"What?"

"Freddy's buying the farm!"

"What??"

"Well, not just me," he corrected. "The entire Blackberry Acres community."

"I don't understand." I took off my jacket and put my purse down.

"We came into some money and want to invest in property."

"How much money?"

"Don't you worry about that," said Mama. "We're working out the details. But the good news is that we can keep the land from being turned into a shopping mall."

I sat down on the sofa and looked over at Freddy, suddenly feeling angry. "Do you even like coming over here? Or has this just been some long con to steal an old lady's land out from under her?"

"Sarah!" said Mama. "Don't be rude. And I can manage myself perfectly fine. I'm not that old."

"I love spending time with Polly," said Freddy. "I'm sorry. I realize this must have taken you by surprise."

"You think we're just hillbillies you can trick into doing what you want."

"That's enough!" said Mama in a tone I hadn't heard since I was a disrespectful teenager.

"Fine," I said. "It's your land. Do what you want with it." I stomped up the stairs, as though I were still a disrespectful teenager, and slammed my bedroom door for good effect.

I lay on my bed and stared at the spot of ceiling above it that I'd been staring at my entire life, covered in smoke-smudged white paint. I should have forced Mama to talk to me earlier about her plans. I wasn't a child anymore, and I had a responsibility to help her. But I hadn't, because the thought of doing so made me uncomfortable. And I'd let Freddy take over the job of helping her deal with Daddy's death.

I didn't trust him. I didn't like him. Sure, we'd had that one weird, stoned night together, but I'd only wound up at Blackberry Acres then because I'd been touched by how kind he was to Mama. I didn't see it as kindness anymore. He was just one more man trying to get something from her, and he'd caught her off guard with his approach. Jimmy Reid she'd expected, but, charmed as she was by his love of folk songs, she never saw Freddy Abbott coming.

We barely spoke to each other at supper. I established that her agreement with Freddy was only verbal and confirmed my suspicion that his offer was far less than what I was certain she could get on the open market. "It's what I want, Sarah," she insisted. "It would have killed your daddy to see this place turned into a parking lot."

"Well, cancer already killed him, didn't it?" I regretted saying that as soon as the words were out of my mouth.

I called Bob that night.

"I'm coming up this weekend," he said, as soon I'd finished telling him about Mama's real estate deal. "Let me talk to this Freddy."

The next morning, when I went into the general store, I made sure to tell Mrs. Hickam about Freddy's offer. That afternoon, Pastor Davis paid Mama a friendly call. I stepped out, thinking it best to avoid the impression we were ganging up on her. I wandered aimlessly along Mitchell's Creek. Spring was in full eruption now—the riverbanks blanketed with purple phlox and the trees overhead a dozen darkening shades of green. The air was damp and smelled of earth and growth and pine needles. The creek burbled, birds sang, and the forest pulsed with the promise of new life. The beauty of it filled me with a sort of ecstasy, despite my troubles.

When I got back to the house, Mama's guest was gone and she was sitting at the dining table with a cup of coffee. "What did he want?" I asked as I hung up my cardigan.

"What do you think? And how did he come to know my business anyway?"

"It's a small town. News travels fast."

"The only people who knew this news were you, me, and Freddy."

"I thought the offer was from the entire Blackberry Acres community. That's a lot of people who might have mentioned it in town."

Mama took a drink and slammed her cup down. "I don't understand why you're so angry with Freddy."

"I don't understand why you're so enchanted with him!"

She stood. "I'm going for a walk. You don't have to wait for me for supper."

Mama and I gave each other the silent treatment for the next two days, exchanging nothing but glances and bland pleasantries as we took our meals together and went about our business. I was waiting for Bob's visit, hoping that would break us out of our stalemate one way or another.

On Friday we were eating lunch in silence—Mama staring out the window, me reading the paper, munching a grilled cheese sandwich, when I saw the mailman's car and stood. I'd gotten one acceptance and one wait-list offer so far for graduate school but still hadn't heard from Chicago.

The mailbox was full—mostly junk, a credit card offer, a seed catalog, the electric bill. But there at the bottom lay a thick envelope

THE BALLAD OF LAUREL SPRINGS   155

from the Art Institute. I tore into it immediately, and only read the first line: *We are pleased to offer you a position* . . .

I ran back into the house, and Mama looked up. "What's the matter?"

"I got in! To the Art Institute of Chicago!" But before Mama could say anything, I felt my stomach turn. I dropped the mail on the floor and ran to the bathroom, where I promptly threw up.

When I came out, Mama was waiting for me at the bathroom door with a wet cloth to wipe my face. "That's wonderful news, Sarah. Are you feeling alright?"

"I have been a little nauseated the past couple days. Maybe it's a stomach bug."

"Come lie down on the sofa."

She put a blanket over me and sat in the easy chair opposite.

"Thanks, Mama."

"When was your last period, honey?"

"What?"

She raised her eyebrows at me, and I crumpled. I had known, hadn't I? Deep down I had known for at least a week now but had refused to admit it. "I think I'm about three weeks late."

Mama couldn't completely hide her smile. "Morning sickness runs in our family. Your aunt Kate like to died from the vomiting her first time around. Hopefully it won't be that bad for you."

I could feel my nose getting hot and tears beginning to form. "What am I going to do?"

"You're gonna have a baby, darling! Just move the wedding up a few weeks, and no one will bat an eye."

"But how can I . . ." I didn't bother finishing the thought out loud. Mama would never understand. I was supposed to be starting my master's in the fall in Chicago.

I knew I didn't have to have the baby. But I also knew I did have to have the baby. Maybe I wasn't as liberated as I liked to pretend.

Mama took care of me for the rest of the day, and it was nice. I felt like a child again, sipping ginger ale from a straw. When Bob got there the next morning, she went upstairs to give us some space, so I could tell him the news.

At first, he was thrilled. "That's fantastic!" he said, picking me up off my chair in an aggressive hug. He put me down, and then seemed to think it through more thoroughly. "I don't have any money. My salary is awful. But I'll find us an apartment."

"In Chicago?" Our eyes locked. I'd already faced up to the fact that we couldn't move there. But Bob needed a minute to figure it out.

"Maybe we should postpone?"

Mama appeared conveniently at the bottom of the stairs. "I've been thinking. Maybe I shouldn't sell to Freddy."

I'd all but forgotten about the farm in the past twenty-four hours, but still felt relieved. "Thank goodness. We should advertise. Get a realtor to help."

"Maybe I shouldn't sell at all."

"What do you mean?"

"I could lease the land to Mac Folsom. That would bring me an income, and we could all stay in the house."

"We?" I asked.

"All three of us and the baby. I could watch after it, while you go to school in the week. You got accepted to UT, right?" Apparently Mama had been paying some attention to my mail. "I know it's a long commute, but if you schedule your classes right, it won't be that bad, will it? And you can both stay with Bob's folks in Knoxville when you need to. All until you get on your own feet and buy your own house for your family."

I looked at Bob. I wouldn't have Chicago, but I would have my master's degree.

"Thank you, Polly," he said. "That's a generous offer."

"Could we have a day to think about it, Mama?"

"Of course, honey. Who would like tea?" She went to the kitchen to put on the kettle, softly humming "Little Sparrow" under her breath.

My mother, the woman I'd known my whole life as constantly working, singing, full of energy and optimism, returned that day from wherever she'd been since Daddy died. The TV retreated into hibernation as she made us tea, then lunch, then got to work on a basketful of mending she'd been neglecting. Bob and I went for a walk after lunch to talk, and he watched helplessly as I threw up into a bush. In retrospect, I think that moment clinched it for him. We were both out of our depth, and Mama seemed so sure of how to proceed.

When Bob left after supper, I had a chance to talk to her alone. She was knitting and singing an old hymn.

"Do you trust Mac?"

"With my life. He was good friends with your father, and he did things for our family—for me—that I'll never forget."

"What things?"

"It's a long story. I'm too tired to tell it now." Her voice was firm and fierce, and I understood she meant that I should never ask about it again.

Bob and I were married the next month by Pastor Davis. Bob's parents came, and a few of our college friends made it as well. Mama cooked for two days straight, and everyone came back to the house after to eat and socialize. Twice I had to excuse myself to be sick, but otherwise it was a wonderful day.

That same week, the sheriff's office announced that they'd arrested a suspect in the murders. Apparently one of the girls had an ex-boyfriend who had followed her down from Ohio and then killed her and her friend in a rage. This briefly took some of the local scrutiny off Freddy. But just a few months later, the sheriff raided Blackberry Acres after an anonymous tip that marijuana was being grown on the property. Not long after, the place was up for sale again. Jimmy Reid bought it, and word is that he wants to build a new motel on the property. Freddy disappeared after that. Some of the girls stayed in Douglas County. I still see Sunshine around town.

My baby girl, Carrie, is lovely. I think about Chicago now and then, and feel the tug of regret. But my life is filled with beautiful moments. Snow is lightly falling on the fields outside, and a great, glowing fire keeps this sturdy old house warm. I am studying at the dining table with a pile of books in front of me, Bob is typing on his Selectric at the desk he's set up in the living room, and Mama rocks Carrie in the same chair where she rocked me as a baby, softly singing her to sleep.

I wish I were a little sparrow
And I had wings that I might fly.
I'd fly away to my false true lover
And when he speaks, I would be nigh.

But I am not a little sparrow,
Nor have I wings that I might fly.
So I'll just sit in grief and mourning,
And try to pass my troubles by.

Perhaps I am missing out on some adventure or some other version of myself that could have been. But this moment in the firelight, watching my baby sleep as Mama's voice fills the room, feels perfect.

THE KNOXVILLE GIRL

CARRIE
(SARAH'S DAUGHTER)
1985–1993

I want to say that the accident of where I was born is not important
to me in any fundamental way, but I know that isn't true. I was
as formed by the place where I grew up as by my parents, my
genetic predispositions, or anything else, most certainly in the way
I saw the world and what I knew to be my place in it. Is it like this
for everyone? Probably not. Some places are more resonant than
others. Or more distinctive. Or more inescapable. Not that I had
any trouble escaping when the time was right. But did I really leave
my Appalachian mountain home behind? Or does the old chestnut
hold true: you can take the girl out of the hollow, but you can't take
the hollow out of the girl?

I can still sing the Appalachian ballads my grandmother taught me
as a child. Perhaps it is to my detriment that I never had a child of my
own to pass the songs down to; on the other hand, the preservation of
traditional music is probably not a good enough reason to bring new
life into this world. Grandma Polly knew a lot of the old songs, and she
loved to sing. She lived with us until her death when I was eight and
often sang to herself as she kneaded dough or worked at her sewing
machine or, later, when she was too sick to do much more than just sit.
Still she sang, and I loved her songs—especially the murder ballads.
These seemingly cobwebbed and moth-eaten tunes told shocking

stories, most often of men killing their girlfriends and dumping their bodies into rivers.

Now I'm disgusted by the endless variety of TV shows about women being murdered, repulsed by the steady stream of true-crime exposés, narrated in husky tones, shocking us, warning us, titillating us. But as a child I was fascinated by those songs. And I see how they all speak of the same thing. There will always be a few who murder, and many who want to hear about it.

"Sing 'The Knoxville Girl'!" I'd plead to Grandma, as she idly worked on a crossword in her favorite easy chair. It was my favorite ballad, since it mentioned the city where I was born. Grandma sang loud and clear, and even though the singer is supposed to be a man, I thought the tune suited her voice:

They carried me down to Knoxville and put me in a cell,
My friends all tried to get me out but none could go my bail,
I'm here to waste my life away down in this dirty old jail,
Because I murdered that Knoxville girl, the girl I loved so well.

When she finished, the words hung in the stale air of our living room. The song was horrifying and marvelous, though I struggled to understand it.

"Why would a man kill a girl he loved?" I asked.

I was very young then and didn't yet know much about the world.

I grew up on the edges of a tourist town, Tates Valley. My upbringing was rural, but less parochial than might otherwise have been expected in southern Appalachia. People were constantly coming and going, both to play in the garish amusement parks built up around the small mountain village where I went to school, and to work providing the infrastructure that housed, fed, and entertained those tourists. It was an odd place. A few people had a lot of money, and a lot of people worked for them, cleaning motel rooms and serving fast food. But I was just a kid, not yet aware of what made where I lived different from other places.

When I was little, we lived just outside of town, on what had been my grandparents' farm. My grandfather had died before I was born, and it was just Grandma Polly, my parents, and me in the house. I loved my grandma dearly. She told me stories, sang her funny old songs, played ceaseless games of pretend with me, and generally indulged me. I could tell that she appreciated my interest in things she cared about. Mom completely rejected what she called Grandma Polly's "hillbilly nostalgia"; she hated the clinking of hammered dulcimers and found anything quilted dowdy and oppressive. Grandma told me she'd tried to teach Mom her ballads, but my mother was never interested. The tension between them was a constant of my childhood, each woman taking offense at the other's innocent comments, reading malice into them that I couldn't find. Mom had wanted to leave Tates Valley. She said so at every opportunity, almost as though she were trying to prove it to me, my father, or Grandma. But something had trapped her. I now suspect it was her own timidity. But whatever had kept her in Tennessee, she blamed Grandma for it and poured resentment on her at every opportunity.

Still, other than the matriarchal bickering, my early childhood was mostly idyllic. I remember running through fields, jumping in the creek, and sledding in winter. Then when I was eight years old, everything changed. First, my grandmother died. Then my father left. He was offered a job in Chicago and apparently decided that he wanted to go there alone. My mother and her siblings sold the farm, but because of their various disagreements, legal and otherwise, Mom never got the money she expected from the sale. The next thing I knew it was just her and me, still stuck in Tates Valley, living in a grim apartment complex in town, and meanwhile the family farm was being turned into condominiums.

Not that I thought it was grim at the time. I missed the fields and the creek, but on the plus side, I could go roller-skating in the parking lot. I must have missed my father, but the memory of that missing has faded, and what remains are images of school, books I was reading, and games I played in the neighborhood around our apartment.

The complex had two stories, and the redbrick buildings made a U shape around the parking lot. We had a two-bedroom apartment on the ground floor. The walls were covered in cheap wood paneling; the kitchen floor was peach linoleum. All of our furniture was boxy and ugly, except for Grandma's antique cherry dining table, which just made the particleboard pieces look even more dismal. Why was everything so unattractive in the eighties? When I look back on my childhood, I remember ugly clothes, ugly hairstyles, ugly cars; everything plastic and disposable. The town of Tates Valley, where farmland was being converted to strip malls seemingly on a weekly basis, was especially hideous, even though—or perhaps even more so because—it was surrounded by the sublimity of the mountains. Everything lovely about the landscape was being systematically destroyed and replaced with cheap plastic and pavement, and I had a sense of not existing in quite the right moment. I knew things didn't used to be so aesthetically awful, even if other aspects of the more distant past weren't so appealing, like the lack of women's rights or indoor plumbing.

The apartment probably felt cramped for my mother, or maybe she was reveling in her independence, I don't know. The details of my parents' separation have never been made clear to me. My mother was the kind of person who would put a positive spin on any situation, so if she was mourning the loss of our former life, I didn't know it. Occasionally she would have a girlfriend over, and I would overhear crude, sarcastic comments about my father, but she hardly mentioned him at all in front of me.

I wasn't allowed to play in the parking lot in front. It opened onto the main road through town, and Mom deemed that unsafe. But the back parking lot was allowed. I could roller-skate or drag my dolls around or take my paints outside. Beyond the parking lot was a scraggly bit of woods that went about thirty feet back before hitting another road and residential neighborhood. The woods were my favorite place to go play pretend, no toys required. As an only child, I played a lot of pretend. Sometimes I even sang to myself. If I had thought anyone could hear me, I would have been mortified, but I usually had the woods all to myself.

On one warm March day, I had wandered back into the woods after school, carrying a book to read, but more intent on some game I had made up for myself that involved hopping from the roots of one tree to another, carefully avoiding touching the ground, lest it result in some imagined calamity. I was wearing my usual outfit of giant T-shirt over lumpy jeans. I still had baby fat, though I was only just beginning to mind it. But otherwise I didn't worry much about my appearance.

At age ten, I knew all the words to "The Knoxville Girl." Without thinking, I sang the song in my warbly, little-girl voice:

> *I met a little girl in Knoxville, a town we all know well,*
> *And every Sunday evening, out in her home I'd dwell.*
> *We went to take an evening walk about a mile from town,*
> *I picked a stick up off the ground and knocked that fair girl down.*
>
> *She fell down on her bended knees, for mercy she did cry,*
> *"Oh Willy dear, don't kill me here, I'm unprepared to die."*
> *She never spoke another word, I only beat her more,*
> *Until the ground around me within her blood did flow.*
>
> *I took her by her golden curls and I drug her round and around,*
> *Throwing her into the river that flows through Knoxville town.*
> *Go down, go down, you Knoxville girl with the dark and rolling eyes,*
> *Go down, go down, you Knoxville girl, you can never be my bride—*

Hearing the crunch of leaves and sticks behind me, I stopped singing and spun around. An older girl was watching me from a few feet away. To me she looked spectacularly grown-up, wearing a stone-washed denim miniskirt and matching jean jacket, a big, blond mass of hair-sprayed frizz rising above her head. Her arms were folded and she was observing me, while rhythmically chewing gum.

"Don't stop," she said. But I was frozen in shame, as well as a little awe. "What happens next?"

"I don't remember the words," I muttered, staring down away from her.

"Sure you do. Don't mind me. I really liked the song. You have a real grown-up voice."

My embarrassment melted quickly in the glow of her compliment. I looked up. "Thanks."

She came closer. "I'm Devon. We just moved in here last week."

"I'm Carrie."

"What grade are you in?"

"Fifth."

"I'm in seventh." By now she was standing close to me, leaning on a tulip poplar. "Come on, sing the rest of the song. It's really good."

I couldn't look directly at her when I sang—that was too intimate. So I shifted my weight from foot to foot and stared through the trees into the back parking lot. I could feel Devon looking at me. She stopped chewing her gum and watched, silent and intent.

I started back to Knoxville, got there about midnight.
My mother she was worried and woke up in a fright,
Saying, "Dear son, what have you done to bloody your clothes so?"
I told my anxious mother, I was bleeding at my nose.

I called for me a candle to light myself to bed,
I called for me a handkerchief to bind my aching head,
Rolled and tumbled the whole night through, as troubles was for me
Like flames of hell around my bed and in my eyes could see.

They carried me down to Knoxville and put me in a cell,
My friends all tried to get me out but none could go my bail.
I'm here to waste my life away down in this dirty old jail,
Because I murdered that Knoxville girl, the girl I loved so well.

I finished abruptly and looked over at Devon. She smiled. "Where did you learn that?"

"From my grandma. It's an old song."

"Why did he kill her?"

"I don't know. The song doesn't say."

She was chewing her gum again, fast. "I bet she cheated on him. Is it a true story?"

"I don't know."

"Can you teach me the words?"

"Sure." I acted casual, but in truth my heart was swelling. At school I had a hard time making friends even with kids my own age, and here was a super-cool twelve-year-old asking for my time.

We sat beside each other on the roots of the tulip poplar. I sang her each verse, one at a time, and she sang it back to me. She couldn't carry a tune, but I was supportive. Anyway, she seemed more interested in the lyrics than the music. She annotated the song as we went through it, adding her thoughts and opinions on the words.

"He, like, says she can never be his bride. So they must have been engaged. It's messed up."

I agreed. That was what I'd always loved about the song. "But why wouldn't he just break up with her?" I asked.

"He must have been real angry."

"I always thought it was kinda crazy that he tells his mom he's covered in blood from a nosebleed."

She grinned. "That'd be a gnarly nosebleed." She stood up. "I better go. Thanks for teaching me the song."

"No problem."

"You can come by sometime if you want to watch TV or whatever. We're in apartment five."

"Okay."

I watched her walk away, thinking that this could be a life-changing moment for me. I now had a twelve-year-old friend in apartment five. The only problem was that I certainly didn't have the courage to go ring the doorbell on apartment five. In fact, I would have squandered this golden opportunity at intergrade friendship if Devon hadn't found me a few days later, reading on the back steps of the apartment complex. I had just gotten into Edgar Allan Poe. The reading was sometimes tough going, but my mother had bought me an illustrated hardcover edition of his collected stories, and the macabre illustrations made up for the dense paragraphs. The book was huge, and I had it propped up on my knees as I read, gruesome cover art of "The Tell-Tale Heart" facing outward. Devon must have been watching me for a moment before I noticed her. When I finally looked up from the Rue Morgue, she was standing about five feet in front of me, wearing skintight jeans and that same jacket. Her hair was pointed extravagantly upward in a side ponytail. She smiled. "Hey."

"Hi."

"Cool book."

"Oh, yeah. Have you read it?"

"We had to read some story by him in school, but it didn't have that awesome picture."

"You can borrow it sometime if you want."

"Cool, thanks." She looked away from me but didn't move. I wasn't sure if I should go back to the book or not. Then she looked back. "I was gonna walk down to the Shell station and buy some candy. You wanna come?"

"I'm not allowed to walk on the main road."

"Is your mom around?" I shook my head. "Then she won't know, will she?"

Her logic was sound. She talked as we walked, sometimes having to shout over the sound of cars. Her mom wouldn't be home until ten thirty, when she finished her shift at TGI Friday's. That was her schedule most nights, so Devon spent a lot of time walking around town on her own or watching TV. They'd just moved here from Florida a month ago. Devon's mom had a boyfriend who she thought they could move in with, but then he got arrested and lost his job, so they had to get this apartment instead. My eyes widened at the arrest detail. Devon threw it in quite casually, like it was no big deal. I didn't know anyone who knew anyone who'd ever been arrested. I wanted to ask what he'd been arrested for, but thought it might be rude. Instead I offered up pointless trivia about my family. "You know, my great-grandfather used to own this Shell station, although I don't think it was called Shell back then. It was before I was born."

"Wow, your family's been here awhile, huh?"

"Forever, as far as I can tell. Although Grandma always said we were English, Dutch, and Irish, so I guess not really forever."

"Too bad you don't still own it. You'd be rich."

The whole reason I knew about the gas station was that my grandma would mutter to herself whenever we passed it on our trips into town when I was little. I'd gotten the distinct impression that selling hadn't been her idea, and she'd held on to her resentment over it into old age. "Just like Daddy to sell the station out of the family. And to have that colored boy working there."

My mother would yell from the driver's seat, "Mama! That's a prejudiced thing to say."

"Well, it's true. Daddy hired that colored fellow Raymond back when he still owned the store. Folks talked about it, let me tell you. Now I hear from my sister that Raymond's son works there still. Daddy wouldn't give us the gas station, but he made sure the Raymonds had jobs for life."

"What did you want with a gas station anyway, Mama?"

"Times were hard, Sarah. You know as well as I do. Farming killed your daddy."

"Cancer killed Dad." And the two women would sink into silence, the gas station forgotten.

As far as I was concerned, the Shell station was a garden of earthly delights. Candy, chips, sodas, pens of a wide variety of colors—what more could a girl want? We were chasing around, debating what snacks to buy, laughing, when Devon rounded a corner and ran head-on into the young man stocking sandwich crackers, causing him to drop a handful of Captain's Wafers cream cheese and chive.

"Watch where you're going, man!" He was cute, with square glasses and a flattop. And I was uncomfortably reminded of my grandma's comments by the fact that he was Black.

"Sorry, dude!" said Devon, immediately bending over to help pick up the crackers.

Something in her demeanor or the ridiculousness of the situation made him laugh. "No big deal. You just startled me. You're not trying to boost anything, are you?"

"Huh? We just came to buy some candy. With money. See?!" She opened up her purse and showed him her huge pile of quarters.

"Alright, girls, just slow down, okay?"

She grinned at him, then turned back to continue our discussion of the relative merits of Lemonheads versus Atomic Fireballs.

Devon chewed gum loudly on the way home. "Seriously, you should come up to my apartment anytime. My mom's, like, never there. We can listen to music or whatever."

"Okay. That sounds cool." In fact, it sounded like the greatest invitation of my life. I hadn't had a best friend since second grade, when Katie McMann had moved to California. I was too smart. I was too quiet. I read too much. I was chubby. I couldn't run. We didn't have cable. I spent too much time talking to my mother about art history and not enough learning the pop culture references that came naturally to my classmates. For whatever combination of these reasons, I had no real friends. I prayed for assigned seating at lunch, so I didn't have to try to find classmates who'd let me sit with them. I prayed for rain, so that I didn't have to wander the playground at recess, aimlessly seeking someone to play with. I prayed to grow up quickly and become a different, popular person.

At the time I didn't question why Devon wanted to hang out with me. It was too precious a miracle to examine closely. Later I came to realize that, despite seeming so cool to me, she too was not popular at school, though for different reasons. She must have been bored and lonely, and I was probably the only person living in her immediate vicinity who wanted to spend time with her. I thought our friendship was an act of charity on her part. Now I see that we both benefited and came to depend on each other in different ways.

Mom never knew that I walked on the main road that day or that the reason I was particularly uninterested in her tomato soup that evening was that I had consumed half of a jumbo box of Lemonheads and a bag of Fritos just two hours earlier.

When I finally did visit apartment five, it was because Devon had found me roller-skating in the parking lot and invited me in. I felt like I was entering a magical realm, but it was actually dingy and dark. Devon's mom wasn't a big cleaner. The TV was on in the living room, tuned to a game show, even though no one was home. Dirty dishes towered on the kitchen counter, beside empty fast food boxes and beer bottles. The blinds were all closed, and the air was musty. My excitement quickly turned to unease.

Devon's room was covered with posters: the Doors, *Friday the 13th*, an Escher print. She plopped on her unmade bed, and I followed suit. "Mind if I smoke?" she asked.

I was secretly scandalized, but shook my head casually. She opened the window and pulled a pack of Virginia Slims out from under her mattress. "You get your report card today?" asked Devon.

I nodded. My straight As were marred only by an A- in science. But I didn't want Devon to know that.

"I failed social studies," she said. "And English."

"Are you gonna be in trouble?"

She rolled her eyes. "Not really. Mom will probably ground me, but she usually forgets after a day or so. You don't have to worry, do you? You're real good at school."

I looked down at the ugly brown carpet. "I guess."

"You shouldn't be embarrassed. That's good. The funny thing is, I like social studies. I just forgot to turn in some assignments. And I guess I skipped class a couple times."

"What do you do when you skip?"

She shrugged. "Just wander around town."

The idea of wandering around town during school was unimaginable. I was beginning to feel panicky in the dark room, with the cigarette smoke and talk of juvenile delinquency. Devon stubbed out the Virginia Slim and tossed it out the window. "You wanna play a game?"

"Sure."

"Let's pretend we have magic, okay? I'm going to be a vampire, but, like, a nice one. You can be whatever kind of magic person you want to."

I nodded. "I'll be a witch. But a nice one. A pretty one."

And we spent the next hour playing pretend. That was the funny thing about Devon. Even though she smoked and skipped class, she still enjoyed playing like a child.

When it was time for me to go home for dinner, I asked if she wanted to come. My own apartment felt comfortable and clean, after the trip to apartment five. Mom was in the kitchen, standing over a steaming pot. She was thin with fashionably permed, shoulder-length brown hair.

"Hey, sweetie, I was getting worried," she called.

"Sorry, Mom. I was playing with my friend Devon."

Mom turned then and saw that I wasn't alone. "Oh, hello there!" she greeted Devon, who was standing awkwardly in the doorway.

"Hi."

"Can Devon stay for dinner?"

"Sure."

We had spaghetti. Devon ate a lot, like she was starving. Around my mom, she got quiet.

"What grade are you in, Devon?"

"Seventh."

"So it won't be too long before I get you at TVHS." Mom was the high school art teacher. "Do you like art?"

"Yeah. I like to draw."

"Fantastic. If you ever want to borrow any of my supplies, just let me know. Carrie has plenty of her own too that she'll let you play with, I'm sure."

"That sounds cool."

"Where's your mom tonight?"

"Working. She works most nights at TGI Friday's."

"That must be hard. Well, please feel free to come by here whenever you like."

"Thank you." Devon smiled. I could tell she liked my mom. Other kids always liked my mom. Everyone wanted to drive in our car on Girl Scouts field trips, even though no one liked me, because Mom let them turn the radio to the Top Forty station and play it as loud as they liked. I liked my mom too, so I understood. But I didn't want Devon coming over because Mom was nice and made good spaghetti. I wanted her coming over for me.

She started coming over for both of us. I'm sure my mom's attention meant a lot to her. Even at my young age, I could sense that her mother wasn't quite right. The first time I met her, it was around two in the afternoon. Devon and I had been playing ghosts and vampires in the woods, when Devon wanted to go in to get something to drink. I followed her into apartment five and waited in the living room while she grabbed some Sprites. I stood against the wood-paneled wall, still ill at ease in that dank apartment. Then I heard a voice coming from the bedroom. "Devon!"

Devon ran out of the kitchen with the Sprites, and yelled, "What, Mom?"

"Bring me some aspirin! My head is killing me."

Devon dropped the Sprites onto the couch and jogged over to the bathroom. Her mother emerged from the bedroom slowly in a tattered blue satin bathrobe, looking, as my grandma used to say, like she'd been rode hard and put up wet—eyeliner and mascara smudged across her face, platinum-dyed hair huge and messy, doused in hair spray yesterday and tossed and turned on all night. She leaned against the hallway wall and pulled a pack of cigarettes out of her pocket. She put one in her mouth and felt around in her pockets. "Fuck," she muttered under her breath, and walked on into the living room, only then noticing me. She looked surprised and took the cigarette out of her mouth. "Who are you?"

"Carrie. I live in apartment sixteen."

"Devon, why didn't you tell me you had a friend over?!"

Devon walked back into the room with two aspirin in her hand. "I hadn't even seen you, Mom. We were just headed back out anyway."

"God, I must look a fright. Nice to meet you, Carrie."

"Nice to meet you."

"Sorry about my appearance. I had a late night at work."

"We're going back outside," said Devon, grabbing the Sprites and heading toward the door.

"Wait, honey. Why don't you have some breakfast with me? I'll make pancakes."

"Mom, I had breakfast, like, six hours ago."

"Alright, well, lunch then. Don't you want pancakes? Your friend can stay."

I desperately wanted out and away from this woman. But when Devon turned to me, I shrugged, not sure how I should respond. "Are you hungry?" she asked.

"Sure."

We sat in front of the TV watching figure skating while Devon's mom fixed the pancakes. "Devon!" she called. "Have you seen my lighter anywhere?"

"No." Devon winked at me, and I realized it must be secreted away in her room.

Devon's mom brought the pancakes into the living room on paper plates. She put a stick of butter and a bottle of Aunt Jemima on the coffee table. There was no knife. Devon grabbed the butter and rubbed the end of the stick directly on her pancakes, then handed it to me, so I did the same. Devon's mom sat beside us and doused her pancakes in syrup. "I saw Walter last night," she announced.

Devon poked at her food. "I thought he was in jail."

"He got out. And I think I can get him a job as a busboy at Friday's."

Devon shoved a forkful into her mouth. "He misses you," said her mother.

Devon chewed silently. Her mom turned to me. "Where do your folks work, Carrie?"

"My mom teaches art at the high school. And my dad is a journalist in Chicago."

"Ooh, that sounds exciting! You get to visit him often?"

I shook my head. "No. His apartment is very small."

Devon's mom nodded. "Yep. I heard that one before."

I didn't exactly know what she meant, but I got the drift.

Mom had wanted to get out. She said so all the time. When I was little, she would get in arguments about it with Grandma, not the sort that included shouting or slamming doors, but the passive, simmering kind that lasted for days. She blamed Grandma for keeping her here, trapping her in Tates Valley, driving my dad away. Grandma thought Mom was ungrateful for what she had and where she lived. A lot of Mom's sentences started with: "If I'd gone to the Art Institute and lived up to my potential . . ." Grandma would reply, "Why didn't you? Who stopped you?" It was a question Mom never seemed to answer.

She had gotten her master's in art history at the University of Tennessee and intended to get her PhD. But then came whatever happened between her and my dad. Or maybe she lost her nerve. Or maybe deep down she didn't want to write a dissertation on El Greco. Or didn't want to leave Tennessee. I don't know. In any case, she wasn't the only one. She had a whole circle of friends—fellow teachers from the school, actors from the dinner theaters, hippies who had come to the mountains to grow weed and throw pottery—who felt they didn't belong here. So many big dreams melted down into handicrafts to sell to Yankees from Ohio, warped into comedy routines to entertain traveling hordes from Georgia, or, in my mother's case, shriveled into lesson plans on chiaroscuro. I think she was a good teacher. I stayed far away from art class in high school, but other kids always seemed to like her, and I know she was a beacon for the social outcasts already attracted to art and further drawn in by the example of an adult as uninterested in the fate of the school football team as they were. Mom hated country music, loved independent film, and wore a lot of black. She was active in local environmental advocacy groups and protested outside the paper mill that was polluting our rivers. She was a registered Democrat and a card-carrying member of the ACLU. To those kids, she was an idol.

Mom hated the tourist attractions that drove our local economy. She thought it was all impossibly tacky, and it was, of course. Strange things came and went: laser light shows, miniature golf with live bunnies, museums of reptiles and Elvis memorabilia. I suppose I didn't know just how odd it all was until I left, and then by the time I came back, it had become much more normal, mom-and-pop outfits slowly bought out by corporations, the singular weirdness replaced by franchised vulgarity.

The biggest attraction in town back then was Frontier City, at least to my young mind. It was an Old West–themed amusement park with some liberal doses of hillbilly thrown in, as well as a dash of Civil War reenactment. You could mine for gold, buy taffy and plastic bric-a-brac in an imitation Dodge City, watch a live rodeo, and ride a roller coaster called the Rebel Yell past a moonshine still. I had only been there once when my babysitter whose boyfriend worked there selling cotton candy got us in for free, so she could make out with him while I gorged on spun sugar. I was secretly obsessed with going back. Secretly, because my mom didn't approve of amusement parks. She said they destroyed imagination, and Frontier City was an abomination of bad taste and overpriced to boot. It was hard to argue with any of that, so I stared at the Frontier City billboards we drove by on the way to school, silently daydreaming of fudge and Ferris wheels.

So when Devon asked one Sunday morning if I wanted to go to

Frontier City, I did not hesitate. She could get us in for free, because her mom's friend was a ticket taker. I had to ask Mom's permission, which was slightly embarrassing, but well worth it. She wanted to know if Devon's mom was coming. She was supposed to drop us off on her way to TGI Friday's and come back to pick us up at the end of the day. I left out the TGI Friday's part, leaving my mother with the strong implication that Devon's mom would be with us all day at the park. Permission granted, we were off, for what I was fairly certain was going to be the greatest day of my life.

And who's to say it wasn't? Do days ever get better than they are when those first childhood wishes are fulfilled? I can think of a day in Tuscany when I was a good bit older, filled with sunshine, art, porcini, wild boar, and Chianti; or that one time I got snowed in with my then-boyfriend when we were still in the first, mysterious flush of love, fucking, drinking coffee and bourbon, watching DVDs, and reading aloud to each other. But did I enjoy those days more than that one at Frontier City? It was almost Halloween—my favorite time of year— and the trees had just exploded into warm, rich color. Spooky ghosts and witches frolicked in the Old West storefronts. An old coal-burning train puffed black smoke into the air, burning our nostrils and dusting us with ash. We ran from ride to ride, determined to go on them all at least once. Our favorite was the rickety old wooden roller coaster, the Grizzly, which we rode four times. We ate corn dogs, caramel apples, and popcorn, washed down with Slush Puppies and Cokes. We played with the toys in the souvenir shops, even though we'd spent all our meager funds on junk food.

Late in the afternoon, worn out from rides and stuffed with sugar, Devon dragged me into an old-timey photo shop. We picked out dresses, but the photographer sighed when she realized we had no money. "Where's your folks? I bet they'll buy a picture for you."

"They're getting supper in the restaurant across the street," Devon lied.

My pink dress had huge puffy sleeves and I held a parasol over my head. Devon chose a giant hat with a black feather and a dress that made her look like an underage prostitute.

"I can hold on to the picture for you," said the photographer, after we'd changed back into our normal clothes. "Bring your parents on over when they're done."

We nodded and ran out of the store, giggling.

When we finally stopped, out of sight of the photographer, I heard the sound of a choir singing. Looking around, I saw a group of old men and women in a nearby pavilion, standing in rows and holding hymnals.

"What's that?" I asked.

"The gospel singers," answered Devon.

"Like in church?"

She nodded and walked toward them. The old folks were clearly not professional singers. They warbled in unison: "*God leads His dear children along. Some through the waters, some through the flood, some through the fire, but all through the blood.*"

To my shock, Devon began singing along. She seemed to know all the words and sang out clearly. When the choir finished, she clapped, and I clapped too, afraid to seem unappreciative. We walked slowly away from the pavilion.

"How did you know that song?"

"We used to go to church in Florida. Before Mom started dating Walter. I liked the songs. I wanted to join the choir, but then we stopped going."

The sun was getting low, and the air was growing crisp. I wished I'd brought a jacket. "What time is your mom coming?" I asked.

"Six."

"Should we head to the entrance?"

"Yeah, in a minute." Devon seemed distracted. She was staring at a Halloween-themed decoration, a scarecrow surrounded by pumpkins.

"What is it?"

"I want a pumpkin."

"Oh, they sell them out front at Kroger or Food Lion."

"No, I want one of those pumpkins."

"What?"

Devon gave me a wicked smile. "Come on, it's not like they're gonna miss one pumpkin."

She was already scrambling over to the display. I looked around to see who might be watching, waiting to arrest us for pumpkin theft.

"Where are you gonna put it?"

"My backpack." She'd already picked out a small pumpkin and was removing it from the feet of the scarecrow. "Here, take it, while I make room."

She reached the pumpkin out toward me. My throat went dry as I took it. I imagined my mother getting a call from the police. I imagined being asked why I'd done it. I had no idea.

Devon opened her tattered backpack wide, and I slid the pumpkin in. She zipped it up and put it on her back. It obviously contained a pumpkin. I felt nervous the whole time we made our way out of Frontier City.

Devon's mom was twenty minutes late to pick us up. We sat on the curb waiting. "You gonna make a jack-o'-lantern?" I asked.

"Yeah! Should we go back and get a pumpkin for you too?" Devon laughed.

"No, it's okay."

"You can help. I'm gonna make it look like a vampire."

Devon's mom didn't seem to notice the pumpkin in her bag, or question where it came from when Devon took a butcher knife to it later that evening.

I spent two weeks with my dad in Chicago that summer, and when I came back, Devon had a boyfriend. He was two years older than Devon, which meant he was a million years older than me. His family owned a motel, the River Vista. The day after I got back, Devon asked if I wanted to go swimming there in the motel pool. Mom said sure, as long as an adult was going to be present. I told her definitely, figuring that at fifteen James was basically an adult.

James was skinny. He looked spectacularly gawky, standing at the gate to the swimming pool in nothing but his trunks when I first met him. His shoulders seemed too big and bony for his torso, and his swim trunks looked in danger of falling right off his gaunt hips. A mop of dark hair contrasted with ghastly pale skin, the shade that can't tan, and a small but distinct rattail trailed down the back of his neck. His face, accented with big, dark, lash-framed eyes, was almost attractive yet slightly off. His nose was crooked, and when he smiled, it looked as though he had one too many teeth crammed in his mouth.

"Hey," said Devon. She had been going to the pool every day and was perfectly bronzed from head to toe, wearing a Baja sweatshirt over her swimsuit.

"Hey," said James. He opened the gate for us.

"This is Carrie."

James nodded at me, and I nodded back. "You wanna swim?" he asked Devon.

"Sure." She pulled off her sweatshirt to reveal a pink bikini.

I had on a giant souvenir T-shirt from Chicago and dreaded the moment I had to take it off to reveal my one-piece suit and still child-like tummy. Devon jumped into the pool, and James followed her. "Come on, Carrie!" called Devon.

I pulled off my shorts and T-shirt and jumped in. Devon splashed me in a playful way, and I splashed back. She didn't really treat me differently than before I'd gone away, but her attention was divided between James and me. He kept swimming very close to her, trying to sneak up from behind and pull her underwater. "Stop it!" she yelled, but she was laughing. James had a sly smile. As soon as she turned her back on him, he was at it again.

Later, the three of us stretched out in a row on reclining chairs by the side of the pool. Hot, thin strips of plastic dug into my thighs. A motel guest, a large, bald, middle-aged man, waded into the pool.

"I'm bored," said Devon.

"Wanna get out of here?" asked James. He sat up and turned toward Devon.

"Yeah. Where should we go?"

"You know about the Happy Camper murders?" asked James.

"No," said Devon.

"It was about ten years ago at the Happy Camper RV park just down the road. It's a campground, and they also have these little cabins down on the river. These two girls were murdered in one of the cabins."

"Oh yeah?" Devon sounded casual, but I knew she was intrigued.

"You can see just where it happened. You wanna go?"

"Sure," said Devon.

I knew I shouldn't go anywhere else with them. I wanted to go home. But I didn't know how to say that without sounding like a baby. They'd both gotten up and were throwing on clothes over their bathing suits, so I did the same.

We followed James along the river, which paralleled the main road. We walked through back parking lots that occasionally gave way to wild riverbank where we had to scramble to keep upright. The river was narrow with steep banks still covered in thick foliage and trees, despite the development all around. Once we walked a ways from the River Vista, James pulled a pack of cigarettes out of his back pocket and handed one to Devon. I was relieved that he didn't offer one to me.

"So who murdered these girls?" asked Devon.

"Some guy they met on the strip. They were on vacation together and went out to meet boys, I guess."

"How old were they?" she asked.

"Like, seventeen or so. Anyway, they took a guy back with them to their cabin. One of the girls went out on the back porch to smoke a cigarette and give the other two some privacy. But when she came back in, she found her friend drowned in the bathtub. She tried to run, but the man caught her and strangled her, then dumped her body in the river."

Devon grinned at me. "Just like in 'The Knoxville Girl'!"

"What's that?" asked James.

"This song Carrie knows about a murder."

"How's it go?"

I felt my cheeks flush. "Oh, I don't know."

"Sure you do," said Devon. "Sing it, Carrie. You sing it real good."

I gulped hard, then performed a condensed version in too high a key, so that my voice wavered on the high notes. I expected James to laugh at me, but he listened intently. When I finished, he nodded in approval. "That's fucked up."

"It's an old song," I said.

"People have always been fucked up, I guess." Devon tossed her cigarette on the pavement.

"The place is just down here," said James.

RVs and campers were parked in rows stretching from the road almost all the way down to the river. Five tiny log cabins overlooked the river. Everything about the place was shabby and run-down— visible mildew climbed up the sides of the cabins, the patches of landscaping between the parking lot and the structures were over- grown with weeds and tall grass, and the parked RVs all seemed to be in need of a wash.

We walked down to the cabins.

"Do you know which one it was?" Devon asked James.

"Yeah. The second one, there." It made no difference really. The cabins were all identical. Still, we crept up to the back porch of this particular one.

"Someone's staying in there." Devon pointed to the window. We could clearly see suitcases by the door. "Anyway, what is there to see?"

"Folks say it's haunted."

"So? Where are the ghosts?"

"You gotta wait for them."

We stood in silence for a moment, staring at the run-down little cabin. I could smell the smoke from someone's grill and realized I was getting hungry. My thighs were chafed and stung from walking in my still-wet bathing suit. I really wanted a shower.

Suddenly I felt a hand on the back of my neck. At the same moment, both Devon and I screamed. James guffawed. He had slipped behind us and grabbed us at the same time. An older woman came onto the porch of the next cabin over and squinted at us. "Everthing alright over there?"

"Yes, ma'am," said James in a surprisingly authoritative voice. "We's just fooling around. Sorry to disturb you."

She disappeared back into her cabin, and we all burst out laughing. I couldn't stop. All my anxiety about disobeying my mother dissolved into giggles.

Devon began spending a lot of time over at the River Vista. Some- times she invited me along. One day when we showed up to swim,

James wasn't waiting at the pool. We waited on the uncomfortable beach chairs for a few minutes, until Devon tossed off her sunglasses in irritation. "I'm going inside to find him." Not wanting to be left alone, I followed.

Devon marched up to the front desk. She was wearing cutoffs and a torn Madonna T-shirt over her bathing suit. The gray-haired woman at the desk gave us a long stare.

"I'm looking for James," said Devon.

"He's makin' beds. I done told him he can't go out and play till it's done." I almost giggled at the way she said "play," as if he were a little boy, but stopped myself, because the woman frightened me. She looked too old to be James's mother. Her hair curled tightly around her head, and she wore thick, black-framed glasses. "Can't keep no help on these days. You hire 'em, then three weeks later they're up and gone."

"Can we go see him?" asked Devon.

"Can you make beds?"

My mother would definitely have answered no, but Devon nodded on my behalf.

"He should be around room twenty-two by now. Down that hall there. You can help him, but I ain't gonna pay you."

We walked down a wallpapered hallway badly in need of updating. When we got to room twenty-two, it was shut, but we could see an open door down the hall. James was inside, sure enough, making a bed.

"Hey," said Devon. She stood in the doorway, arms crossed.

"Oh, hey! Is it two already? Shit. I gotta finish these rooms before three."

"I thought we were swimming."

"Sorry, like half the staff has disappeared, and my mamaw's making me do this."

"Okay. So I guess we'll just go home."

"You guys can swim. I'll meet you down there."

"This is so lame."

"Sorry, Devon. But I really do have to do this. Listen, when I'm done, we can get out of here. I've got my dad's keys."

"Oh yeah?"

"Yeah. We can go swimming up at Mitchell's Creek."

"Okay. We'll be down by the pool."

Devon motioned for me to follow her, and we went back outside.

"You don't think we should stay and help James?" I asked.

"Yuck, no. No one's paying us to be fucking maids." Devon hadn't used to talk like that to me.

Back at the pool, she tore off her clothes and cannonballed into the water. I jumped in after her. She emerged, gasping for air. "What's Mitchell's Creek anyway?" she asked.

"A swimming hole in the national park. It's really cool." The swimming hole wasn't far from my grandparents' old farm, where we used to live, and Mom had been taking me to swim there for as long as I could remember. The water was freezing, but I loved it. There was a natural rock slide, where you could ride the rapids. "Does James have a driver's license?" I asked.

"He's fifteen. He's got a learner's permit."

I knew I shouldn't get in the car with James driving, but I did. Just like I knew I shouldn't walk along the highway, or go to the pool with no adult around, or hang out with Devon while she smoked. But I did. All of it was thrilling and just the tip of an adolescent iceberg of I-knew-I-shouldn't-but-I-dids.

James opened the door of his dad's Buick for Devon, but she ignored him and got in the backseat to sulk. He motioned for me to get in the front, so I did, nervous to have to make conversation. The car was hot from sitting in the sun and had a sticky-sweet smell.

James gave me a sideways glance as he drove. "You know Mitchell's Creek?"

"Oh yeah. My mom and I have been coming here since I was little."

"Your mom's the art teacher, right?"

"Yeah."

"She's cool. I took art last year."

"Do you like to draw or paint?"

"My favorite thing was making paper."

Mom was really into papermaking that year. I had spent countless rainy Saturdays making paper, and found it completely boring. But I didn't say that. "Yeah, we make paper sometimes at home."

"Nice." He smiled at me. He had patchy stubble on his cheeks, much lighter in color than his dark hair. It's possible this was the first time a teenage boy had ever smiled at me, at least that I was aware of. "I was thinking about going to art school, but I don't know. My mamaw wants me to take over the motel when I grow up."

"Do you want to?"

"Not really. But I don't really want to do any job, you know?"

I was planning on becoming a novelist, a film director, or a movie star, so, no, I did not really know. "Running a motel must be a lot of work."

"Mamaw sure doesn't seem to enjoy it."

Devon let out a loud sigh from the back. "How far is this place? I'm getting carsick." We were winding up into the mountains on a two-lane highway.

"Not much farther," said James. He smiled into the rearview mirror. "Keep your pants on."

Devon glared. "My pants are wet."

"Well, don't worry, we'll be back in the water soon."

She rolled down her window and stuck her arm out. James turned to me. "Does she get this pissy with you?"

I had no idea what to say, but Devon hit James in the back of the head. "Shut up!"

"Hey! I'm driving!"

She was silent the rest of the way. James parked on the side of the road, and we made our way down a steep bank to a small, pebble-strewn beach. A couple little kids splashed in the shallows, while their mother looked on from a blanket on a rock. We walked past her to another large boulder high up above the rapids and put down the towels James had grabbed from the motel.

Devon pulled off her shorts and jumped right in. She came up immediately and screamed at the cold. James laughed. "You didn't tell me how cold it was!" she shouted.

He jumped in after her. She kicked him under the water, and he laughed and splashed her. She began to laugh too.

I knew all too well the sensation of jumping in, yet it was always a shock. I slid down the side of the rock into a deep pool. As the water reached my heart, I gasped, and for a moment I thought I couldn't breathe.

James showed Devon how to go down the rapids, hollering the whole time. You had to give up control to the water and always wound up slightly beaten against the rocks. When they got to the calm shallows and motioned for me to join them, I took a deep breath and flung myself into the narrow chute that created the natural water slide. I had gone down these rapids dozens of times before, with my mom watching. But something went wrong this time. The current thrust me into a rock on my left and my ankle hit it and turned at an unnatural angle. I yelled in pain.

James immediately recognized the tone of my scream and hurled himself against the current in my direction. It was not easy to swim against that current. I used to try it for fun and always gave up sooner or later, letting it push me back to the shallows. But James managed to reach me as I continued down the chute at a lopsided angle. He grabbed me and held me tight, as the current pushed us along together. I didn't have time to feel embarrassed—besides, I was in too much pain. My ankle throbbed. Still, I managed to notice the slick warmth of James's skin next to mine.

"You okay?" he shouted over the roar of the water.

"Yeah!"

Then we were in the calm shallows, disaster averted. Devon and James helped me to shore, and we all looked at my ankle. Already it was purple and badly swollen.

"Looks like you sprained it," James said. "You might want to keep it in the water. Ice would be good for it."

I nodded.

"Shit," said Devon. "Looks gnarly."

"Do you think you can walk on it?" asked James.

"Yeah, I think so."

"Well, maybe I should drive us on back home."

"Oh no, don't let me stop you guys from having fun. I can just sit here, if you want to have another swim."

They looked at each other, trying to decide. "We should get you home," said James. I felt grateful and realized that I wanted my mother. Devon didn't protest and went back to pick up our towels.

I wrapped a towel around my chest, as though I had breasts to balance it on. James wrapped a towel around his waist and offered me his arm. "Let me help you up the bank. You don't want to fall and twist it again."

When I hobbled into our apartment, Mom was chopping vegetables in the kitchen. "Hi, sweetie! You have fun?"

I was ready to come clean. It was one thing to tell little fibs about what adults would be present at the swimming pool and a whole other to concoct an entire story about how I'd injured myself.

"I sprained my ankle. Don't be mad."

She put down her knife and came over to me, wiping her hands on her jeans. "Oh, honey! Let me see. Why would I be mad?"

I sat on the sofa and stretched out my leg. Mom gently touched my hot ankle with her cool fingers. "We went to Mitchell's Creek."

Mom stiffened. "You and Devon?"

"And James."

"How'd you get there?"

"James drove."

"I thought he was fifteen!"

"He is. He has his learner's permit. His dad came too." So I caved a little, unable to admit to the whole naughty truth.

"Well, you should have called me and asked permission. And Devon should know better too. Did she tell her mother?"

"Her mom's at work."

"I see. Listen, just because Devon's mom lets her get away with murder doesn't mean you should just follow along. Do you understand, Carrie?"

I nodded.

"I mean it. I like Devon, but she doesn't really have anyone looking after her."

"Yeah, I know."

"And listen, I know James Reid. He's not a bad kid, but he's not very focused. He almost flunked out of art, which is a challenge, believe me. But he skipped class half the time and was doing God knows what. I don't want you riding in a car with him, even if his dad is there."

"Okay. But he was really nice to me. He came and got me in the rapids when I hurt my foot."

"Well, I'm glad. But that doesn't change my opinion."

"Okay."

"Now, let's take a look at this ankle. Does it hurt to walk?"

"A little."

"Well, just stay here for now and keep it elevated." She disappeared into the kitchen and brought me back an ice pack. "Good thing your grandma's not around to hear about you hanging out with a Reid boy."

"Why?"

"She hated the Reids. Bad blood between our families went way back. James's grandfather tried to buy the farm from Grandma after your granddad died. She practically spit in his face."

"Grandma?!"

"Yeah. She was spunky back in the day." She kissed me on the forehead. "I'll get you some dry clothes." I was still young enough that my mother's kisses could make me feel better.

When school started again in August, I saw less of Devon and none of James. She never officially told me they'd broken up, but we didn't receive any more invitations to the swimming pool. And Devon was in eighth grade now, so it was only natural for her to drift away from me. Luckily, I had distractions. That year I actually made a friend my own age. Ashley Kreigler moved with her family from Michigan, and we became best friends. It was a much more natural friendship than with Devon. We were the same age, and we were both book-smart and labeled nerds by the other kids in our class. Ashley didn't smoke or have boyfriends or talk me into doing things I knew I shouldn't. My mom loved her.

Ashley even helped when I did a social studies project on southern Appalachian ballads that year. I'd prepared a presentation, and Mom got me a poster board. I was going through her old art history books looking for images to illustrate the murder ballads. It was a Thursday afternoon, and I thought I'd go knock on apartment five to see if Devon was interested.

When she came to the door, she looked awful. Her eyes were red and puffy; her hair was uncombed. "Hey," she said.

"Hey. I'm working on a school project about murder ballads. Do you want to help?"

"Um, I don't think so. I'm kinda tired."

"Are you sick?"

"No, no, I'm fine. Just tired."

I went home and called Ashley, whose mom let her come over after dinner for an hour to look at pictures with me. Mom made us popcorn and we sat in the living room with her books spread all around us. I'd typed up the lyrics to some of the songs, and Mom had printed them for me at the high school. But she was still dubious of hillbilly nostalgia. "These songs are always told from the man's point of view. Why don't we ever get to hear from the victims?"

"We can't. The women are always dead by the end of the song," I replied.

Ashley leaned back against the side of the sofa, her long, spindly legs tucked under her. She was pale with brown hair and thick eyebrows that she wouldn't begin plucking until sometime in high school. She read the lyrics to "The Knoxville Girl" in silence.

"Sick, right?" I asked. "Why did he kill her? The guy never says."

"Maybe she was pregnant." Ashley had developed an advanced understanding of unwanted pregnancy by secretly reading her mother's romance novels.

"But then that would mean he also killed his baby!"

"Exactly. If he didn't want a baby, and found out she was pregnant, then that's why he killed her."

I looked at my mom, who was munching popcorn on the sofa, to see what she thought about this theory. She'd stopped chewing and was giving Ashley a worried look. I got the feeling she wanted to change the subject. "Your grandmother always said this song was written about her great-aunt."

I dropped my scissors and gaped at her. "What? She never told me that!"

"She probably didn't want to freak you out. But, yeah. That's the family story."

"Wow," said Ashley.

I couldn't believe that Grandma would have kept such a tantalizing secret. But then I thought about how it didn't really make sense. "The song's been around for centuries," I insisted. "There's an older British version called 'The Oxford Girl.'"

Mom was unfazed. "Yeah, I know. But the American version was written about Grandma's great-aunt. I'm pretty sure."

Even at that young age, I'd already become aware that my mom often took an overly artistic approach to facts. "Who was this person who got murdered anyway?"

"Grandma's grandma's sister. She was just a teenager. And her boyfriend killed her up by Laurel Springs."

"Then why's the song about Knoxville?" asked Ashley.

"I don't know. Details get mixed up in folklore. But I'm pretty sure it's about this girl, Polly. Grandma Polly was named after her."

I shook my head. "I'm not convinced. Lots of people get murdered."

"Not that many, I hope," said Mom.

"Could I have some more Coke?" asked Ashley.

Ashley was practical, not into horror or the macabre like Devon. That was what I missed the most about Devon. She was a great one for ghost stories and playing Bloody Mary and making you believe it was all real. But without realizing it, I had probably pushed her away as much as she'd pushed me. I didn't see it that way at the time. But I soon came to prefer the comfortable, understandable company of Ashley. Then the next year, Devon went to high school, and my mom bought a small house, so we moved. I lost track of Devon completely.

When it was time for me to start applying to colleges, my mother saw to it that I didn't make the same mistakes she felt she had. She encouraged me to go as far away as I wanted. And in a surprise twist, my dad reappeared. Suddenly racked with guilt, I guess. He invited me to start spending the summers in Chicago and promised financial support for college. I loved Chicago but was less crazy about my step-mom, so I ignored their hints about applying to Northwestern and set my sights on Boston University.

I decided to stay in Tennessee the summer after my high school graduation to work and save money for school. I got a job in the kitchen of the Pizza Palace on the strip. The place was awful, almost awful enough to put me off pizza forever. For years I couldn't even eat tomato sauce of any kind—the sweet smell brought back too many hot, sweaty memories. But the work was mindless, and once I'd gotten to the point where I could compose a Pizza Palace Pepperoni Supreme in my sleep, I was able to relax and let my mind wander. The evening manager, Luke, always turned the radio in the kitchen to the country station, and I soon began singing along with Garth Brooks and Billy Ray Cyrus against my will. (Despite my interest in folk music, I had cultivated far too alternative a personal style to have any respect for the crass commercialism of Top Forty country.) But Luke was alright. I also developed a crush on my coworker Caleb, who was on summer break from UT, where he was prelaw. He wasn't particularly interesting, but I had managed to make it through high school without ever going on a date or having a real first kiss and was beginning to give up hope. Caleb sometimes brought pot to work that he would share with me in the back parking lot when our shift ended.

One day when I was going to work, Mom asked if I could stop for gas on the way home. I stopped at the Shell station, since it was just down the street from the Pizza Palace. I recognized Devon at once, standing behind the register, when I went to pay. She'd never been particularly good-looking (nose a little narrow, eyes a little too wide, face pocked with hints of acne), but she'd always had style. Now she had dyed red streaks in her naturally blond hair, tied back in a ponytail. Her fingernails were painted black, and she was wearing dark lipstick with a nose ring and multiple ear piercings. In comparison, I felt square, still wearing my Pizza Palace polo shirt. I had no makeup and no piercings beyond the normal old earlobes. My hair was a boring shade of brown.

She recognized me too. We smiled at each other. "Oh my God, Carrie! Holy shit, it's been like a million years!"

"How are you?"

"Whatever. I'm fine."

"I'm working at Pizza Palace." I pointed to my shirt.

"Nice. You know Caleb?"

"Oh yeah. I do."

"He's okay but kind of a dick."

I had no idea what that meant but was too embarrassed to admit it, so I nodded. "Yeah."

"We should hang out!" she told me. "Do you work tomorrow?"

"Um, yeah. But I get off at nine."

"Yeah, I have to be home with my daughter tomorrow night."

"Your daughter?" I knew girls got pregnant, of course, knew of girls who'd had babies, but the thought of someone I was friends with having a child was shocking.

She smiled and pulled her wallet out of her back pocket. She flipped it open to show me a picture of a scrawny girl with a crown of brown curls. "Her name's Lydia."

"She's really cute. I'd love to meet her."

"Yeah, that'd be fun. Listen, let's exchange numbers." She printed out some blank receipt paper and began writing on it.

She called me two days later in the afternoon. "You working tonight?"

"Yeah."

"Cool. My mom's staying with Lydia. You wanna meet me at the Shell station when you get off? We can go somewhere to chill."

I had no idea where she had in mind but played it cool. "Okay, sounds good."

My mom dropped me off at the Shell station at nine. Devon was standing out front, smoking, dressed all in black and skintight jeans, even though it was still a balmy eighty-five degrees. She was tiny, naturally thin with a boyish figure that made me feel pudgy and self-conscious. At least I'd had time to go home and change out of my awful Pizza Palace shirt into a pea-green scoop-neck tee that I liked to wear with a lavender scarf tied around my neck in a retro fifties style. The outfit made me feel like Sandy to her Rizzo.

"Hey." She smiled. "Cool scarf."

"Thanks." The warm air suddenly made me feel very hot, and I wanted to rip the damn thing off. But now that she'd complimented it, I couldn't.

"Wanna go for a drive?" She stubbed out her cigarette and pulled car keys from her pocket.

"Sure."

She led me to her battered Ford Fiesta and opened the passenger door. She picked up empty Coke cans and fast food containers and threw them in the back of the car. "Sorry about the mess."

"No problem."

She went around to the driver's seat, turned on the engine, and popped a tape into the cassette deck. "It's a mix tape. Hope you don't mind."

"Of course not." Nine Inch Nails screeched out. Devon rolled down her window halfway, and I did the same with mine.

"It's so great to see you again!" she said.

"Yeah, it is! I can't believe how long it's been. Where do you wanna go?"

"How 'bout Lookout Point? You know that place?"

"Sure." True to its name, Lookout Point was a lookout on the edge of the national park. You could walk about a quarter of a mile from the parking lot to an observation tower with views east across the mountains and west across the valley. I had never been there at night. I wasn't even sure if it was legal to go there after dark. But Devon was driving with a sense of purpose.

She lit a cigarette. "Want one?"

"Okay." I had tried cigarettes a handful of times. I wasn't sure I really liked smoking, but at that moment it seemed like the perfect thing to be doing, as the warm night air blew through Devon's shitty car and we listened to industrial rock music.

"It's funny to be smoking with you! I still think of you as a little kid. I would never have let you smoke when we lived in those apartments."

"Yeah, that's true. You never offered me a cigarette."

"I felt protective. You were such a sweet kid. I must've already had a maternal instinct." She flashed me a grin.

"What's it like, having a kid?"

"Aw, it's alright. Lydia's so sweet. Don't get me wrong, though, it's been really hard. And my social life definitely suffered. It's hard to find any guys who want to date a single mom."

"What happened to her dad?"

"What do you think? Heard I was pregnant and split. Just like my dad. And your dad."

"My dad's actually come back."

"Good for him." Her voice throbbed with sarcasm. She stopped at a red light and shook her head. "Sorry. That really is good."

"Yeah. He has a new wife. I think she guilted him into it. But she's kind of awful. She's always buying me sweater sets and telling me I should get a perm."

"So are you headed to college next year?"

I'd been dreading the question. For most people in Douglas County, Boston might as well be the moon—at least, that's how they reacted when I told them where I was going to school. "Yeah. I'm going to Boston University."

"Wow! Good for you! I'd like to go to college if I could ever save up some money. I mean, obviously nothing like Boston University. But the community college maybe."

"Yeah, that'd be good."

"What are you gonna major in?"

"English."

"Cool."

"You know, I wrote an essay last year about murder ballads. Do you remember 'The Knoxville Girl'?"

"Of course! That's so cool. What was your paper about?"

I stopped myself from saying "misogyny," worried she wouldn't know the word. I was careful to keep my language simple with Devon, a skill I had been developing my whole life. "Men killing women. I compared the old ballads to horror movies."

"Cool! We never did anything like that in my English classes."

"It was a college prep independent study unit."

"I should definitely go to college. I could kick ass at that. What was your paper called?"

I winced. "'The Same Old Song: Misogyny in Traditional Murder Ballads and Contemporary Horror Films.'"

"What's *misogyny* mean?" She sounded genuinely curious.

"It's just a fancy word for men hating women."

"Huh."

"What?"

"I don't think men hate women, really. Do you? They just don't give a shit about us."

I smiled. "You would kick ass at college, Devon." She looked genuinely pleased by this, in a way that made me sad. "How's working at the Shell station?"

"Fucking awful. The hours suck and the night manager is a total creeper who can't keep his eyes off my tits. But whatever. It's a living." She flicked her cigarette out the window, so I did the same. "The daytime manager's a good guy, at least. He worked there when we were kids. Do you remember? He was a cute Black guy with a flattop? We drove him crazy running around on sugar highs."

"Yeah, I think so."

"He's married, though."

"Oh, so you *like him* like him?"

She rolled her eyes. "We had a thing, but it didn't last because of the wife."

I was too surprised to say anything about Devon's apparent affair with an older, married Black man. We were out of town now, winding along a dark mountain road. There were hardly any other cars out this late. I put my hand out the window to feel the current of warm air rushing by. A full moon was rising above the mountain looming ahead, giving the forests and fields a silver glow.

Devon parked at Lookout Point and we got out. "Come on," she said. "Let's walk to the tower."

I wanted to ask if it was safe in the dark, but I said nothing. The moon actually made it easy enough to follow the trail. I tried to ignore the forest sounds, the chirping of insects and the rustling of God knows what. "What if we see a bear?" I asked.

"Just act big and powerful. That's what they say."

I knew that. In the daylight, that sounded reasonable. But now?

Devon didn't seem to notice my unease. "So, how well do you know Caleb?" she asked.

"Oh, we've just been working together a of couple weeks. How well do you know him?"

"Pretty well. He's one of those guys who's always around."

"He's kinda cute. . . ." I immediately regretted saying it.

"Do you like him?" Devon was excited.

"I don't know."

"I don't think he has a girlfriend. You should go for it."

"I don't know."

"Does he still sell weed?"

"Yeah."

"Do you think you could hook me up?"

"Sure." I didn't really know what that meant. I hoped it was as simple as giving Caleb her phone number, since I really didn't want to get in the middle of a drug deal.

"I wish we had some now," she said.

"Yeah."

We came to a clearing and the observation tower. When we got to the top, I stared, speechless, at the view. I'd seen it a dozen times before, but never in the dark with a thousand stars above me. The mountains loomed before us, massive even in the light of the moon. From a spot like that, you could think they went on forever, peak after peak, as limitless as the ocean.

Devon lit a cigarette and leaned out over the railing. "Fucking gorgeous, isn't it?" I nodded.

For a moment we were both silent, Devon smoking, me staring into the darkness. She tossed her cigarette, then to my shock opened her mouth and began to sing: "*Amazing grace, how sweet the sound that saved a wretch like me.*" Devon had a wobbly but vibrant alto that seemed to fill the great emptiness before us. I smiled at first, thinking she must be making some sort of joke. But she sang loud and clear, struggling to stay in key, but with no hint of irony. "*I once was lost but now am found, was blind but now I see.*"

My face stiffened, but she wasn't looking at me anyway; she was staring out at the mountains. She turned to me and burst out laughing. I laughed too, relieved that the strange moment was over. It is oddly intimate to stand beside someone singing a cappella.

"Something about being up here makes me want to just scream or sing, you know?" She then howled like a wolf, as though to demonstrate. "Come on, Carrie!"

I howled. At first I felt ridiculous, but then a feeling of exhilaration washed over me. I turned my neck up toward the sky and howled again as loudly as I could.

"Yes!" called Devon in support. And we howled together at the moon.

The next time I saw Devon, she invited me over to her trailer. At her request, I'd brought along twenty dollars' worth of Caleb's weed. It was after work again, and her daughter was already in bed. The small, cramped space was filled with toys and kid paraphernalia.

"Want a beer?" she asked as she dumped a pile of generic Barbie dolls out of a chair for me to sit in.

"Sure."

She handed me a Bud Light and sat down. She was wearing a pair of cutoff shorts that looked like they might not survive another spin cycle. "It sucks missing Lydia's bedtime. I wish I could change my schedule so I could get home in time to put her down."

"You can't ask for different hours?"

"Not really. I put in requests, but my boss never seems to pay any attention."

"I thought you guys were . . . friends?"

"I think he goes out of his way to make sure he's not favoring me."

There was a knock at the door. Devon hadn't mentioned that she was expecting anyone else, but she didn't look surprised. "Come in!" she shouted, without bothering to check who it was.

The door opened to reveal a tall young man with dark hair. Something about him was familiar. "Hey," said Devon. "You remember Carrie? She used to live next to me when we were kids."

He smiled at me. "Whoa! You're all grown-up!"

And then I realized it was James. *He* was all grown-up—no longer so skinny. His upper body had caught up to his height, his chest had filled out, and his face had matured. He was wearing jeans and a preppy polo shirt, but a shoulder tattoo peaked out from under one of its sleeves.

"What's it been?" he asked. "Five years?"

Devon got up and went to the fridge. "Carrie's starting college in Boston in the fall." She handed James a beer.

"I'm working at the Pizza Palace this summer," I told him.

"Cool. I've got two more years at UT. But I help out at my family's motel in the summers." He collapsed into a chair.

"How's that?" I asked.

He shrugged. "Okay. Same damn thing since I was eleven."

Devon sat back down, propping her feet up on the back of James's chair. "God, I hate this town," she said.

"Why don't you leave, then?" He popped open his beer and took a swig.

"I don't have any goddamn money. And I have a little girl, remember?"

I had wondered if James was Lydia's dad. But he replied, "Yeah, well. That's not my fault."

Devon grinned at me. "Everyone wants to get out of this town, but nobody ever leaves. Except you."

James took a small pipe out of his pocket. "Should we smoke?"

We passed it around. "You got this from Caleb?" he asked.

I nodded.

"You can get better shit in Knoxville."

"Then go smoke up in Knoxville!" snapped Devon. "Why do you even come back here for the summers?" I couldn't get a grasp on her relationship with James. Were they a couple? There seemed to be tension, but then why had he come over anyway?

"My family needs my help."

"The weed seems good enough to me." I giggled.

Devon smiled. "Remember that time we all went to the murder cabin?"

"What?" James drew on the pipe, then held it out to me.

"I remember! God, I haven't thought about that in years. The Happy Camper murders."

"Oh, right," said James.

"You were the one who took us." Devon gave his leg a flirtatious kick.

I took a hit and handed the pipe off to Devon. "I wonder what the real story was there. Do you think the guy was just a psycho? Did he rape them? Did anyone ever say?"

"I don't think so," said James. "More likely, it was a drug deal gone wrong."

"Or maybe he was just an asshole, and when he wanted to hook up and the one girl said no, he lost his temper." Devon paused to inhale. "Then when the other girl saw what had happened, he had to kill her since she was a witness." She passed me the pipe. "Who wants a Hot Pocket?"

After a couple hours of Hot Pockets and music videos, I got up to leave. "This has been fun," Devon said. "Just like old times."

"Yeah, except your little friend got hot!" James winked at me.

I tried very hard to concentrate on the lines on the road as I drove home. But my mind kept going back to James's wink. Did I like him? He was cute, so there was that. And he had called me hot. That was what it came down to. My lack of self-confidence, my vanity. I plotted new excuses to hang out with Devon, so I could find out more about him. Were they going out? Had they recently broken up? Did he have a girlfriend? Did he want a girlfriend? Did he like me?

I made plans to meet up with Devon and her daughter that weekend to go to the public pool. In the meantime, I went to the mall with Ashley and managed to casually bring up my encounter with James.

"I don't get it," she said. "Are they, like, dating?"

"I don't know."

"Well, it's shitty for him to flirt with you if they are."

"Yeah."

We were sitting across from each other at a small table in the food court, almost shouting to be heard over the large water feature gushing behind us. Ashley dabbed at her pizza with a napkin to soak up the grease. "What's she like now? Do you guys have anything to talk about?"

"She's into music. It's kind of awkward. I mean, what do I know about having a kid?"

"Yeah. And what does she know about college?"

"She'd like to go to college if she could." I dunked a fry into a pot of ketchup.

"I thought she flunked out senior year."

"Really?" I honestly didn't know if that was true.

"That's what I heard."

"I don't know. She's had a hard time, you know. Her mom wasn't a great mom."

"And now she's smoking pot with her little girl in the house!"

I let the chicken tender I was about to eat drop back into its greasy container. "It wasn't like that! We just watched TV."

"Come on, Carrie! If you had a kid tomorrow, would you ever do that?"

"Well, I'd have to at least kiss someone first for that to ever be an issue, wouldn't I?"

Ashley softened. I knew she pitied me for never having had a boyfriend. "Don't worry. I'm sure it will happen soon enough. And of course you'll make sure you don't get knocked up."

"Look, maybe it was a little irresponsible. You're right. I shouldn't take pot over there again. I'm gonna hang out with her and her daughter this weekend, so I'll see what kind of mom she really is."

On Saturday morning, Devon called me. "I just heard from James," she said. "You remember his family's motel? He said we could go swimming there if we want instead of paying to go to the pool."

My heart leapt. I put on my favorite shorts and a low-cut top over my bathing suit. The motel looked exactly as I remembered it—in fact, it didn't look like any real maintenance had been done in the ensuing years. A couple kids played in the shallow end of the pool, while their parents napped on plastic chaises. James was sitting on a chair, wearing only swim trunks and sunglasses. He was still very pale, with patches of dark hair on his chest. When he saw me, he waved. "Hey, Carrie!"

"Wow, this really take me back!" I exclaimed.

"I know, huh? This place never changes."

"Do you have to work today?"

"I can take a couple hours off to hang out with you and Devon and Lydia."

I sat down beside him. "Are you planning on taking over the family business when you graduate?"

"Hell, no! I hate this shithole. How 'bout you? You must have big plans."

"I'm not sure. I can hardly decide on a major."

"But you're getting the hell out of Dodge, whatever you do."

"Yeah. I can't imagine living here as an adult."

"Smart girl. But then again, you always were."

Before I could reply, Devon appeared, followed by an adorable little girl with a mass of dark-brown curls.

"James!" Lydia ran over to James, and he picked her up.

"Hey, pumpkin! How are you?"

"Lydia!" called Devon. "No running by the pool! I've told you this."

"Who are you?" asked Lydia, looking at me.

"I'm your mom's friend Carrie."

"I'm Lydia."

"Nice to meet you."

She jumped off James's lap and rushed toward the pool, but Devon grabbed her. "Lydia, look at me. No running by the pool, okay? You've got to be more careful."

"Okay, Mommy."

Devon began peeling off her shirt and shorts. "I'd better go on in with her."

Devon and Lydia sat on the steps in the shallow end. I tried to go in deep enough that the bulk of my body was submerged. Devon was unselfconscious in a tiny, mismatched bikini. James jumped in and tossed a beach ball to Lydia. "Catch!"

She giggled and threw the ball back toward him. He paddled over to her with the ball and tossed it to her gently. Devon left the two of them in the shallow end and walked farther out toward me. "She loves James."

"That's sweet."

"Lydia," she said, "thank Uncle James for bringing this super-fun beach ball!"

"Thanks, Uncle James!" shouted Lydia, splashing her hands on the surface of the water. Devon smiled at him, and he winked. I felt a little disappointed to see how easily he distributed winks.

Then she grabbed her daughter into an embrace. "Come here, you little mermaid! Show me how you swim!" Devon held her gently on her tummy, while Lydia kicked her legs and scooped water with her hands. "Good job!"

"That's great, pumpkin!" James grinned down at them.

They looked like a family. Devon softened as she watched Lydia play. It reminded me of the girl she had been when we first met—trying to be cool, but still innocent enough to play in the woods.

James splashed in Devon's direction. "I've got an idea. What do you think about taking Lydia up to Mitchell's Creek later this week?"

"Okay. I need to double-check with my boss, but I think I've got Thursday off."

"Don't let him dick you around like he always does," said James.

Devon covered Lydia's ears. "Language, Uncle James!"

"What's Mitchell's Creek?" asked Lydia, intrigued.

"It's a place to go swimming. But not in a pool. In an actual creek in the mountains," explained James.

"Cool! I wanna go, I wanna go!"

"Okay, sweetie," said Devon.

We met up in the afternoon that Thursday at the swimming hole, and Devon brought along her mom to help keep an eye on Lydia. We spread out a blanket and cooler on one of the big river rocks overlooking the rapids; then James took Lydia down to a calm shallow spot to play. I sat on the blanket, watching them, idly eating cherries. The creek was surrounded by dense woods, their bright summer foliage stained a lurid variety of greens.

Devon's mom got out a cigarette. "I can't believe you kids are all grown-up! And I'm a grandma."

It *was* hard to believe. I don't think she was forty yet. "Well, you look great," I said.

"Thanks, sweetie. It's the cigarettes. They'll probably kill me, but they do keep me thin."

We took turns swimming in the cold water, then warming up in the blazing sun, until we all gathered on the blanket to eat a picnic supper. My suit was still wet but I pulled my shorts on over it anyway to cover my thighs. The sun was only just beginning to dip toward the tree line. Devon's mom volunteered to take Lydia home and put her to bed.

As soon as they left, James pulled his pipe out of his pocket. "Shall we?"

I hesitated. I knew I had to drive home along the mountain roads. But when he offered me the pipe, I said, "Just a little, I guess."

When Devon had done a few rounds, she stood up and pulled off her shorts. "I'm going back in."

She went to the edge of the rock and in one fast, smooth movement dove into the water headfirst. James jumped up in alarm. "Devon!"

After a moment her head bobbed up all the way on the other side of the creek. "You asshole!" shouted James. "You don't fucking dive into a place like this!"

"Oh, come on. I've been coming here for years. I know this place like the back of my hand."

"Idiot," said James. "It's a creek! Rocks move."

He turned and walked away into the dusky woods. I felt pleasantly high and uninhibited, so I followed him. It wasn't possible to get far into the forest. The bank back up to the road was steep, and the ground was thick with laurel. James sat on a stump, just out of sight of our blanket. The air hummed with chirping insect sounds. "Hey," he said as I approached.

"She shouldn't have done that."

"Devon's like that." He ripped bark off the side of the stump absently.

I leaned on a tree across from him. "Are you guys together?"

"No. You know, we've been friends, and gone out, and been friends, and hooked up for years. It's bullshit. Then she got with Lydia's dad. He's married, did she tell you that?" I shook my head. "Fed her some line about how he was gonna leave his wife, but of course, that never happened. I've been like Lydia's dad all this time, and what thanks do I get?"

"I'm sorry."

"Not your fault." He looked up at me. "What about you? Do you have a boyfriend?"

"No."

He grinned. "That's hard to believe."

My insides turn to Jell-O.

"Come on, a pretty girl like you. What, do you love them and leave them?"

I gave a forced chuckle and shook my head.

He stood up. "Come here."

I wasn't sure what he meant. I was only standing a foot away from him. But he motioned for me to come closer.

"Let's try something," he said, and put his hand around my waist. He pulled me in close, so that my breasts were right up against his naked chest, then bent down and kissed me. It was wet and sloppy. I was excited, but scared too, and had no idea what to do with my tongue. We made out for a minute or five—who knows? I could feel James's erection on my leg.

I heard rustling in the forest, and James pulled away from me swiftly. He put his finger to his lips.

Devon appeared. "Hey. Sorry I scared you."

"Forget about it," said James. I stood frozen, no idea what to say or do.

"It's getting dark out here," said Devon. "Don't you want to come back out to the rock?"

Together we walked back to the blanket.

Devon nudged James. "Did you bring anything else?"

"Like what?"

"You know . . . in case we really want to party."

"I don't have anything on me. I could give Stacey a call."

"No, don't worry about it. Just give me a cigarette."

"Don't have any of those either."

"Jesus Christ! We should get out of here anyway. It's getting dark."

"Whatever you say, princess."

I sat in my mom's car for a minute before starting the engine, trying to gauge how high I was. The last of the light had faded, and the woods on either side of the road blinked with fireflies. Just as I turned the ignition, James knocked on the driver's window. I rolled it down.

"Hey," he said. "Today was fun."

"Yeah, it was."

"Can I give you a call sometime?"

"Sure."

"Great. You got a pen?"

The next few days were exquisite agony. I replayed the moment in the woods again and again, its details becoming simultaneously fuzzier and more heightened as they were repeated on loop in my imagination. I found myself jumping every time the phone rang. I kept running to the phone before Mom could, not wanting to have to explain James to her.

But three days went by, and he didn't call. I went through the motions at Pizza Palace, more distracted than usual. Luckily, Luke was not an attentive supervisor. He was too busy lip-syncing to Garth Brooks to notice as I accidentally doubled the amount of cheese on a medium pepperoni and popped it into the oven anyway.

Caleb gave me side eye as he spread tomato sauce onto dough. "Rough night?"

"Why do you ask?" I slammed the oven shut.

"You look tired."

"No. I'm fine." I took his pizzas and began applying cheese.

"You're friends with Devon Kerr, aren't you?"

"Yeah."

"Do you know if she's still dealing out of the Shell station?"

I looked up at him before turning back to the oven. "Dealing? You mean, drugs?"

He rolled his eyes. "Yeah."

"I don't think so." I spoke softly so Luke couldn't hear us over the country music he was blasting. "She asked me to get pot from you, remember?"

"Not weed. Devon deals crystal."

"Meth?" I knew I sounded stupid and naïve.

"Yeah. Has been off and on since high school. I thought she'd gotten out of it after the kid came along. But I heard from an acquaintance that he got a little something extra with his gas last week at Shell."

"I don't know anything about that."

He shook his head. "Yeah, obviously."

"Sorry, I'm not part of your drug underworld."

"Hey, I just sell my cousin's weed that he grows in the backyard to friends for pocket money. Devon's in another league."

"If that's true, then why's she working at the Shell?"

"I don't know. She's your friend. I assumed she'd gotten clean for her baby until I heard this rumor."

"Well, maybe that's all it is." I slid the pizza in the oven, trying to convince myself that Caleb was mistaken.

"Maybe." Caleb obviously didn't think so. "But she did look pretty high when I saw her at McGrady's last Friday."

McGrady's was the local tavern. It only served beer, since hard liquor by the glass was still illegal in the county. I'd never been there and had assumed that it was only frequented by bikers and alcoholic old men. "How could you tell?"

"Well, she and her boyfriend were all over each other. Just really messy, you know. Not the way normal people act in public."

"Her boyfriend?" I had completely lost focus on the cheese and stood completely still, staring at Caleb.

"Yeah, you know. That guy she's always with—he's a couple years older than us, I think. Jason maybe?"

"James?"

"Yeah, James."

I felt sick. The oven timer blared, and I turned to fetch the pizza. It was a rubbery mess.

"What the fuck is that?" said Luke, paying attention for the first time that evening to his employees.

"I think I might have overcheesed it."

"Jesus. Well, give it to the customers anyway. We'll see if they complain."

Caleb was just repeating gossip. People spread false rumors all the time, exaggerated, took things out of context. Yet some part of me knew it was all true. Devon was interested in drugs, that was undeniable, and the thought of her dealing wasn't really that surprising. And of course, James and she were in some sort of relationship. I knew the most sensible thing for me to do was to leave both of them alone. But my mind worked on the truth and twisted it to something more palatable. James seemed fed up with Devon. Maybe he knew she wasn't right for him. And Devon must have known that drugs weren't right for her. She'd gotten clean for Lydia, Caleb had said. Maybe she'd just fallen off the wagon briefly. Maybe it was just a simple mistake. Everyone made mistakes.

When I got home that night, Mom had left a note on my bed: *James called, 9:15* with a return number. I felt like squealing, but I didn't. It was past eleven, so I waited until the next day to call back. Besides, I didn't want to seem too eager.

I caught up with him the next afternoon, my heart pounding so hard that I wasn't really sure I could keep my voice steady if he answered the phone. I actually prayed I would get his answering machine, I was so scared to talk to him. But he picked up right away. "River Vista Motel, this is James."

"Oh, hi! It's Carrie."

"Hey, Carrie, how are you?"

"Good, good. Are you busy?"

"Yeah, I'm just working the front desk at the motel. Hey, do you want to get together tonight?"

"Okay." My hands were shaking as I spoke.

"Cool. Are you working?"

"No, it's my night off."

"Should I pick you up then? Does seven work for you?"

"Sure. My house is on River Road. Do you know where that is?"

"Yeah, I think so."

"We're five eighty-six."

"Alright, I'll see you tonight."

I had four and a half hours before our date. I opened my closet and stared at the row of shirts hanging there. I had just bought a cute sundress, but I didn't want to look like I was trying too hard. I chose a green T-shirt that I knew showed off my breasts, though not too much. Then I was faced with what to do to stay calm for the next four hours and twenty minutes.

Mom served dinner as usual at six thirty. I didn't know if I should eat or not. Were we going to get dinner when we went out? I didn't want to be starving if James and I didn't get food. But nerves were forcing my stomach to churn uncomfortably. Mom put a huge plate of stroganoff in front of me. I could barely stand to look at it.

"I'm going out tonight." I tried to sound casual.

"Oh yeah? With Ashley?"

"Um, no. With James Reid."

She looked up from her noodles. "Oh. Like a date?"

"No, nothing like that. Just hanging out. Devon may be there." I was embarrassed. And I knew my mom would not approve of James. She would think he wasn't right for me, not smart enough, not motivated enough. I probably knew deep down that she was right, but I was too smitten to admit it to myself.

"Okay. What's he doing these days? Is he in college?"

"Yeah. He's studying business at UT."

"Oh, okay. Good for him." She dropped it. Mom was always care-ful not to pry too much into my social life. She knew how awkward having her work at my high school could be and tried to compensate with discretion.

I ate a portion of my dinner and told Mom I'd finish the rest when I got home. I got everything ready to go, trying not to stare out the front window. Then I watched the news with her in the living room.

7:02.

Wheel of Fortune came on. My mom was knitting and hardly watch-ing the TV, but she didn't turn it off. I kept watching to avoid staring out the window. The first puzzle went by, the second. 7:11. No James. Should I call him? I decided to wait until 7:20.

I went to the phone in the kitchen so that my mom wouldn't hear. No answer. A voice-mail greeting: "You have reached the River Vista Motel. Please leave a message, and we'll get back to you as soon as possible."

I hung up, embarrassed to leave a message, then went to my bed-room and tried to read *The Sound and the Fury* because my English teacher had said it was the greatest American novel.

8:01. I officially gave up, threw the book across the room, and began to sob.

I cried for a solid ten minutes or so. Foolish, I know. But that is how I was as a girl. I fell easily, hard. I did not think rationally about the objects of my affection; I idealized them. I wanted too much—great love, commitment. I was miserable with wanting. So I cried and cried. I cried because I knew something was wrong with me. I had never had a boyfriend. I was going to be alone forever. I was a freak.

I didn't realize then that I had already gotten the best James had to offer—an ephemeral moment in the woods. A hot make-out session on a humid summer's night, surrounded by dazzling fireflies, illicit, hidden. What could be better than that? Why couldn't I have just enjoyed that moment, the process, the longing for more? Only a fool would want more than that.

I stopped crying, went to the bathroom, and washed my face. I held a cold rag over my eyes. I was done crying. I was done with James. I would not see him again, and if I ran into him, I would not talk to him. Fuck James. I might feel pathetic, but I would not act pathetic.

When my mom found me eating low-fat ice cream in the kitchen, I'm sure she could see my eyes were puffy.

"You okay? What time are you going out?"

"He didn't show." Before she could reply, I waved my hand to stop her. "It's okay. He's an idiot. It's no big deal."

She gave me a pitying grin that made me avert my eyes in embarrassment. "Want to watch a movie?"

"Yeah."

James did call the next day. I was at work and Mom was out, so he left a message: "I'm really sorry about last night. Something came up last-minute. Let me make it up to you. I'm free tonight. Give me a call."

I did not call, and it felt great.

I did call Devon a couple days later, feeling vaguely guilty about the whole thing. I left a couple messages for her but didn't hear anything back, which felt ominous. Maybe she'd found out about James and me. Maybe she was on drugs. Maybe she was just really busy.

I put Devon out of my mind, did my shifts at Pizza Palace, scoured the library for reading material, hung out at Ashley's house, went for hikes with my mom. The summer seemed endless. With the exception of the James incident, life had fallen into a calm, comforting rut. I was in stasis, able to avoid the maturation process for a few more weeks and curl up on the couch with my mother every night.

My mom booked a motel on the beach in South Carolina for a few days, and I got time off from the Palace. We traveled together peacefully, swimming in the surf, gorging on seafood. When we got back to Tennessee, I unloaded the car, while Mom ritualistically played back the messages on our answering machine. As I dragged suitcases to the door, she shouted for me. "Carrie? Devon's called you three times while we were gone."

I dropped the bags and went to her. "Did she say why?"

"No. Just said to call her back."

I felt mildly panicked. Had she found out about James? I didn't want to return her call, but it seemed irresponsible to ignore her. After unpacking and eating supper, I took the phone into my bedroom.

"Hello?"

"Hey, Devon, it's Carrie. Sorry I didn't get back to you sooner. Mom and I were at the beach."

"Oh, that's okay. Can you come over?" Her voice was urgent.

"Um, right now?" I was exhausted from the seven-hour drive.

"Yeah. I really need to talk to someone."

Something in her voice told me I should go. I asked Mom if I could take the car, and got to Devon's trailer fifteen minutes later. She opened the door for me and smiled weakly. She looked awful—hair messy, dressed in an ancient hot-pink sweat suit.

"Are you okay?" I asked.

"Not really." She sat down at the small table, and I sat across from her.

"What's wrong? Is Lydia okay?"

"She's asleep. She's fine. It's me. I've been feeling really shitty. Oh, man!" She ran her hands through her tangled hair.

"I'm sorry. Can I do anything to help?"

"Probably not. The thing is, I've fucked up."

"How?"

"I'm pregnant."

"Oh."

"Yeah."

I tried to think of the right thing to say. Obviously not "congratulations." But before I really thought it through, I blurted out the first question that came to my mind: "Is it James's?"

"I'm not sure."

"Who else have you been with?"

"Just this one other guy. It's either his or James's. I can't be sure."

"What are you going to do?"

"I don't fucking know. I can't have another kid, Carrie! I can't. It's been so hard. I can't go through it all again! It's already starting. I feel like such shit! I'm so tired. I had to run away from the cash register tonight to puke in the back of the station."

"Do you know where you can go to . . . take care of it?" Despite being raised on pro-choice feminist gospel, I felt unable to say directly the words I meant.

"Yeah, I think so. But I don't want to do that either. I don't want to kill my baby!"

Why was she coming to me with this? I was just some girl who'd wandered back into her life after years of absence. "Have you talked to your mom about this?"

"My mom's an idiot."

I couldn't really deny that. It began to occur to me that Devon didn't have any girlfriends. In the time we'd spent together, I'd only really heard her talk about spending time with James. "Have you told James?"

She shook her head.

"I think you should."

"He's pissed at me right now."

"Well, surely when you tell him this he'll get over it."

"When I tell him it might not be his?!"

"You don't have to tell him that."

"He knows about the other guy. That's why he's pissed."

"Oh."

Devon picked up a napkin from the table and began ripping it into tiny strips.

"I'm sorry, Devon."

"I know."

"Can I get you anything? You should probably get some rest."

"Yeah. Do you mind just staying awhile? We could just watch some TV. I don't want to be alone."

We watched Letterman on the sofa, in silence. After a little while, her eyes began to droop shut. Eventually she drifted off, and I showed myself out. As I drove back to my mother's cozy little house, I felt a sense of relief that nothing more had happened between me and James. I wanted out of that situation. I would be a good friend to Devon, support whatever decision she made. But I would stay minimally involved.

I called the next day to check on her, but didn't hear back. A couple of days later, on my night off, she called in the early evening.

"Carrie?" I could hear that she was crying. "I told James. He was really pissed."

"It's gonna be okay, Devon. You don't need James."

She sobbed into the receiver.

"It's gonna be okay, I swear. Whatever you want to do, I'll help you."

"I just hope he calms down soon and forgives me."

"I'm sure he will."

"Hey, Carrie, will you promise me something?"

"What?"

"If anything ever happens to me, will you keep an eye on Lydia?"

"What are you talking about? Why would anything happen to you?"

She sniffled. "I don't know. Sometimes I just get a weird feeling. . . . I know my mom would take care of her, but you're so smart and really have your shit together, not like everyone else around here. I'd just like to know that you were watching out for her. If anything ever happened."

"Of course I would. But that's a ridiculous thing to worry about."

"I'm gonna go check on Lydia. But can you come over later?"

I didn't think that much of what she'd asked. Devon was just upset. But when Mom got home a little over an hour later from her land conservation meeting, I called Devon right away. I'd be able to take the car and visit her.

Her mood had dramatically improved. "Hey, Carrie. I was just about to call you. I'm actually headed out."

"Out? Where?"

"To see James. He called and said he was sorry for how he reacted. I'm going over to his place, and Mom's staying with Lydia. Thanks for earlier. You're right—everything is going to be okay!"

I had my doubts about that, but it wasn't really my concern. I had other things on my mind. It was my last week at home, and I'd started packing.

My mom woke me up the next morning. "Carrie . . . Carrie . . ." she was saying, gently shaking me. My eyes opened slowly. "Carrie, I just had a phone call with some bad news."

As I struggled to focus, I saw that her face was strained, like she was holding back tears. "What is it, Mom?"

"It's Devon. She was in an accident last night."

"What?" I sat upright.

Mom nodded, and began to cry. "I'm so sorry, Carrie. She was killed."

I had never known anyone who had died before, except for my grandparents and other geriatric deaths that made a certain kind of sense. I couldn't grasp it. "What?"

"She was in a car accident late last night. Well, technically, early this morning. Drove off the side of Highway Eleven into a tree."

She must have been going home from seeing James. I didn't move or speak. Mom threw her arms around me, but I felt my body stiffen.

The rest of that day was foggy and confused. At some point I called Ashley, but she was awkward and didn't know what to say. I read and reread the brief article in the local paper about the accident, but it didn't offer any details to help me understand what had happened. That afternoon, I asked Mom if I could borrow the car early for work.

"Are you sure you're up for work tonight? You might as well just quit that job anyway. You're only here for another week."

"I think I'd like the distraction."

"Okay. Be safe." She grabbed me to her and squeezed.

I don't know if I knew where I was headed when I got in the car. I hadn't thought things through. But I headed to the River Vista Motel. A young Latina woman was sitting at the front desk. "Hi," I said. "I'm looking for James."

She nodded and pointed down the hall. "James, cleaning that way."

"Thanks." Even though I'd driven there to find him, I was surprised by how easy it was. I walked down the hall, peering into a few open rooms, until I saw him, wearing khaki shorts and a polo shirt, making a bed, just like all those years ago.

"You still clean the rooms here?"

Startled, he dropped the pillow he was puffing. "Shit. You scared me."

"Sorry."

"We're still short-staffed most of the time."

I walked into the room and stood across the double bed from him. "What happened last night?"

He looked down at the duvet.

"I know she was headed to your house. We'd just talked on the phone before she left."

"Yeah, she told me that she'd talked to you. She came over."

"And then what?"

"I don't know, Carrie, what do you want me to say? We got fucked up."

"Fucked up?"

"Yes, okay. We got high. Devon was always high, you do realize that, don't you?" His voice had become louder, almost angry.

"But she was pregnant."

"Yeah, I know."

"Why would you give her drugs if she was pregnant?"

"I didn't force them on her."

"That could have been your baby!" All the emotion I had not known how to express that day suddenly boiled over into rage. I realized I was screaming. "You just killed your goddamn baby!"

"Please. All I did was give her what she asked for." His expression was calm, defiant.

"What is wrong with you? Why did you let her drive?"

"Don't fucking blame this on me. Devon was fucked up."

"What is wrong with you?" I could feel tears coming.

"And that wasn't my baby. It was probably just another little nigger, like Lydia."

I had to get away from him. I never wanted to see him again. I got to my car, locked the door, put my head down on the steering wheel, and sobbed. When I felt calm enough to drive, I went to the Pizza Palace and quit my job. Luke could see what a mess I was, so he didn't object. I drove home and went to my mom's room, where the light was on. She was sitting up in bed, reading. I crawled under the covers into her arms and stayed there for a long time.

I loved college and I loved Boston. I loved my classes, the bookstores, the coffee shops, the art house cinema, and the concerts at Berklee. I had gotten lucky and loved my roommates too. I loved it—and yet some part of me did miss the familiar. I missed Mom and Ashley. And I missed something else as well, less tangible, but more intense—a sense of place. Sometimes I looked out the window of my dorm across the city and felt oppressed by the lack of height in the landscape. The buildings were tall, of course, but buildings are not land. There were hills, of course, but hills are not mountains. I saw great beauty in the gray expanse of the Charles River and the spires of Harvard peeking up through the blanket of autumn leaves. But I missed living in a valley amongst highlands. It was as simple as that. I don't know if someone raised in a flat landscape can understand, though I'm sure the prairies exert their own nostalgic pull on those who have abandoned them for more topographically varied lands. I'm sure that for those who grew up by the sea, the pull of the ocean is similar. I love the sea. But I am from the mountains.

When I came home for Christmas that year, I called Devon's mom and asked if I could come over to see Lydia. She gave me a big hug when I arrived, a cigarette in her hand. "Thanks so much for calling, Carrie! It really means the world to me to see you. We haven't heard from many of Devon's friends."

Lydia was playing with some battered Barbie dolls on the floor. "This one's a princess," she told me as I sat with her. "This one's a mommy."

I looked over at Devon's mom, who shook her head sadly. Lydia was bright and happy, a normal little girl. I had high hopes for her and still do.

Not long after Devon died, Lydia's grandma joined AA and got married. They all lived in a tidy little house by the river. Lydia is smart, with a sarcastic edge that reminds me of her mom. But she's making better choices—working on a degree at the University of Tennessee. She is my hope that things can get better, and I want to have hope. I try to send her a check each year on her birthday and visit every time I go home to see my mother.

I live in New York now but still visit Tates Valley at least once a year. Even so, I always brace myself for the inevitable changes—farms disappeared into strip malls, hollows carved open by four-lane highways, forests laid bare and paved over to accommodate the never-ending trail of cars, coming and going, spewing exhaust, which then transforms even the air to smog. The old constantly replaced by the new, the cheap, the tacky; nature mutilated beyond all recognition.

The biggest surprise of growing older has been to see how quickly and dramatically the world around me can change. In childhood, circumstances felt eternal, but now nothing seems to last. Landscapes transform; nations dissolve; climates change; people die. No wonder we cling to the fragments that somehow survive from one generation to the next—the stories we learned from our parents, the songs our grandmothers taught us.

Mom is still in Tates Valley. Although she loves to visit me and go to galleries and museums, after a few days she's always eager to get home. "I always wanted to leave Tates Valley, and now I can't wait to get back," she reflected the last time we were together, sitting in the back of a taxi headed to LaGuardia Airport.

"Why didn't you ever leave, Mom?"

"That's a long story. It's more complicated than you might realize. My father was dying, Mama needed help with the farm. . . ."

"It doesn't sound that complicated."

She gave me a look that only mothers can, a look to make you feel like a small child again. "You don't know. There's a lot you don't know. But what does it matter now? The past is past."

I dropped it. I don't want to go digging into my mother's past if she doesn't want me to, and I'm not interested in dark secrets anymore. I'm not drawn to the shadows, like when I was a kid. I can't watch TV shows about women being raped and murdered, and I don't sing murder ballads. Fall is no longer my favorite season. I find myself more thrilled each year by the annual miracle of spring.

POWER IN THE BLOOD

LYDIA
(CARRIE'S "GODDAUGHTER")
2011–2013

I f I had to do it over again, I would do everything differently. Obviously. It's hard to pinpoint exactly where the mistakes began. Probably with my parents. Probably before I was born.

I don't want to make excuses for myself. My childhood was hard. So what? My mom died when I was five, and I never knew my dad. I was raised by my grandma, who tried her best. She had screwed up with her own daughter, my mom, and I know that ate away at her. After my mom died and Grandma adopted me, she joined AA and tried to turn her life around. She was a waitress here and there—seems like she'd worked at every restaurant on the strip at some time or another. She met Ted at an AA meeting. He made a decent living as a plumber, so I guess you could say our lives improved when she married him, and we moved into his brown split-level in a patch of woods off the highway. But Ted was a hard man, very strict with me. He paddled me whenever he thought I got out of line, always over Grandma's objections. It wasn't full-on abuse, depending on your stance on that sort of thing. But I never thought of him as my grandfather. It was more like a drill sergeant had adopted me.

He also got her going to Mount Zion Church of God. Kids at

school would make fun of me for going there and say that we were snake handlers. There wasn't any snake handling in the years I went to Mount Zion, but it wouldn't surprise me if there used to be. Reverend Maples did speak in tongues and perform the occasional miracle. In second grade when I got strep, Ted wouldn't let Grandma take me to the doctor and instead had Reverend Maples come pray over me. The next day when my temperature went up to 104, she sneaked me out to the urgent care clinic in CVS.

Church wasn't just on Sunday morning, and it didn't just last an hour. You never knew how long you'd be stuck in there; it all depended on how many people testified that day and how inspired Reverend Maples got. It felt like my whole life was school and church. I wasn't allowed to go to school dances or wear shorts and tank tops. Ted didn't approve of going to the movies, even to see something G-rated, because the demons from the R-rated movies might somehow get into the theater. The songs we sang at Mount Zion were all about blood—"Nothing but the Blood of Jesus," "Power in the Blood," "There Is a Fountain Filled with Blood." We were always reminding ourselves that Jesus was a man and that he died and bled and bled. I absolutely believed that demons were real and the devil himself walked the earth, looking for weak people like me to tempt away from salvation.

When I was little, it all scared the shit out of me. At age six, I accepted Jesus Christ as my savior, and as I grew up, I testified to His miracles more than once. I was devout. I believed in it all—the miracles, the hellfire, the bloody grace. After all, I was praised for putting on a good show in church and punished for showing any disobedience. But as I got older and started thinking it through, the church stopped making sense. Grandma was so proud of being born again, but that idea never sat right with me. You could get saved and everything from the past was just forgotten, but if you hadn't taken Jesus into your heart, you could live like a saint and burn in hell. It took years to get all the nightmare images of damnation out of my head, years before I could find it all funny.

I guess I wasn't the only one struggling with the theology, because Mount Zion shut down a few years ago. The squat brick building became a Catholic church, which really pissed Ted off. He loved to talk about how much he hated Catholics, but what he really meant was that he hated Mexicans.

I met Finn when I was sixteen. Grandma had given me her old Saturn as a birthday present when Ted bought her a newer car. That meant I could get a job at a go-kart track and, when I wasn't working, escape. I started lying a lot about when I had work and where I was going in the car. The truth wasn't that awful—I wasn't drinking or doing drugs, at least not much. Sometimes I drove to Knoxville to hear music in clubs. Sometimes I drove up into the mountains to get peace and quiet. Sometimes I just drove, anywhere, to get away.

I'd seen Finn in the halls of Tates Valley High School but had never talked to him. He was two years older than me and infinitely cooler. I didn't actually meet him until after he'd graduated and was playing bass in a rock band at a show in Knoxville. He asked me out the next day, and I had my first kiss.

We became serious fast. Up until then, I had thought guys were never going to be interested in me, but Finn liked me right away. He said he liked my style, which in those days was mostly thrift-store sweaters thrown over leggings. He was hip, always up on the latest music, friends with all the local bands, and he wore wire-rimmed glasses, which gave him an undeserved look of wisdom, even though he was only halfheartedly attending community college.

Finn was kind to me, and I felt safe with him. Looking back, I see that I was so incredibly young, and we moved so fast. We should have waited. We should have taken time to grow up. But we were impatient. It wasn't enough to date and make out. It wasn't even enough for us to have sex. We wanted the whole package, both of us. He first asked me to marry him when I was just seventeen. A tiny part of me thought he was crazy, but the rest of me was too happy to listen to that cautious 5 percent. It's hard to say why he was in such a hurry. He's always been impulsive. And he's always loved big, romantic gestures. Whenever we would fight, he'd come home with roses or a song he'd written me. I told him I had to wait to graduate from high school, but as soon as I did, we moved in together.

His parents never approved of me. They weren't rich but had

enough to look down on me in my Goodwill clothes and twenty-year-old car. And they thought I was trouble, because I'd been raised by my recovering alcoholic grandmother in the Pentecostal church. I understood just what their looks meant because people had been looking at me that way my whole life.

I felt I belonged with him, in a way I had never felt with Ted or even with Grandma, who tried her best but sometimes seemed so unlike me. She and I didn't even look alike—me with my dark eyes and frizzy hair that's almost black, her with pale-green eyes and hair that went from peroxided blond to white sometime during my childhood. I would stare in the mirror as a teenager and wonder just where the hell I had come from. I knew she was my grandmother—but I could barely remember my mom and had never known my dad. I felt out of place in this world, until I met Finn. Going home had always filled me with dread. I could never feel quite comfortable in the place where I lived with Ted there. But I loved coming home to the tiny apartment I shared with Finn. It was all ours. I decorated. I started cooking. I planted flowers in the window box. Finn had dropped out of college by that time and given up the rock band. He got a job with a moving company and made sure I went to school at the University of Tennessee in Knoxville, always telling me how smart I was, how I could do anything. Then I found out I was pregnant. Honestly, I was thrilled. A little scared, of course, and we knew money would be tight. But I didn't feel too young. We went ahead and got married, and we were both just so, so happy in those months as my belly got bigger and my little girl began to kick and twirl inside me.

The night before she was born, when I wasn't sure yet if the contractions were real or just a false alarm, I lay in the darkness of our bedroom, trying to get some rest. But I was too excited, literally too pregnant with possibility to sleep. I made a vow to myself in the darkness. I would give her all my love. I would always be there for my daughter. I would always put her first.

My girl, my Grace. How could she have come from within me, and now I'm not even allowed to be in a room alone with her? How did I fail so completely?

I was lucky to get assigned to our local school for student teaching, and it was a comfort to be back at my high school. The halls were familiar, the students too. Tates Valley is an unusual place to grow up. Tourists come for a quick visit, spending an hour here at the arcade, a day there at the water park. Or they just see a blur of billboards and neon signs on their way to the mountains. But it's a different place when it's where you live. I understood the students' lives there, because they'd grown up like me—sneaking cigarettes in the parking lots of outlet shopping malls, stuck in traffic jams behind endless streams of Georgia/Ohio/Florida plates, their parents struggling to get by on seasonal paychecks or tips. As soon as they were old enough, everyone got a job somewhere awful in the summer, if not year-round—a pancake restaurant, a wax museum, a miniature golf course. People are constantly coming and going—not just tourists, but workers also, and as a kid, that means friends disappearing as abruptly as they first transferred into your school. It's a small town at heart, but one where a lot of cash is constantly changing hands, and that invites a certain amount of vice. A kid who's paying attention can learn plenty about human nature and capitalism growing up in a tourist town.

Finn got up early on my first morning of student teaching and cooked me breakfast, wearing boxers and a T-shirt with my paisley apron over it. Grace was still asleep, and we enjoyed the quiet, sipping coffee together, munching bacon. Finn leaned back in his chair and grinned. "You're gonna do great, Mrs. Caton."

"I'm nervous."

"No need. You're an awesome teacher."

"What if the kids are mean to me?" I asked, half-kidding, half-sincere.

"Then you'll be mean right back. Don't pretend like you're not a badass."

I smiled. And Grace started crying, so I got up and got her dressed to go to Finn's parents' house.

I was excited to start teaching. When I first went to college, I didn't know what I wanted to do with my life. I'd majored in English, because it had always been my favorite subject. My aunt Carrie had encouraged my love of reading all through my childhood, sending me books in the mail, urging me to write stories and send them to her, which was a thrill because she was a professional writer. But when I got pregnant, I needed a practical plan, so I'd added an education minor and began working towards getting my teaching license. I'd had a lot of jobs through the years, but this was the start of a career.

I had bought a special first-day-of-school outfit—a pencil skirt, because that was what I thought professional women wore, and a short-sleeved, button-up shirt that was too big and ballooned out even after I tucked it in. The skirt had a tag in the back that was incredibly itchy. It bothered me for the entire drive to school. And once I got there and started walking up and down the hallways, my new black ballet flats began to give me blisters, the rough synthetic leather chafing against the tender skin on my heels.

I was assigned to Mrs. Holmes, who'd been my English teacher just a few years earlier. She wore her dyed blond hair in a bob and always had on bright-red lipstick. And when the trial started, it turned out she had a real love of the camera. She must have been interviewed a dozen times by every media outlet that came to town. She didn't bother to get up from her desk when I came into the class that morning. I had to clear my throat to even get her to look up from her cream cheese and bagel. "Hi, Mrs. Holmes."

"Oh. Hi there, um . . ." I was opening my mouth to remind her of my name when she recalled it: "Lydia."

I smiled, aware of how awkward I looked, holding my purse and tote bag in front of me, oozing nerves. "It's so great to be here! I'm really excited!"

She chewed her bagel and gave me a skeptical look. "Pace yourself, honey. You're gonna need that enthusiasm when we're a few weeks in."

I nodded. She popped the last piece of her breakfast into her mouth and stood up. "Well, we'd better find someplace to put you."

Mrs. Holmes eyed a table set off to one side of her desk, covered with stacks of papers and files. "I'll clear you a space at this table.

You'll mostly be observing this first week or so. But don't worry, I'll find plenty to keep you busy." Her black slacks were taut around her rear, perilously close to bursting a seam as she bent over to rearrange the stacks and clear a space for me. "You still live in town?" she asked.

"Nearby."

"Good. Then you know nothing ever really changes around here."

Mostly that seemed true. The bells rang out just as I recalled from my own days in Tates Valley High, met by the cacophony of class changing. The smells were familiar: pubescent perspiration, drugstore perfume, pencil lead, and disinfectant. The girls still wore leggings; the boys still showed off their first-growth stubble. The kids all had smartphones, but otherwise high school was high school.

I was supposed to be observing that first week and taking notes. Mrs. Holmes taught senior English, so the kids were both jaded and anxious to get going with their final year of school. They were moderately well-behaved, if vacant and completely disengaged from the study of British literature. I watched as Mrs. Holmes's already minimal energy levels flagged throughout the day. By sixth period, she seemed checked-out completely, yawning, texting on her phone during the class change. But I was excited because the last period was the honors class. Finally, I thought, we'd get the enthusiastic students. They'd been assigned *Tess of the D'Urbervilles* as summer reading, one of my favorite books, and I was looking forward to the discussion.

Mrs. Holmes went over the classroom rules for the fifth time that day, then gave a brief lecture on Thomas Hardy. She had the enthusiasm of an automated messaging service. Kids were on their phones, dozing, doodling—and these were honors students on the first day. I could see that some things had actually changed. In spite of Mrs. Holmes, I had loved this class, because I loved books.

Mrs. Holmes's monotonous drone was interrupted by an electronic jingle that caught everyone's attention. All eyes were on her vibrating phone, sitting prominently in front of her on the mini lectern on her desk. "Excuse me for a minute," she said, and to my amazement took the call, turning her back to the class and me.

I could only make out a few words here or there: ". . . well, have

you tried? . . . no, not that . . . of course I'm busy . . . can't you just
use . . . alright . . . I've given you the best years of my life! . . . you
know I care . . ."

She hung up and came over to me. "Lydia? Could you take over
here for a minute? I've got a family emergency."

This was against the university's student teaching policy, so I
hesitated.

"It's not a big deal," Mrs. Holmes went on, obviously irritated with
my lack of response. "Just lead the discussion on *Tess*." She lowered
her voice. "You've read it, right?"

She had given me an A+ on my essay on *Tess of the D'Urbervilles* five
years earlier. I'd written a term paper on Thomas Hardy in college.
And I'd reread the book just the month before to prepare for this
student teaching. I nodded.

"Okay. Be back as soon as I can." She grabbed her purse and
headed for the door.

I walked to the lectern, aware of my throbbing feet, my itching
skirt, and twenty-seven pairs of adolescent eyes on me. The students
were all staring now, their attention rapt with the unexpected drama.
I cleared my throat. "What do you think of the character of Tess? Is
she a strong character? Or a helpless victim?"

Silence. I tried to meet students' eyes, but they were all looking
down, out, away. I felt my cheeks growing hot. I looked around for
someone to point to and force into conversation. But before I could,
a hand went up in the back of the room.

That was the first time I saw him. A boy, I guess, like all the others.
A seventeen-year-old boy at that time, tall, with coal-black hair cropped
close to his light-brown head, wearing a plain white T-shirt and jeans.
Latino, I assumed. I nodded at him, and he spoke in a deep, confident
voice: "She is strong. She supports her family the only way she can
in the end. Terrible things happen to her, but she keeps trying to pull
her life together."

I nodded. "What do you the rest of you think? Do you agree?"

More silence, but after a moment, a girl in the front stuck up her
hand. "She puts up with way too much from Angel. She should have
gotten rid of him on their wedding night."

"But what could she have done?" I asked. "She didn't have a lot of options as a woman in that time."

"Okay, I get that maybe she couldn't just divorce him. But she's too nice to him! He treats her like crap and she keeps apologizing."

I smiled at her response. It seemed to me that the students were waking up. Another girl beside her raised her hand. "She should have told him about Alec from the beginning. It wasn't right to wait until they were married."

The first girl rolled her eyes. "She shouldn't have had to tell Angel about Alec at all if she didn't want to."

The second girl shook her head. "She'd lost a baby! That's a big deal—especially back then. It was wrong not to tell him."

The boy in the back raised his hand again. "She did it because she was scared of how he'd react. And she was right—he bolted. Even though he'd just told her he'd done the same thing, except worse, if you think that having sex before marriage is wrong. Because he chose to do it. She was raped."

The second girl wasn't having it. "Angel was a nice guy. He hadn't done anything wrong. And she lies to him!"

"She doesn't lie," he replied. "She just doesn't tell him the whole truth. And he's only superficially nice. When she needs him most, he abandons her. Both the men in her life hurt her, just in different ways."

"Why do you think they hurt her?" I asked.

I looked around the class, but no one else wanted to engage. The boy cleared his throat and to my amazement quoted the text by heart without looking at the book or his notes: "'*He won't hurt me. He's not in love with me.*' That's what Tess says about the farmer she works for. Even though he's a jerk, she's not afraid of him, like the men who love her."

He spoke clearly and with assurance. I noticed his eyes then. Deep-set and dark beneath heavy brows, those eyes looked older than his years, as though they'd already seen all the world had to offer and were worn out. (Can eyes look like that? Am I just spouting some poetic hindsight bullshit?) His stare was so intense that I found myself looking away, down at Mrs. Holmes's useless notes.

Mrs. Holmes returned to class the next day, and I didn't have to do any more real teaching for the next few weeks. She did ask me to grade the first batch of essays the students wrote on the summer reading. By that time, I had learned the boy's name: Alex Greggs. He didn't always turn in his assignments or even come to class. But when he did show up, he was obviously the smartest student in the room. His paper happened to be at the bottom of my grading pile, and by the time I got to it, I was braced for more faulty constructions, incoherent arguments, and missing thesis statements. But Alex's paper was clearly written, original, well thought out, even elegant in its construction. I still remember the title, same as one of the sections of the book: "The Woman Pays." I gave him an A+.

My relationship with Finn had changed after Grace was born. The birth was hard on me physically, and for a long while after, I didn't want to have sex. Then as I began feeling better, we were always so tired with school and work and the baby. Some days Finn and I hardly even had time to talk to each other.

But it went deeper than sex. Finn used to read the books I was reading for my English classes in college, because he wanted to be able to talk to me about them and he wanted to learn. But he hadn't cracked open a book in years. He was always so exhausted when he got home from work that all he wanted to do was plop in front of the Xbox. He started hanging out more with his older brother, Roy. When we were first together, Finn had called Roy a redneck, which was accurate, and avoided him except for family gatherings. But at some point Roy started coming around more, and Finn's attitude toward him softened. They took to going fishing and hunting together on the weekends. Finn grew a beard and bought a gun. I freaked out when he brought it home, but he just laughed and called me a liberal.

"I thought you were a liberal!" I replied.

"Yeah, sure. About social issues."

"Isn't not-getting-shot a social issue?"

"Lydia, it's for hunting. I don't want to have to always borrow Roy's rifle. Don't worry. I've got a case and a lock."

The truth is Finn didn't know anything about politics. When I met him and he was in the music scene, he would talk about voting for

Obama because he thought it was cool. But Roy got him listening to talk radio in the car, and suddenly Finn was telling me he'd become a libertarian, as if he had any idea what that meant.

We were too caught up in life, in making ends meet, and at some point I began to realize that he had settled. Settled into this life, settled down from his rock band past, settled for what we had, uninterested in looking for anything new. I felt it for a long time before I said anything.

One Saturday evening, he was grilling in the backyard and Grace was splashing in her kiddie pool, while I watched both of them from the small deck overlooking our yard, nursing a beer. It was nice. I was enjoying student teaching. Finn had been made manager at the moving company, and we were able to rent that sweet little house. I was thinking, *This is good . . . and yet . . . and yet . . . Is it enough? Is it what I want?*

I went over to the grill, where Finn was staring intently at his burgers. "Do you ever think about leaving?" I asked.

He didn't look up. "Leaving where?"

"Tates Valley. We used to always say we were gonna get out of here when we got older."

"We were just kids."

"Mommy, look at me!" Grace shouted from the pool, and I turned to watch her hit the water to make it splash as high as she could.

"That's good, sweetie!" I turned back to Finn. "But really, what's keeping us here?"

"Um, my job, your school, my family."

He didn't get it. I knew he didn't get it, but I needed to confirm this feeling. "We used to talk about moving to New York."

He let out a mocking laugh. "What would we do in New York?"

"Mommy, look!" I didn't turn this time.

"I could teach in New York. You could manage a moving company in New York. Or try something different. Be whatever you want to be."

"We're barely getting by in Tennessee. With my parents helping out! How do you think we could afford a place in New York?"

"Okay, not New York, then. But don't you ever want to see more of the world? I mean, what's keeping us here, anyway? The humidity and the racism?"

He looked up, and I could tell he was getting angry. You get to know these things when you live with someone. You can actually feel the moment when a discussion veers into argument. I could calm him, or I could keep needling.

"Mommy, look, look!"

"I'm happy here," he said defiantly as he flipped his burgers.

"You've changed," I replied. I went to stick my feet in the pool and watch Grace splash.

Mrs. Holmes suggested I work with the honors students on their college admissions essays. We had brief one-on-one meetings during class, but I asked her if I could volunteer to stay late some days and do more in-depth tutoring. She cocked an eyebrow at me. "Volunteer?"

I nodded.

"It's your life. If you want to spend more of it than you already do in these hallowed halls, then by no means am I going to stop you."

I had a handful of students in mind who I thought could use the extra help. Most struggled with writing, even though they'd gotten into the honors class. But a couple, including Alex, were fine writers; I just thought their essays could be stronger. Alex was so smart. Still, looking at him, I thought it was a miracle that he'd made it into the honors class. You could just tell he came from a bad place—cheap, awkward clothes, always tired, probably hungry, already exhausted at eighteen. He reminded me of me.

We met one afternoon after dismissal in Mrs. Holmes's empty classroom. It was the first time I'd ever been alone with him. He drifted in a couple minutes late, in the way I'd grown used to in class. He didn't seem particularly concerned with tardiness or absence or giving the teacher the impression that he was eager to be there. Usually he was by himself, something of a loner, though definitely not an outcast. He was one of those kids who gave off an ineffable coolness that other kids respected instinctively.

"Hi, Miss Caton."

"It's Mrs., Alex."

"Aw, my bad."

"No problem. Have a seat."

We took a look at his essay. I'd made notes on it, but I really wanted to convince him to start over. He'd written about losing a cross-country race, and it was fine but not as strong as it could have been. I suspected he had a story in him that would win over an admissions committee but wasn't ready to share it.

"Did you write this for a specific application?"

"It's answering one of the Common Application prompts."

"Okay. Do you know where you're applying?"

He leaned back in his chair and crossed his arms in a defensive pose. "I don't know. UT, I guess."

"Okay. Anywhere else?"

"I don't know. I don't know if it's worth it."

I was shocked. He was easily the smartest kid in the class.

"What do you mean? It's absolutely worth it! You have to go to college."

"Everyone says that. But really, what's the point?"

"Are you kidding? You know what the point is. To get a good job. And to get an education. To live up to your potential."

"I don't know if I can get in anyway."

"Oh, come on! You're the best student in the class!"

That got his attention. He looked down at the ground, suddenly shy, as though he wasn't used to getting a lot of compliments. "My grades aren't that great."

"Why not?"

"I don't always turn in assignments when I should. Or make it to class."

"Okay. Well, I'm guessing you already know that needs to change. In the meantime, that makes your essay all the more important to make up for weak grades."

He leaned forward and looked at his paper on the table. "Yeah, okay."

"This essay is well written. But there's nothing special about it. I hardly know anything more about you after reading it."

"You think I should write from a different prompt."

"I think you should write something you care about. That's what really matters."

"Like what?"

"What makes you special? Why are your grades lower than they should be? What is going to interest someone in admissions about you?"

He put his hand to his head and rubbed his temple. "I don't want to write some sob story."

"Do you have a sob story?"

"No. Maybe. I don't know. But I don't want to just write about how my dad left and my mom left and I was raised by my grandma."

"Why not? If that's your story, you should write it."

"It's not my story. It's my life."

I tried to will him to look me in the eye, but his gaze was fastened on his lame cross-country paper. "I get it. It sounds like a hard life. I was raised by my grandma too." He looked up, and finally I had the attention of those big, dark eyes. "I don't like to talk about my family situation either. But it's okay to write about it. I know it may feel cheap, but it's an important part of who you are. That's the kind of thing an admissions committee wants to know about."

He was silent. I could see I was going to have to drag the story out of him. "When did your family first come to Tates Valley?"

"My family's been here forever. My dad's family, anyway. My mom and grandma moved here from Mexico a couple years before I was born."

"So your dad's white?"

"Yeah. How about you?"

"How about me what?"

"What are you? Latina? Mixed? Something else?"

"Oh! I'm just white."

"I see. I just thought . . . because of your hair . . ."

I tried to steer the subject away from myself. "Is your dad around at all?"

"Nah. He split before I was born. I used to spend time with his mama, but she died two years back. My mom hung around until I was two and then she split. So I was raised by her mom, my *abuelita*."

"That's your essay, Alex. Let them know about the challenges you've faced. Tell it in a natural way. Focus on how it's made you the person you are."

He didn't look convinced, but he flipped over the old essay and began to jot down some notes. We worked together for about an hour, talking about ideas, working out a structure. He was reluctant to open up but gradually began sharing more. When we were done, I asked if he needed a ride home.

Looking back, that was probably my first big mistake. I did worry as we walked to my Corolla; I knew maybe it wasn't the right thing to do. I worried that the mock turtleneck I was wearing drew too much attention to my breasts. I worried that my car was littered with Goldfish crumbs and applesauce that Grace had squeezed from one of those little pouches.

At the same time, it all seemed perfectly natural. Alex was easy to talk to. We buckled our seat belts, and I turned the key in the ignition. "Where to?"

"You know the River Vista Motel?"

"That's where you live?"

"Yeah. It's not a motel anymore, just apartments."

It was only a couple miles, but leaf-season traffic clogged the streets. You have to be extra careful driving in a tourist town. When people go on vacation, their minds go on vacation too. They forget basic traffic laws and get distracted by neon signs and billboards. Their kids are yelling at them from the backseat to stop and take them to the fudge shop. You should expect cars to stop suddenly for no apparent reason, pull out in front of you without indicating, or even drive the wrong way. And, especially in October, you should expect a lot of traffic.

"God, I hate driving here," I said as a truck stopped abruptly in front of me, in the middle of the road, to let out two teenage passengers.

"You live in Tates Valley?" asked Alex.

"Yep. Born and raised. And still here, as you can see."

"Did you go to the high school?"

"Sure did. I had Mrs. Holmes for senior English too."

"No shit!" He realized he'd used a vulgarity. "Oh, sorry."

"It's okay, Alex. I don't care." Perhaps another small mistake. They begin to pile up slowly, eventually snowballing into disaster.

"That's where I work," he said, looking out the windshield to the Hillbilly Playhouse, a dinner theater.

"You wait tables?"

"Sometimes. I also play in the show."

"Play?"

"Yeah, when other musicians call in sick. I play the banjo."

"You're kidding!" I laughed at the image of him in a bluegrass band.

"No, why's that funny?"

"I don't know. You just don't look like a banjo kind of guy."

"Because I'm Mexican?"

"Oh, I didn't mean—"

"I'm just messing with you, Mrs. Caton. My grandma taught me to play. The one from here."

"I'd love to hear you sometime." I was pulling into the River Vista Motel parking lot.

"Come in. You can hear me now."

A big mistake. No doubt the biggest yet. I parked the car and followed him inside.

The building had still served its intended purpose when I was in high school, but at some point the motel owners had found it more profitable to provide housing for the growing labor force than to compete with the newer, fancier accommodations opening up around town. It was depressing. When the management stopped catering to tourists, they'd obviously stopped worrying about basic upkeep and maintenance. The ragged carpet in the hallway was worn almost bare, and an overhead fluorescent light flickered off and on. Alex led me into what would once have been a suite of two double rooms, still decorated in sad, nineties-era generic motel artwork and linens. A painting of a black bear. Faded burgundy wallpaper. He flicked on the light and tossed down his backpack. "My grandma's at work. You want a Coke or something?"

"No, thanks."

He sat down on one of the beds and motioned for me to sit on the other. Sure enough, he reached under the bed and pulled out a banjo case. I have to admit I've always had a thing for musicians. But I was used to hanging out with Finn and his indie-rock friends. I'd never really listened to someone play a banjo. I mean, sure, I'd heard them before, but I'd always run in the opposite direction of anything associated with country music. I was vaguely aware of the hipster Americana bands that played in Knoxville, but it wasn't my scene. I should have realized bluegrass was cool again, along with artisanal moonshine and Etsy quilting squares. Folk music seems to revive itself again and again.

Without any introduction, he took out the instrument and began to play. His singing voice surprised me. It was higher-pitched than his speaking voice, a smooth, clear tenor, with a Tennessee twang he didn't use when talking, *"I'm just a poor wayfaring stranger, traveling through this world of woe. But there's no sickness, toil, nor danger in that fair land to which I go."*

He didn't look at me at all as he sang. He concentrated on the music, his fingers plucking out the chords on the banjo, his eyes fixed on the bedspread. *"I'm going there to see my father. I'm going there no more to roam. I am just going over Jordan. I am just going over home."*

I was transfixed. I couldn't take my eyes off him, hardly able to believe that he was producing this music. To my untrained ear, his playing seemed flawless.

> *I know dark clouds will gather round me.*
> *I know my way is rough and steep.*
> *But beauteous fields lie just before me,*
> *Where God's redeemed their vigils keep.*
>
> *I'm going home to see my mother.*
> *She said she'd meet me when I come.*
> *I'm only going over Jordan.*
> *I'm only going over home.*
> *I'm just a-going over home.*

I think it was the line about "going home to see my mother" that got me. His fingers lingered over the last chord, and then he looked up. My eyes brimmed with tears. His face fell. "Mrs. Caton, are you alright?"

I gave my head a shake and wiped my eyes with the back of my hand. "Yes! Of course. I'm sorry. That was just really beautiful."

Our eyes met. I could see that the praise had made him happy.

And I felt something, real and intense. At that time, it wasn't anything wrong or to do with sex. It was something much simpler, much bigger than that. It was connection. That breathtaking, rare thing when your eyes meet another human's, and you reach a sort of understanding without words.

I was shaken. And that's when I realized that I needed to leave immediately. I stood. "Thank you so much for playing for me, Alex. I'd better get on home now."

"Thanks for the lift, Mrs. Caton."

"I'll see you tomorrow." I got to the door and down the hallway as fast as I could, and gulped the fresh air outside.

My first mistakes. My first trespasses. Those old songs from Mount Zion haunt me still: "*What can wash away my sin? Nothing but the blood of Jesus.*"

That was how it began. After that afternoon, there was an understanding between Alex and me. We gave each other tiny nods in the hallway. He smiled at me when he came into Mrs. Holmes's class. I don't know if anyone else even noticed. But I think in both our minds we had gone past the teacher-student relationship. We were friends.

Occasionally we met for more tutoring session. More mistakes. I guess some part of me knew it wasn't a good idea because I didn't tell Mrs. Holmes about it, though I did tell Finn that I had to stay late for work reasons. I always gave Alex a ride home. He always invited me in to hear him play songs on his banjo. I didn't run away like that first day. I got to know that awful motel room. He played for me. We had snacks. We had conversations. We talked about literature, music, politics. I told him about my grandma and Ted. I told him about Finn. I told him to start calling me Lydia, at least outside of school. (Mistakes, mistakes.) He was interested in everything, and he read all the time. He would skip class to read Dostoevsky in the parking lot, which I told him was idiotic but secretly admired. He was still at that magic stage in life when everything is possibility. You don't appreciate it when it's happening. He didn't. He thought he had no possibilities. He thought he shouldn't bother applying to college and should just get a full-time job at the Hillbilly Playhouse, for God's sake. But even with school and his job, he had so much time. He could spend hours listening to jazz or teaching himself a new song on the banjo or writing poetry in English then translating it into Spanish. Things I would never dream of doing, because I don't have the talent or ability—but also because who has the time, when you have a child, and groceries to buy, and shirts to iron, and a house that needs cleaning, and a car that needs an oil change and also you should get that strange rattling sound checked out, and you need a haircut, and for Christ's sake, someone needs to take out the garbage.

Instead of going to pick up my daughter from her grandmother, I was eating microwave popcorn with a boy on a bed, talking about Bob Dylan. Of course I knew it wasn't a good idea.

He submitted his college applications, and we no longer had the pretense of meeting for tutoring sessions. But we kept hanging out. We never really talked about it and certainly didn't conspire to be dishonest to people. I don't know if he told anyone about me. His grandma was always at work when I went to the motel. I was vague with my husband, just saying I needed to stay late at school. He didn't seem suspicious.

And at that point, it *was* really just hanging out. I knew it was strange. I knew it wasn't a good idea. But it was just talking, playing music. We went on like that all through the semester.

Then suddenly it was December, and my student teaching was wrapping up. Everything was a busy blur. I was preparing lesson plans, writing Christmas cards, taking Grace to see Santa. She rode her tricycle into our Christmas tree that year and knocked it over. I didn't bother putting it back up.

I went over to Alex's place one last time during the final week in the semester. It had gotten cold. I kept my coat on in the chilly room when we got to the motel. "You want some coffee or something?" he asked, opening the minifridge.

"Sure."

He started making a fresh pot.

"It's my last week at the high school."

"I know," he said, coming over to sit across from me on the bed. The coffeemaker grunted rhythmically in the little kitchenette across from us.

"Good luck with everything."

"Thanks. Good luck to you too. You gonna be teaching for real next year?"

"I hope so."

"You're a way better teacher than Mrs. Holmes."

"Thanks."

We often fell into awkward silences, during which I thought about how I shouldn't really be there.

"I mean it. I wasn't gonna apply to college until you came along."

"Well, that would have been ridiculous. I'm sure your guidance counselor would have talked you into it."

"Okay, but now maybe I can actually get in because you helped me write that essay."

"I just pointed you in the right direction."

"I'm trying to say thank you." He caught my eye. For a moment we were quiet, just looking at each other.

Finally, the silence was too much for me. "You're welcome," I said. He got up to pour the coffee.

Alex was so smart. And I had only ever been with Finn. I'm not trying to make excuses. And I don't want to blame Alex for what happened. But he had swagger, the way he walked down the halls at school. He looked at every girl like he knew they all loved him. And probably a lot of them secretly did.

I drank my coffee quickly and got up to leave. He walked me to the door and put his hand on the knob to open it. But then he stopped. "Thanks for the ride, Lydia."

"Of course." He didn't move, his hand still on the doorknob.

"I had a great time."

"Me too," I said softly, beginning to feel afraid.

"Good night," he said. But he still didn't move.

"Alex . . ." Before I could say anything else, he leaned forward and kissed me on the mouth.

I would be lying if I said I didn't kiss him back. It would be dishonest for me not to admit that a thousand electric shocks reverberated through my body. It would be misleading not to say I lingered, not to note the length and intensity of the kiss. I cannot claim that I didn't want him then, that I didn't long for him to toss me onto the scratchy polyester bedspread and make love to me.

But I did pull away, finally. That is the truth. I grabbed the door-knob and let myself out, running as fast as I could to my car. I went home to Grace, and we sang "Jingle Bells" and watched *A Charlie Brown Christmas*. I tried to put the whole thing out of my mind. I would never go back to that place. I had just two more days at the school. I would never speak to or look at Alex Greggs again. It had all been a big mistake.

Lying in bed that night, I tried to tamp down the memory, admon-ished myself to forget about it. But one of those old blood hymns kept playing in my mind, *Would you be free from your burden of sin? There's power in the blood, power in the blood. Would you over evil a victory win? There's wonderful power in the blood.*

I didn't see Alex for the next six months. I finished my master's and landed a job for the fall at a school in Knoxville. It would be a long commute, but we were looking into leaving Tates Valley to move closer to the city. Grace turned three and we threw a party in the backyard. Nothing much changed between Finn and me. We could have gone on like that and had a good life together.

But my grandma got free tickets to the Hillbilly Playhouse from someone who worked at the new church she and Ted attended. She wanted to take Grace and me. She was always looking for nice things for us to do together, since I refused to come to her house when Ted was around.

I see now that this was another of my mistakes. I could have said no or just made up some excuse to get out of it. I could have sent Grace on her own. But I told myself it would be fine. Alex might not even work there anymore. And what had happened wasn't that big a deal, really.

We met Grandma at the theater. She'd gotten all dressed up for the occasion with long, dangly gold earrings and bright-pink lipstick. "How are my girls!" she asked, as Grace bounded into her arms.

Our waitress had been in one of Mrs. Holmes's English classes, so she treated me with an awkward deference. We got extra helpings of mashed potatoes with our giant turkey legs. The show was pretty awful. An emcee in tattered overalls came out to welcome us and tell a series of redneck jokes that had been dated before I was born. But the audience loved it, and their enthusiasm was especially baffling because no alcohol was served in the Hillbilly Playhouse. Actors came out for a series of skits, revolving loosely around a family feud. There was a dumb hothead hillbilly, a sexy slutty hillbilly, a sassy grandma hillbilly, etc. Grace laughed along with the crowd, especially when the actors did pratfalls, which was often. Grandma laughed too. Bless her heart, but she is not a sophisticated woman. I had the feeling of watching a foreign TV show or a movie from so long ago that it makes you wonder what life is or was like for the people who created it, or why it appeals to them. The odd thing was that I was in my hometown.

Music accompanied most of the acting, but the source of it was hidden until a square-dance scene when the band joined the actors onstage. And sure enough, there was Alex, in a ridiculous flannel shirt and overalls, playing his banjo. I felt sick when I saw him. He looked so out of place on that stage, radiating cool in the lamest of scenarios. His face was blank, his dark eyes focused on his banjo.

When the show was over, the cast invited the audience up to take photos with them. I tried to pull Grace toward the exit, but Grandma wanted a picture. "Come on, Lydia! I can put it on my Facebook!"

Reluctantly I followed her toward the stage and saw where the band had been hidden. I knew at that moment that seeing Alex was inevitable and felt overwhelmed by dread. I was sweating even though the theater was frigid with air-conditioning. I didn't want to be in that bizarre place anymore. I wanted fresh air. I didn't want to be anywhere near him.

"Mrs. Caton?" I could hear the surprise in his voice before turning to face him.

"Alex! So nice to see you." He came right over to us. "This is my grandmother, Sue. And this is my daughter, Grace."

He shook Grandma's hand and asked Grace for a high five. "Would you like to see my banjo, Grace?"

"What's a banjo?" she asked.

"It's the instrument Alex plays in the band, sweetie. Kind of like a guitar."

He brought it over and let her pluck at the strings. "How are you doing?" I asked.

"Good. I got into UT. And I even got a scholarship. I start in the fall."

"That's fantastic, Alex! I'm so glad to hear it."

"Can we get a picture with the band?" Grandma asked.

Alex gathered his bandmates, and we posed for a photo. I was standing next to him, holding on to Grace in front of me. Grandma handed her phone to one of the actors; right before she snapped the picture, Alex said, "I can't believe you're here," under his breath. I turned to him and we shared a look—a mutual half-smile to say, *We both know this is a ludicrous situation.* Unfortunately, that look was captured in the photo that Grandma put on Facebook. Later the local paper found it and put it on the front page, with Grace, Grandma, and the rest of the band cropped out, so that it was just Alex, in his patched overalls, and me, staring at each other.

"I'll tag you, Alex! Are you Facebook friends with Lydia?"

"No, I don't friend any of my students on Facebook," I interjected.

"Oh, well, friend Alex, so I can tag him! He's not your student anymore."

So I did. I friended Alex. And he PMed me. And I agreed to meet him one Tuesday afternoon to catch up. That's when the mistakes started getting really big.

He suggested we go for a hike, and it seemed like a nice idea. Grace was supposed to be staying with Grandma that day anyway, and the weather was nice—not too hot. I picked him up at the River Vista, and we drove into the mountains, catching each other up on the past few months. He'd belatedly dedicated himself to school in his last semester—because of me, he said, although I don't know if that was true. But he did seem more focused than before. "I know this is my shot, getting into UT. I'm not gonna screw it up."

"You've just got to put school first. Don't let anything else get in your way. Don't be like me and get married and pregnant!"

"Aw, your little girl is sweet."

"Yeah, she is. But I'm just saying. No distractions, Alex. Go to class, get shit done."

We decided to walk to Laurel Springs, a short hike above Mitchell's Creek up on Jones Mountain. A few other cars were parked at the trailhead, but we didn't see anyone else around as we started walking. It was a beautiful June day. The forest was a hundred shades of green, thick with foliage, laurel and rhododendron on the hillsides, oak, hickory, and pine towering above us. The warm air buzzed with insect noises, birds, and the shuffling of squirrels or God knows what through the leaves. The walk was steep and for a while we stopped talking, as our breath grew short and my T-shirt became wet and sticky against my back. Then we came to a clearing and saw the brown wooden sign that marked the spring. Water bubbled up below a gigantic oak tree that looked as if it had stood here for centuries, somehow saved from logging and the carelessness of human progress. Alex went over and scooped a handful of water that he promptly swallowed.

"Is that safe?" I asked.

"Sure. People pay three dollars a bottle for mountain springwater."

"I'm pretty sure that's been treated."

He leaned back against the tree. "You know, folks say this place is haunted."

"Oh yeah?"

"Yeah. According to my grandma, a girl was murdered here by her boyfriend, like a hundred years ago."

"Seriously?" I ventured over to the spring and bent to let the frigid water flow over my hand.

"That's what Grandma says."

The water became too cold to bear, and I stood up. I started to take a step back, but Alex gently grabbed my arm. Our eyes met. "Alex . . ."

"Lydia." He said my name calmly, for no other reason than to say it and show me that he could say it with confidence.

"This is a mistake," I said.

"Lydia." His voice was strong and possessive. I loved the way he made my name sound.

But I did try to pull away from him. He held onto my arm firmly. When he spoke again, his voice was softer, but more urgent. "Lydia."

I let him kiss me then. We moved away from the trail, behind the spring, bodies intertwined as we walked. He sat me down on a large, smooth rock, and we began kissing again.

I will spare you both the details and the euphemisms. We had sex.

I don't want to make excuses. But Alex was not an innocent. He'd slept with plenty of girls. I'd only ever slept with Finn.

Afterward, we lay back against the smooth mountain stone, side by side. He spoke in a hushed voice. "I love you, Lydia."

For some reason, his declaration didn't sound foolish to me. I knew he was eighteen. I knew I had been his teacher. I knew what we had done was a terrible mistake. But it didn't sound foolish to me, because I felt it too.

We walked down the trail, mostly silent. What was there to say? In the car, I began to panic.

"What have I done?" I wasn't really talking to Alex. I just couldn't tamp down the sense of dread now beginning to pulse through me.

"It's okay." His voice was not convincing.

"I'm married. I have a daughter."

"It will be okay."

"We can never let this happen again."

"I meant what I said. I love you."

"Alex, you can't love me. You're just eighteen. You need to forget about me and go to school in the fall and make a life for yourself."

"Don't do that. Don't act like I don't know what I'm feeling because I'm only eighteen."

I glanced at him in the passenger's seat and could see how bothered he was by what I'd said. I didn't really care what he was feeling at that moment, though. I had the air-conditioning turned up high but was sweating. I felt like I might vomit.

I didn't get out of the car when I dropped him at the River Vista.

"Can I call you?" he asked.

"I'll call you." Before he'd seemed pissed, but now he looked like he might cry. I softened. "I will. I promise. I just need a little time to think things through."

As I drove toward home, I began to cry, and soon I was sobbing. I had to pull over in the parking lot of a flea market. After a moment, I heard a tap on the window. I looked up and saw a large, middle-aged woman staring at me. I rolled down the window. "You alright, honey?" she asked.

I nodded.

"You sure? What is it? Man trouble?"

I nodded again.

"He ain't worth it, honey, trust me." I smiled and assured her I would be okay.

Something about that interaction shook me out of my panic. I wiped my eyes and stopped crying. Then I drove home fast, so I could tell Finn everything.

You might have thought the mistakes couldn't get any bigger. But I have a real talent.

It's hard to explain what I was thinking at the time. Partly, I couldn't imagine keeping a secret that big. I already felt so guilty, and the only way I knew how to get rid of the guilt was through confession. (*Thanks, Mount Zion!*) As I drove, I went over and over it in my head and began to convince myself of crazy things. Finn hadn't seemed that into me in a long time. Maybe this would be sort of a relief for him. I would give him permission to sleep with someone else too. We could just talk it through.

Grace was still at Grandma's when I got home. Finn had just gotten home from work and was drinking a beer on the couch with some baseball game on the TV. "Hey," he called as I came in, not bothering to look up.

I put down my purse and walked over in front of him.

"What's up?" he asked. He'd changed out of his work clothes into Hawaiian shorts and flip-flops, which gave him a slightly goofy look.

"Can you turn off the TV?"

He sat up straight and punched the buttons to turn it off.

I sat down in the easy chair across from him. "I've done something bad."

"What? Are you okay?"

"Yeah, I'm fine. I'm really sorry."

"What is it, Lydia?"

"I slept with someone."

"What?" His voice immediately switched from concerned to enraged.

"This afternoon. It was a mistake. I'm so sorry! I knew it was a mistake as soon as it happened and I came home to tell you."

"Who?"

"One of my students from Tates Valley."

"What the fuck, Lydia?!"

"Not a student there anymore. He's graduated."

"What is wrong with you? You're cheating on me? With a *student*? If anyone finds out, you could lose your job!" He was standing now, pacing, shouting.

"No one will find out. And anyway, he's eighteen now."

"Oh, okay," he sneered. "No big deal, then."

"I know it was a bad thing to do." I stood up too. I wanted to calm him somehow. I had this crazy idea of putting my arm around him, but as I inched toward him, I knew it would be catastrophic to try to touch him. "I love you. It was a mistake. I'm only telling you because I don't want to lie."

"What were you thinking?"

"Well, I mean, you and I haven't—"

"We haven't what? Are you seriously about to blame this shit on me?!" He was walking toward me now. I had never been frightened of my husband, and I wasn't then. But I could feel a rage in him that I had never experienced before.

"We haven't had sex in months. You don't seem interested in me in that way anymore."

"What? You're always busy. You never have time."

"I'm sure that's true. But I haven't felt like you wanted me in a long time."

"So you had sex with a teenager?!"

"I realize that was not a good response. But since it's happened, maybe we should talk about what we want from our relationship. Do you ever think about sleeping with other people? Maybe we should try an open relationship."

"No, I don't want to think about it, and I don't want a goddamn open relationship! I want you to get the fuck out of my house!"

"Finn . . . I've gotta pick up Grace in half an hour."

"Jesus Christ. Fine. I'll go." He grabbed his keys and headed toward the door.

"Finn, please! Can we just talk?"

"Fuck you, Lydia!"

And the door slammed.

I managed to keep it together that evening while I gave Grace supper and a bath. After I tucked her in, I burst into tears and sat in the hallway outside her room crying for maybe ten minutes. Then I pulled myself together.

Finn came home around midnight, drunk, and passed out on the sofa.

We managed to not speak to each other for three full days, except for essential interactions, and Finn stayed camped out on the sofa at night. Finally, on the third day, he came up to me when Lydia was in bed, and I was doing the dishes. "I've decided not to leave," he said.

I turned off the water and faced him. He looked exhausted.

"At least not for now."

"I'm glad."

"I'm not forgiving you."

"Okay."

"But I don't want to disrupt things for Grace."

"Me neither."

"Honestly, Lydia, I don't really give a shit what you want right now."

I felt hot, stinging tears welling in my eyes and tried to force them back.

Finn continued, "I'm gonna come back to sleeping in the bedroom, so she's not confused."

"Okay."

"I don't know when I'll be able to forgive you. Or if I even can."

"Okay."

"Can you promise me that you won't see that boy again?"

"Yes."

"Good." He turned and left the kitchen. I didn't know what else to do, so I turned on the water and finished washing the dishes. After three days of awkward silence, I felt relieved. He wasn't leaving. He had talked to me. It was progress.

I fully meant to keep my word to Finn. I deleted Alex's information from my phone and unfriended him on Facebook. But a week after our day at Laurel Springs, he started texting me.

> Hey Lydia. I'm sorry u got upset last week. I know I said I wouldn't call but I miss u. Call me.

I figured I owed it to him to write back.

> Alex, I'm sorry I haven't called. My husband found out about us and it's been bad at home.

I knew better than to try to explain that I had confessed for no good reason.

> Oh shit.

> Yeah. I can't see you again or talk to you.
> My marriage is on the line.
> I'm sorry. I didn't mean to hurt you.
> Please just forget about me.

He didn't reply for a few hours, and I felt a weight lifted. Maybe it was that easy. I could just send a text and make Alex disappear from my life.

Later that night, my phone rang. I was reading in bed; Finn was downstairs watching the Braves. It was Alex. I knew I shouldn't answer but found myself picking up the phone.

"Don't be mad. I know you asked me not to call."

I'd forgotten how sexy his voice was. I didn't say anything.

"I miss you."

"I can't talk to you. I'm sorry."

"Please don't hang up."

"I can't. I made a promise."

I hung up the phone, put it in sleep mode, and hid it under a pillow. But I couldn't sleep. After an hour of tossing and turning, I peeked back at the phone. Eight missed calls. A series of texts:

I have to talk to you. I'm going crazy.

I've never felt like this before.

I LOVE U.

Finn was so angry with me, and there was no one else I could talk to about it. The thought of talking to someone who didn't hate me was comforting. And Alex was obviously upset. I called. I'd turned out the light and the room was dark except for the streetlight coming through the closed blinds.

"You called!" he said.

"I shouldn't have." I spoke softly, in case the baseball game had finished.

"I'm glad you did."

"I do care about you. But you don't know what it's been like here. This is the only way I can save my marriage."

"Maybe your marriage isn't worth saving."

"Maybe. But I have a little girl. She's only three. I don't want to destroy her life."

"It wouldn't destroy her life."

"How do you know? We both came from fucked up families. I'm trying to do better for her."

He was silent. I didn't know what else to say. "Alex? Are you there?"

"Yeah." I realized from his voice that he was crying. It shocked me. He'd always seemed so confident and in control.

"Are you okay?"

"I don't know." His voice was choked and small. He sounded like a little boy.

"I made a horrible mistake. It was wrong of me to ever go home with you. It wasn't appropriate." It was the first time I had ever admitted as much out loud.

"Don't you love me?"

"I do. But we can't be together. I want the best for you, which is why when you hang up, you must forget all about me. Pretend this never happened."

He sniffled softly, but said nothing.

"I'm going to go. I'm so, so sorry. Please know I do care about you, but we mustn't talk again."

I hung up and stuffed the phone back under the pillow. I know it will sound crazy, but I hadn't fully realized until that moment that he was just a kid. I had fooled myself into thinking otherwise. But I was wrong. He was a scared, lonely boy, and I had hurt him. It felt worse than hurting Finn. It felt worse than anything I'd ever felt before.

I didn't hear from him for about a week. Finn wasn't really speaking to me, but I made the most of those summer days with Grace. We went to the county pool. We went to story time at the library. We went to the movies. Grace sat in my lap and turned around for a hug whenever anything scary happened on-screen.

We were walking home from the playground when I got a text from Alex:

> I really need to c u.

I erased it and didn't reply. About an hour later, another text:

> Please. I need help.

Twenty minutes later:

> Really. I wouldn't bother you if wasn't important.

Finally I wrote back:

> I'm sorry, but I CANNOT SEE YOU. Please stop.
> Erase my number from your phone.

He didn't stop. The texts continued for the next few days. He would cycle through emotions. Sometimes sweet, sometimes angry.

He loved me, he needed me, he was so sad, he was so pissed off, fuck you, bitch, go to hell!, why? why? why? Sooner or later, Finn was going to see one of the texts.

And of course I knew it might not stop with texts. So it wasn't that surprising when he showed up one Saturday morning.

I was making breakfast, and Finn was in the shower. I heard a knock, which was strange because we had a doorbell. I left Grace at the kitchen table with her yogurt and went to the front door. We still had a baby gate between the kitchen and dining room, and I locked it behind me, so she wouldn't be able to come in.

I tensed up as soon as I opened the door. My first thought was Finn. I could hear the shower running and knew I had to get Alex away from the house before he got out. Alex looked awful, like he hadn't slept or bathed in a while, his chin rough with stubble. But I was too agitated to feel badly for him. "What are you doing here?"

"I had to see you. I'm not doing so well. I just need to talk."

"No. Go! Just please get out of here. My husband is in the shower, but if he sees you, he's going to freak out." I began to slam the door, but he pushed his arm in the way.

"I can't go. I'm losing my mind. I feel so alone."

"I'm sorry, Alex. I can't help you. I have to think about my daughter." Gently I moved his arm back out of the doorway. He didn't resist my touch. Briefly, I squeezed his hand.

"Good-bye, Alex." I slammed the door and dead-bolted it.

I went back to the kitchen and heard Finn getting out of the bathroom. "Who was knocking?" Grace asked.

"No one, sweetie. Just a salesman."

"What's a salesman?"

"Someone who sells things."

A few minutes passed. Then another knock at the door, this time louder. Finn had just come downstairs, dressed in khaki shorts and a T-shirt. "Who's that?" he called from the living room.

My heart began to pound as I heard him opening the door. I went into the living room, and I could see the look on his face as he realized who the disheveled kid on the doorstep was. "You need to leave," Finn said in a calm, steely voice.

"I'm sorry," I said weakly from behind him, tears beginning to collect in my eyes. "I've told him I can't see him again."

Alex lunged for the door. "Please, Lydia. Just let me talk to you. I love you."

Finn blocked him. "Get off our property now."

He slammed the door and turned to me. My cheeks were hot and wet with tears. "I'm so sorry," I said.

"He needs to go."

"I know."

"Mommy, who was that?" Grace called from the kitchen.

"No one, sweetie. Don't worry." I went back to her. Then the doorbell rang.

From the kitchen, I heard Finn yell, "I said, get the fuck off my property."

"Why did Daddy say 'fuck'?"

"He shouldn't have, sweetie. It's a bad word."

"But why?"

I couldn't focus. I started back to the living room, just in time to hear Alex taunting Finn: "I made your wife scream. She was begging me for more."

"Alex, shut up and go!" I shouted.

"Mommy, what's happening?" Grace cried from the kitchen.

Finn slammed the door once again. His body was tense, and he wouldn't look me in the eye. He went to the hall closet and pulled his rifle case from the top shelf.

"What are you doing?" I yelled.

"Go to Grace," he said, still not looking at me.

"Put that away!"

"Go to the kitchen."

"Mommy! Where are you?" Grace could hear us yelling and was starting to sob.

I ran to the kitchen. She was standing at the baby gate, crying and afraid. I tried to hide the fact that I was crying too, but I couldn't. So I held her as tight as I could. "It's okay," I said. "It's okay. It's all going to be okay."

There was another knock at the door. I heard Finn go outside.

Maybe Alex wanted to die. That didn't occur to me at the time. He always seemed content and self-assured. I didn't think he was prone to depression or in any real trouble. But now I look back and see it differently. He'd had a hard life. He was bitter. He felt alone. And I crushed him. I know that now. He put all these foolish hopes on me, and I destroyed them.

So maybe he wanted to die. He'd said as much in some of his texts, but I hadn't taken it that seriously. He'd said he was desperate, he needed help, he couldn't go on anymore.

Thinking of it that way makes me feel sorry for Finn. He didn't want to be in that situation. Alex and I forced him into it.

I heard the first shot. Then another. Grace didn't particularly seem to notice, but I was shaking with fear. "Sweetie, Mommy needs to go check on something. Would you like to watch *Sesame Street*?"

Grace nodded, her soft little face covered in red splotches from crying. I gave her my phone and put on the show. Then I went to the front door.

There was so much blood. Alex was lying on his back on the ground a few feet from the house. His white T-shirt was soaked red where he'd been shot in the chest, and a pool was already collecting below him. His eyes were open but uncomprehending.

Finn was leaning against his truck, still holding the rifle. He didn't seem to see me. He was staring at Alex. He looked terrified.

I didn't scream. In fact, I think I stopped crying at that moment. It was as if the shock of it shook the emotions out of me. Without ever looking over at me, Finn said to himself, "I gotta get out of here."

He got in the truck, throwing his rifle on the seat. I didn't try to stop him. I went to Alex and sat beside him, taking his hands, touching his cheek, desperate for a sign of life. Finn pulled out of the driveway, and I stayed on the ground for a long moment. I could feel the warm, thick blood on my bare legs and arms and smell it too, sweet and metallic. I knew Alex was gone, but I wanted to bear witness.

There's wonderful power in the blood.

I stood up. I went to the next-door neighbor's house—I think her name was Leslie. I used to wave at her politely, but we had never spoken. I rang the doorbell. She opened the door, still wearing her pajamas, and audibly gasped.

"Someone's been shot in front of my house. Can you call nine-one-one?"

She nodded and pulled a phone out of her pocket. She pressed the digits, then handed the phone to me. I told the dispatcher that my husband had shot Alex Greggs on our property with a rifle, and saw Leslie's eyes get wide.

It honestly never occurred to me to lie. By now it should be clear that lies don't come naturally to me, except when I'm telling them to myself.

They told me the ambulance was on the way. "Could you go to my daughter?" I asked Leslie. "She's alone in the house, and I don't want her to see me like this."

"Of course," she said, this kind, amazing stranger. I know that later on reporters approached her, but she never talked to any of them. I will always be grateful to her.

The ambulance took Alex's body away. The police came at some point and took me to the station. Someone, Leslie and I, or maybe the officers, managed to call Finn's parents, because Grace wound up with them that afternoon. And at some point Finn drove back to the house, past the two police cruisers and giant bloodstain in the driveway, and parked his truck in his usual spot with the rifle still sitting on the passenger's side of the cab. He was immediately arrested.

As soon as he was taken into custody, Finn confessed. His story corroborated mine, so they released me. I was exhausted, completely spent. But they were still searching our house, and I wasn't allowed back there, so I went to Walmart to buy clean clothes. Then I went to my in-laws' house to pick up Grace.

Finn's mother opened the door. She'd given me plenty of scornful looks in the past, but the way she stared me down that evening surpassed them all. "I always told him you were nothing but trash."

"I'm sorry, Jeanine. I really am sorry for it all. But I need to pick up Grace."

She knew she didn't have a choice that day, though no doubt she was already concocting plans. She left me on the porch and went to get

Grace. The truth was I probably should have left her there, because the only place I had for us to stay was Grandma's—with Ted. But I needed Grace with me that night even if it meant staying with him.

She looked so small and frightened, clinging to her favorite stuffed bunny. As soon as she saw me, Grace ran and threw herself against me, hugging my neck. I wrapped my arms around her and felt a little peace for the first time all day.

But once I had tucked her into bed at Grandma and Ted's, I was left alone with the terror, grief, and guilt. I lay awake beside her on the pullout sofa, unable to push images of Alex from my mind, with one of those awful hymns going around my head. *Come, there is safety in the blood, hide you in the blood of Jesus. Now plunge beneath the crimson flood, hide you in the blood of Jesus.*

At least Grandma didn't judge me. Over the next few weeks, it started to feel like she was the only person in the world who didn't think I was an evil whore. Ted was a different story, of course, but he kept his distance. It must have been obvious by then that I was way past salvation.

I went to see Finn the next day. He was in need of a shave and looked worn-out and small in his oversize orange prison clothes. I sat across a table from him in a visitors' room at the jail. Neither of us spoke for a minute or so.

"I'm sorry, Finn," I said finally. "I'm so sorry."

"Why did he come to the house?" He sounded confused, like he was still trying to understand what had happened.

"I don't know."

"How's Grace?"

"Fine. A little confused, but she just thinks she's on vacation. We have to stay at Grandma's because the police won't let us back in the house."

"Why didn't you go to Mom and Dad's?"

"Your Mom and Dad aren't real happy with me at the moment. Have they been here?"

"Yeah. Mom's starting a GoFundMe to raise bail. They talked

about it at church this morning and I guess a lot of people started donating."

"Wow." People were donating money to bail out a murderer. I didn't understand it. But that was because I hadn't yet heard my mother-in-law's pitch.

"Hopefully, I'll be out of here soon."

I thought Finn was delusional. He seemed that way. His voice wasn't normal, and he was kind of staring off into space, hardly looking at me or at anything around him. I was worried for him. Of course, I was angry too. Beyond angry. I couldn't believe what he'd done; it was the worst thing I could imagine. I will die with the image of Alex's bloody body permanently etched somewhere deep in my mind. But I knew too much about Finn for him to ever be just that one horrible act to me. "I love you, Finn. I wish you hadn't done it. But I do love you."

"I know."

Four days later, I was shocked to see his truck pull into Grandma's driveway. I ran out into the driveway before Grace could see what was going on. Finn got out of the truck, dressed in civilian clothes. "You raised bail!" I said. "That's great."

But I didn't think it was great. Standing across from him, I felt scared—not that he would physically hurt me, but because I was beginning to realize I had no idea what he would do next.

"Can I have Grace for the night?"

"The night?"

"Yeah. I thought she could go back and forth between us."

"Are we not together anymore?"

He didn't reply or even look me in the eye. I was overcome with rage. It was the fact that he didn't even bother to tell me about the decision he had made. That he was leaving me, as if what I had done was worse than what he had done.

"Okay, fine. Let's get divorced. But no, you can't have Grace for the night. You're out on goddamn bail for murder, and I'm her mother!"

"I thought we could be civil about this."

"Well, then you shouldn't have shot my friend in the chest!"

He guffawed. "Your *friend*?"

"Fuck you, Finn."

I went back in and slammed the door.

The police had issued a statement, and the local news were all over it. Naturally, they reveled in the sordid details. They also interviewed Alex's grandma, whom I'd never actually met, sobbing and talking fast in Spanish, dubbed over with an English-speaking voice: "What would that woman want with a boy?"

Grandma loved having Grace around, but kept giving me mournful looks. One night after my daughter was in bed, she brought me a cup of tea and started to cry.

"I'm so sorry, Lydia. I tried my best to make things right with you."

"Grandma, this mess isn't your fault."

"I don't know, Lydia. I know things weren't easy for you growing up. Maybe I should have told you more about your mother—"

"I don't care about my mother."

She gave me a tortured look. I knew there were things she wanted to tell me, but I didn't want to hear them.

It took a few days for the news to go national, as far as I can tell. I think the fancy lawyer Finn's parents hired had something to do with that. I was fixing Grace a sandwich in the kitchen when Grandma called out from the living room: "Come quick, Lydia, you're on CNN!"

Sure enough, footage of our neighborhood was on TV, as well as our house, still cordoned off with police tape. A menacing narrator explained, "No one expected scandal and murder in this charming southern neighborhood."

My Facebook profile picture, taken two years earlier when we took Grace to Myrtle Beach, flashed on-screen, tinted a frightening red. "Neighbors thought Lydia Caton was a caring young wife and mother. Little did they know, she was a predator."

A couple of the boys from Mrs. Holmes's English classes appeared in front of the camera. "She hit on me," said the first one, whose name I couldn't even remember.

"She came on to all the boys," the second agreed, nodding.

"I just ignored it," said the first one. "I've got a girlfriend. But I guess Alex was just more vulnerable."

Then there was Mrs. Holmes. "I can't believe this was happening right under my nose! I feel so terrible for that young man, getting caught in her web. The thought that I could have somehow put a stop to it . . ." She shook her blond bob slightly and put her hand over her eyes, apparently overcome with emotion.

The picture we'd taken at the Hillbilly Playhouse flashed on the screen. The camera zoomed in on Alex and me, until our faces became pixelated blurs.

It was so outrageous that I laughed. I looked over at Grandma, but she wasn't laughing.

Finn's parent were next. "We never trusted her," my mother-in-law said. Her husband sat beside her, silent and stone-faced. "We tried to get along, because Finn loved her. But when he found out about her betrayal, it was too much for him. He's just so tenderhearted. And then for her to rub his face in it, bringing that boy to their house."

Finally, Finn. He was wearing the one tie he owned, the one I'd bought him for our wedding, which he'd only ever put on since for other people's weddings. "I don't remember it happening, but I know that I did it, and I'm deeply sorry. I want to especially express my regret to Mrs. Rodriguez."

He looked directly into the camera, eyes wet and sparkling.

Grandma looked over at me. "Sweetheart, I think you need to get yourself a lawyer."

It was another week before I finally took her advice. By that time, I'd been served papers informing me that Finn's parents were suing me for custody of Grace. Apparently their church's GoFundMe campaign didn't stop at getting murderers out of jail. It also provided funding to take a mother's child away from her. Good Christian charity.

I knew my lawyer was a terrible lawyer as soon as I set foot in his tacky, messy office, located in a run-down strip mall on the outskirts of Douglasville. But I'd left messages with over a dozen attorneys, and he was the only one who'd even returned my call. Besides, I had no money. Grandma had promised to help as much as she could, but she was having to go behind Ted's back to slip me cash. I'd been applying for jobs all over Douglas County and couldn't even get hired to clean up after kids at the arcade. I was toxic in Tennessee. Everyone knew the story by then, and everyone hated me.

My terrible lawyer told me I should be prepared to at least temporarily give up custody. I barely listened to the rest of what he had to say. Afterward I sat in my car in the parking lot for a long while, unable to move.

Then my phone rang.

It was my aunt Carrie. At first I didn't want to pick it up. I'd always looked up to Carrie more than anyone else I knew. She lived in New York but had grown up here with my mom, and always visited me when she came to town. The thought of having to tell her everything made me feel deeply ashamed. But I was desperate for help.

"Lydia, are you alright?" she asked me.

"No, not really." I started to cry.

"It's going to be alright, sweetie. You're going to be okay."

I knew that wasn't true, but it was still nice to hear her say it. She told me to let her know if I needed anything. And driving home, I got a crazy idea. I know it wasn't rational. But I felt so hopeless and trapped. I threw my things into a suitcase as fast I could, buckled Grace in her car seat, and started driving north.

Grace watched cartoons on my phone as I scanned through radio stations, along an infinite stretch of interstate, through farms and mountains, past little towns marked by identical fast food restaurants and gas stations, some of which we stopped at for snacks and drinks and potty breaks. She fell asleep and peed in her car seat. Virginia seemed to go on forever, until it got deathly dark, and I had to sleep. We spent the night at a Motel 6 that I put on my almost-maxed-out credit card. We got up early the next morning to get back on the road. The land flattened and the towns got closer together, until there were hardly breaks between them. Finally I could see the great towers in the distance, the new World Trade Center, not quite finished, standing above them all. We descended into the Holland Tunnel and emerged in the city. I drove slowly, trying to stay out of the way of taxis, stunned by the honking and pedestrians and one-way streets. We got to Carrie's apartment in Brooklyn sometime around 6 p.m. It took me another twenty minutes to find a place to park. And then we walked up her stoop, and I lifted up Grace to ring the buzzer for her apartment.

"Hello?"

"Carrie?"

"Yes, can I help you?"

"It's Lydia. Grace and I are downstairs."

Carrie buzzed us in, and we slowly climbed to the third floor. She was waiting with the door open. She looked good, as always, in a crisp white button-up shirt and cashmere cardigan. Soft brown hair framed her face in stylish layers. Everything about her appearance looked casually expensive.

"Are you okay? How did you get here?"

"We drove. I'm sorry I didn't call."

"A cat!" Grace shouted, spotting her tabby.

"I don't understand." I could see the concern on her face.

"I just . . . had to get out of there."

"Okay, sit down, sit down. We'll talk it all through."

I took Grace to the bathroom, and Carrie got us water. Her apartment was small but lovely. Everything was cream-colored or beige. I tried to explain as best I could, aware that I sounded a bit manic.

"I thought there was a custody issue?"

"Well, yeah."

"Doesn't that mean you shouldn't leave?"

I knew I shouldn't be crossing state lines with Grace. But for the past two days, I had just pushed that thought out of my mind. I looked down.

"Okay," Carrie said carefully. "You can stay here. But we're going to make a plan, okay?"

When her husband, Tom, got home, she ushered him into the kitchen, and I could hear her trying to explain our presence in hushed tones. I'd met him a couple times when he'd come with her to Tennessee. He was older than her, mostly bald with square glasses.

"Hi, Lydia," said Tom, when they reentered the living room. "I'm sorry about all your troubles."

He spoke to me like he thought I might be crazy, slowly and with caution. I knew then I'd made a horrible mistake. I'd driven all the way to New York, and nothing had changed. I was still a pariah. I'd just made things worse.

After I put Grace to bed, Carrie offered me a glass of red wine. I drank carefully, because I was terrified of spilling it on her fancy beige sofa. "You can stay here for a week, Lydia. That should be enough time to clear your head. But then you have to go home. They could take Grace away because of your pending court case. You know that, right?"

I nodded. "I just had this feeling that I had to get away. Like if I just wasn't in that place, maybe things would be better."

She put her cool, soft hand on mine. "Do you want to tell me about Alex?"

No one had asked me that before. And I realized that I did very much want to tell her about Alex. She listened, making no judgments, at least not out loud. When I was done with my story, Carrie was silent. She poured us each more wine. Then she said, "Lydia, have you ever met your father?"

"What? No. I mean, I didn't even think anyone knew who he was."

"Your mom must have had an idea."

"Yeah, well, she's dead."

Carrie looked down. I felt bad, because I know she was close with my mom. "When you're ready, I think I could help you track him down."

"Do you know who he is?"

"Not for sure, but I have some ideas."

"Why are you mentioning this now? What does my father have to do with anything?"

"I don't know exactly. I just thought it might help you. It might change how you think about yourself."

"Why should I care about a man who obviously never cared about me?"

"It might be more complicated than that. Surely you're learning that some situations are more complicated than they seem on the outside."

I understood what she was getting at. But I didn't want to think about my father.

I spent the next few days playing tourist with Grace, doing everything I could to distract myself from the reality of our situation. I took her to the park near Carrie's house, and we explored half a dozen local playgrounds. We rode the Staten Island Ferry and saw the Statue of Liberty. We went to story time at the library and a playgroup at the Brooklyn Museum. I pushed her stroller to the East River and we stared up at the impossible magnificence of the Brooklyn Bridge and, beyond that, Manhattan. We slept in Carrie's office, sharing a twin-size futon, Grace's warm, silky head burrowed into my shoulder. I have often tortured myself with the memories of that last magical week we had together.

On the fifth day, Carrie got a phone call from Finn's father. I didn't expect her to lie for me. She gave me the phone, and I told him we would drive home the next day.

"You'll drive home tonight," he told me. "Or you'll spend the night in jail."

When I got to their house the next afternoon, I was exhausted. I'd only slept for a few hours in the car, parked at a gas station in Maryland. Finn's mother opened the door when I rang the bell, her expression cold and hard. She pulled Grace inside, away from me, then stepped out on the porch, closing the door behind her. "Despite everything, Lydia, I do believe that you love that child."

"Of course I do."

"Then how do you not see the best thing for her is for you to get out of her life?"

I said nothing but turned and drove away as fast as I could, numb and too worn out to even cry.

In the end, I was sentenced to more time in prison for breaking the custody order than Finn was for killing Alex. Finn put on a hell of a show. Tears and solemn apologies. Bafflement at what he had done. His memory a blank when it came to the fateful moment. The jury found him not guilty of murder, but slapped him on the wrist with negligent homicide.

I had felt sorry for Finn that awful day when he killed Alex. I was outraged—of course I was—but even so, I saw the terror in his eyes and felt pity. But something changed in him afterward. He never took responsibility. And he was never punished. I remember Grace's pediatrician telling me that you have to be consistent when giving a child time-outs, or the punishment won't be effective. But life hasn't been consistent with Finn. He did a horrible thing. We both did horrible things, but he hasn't paid a price.

I took a lot of pills, but not enough. Then I spent some time in the hospital. Carrie came to visit and asked if I wanted to come back to New York with her.

Every day I think of moving back to Tennessee so I can spend my allotted half hour with Grace every two weeks under supervision. But how would that be good for her or me? She's five now, and I wonder so hard what kind of person she is becoming. I know already that she is curious and creative, that she loves to sing and dance. I hope she turns out nothing like me.

I wish the Internet didn't exist. People used to be able to keep secrets. Grace could have grown to adulthood only hearing whispers of rumors. But surely she'll google me one of these days—or one of the mean girls in her class at school will. Maybe it's better that way. Maybe secrets are bad for people. Maybe secrets fucked up my parents and grandparents. But if they did, they kept that secret, so we'll never know.

I try not to feel sorry for myself, but I know the only two people left who care about me are Carrie and my grandma, who keeps calling me, crying. She wants me to come home to Tennessee. She wants to tell me about my mother and confess all the things that she did wrong as her mother, because she thinks that contributed to the wrong thing that I did. Before I can stop her, it starts gushing out: "I was an alcoholic, Lydia. I wasn't paying attention. Half the time I was drunk and the other half blacked-out." I stop her before I have to learn more than I can bear about the past. She wants me to forgive her, and I do. I don't blame her for my problems. And God knows I understand the impulse toward confession, the yearning for forgiveness that is Mount Zion's most lasting impression on me.

Carrie has things she wants to tell me as well. She once e-mailed me a story about my mother that she wants me to read. It's sitting in my inbox, waiting for a day when I feel strong enough to open the document. She also wants to take me home to find my father.

But I don't know if I can ever go back to Tennessee.

Last month, after a long drought, wildfires broke out in Tates Valley, bad enough they even made the national news. (Finally, I'm not the local headline anymore.) I lay in bed that night, staring at my phone, refreshing the feed from the local Knoxville news stations to see what parts of my childhood were being destroyed. Hundreds of buildings were lost. Ten people died.

How can people deny that something is wrong with this world? It's almost enough to make you believe Reverend Maples's sermons about the Apocalypse—the world is ending and Jesus is coming back. But I don't believe that. I believe humans have fucked up our world, and now we're paying for it.

I don't know. Maybe it's the same thing.

They say the fire started up by Laurel Springs—some kids playing with matches. I think of those great tall virgin hardwoods going up in flames, and it makes me sad. Of course, I think of the dead and that makes me sad too. The River Vista Motel burned down. That doesn't make me sad, but I was worried for Alex's grandma. I couldn't find her name anywhere in the papers, so I assume she's safe. Poor woman.

God leads His dear children along. Some through the waters, some through the flood, some through the fire, but all through the blood.

I can't get the blood hymns of my childhood out of my head. I know we can never escape our pasts or even our parents' pasts, and yet I hope against hope that my daughter will find a way.

PRETTY POLLY (REPRISE)

♪

POLLY
(LYDIA'S GREAT-GREAT-GREAT-GREAT-AUNT)
1891

I've been lying here in the hayloft for half an hour or so, since I vomited off the back porch into a blackberry bramble. I'm trying not to think about the smell of manure wafting up through the barn in the summer heat. I've lived around animals all my life, so it's nothing I'm not used to, but for the last week, any scent has turned my stomach, even the sweet smell of molasses. I just need to lie down. I feel so tired and sick and sick of being sick. I threw up eight times yesterday. It is ceaseless, this feeling. I long to lie under the soft quilt on my own bed, but I dare not go back to the house. Ma would know in an instant.

My older sister, Clem, got sick like this when she was first carrying her boy. Ma said then that it ran in our family. I vomited for the first time on Tuesday. That was manageable. I washed my face and went back to work picking tomatoes. Wednesday it happened twice. The second time was a narrow miss. I was washing dishes and had to run out of the kitchen, but I made it to the outhouse in time. Each day has gotten worse. It's only just lunchtime, and I don't know how much longer I can hide this. I feel powerfully thirsty but also like I can barely move.

The only one who knows is Will. I got hold of him after church yesterday and was able to tell him, quietly as I could at the edge of the churchyard, Ma and Pa not more than five yards away. I could see the news came as a surprise to him. It shocked me as well, although I knew well enough as soon as I let him lie with me that this was a possibility. Still, when I realized my monthly was two weeks past due, I tried not to think about what it might mean. It wasn't until this awful sickness took hold of me that I faced the truth of my situation.

Will was good about it. He gave my hand a quick squeeze and told me he'd take of everything. He said he'd find me today so that we can talk things over. If I can just hold on until he comes calling, I hope he'll promise to marry me. I need that promise before I can tell Ma and Pa, and I can't figure any other way out of this fix.

The sick feeling seizes me again, and I let out a pitiful whimper. How can I be sick again with nothing in my stomach? If I lie very still, maybe I can stave off the heaving. My stomach is sore from it, and tiny red spots have begun to spread around my eyes, giving me a ghastly look. I told Mama it was just hay fever.

"Early in the season for that," she said, suspicious.

"I just don't feel myself," I replied.

Do I want to marry Will Reid and have his baby? Not much point in asking now. We met just five months ago. He's a relation of the Reids here in Tates Valley and came from North Carolina to work on his uncle's farm. The day before we met, I attended a quilting bee at Molly Eliot's house, and when we'd finished our work, Ruth Hickam asked Molly if she had a cat around. "Throw a cat on the quilt," said Ruth.

"Why on earth would I do that?" asked Molly.

"See which way it jumps off," replied Ruth. "Whoever it jumps toward will be the next to marry."

We all giggled, and Molly went to fetch her tabby. The poor thing yelped as it was thrown on the quilt, then jumped straight at me. I actually let out a little scream, I was so startled by the ball of fur coming for me, and everyone laughed.

I don't believe in those old wives' tales, but maybe I had it on my mind the next day when I met Will at the revival. He had dark-brown hair and a strong jaw, and I could tell from the look he gave me that he liked me even on that first day of our acquaintance.

The first time he touched me, we were walking side by side on our way home from town, where I'd run into him at the mill. It was a warm April day, and he was carrying a large sack of flour on his back. His sleeves were rolled up, exposing thick, ruddy arms that glistened with perspiration. He gently slipped his free hand around my hip as we walked, and I felt as though my whole body had gone limp. I don't know how I kept walking, the sensation was so powerful. I liked that he liked me, I liked the way his blue eyes sparkled in the sunlight, I liked his crooked grin, and I liked the feel of his rough hand on the thin cotton of my skirt.

I hadn't been thinking of the future. But he would probably be as good a man as any to marry. I might have to move back to North Carolina with him, but I hope he can stay on with his uncle for a while anyway, at least until the baby comes.

This isn't how I meant for it to happen, but I've wanted a baby for as long as I can remember. I doted on my little sister, Pearl, when she was born and begged Ma to let me feed her, rock her, bathe her. I loved everything about her: the soft gurgles she made when sleeping, the feel of her fat cheek against mine when I hugged her tight, the gently sweet smell of her fuzzy head. I didn't even mind helping Ma wash her diapers.

I mean to be a good mother—kind, patient, calm, but firm when it is called for. I will have fun with my child, even when I'm busy, not like Ma, who only ever has time to scold and nag. I will be sympathetic to the terrors and agonies of childhood, rather than punishing. I will always listen. I will try, anyway.

I wish there was someone I could talk things through with before seeing Will. I thought about confiding in Clem, but I don't trust her not to go to Ma. I would tell my friend Violet, but she would never understand. She's read more books than any person I know, yet she doesn't know much about the world. I wonder if she even knows how babies are conceived? Anyway, she hates Will. Always has, since we first met him. Said she didn't like the way he looked at me, and I knew what she meant. He has this way of gazing like he could eat me up with his eyes. But I do like it.

I don't know much about men, but I reckon I shouldn't seem too desperate when he comes. Then again, Will is no fool, and he knows I'm desperate. All there is for it is to pray for him to come through and ask me to marry him. And if he won't promise? What then? I can't bear to think on it. Ma and Pa will never look at me the same. Will Pa let me stay in the house? And even if he does, what will everyone else say? I will be ruined.

I hear a sound and look down from the hayloft to see Pa's hound sniffing around the barn. He looks up at me and starts barking. "Shhh!" I call out.

The dog keeps barking. "Shush, get out of here!"

Pa is out in the fields hoeing, but Ma is back at the house and I don't want her coming to investigate what the old mutt is barking at. I sit up. "Get on out of here!" He finally quiets.

The sick feeling surges in my belly, and I know there's no avoiding it now. I don't have the energy to get myself down from the loft, so I vomit into the hay.

I lie back down. I know I need to eat something. This sickness is so odd; if I let myself get the least bit hungry, then I get sick, yet I can't keep anything in my stomach. I had shoved a stale biscuit in my pocket before I left the house, and I fish it out now. I break off a tiny piece and put it in my mouth. It's a struggle to even work up the energy to chew. This isn't like me. I hardly ever get sick. I've always been lucky that way, and besides, Ma says hard work keeps you healthy. If that's true, then I must be fit as a fiddle, for there's no shortage of work to busy myself with on the farm.

I'm not stupid. I knew this could happen. We were up at Laurel Springs when we first lay together. I'd taken Will up there one afternoon when he'd finished his work for the day and I managed to slip away from Ma. It's a beautiful place, up in the mountains, deep in the forest. A young oak stands tall over the place where frigid water bubbles up from the ground. The spring wildflowers were still blooming, and the soft ground around the spring was purple and white with phlox and trillium.

I told him the old story about Laurel Springs. Folks say it's haunted by the ghost of a Cherokee maiden, who was in love with one of her tribe's fiercest warriors, long ago, before white men came to these mountains. He told her he would marry her when he returned from the warpath, but many months went by, and he did not come back. Her tribe, believing their warriors dead, prepared to move north. But the girl refused to leave the place where her beloved had vowed to return to her. Rather than go with the tribe, she went to Laurel Springs and ate enough jimsonweed leaves to kill herself. Not one day later, the warrior finally returned, and found her corpse waiting for him by the springs.

Will smiled at my story. He pulled me to him and kissed me hard. I had that feeling again that I couldn't move, yet I know I kissed him back.

After a moment he let go of me, then pulled out his pocketknife and began carving on the oak tree. "Don't do that!" I cried.

"Why not?"

"That tree will be scarred for the rest of its life."

"That's the idea," he said as he carved. "Don't you see?"

I didn't like the idea of the wild tree carrying this mark, but I couldn't help but smile when he stood back and I saw our initials: WR + PC.

He put the knife back in his pocket and took me in his arms. "I want to be with you forever."

I have a firm understanding of animal husbandry and knew exactly what might happen if I let him make love to me. But it was the only thing I could do that wasn't proscribed, that gave me a taste of power, that made me feel beautiful, that made me feel alive. Because I knew everyone would say not to. Because I wanted to know what it was like.

I know of one woman in Tates Valley who had a child out of wedlock a few years back. Her father sent her out of the house, and she was shunned. For a while she disappeared with her baby, but then one Sunday she showed up at church. She confessed her sins for all to hear and was saved by Reverend White. I remember her sobbing and shaking in the middle of the chapel. I always wondered if she'd really found Jesus or just pretended to get everyone to leave her alone.

I hear Mama's voice and force myself to sit up. "Polly!" she's yelling from the porch.

I manage to hop down from the hayloft, brush myself off, and shove some more biscuit in my mouth. I do feel a bit better since I started nibbling it. Mama's voice echoes: "Polly, where have you got to?"

I walk to the house, working hard to keep myself steady. "Sorry, Mama!" I call out. "Daddy needed an extra hand with the cart."

"Well, I promised Clem I'd bring over this honey, but the butter needs churning."

"Alright, Ma. I'll do it."

"The cream is in the churn. I'll be back before supper."

I just want her to go, so I can be sick in peace if need be. The churn is on the porch, and I sit in front of it and begin churning slowly as she makes her way up to the road. But as soon as she is out of sight, I let go and lean back in the rocking chair. I don't know how I'll ever finish, and I don't really care. I want to go inside to my soft bed, but I don't have the energy to walk even that far. The wind whistles through the trees; the chickens are clucking. They'll need to be fed, if I can ever get the churning done. Lucky chickens. I wish I could just lay an egg and be done with this. It seems like a much better system.

I hear distant footsteps and open my eyes to see Violet coming down the road. I wave to her weakly. She comes up to the porch, carrying a well-worn copy of *Jane Eyre* that she's been reading to me over the past few weeks.

"You alright?" she asks.

"I feel poorly."

She sits in a chair beside me and puts a cool hand on my cheek. "You poor thing! Let me fetch you some water. You look unwell."

She goes in the house and comes back out with a cup. I drink gratefully. I hadn't realized that I was so thirsty.

"You should lie down," Violet says.

"No time. I have to churn this here butter."

"Let me do that. I came to read to you, but I can churn instead."

I'm too sick to protest. She scoots up to the churn and begins to work. "Go on and lie down."

"I just want to sit with you a minute." It's nice to be with a friend, even though she doesn't know my situation. Violet is so kind. She smiles at me, her teeth jutting out. She thinks she's ugly, but I always tell her she has a memorable face, the sort of face that makes an impression. The sort of face someone can fall in love with. She says no one will ever fall in love with her.

"Rest your head," she says, "on your beautiful golden curls." I touch my messy hair; no doubt it has hay stuck in it from my having lain in the barn. Violet has a way with words.

I close my eyes, and I must fall asleep and dream. I see scattered, frightening images. Violet is churning, talking about Mr. Rochester softly—perhaps that's real. "A brute," she says.

I see Rochester, dark and menacing, riding on a horse. Then I'm in the house, and Pa is playing his fiddle. The song he's playing now isn't quite right; he hits wrong notes and it makes my skin crawl. "Some folks call it the devil's instrument," Pa says with a menacing laugh.

I run away from the horrible music, outside into the fresh air. Will and his cousin are walking toward the porch, holding shotguns, dragging the dead carcass of a black bear behind them.

"We've been bear hunting," says Will. The animal's fur is caked in blood, its jaw slack, mouth agape.

I jolt awake. "Polly!" my little sister is yelling.

"Leave her be!" says Violet. "She's poorly."

I blink. Pearl is on the porch. "Sorry, Polly. But I got a message for you."

Violet is leaning back in the chair, *Jane Eyre* open on her lap. "What message?" I ask.

"From Will Reid."

I sit up straight. Pearl grins, but Violet scowls. "He says to meet him at Laurel Springs. He's on his way now."

"Thank you, Pearl. Don't tell Ma!"

"Of course I won't!"

"You're in no condition to walk all the way to Laurel Springs," says Violet.

I stand and immediately feel queasy.

"You gonna marry Will Reid?" asks Pearl.

"Don't know."

"Violet's right. You don't look real good."

"I can do it." But then before I can hide from Pearl and Violet, I have to throw up off the side of the porch.

"Oh, Polly!" says Pearl. "You oughta lie down."

Violet is immediately by my side with her hand on my back. "Let's get you to bed."

"No. Just fetch me a piece of bread."

"You're hungry?!" asks Pearl.

"Yes! Just get it." I straighten up and meet Violet's puzzled face. "I have to go," I tell her.

She shakes her head. "You would do well to stay away from that man."

"He ain't so bad. And I need to talk to him right away."

"Let me go talk to him for you."

I smile and raise an eyebrow at her. "I'm sure you'd love to give him a talking-to."

"I just want to help you."

"I know."

Pearl brings me the bread.

"At least let me walk you to the path."

I nod, and we link arms. I eat the bread as we walk slowly up the road. I feel a little better since my rest on the porch, or maybe it's just the anticipation of seeing Will. We pass the old peddler who comes round every few weeks selling needles and thread, pots and pans. He slows his mule to let us pass and tips his hat as we go by. I give him a wave. I always enjoy looking at his bolts of cloth, listening to his stories from around the mountains. "I envy him a little," I say to Violet. "His life on the road, camping out under the stars, always moving on. I ain't never been more than five miles from the farm."

"Must be a lonely life."

"But he knows everone in two counties! Spends all day talking to folks."

"That's not the same as having a real friendship." She gives my arm a squeeze. "You know you can confide in me if you're in some sort of trouble."

Perhaps she's not as naïve as I thought. I squeeze her arm in return. The little path off the road up to Laurel Springs is just ahead.

Abruptly, Violet stops walking. "Don't go up there, Polly. I have a bad feeling."

"Don't be foolish, Violet. The stories about Laurel Springs are just nonsense to scare children."

"I know that. But I don't trust Will Reid. I saw him walking with Lacey Franklin on the road last week."

I try not to let her see that this upsets me. I know Lacey Franklin's had her eye on Will, even though she knows he's been courting me. "Ain't nothing wrong with that."

"It wasn't that they were walking together—it was the way they were walking. He had his hand on her wrist and was almost dragging her along. I think she was crying."

I try to think of a good reason Will would be dragging Lacey by the wrist. Perhaps Violet's exaggerating or remembering incorrectly.

"I could come up there with you," she offers.

"I need to do this alone."

"He's a brute, Polly."

I'm startled because that's the same word she used in my dream. "Did you say that when I was asleep earlier?"

Violet's confused. "No. I was silent. Tried to churn as quietly as possible so as not to disturb you."

"Well. I thank you for your concern. But I'll be alright."

Leaving Violet there, I strike out from the road onto the little path. Enough people come this way that it stays pretty clear, even in summer when the undergrowth swells and a soul can get herself lost in a laurel slick for all eternity. I stop short when I see a dead sparrow on the path. I bend over it, despite my horror. Its body is intact, save for a broken wing, and its black bead of an eye seems to look up at me. The poor little bird is perfect, with a tuft of red feathers on the top of its head. I take a large maple leaf and scoop it up off the path, letting the body fall gently into a hollow log. I stuff some leaves on top to shelter it—the best burial I can manage—and say a little prayer for the bird under my breath as I walk up the mountain.

I feel the sickness returning and stop to lean on a chestnut tree, breathing hard. I manage to hold on to my stomach and start back up the hill. I'm sweating hard by the time I reach the spring, despite the breeze. I hope to have a moment to freshen up my face, but Will is sitting there already, leaning against the oak tree, our initials floating over his head.

"Hi there, Polly."

"Oh, Will, I'm awfully sick. The morning sickness stays with me all day long."

He stands and puts a hand on my shoulder. "Here, sit."

I do as he instructs. Something smells, and my stomach turns. "Everthing smells terrible to me. I could swear I smell fish."

"I caught three trout earlier. They's keeping cool in the spring."

I look over and see them now, dead eyes staring up at the sky. "I'm like a bloodhound," I tell him.

"How far along you reckon you are?"

"Not more'n eight weeks."

He's pacing in front of me, and I can tell he's nervous. "You told anyone else?"

"No. Pa'll kill me if he finds out."

"But your folks know we've been courting?"

"I reckon so. I never tried to hide it. Ma likes you."

"And you ain't never been with another man?"

"Of course not, Willy! Why would you ask sech a thing?"

"A man's gotta be sure. You tell me this child is mine, and I have to just take your word."

"You know I'm not that sort of girl!"

He doesn't say anything. His pacing makes me anxious. "Come sit beside me," I say.

He comes back to the tree but stays standing, leaning against it. Still he says nothing. I don't want to push him, so I remain quiet too.

Will looks down at me, and his face softens. "Your condition suits you. Your cheeks are real rosy."

"Oh, it's just a hot day."

"I don't look so pretty in this heat."

Momentarily I forget the sickness and my desperate need for a marriage proposal. I want him to kiss me. But he doesn't. Instead he pulls at the bark of the tree anxiously with his hand, as though he wants to skin it.

Though I know better, I feel my apprehension getting the better of me. "Violet said she saw you with Lacey Franklin last week."

He looks ahead, expressionless. "Maybe she did."

It's like I'm picking at a scab, unable to stop until I make myself bleed anew. "What were you doing with Lacey?"

He shrugs, looks at the ground, and says nothing. His silence stretches and grows, and I feel it like a slap on my skin. Birds chirp, leaves rustle, the springs burble, and Will says nothing.

I take a deep breath and look up at endless layers of green leaves pierced by brilliant sunlight. For a moment, I float above my sickness and my worry to revel in the sublime summer beauty of this place. I am overwhelmed by the feeling of being alive in this moment, warm sun on my face, rough bark on my back, life throbbing all around me in the dense woods, and growing inside me too. It is nearly too much to bear. A blinding ray of sunlight breaks through the canopy, and I squeeze my eyes shut.

I hear Will moving about, pacing again, but I keep still. I'm awfully worn out, and I almost feel as if I could drift back to sleep in the July sun. I wish he would tell me his intentions, one way or another.

Then a sound. Will lets out a low, guttural, inhuman growl, like a wild animal. A brute. I feel pain on the crown of my head, the worst pain I have ever felt, and a roaring in my ears. My eyes snap open, momentarily blinded by sunlight. I put my hand to my forehead and feel something warm and wet, and finally turn to see him looming over me. His face is not like I have ever seen it, twisted ugly with exertion and rage. His arms are raised over me, holding a large gray rock, now splattered dark red with my blood. Before I can scream or run, he drops toward me again. There is no time for fear, anger, sadness, regret, or even shock. I only have time to think, *No, no, no, no—*

And then, nothing.

———

Violet couldn't say what possessed her to go down to Mitchell's Creek that afternoon. It was out of her way, and she knew she was needed at home to prepare dinner. She had no intention of bathing or fishing. But there she was, standing at the water's edge, when she saw the figure caught between two rocks, dark, wet, lifeless. She recognized the fabric of Polly's dress, even though it was soaked through, a dress patterned with wide red and white stripes. She'd seen her friend walk, dance, and work in that dress countless times, and Polly had been wearing it just yesterday, the last time she'd seen her. Violet didn't yet know that her friend hadn't shown up for dinner the night before, and Polly's father had spent all day searching for her. He hadn't thought to look in the creek.

When Violet was a little girl, her mother used to sing the song: "*Pretty Polly, pretty Polly, come go along with me, Polly, pretty Polly, go along with me, before we get married some pleasures to see.*'"

Violet had never cared for those gruesome old ballads about murder and ghosts. But after discovering Polly's body that day, she couldn't get the song out of her head. The melody circled round and round on an endless loop. She wasn't much of a singer but found herself compulsively humming, against her wishes, whispering the words under her breath, "*Oh, he led her over mountains and valleys so deep, he led her over hills and valleys so deep, pretty Polly mistrusted, and she began to weep.*"

Violet took comfort in having been the one to find Polly. Her friend's broken, abandoned body was the worst thing she'd ever seen, but at least she had borne witness. And she was glad of that. She had loved Polly dearly, that laughing, carefree, golden-haired girl, so unlike Violet herself. The heartache of missing her was fierce. At times she thought she couldn't bear it, but slowly she learned to get through the days. Sometimes she would find herself, against her will, humming, "*'Polly, pretty Polly, you've guessed just about right, Polly, pretty Polly, you've guessed just about right: I've dug on your grave the best part of last night.*'"

She wanted rid of the song. She forced herself to whistle happier tunes, lingered in church to listen to hymns, read and reread every book she owned, anything to expunge the plaintive melody and erase the cruel rhymes. But the song haunted her. "*Gentlemen and ladies, I bid you farewell, gentlemen and ladies, I bid you farewell, for killing pretty Polly, I soon will be in hell.*'"

The song had outlived Polly. The song would outlive Violet's mourning.

Later, Elizabeth Munroe would teach Violet that "Pretty Polly" was an ancient song, older than the state of Tennessee or even the United States of America. The song had been haunting listeners for centuries, had haunted its way across the ocean to a new world. How could Violet hope to escape from a tune so powerful, the words repeated generation after generation? How could any of us? The song would outlive us all.

ACKNOWLEDGMENTS

I was raised on the songs and stories of the mountains where I was lucky enough to grow up, and for that I am grateful to my parents, Vandy Kemp and Bill Beard.

I first wrote about Laurel Springs many years ago for a class in my MFA program. The workshop was heated but provided excellent feedback. I am indebted to everyone who participated, and in particular, my classmate Anne O'Neil, whose enthusiasm for the story encouraged me to believe I was onto something worth pursuing.

Around the same time, Paula McGhee told me she had a story I should write about. I agreed and am grateful to her for sharing it with me that day in the Smokies.

I appreciate all the friends who gave their opinions of the many titles under consideration for this novel, including Julia Adam, Joshua Butts, Raelee Chapman, Annie Chen, Erin Coffey, Meghan Formel, Lesley Jenike, and Emily Ting.

And thanks to Declan Smithies for advice and support throughout the long process of writing this book.

Finally, I am grateful for the vision and wisdom of my editor Jackie Cantor. Collaborating with Jackie has been a pleasure and improved the book immensely. And a million thanks to my brilliant agent, Rayhané Sanders, for not only bringing me to Jackie, but also fighting tirelessly on my behalf, to both establish my career and sharpen my writing.

ABOUT THE AUTHOR

Born and raised in East Tennessee, Janet Beard moved to New York to study screenwriting at NYU and went on to earn an MFA in creative writing from The New School. Her first novel, *Beneath the Pines*, was published in 2008, and her follow-up, *The Atomic City Girls*, became an international bestseller 2018. Janet has lived and worked in Australia, England, Boston, and Columbus, Ohio, where she is currently raising a daughter and working on a new novel.

janetbeard.com
facebook.com/janetbeardauthor
instagram.com/janetlbeard